Wooden Shoe Hollow

Charlotte Pieper's Cincinnati German Novel

*To Andrea,
Alles gute,
Don*

Charlotte Pieper at the family home in Golf Manor.

Wooden Shoe Hollow

Charlotte Pieper's Cincinnati German Novel

Second Edition

Edited by
Don Heinrich Tolzmann

LITTLE MIAMI PUBLISHING CO.
Milford, Ohio
2004

OTHER TITLES BY THIS EDITOR
PUBLISHED BY LITTLE MIAMI PUBLISHING INCLUDE

German Pioneer Accounts of the Great Sioux Uprising of 1862, edited by Don Heinrich Tolzmann (2002)—The fascinating firsthand reports of two German-American women who were kidnapped as children and survived to tell the story.

New Ulm, Minnesota: J. H. Strasser's History and Chronology, translated and edited by Don Heinrich Tolzmann (2003)—The history of a frontier settlement founded by Cincinnati Germans in the 1850s.

German Heritage Guide to the Greater Cincinnati Area, by Don Heinrich Tolzmann (2003)—A guidebook to German-American influences as they relate to historical and current events, places, and people in the tri-state region of Ohio, Kentucky, and Indiana.

Little Miami Publishing Co.
P.O. Box 588
Milford, Ohio 45150-0588
http://www.littlemiamibooks.com

First Edition copyright © 1951 by Charlotte Pieper. Published by the Exposition Press, Inc., 386 Fourth Avenue, New York 16, N.Y.

Second Edition with new material copyright © 2004 Don Heinrich Tolzmann. All rights reserved. No part of this book may be reproduced or transmitted in any form or by any means, electronic or mechanical, including photocopying, recording or by any information storage and retrieval system without written permission from the author, except for the inclusion of brief quotations in a review.

Cover design by Print Management, Rebecca Adkins, graphic designer. Copyright © 2004 Little Miami Publishing Co.

Cover includes a photograph of wooden shoes that are on display at the German Heritage Museum located at 4764 West Fork Road in West Fork Park, Cincinnati, Ohio. Photo by Michael Stretch, Print Management.

Printed in the United States of America on acid-free paper

ISBN 1-932250-16-6
Library of Congress Catalog Card Number 2004103039

Dedicated to

Wooden Shoe Hollow

And Cincinnati's German-American

Novelist of the Area

Charlotte Pieper

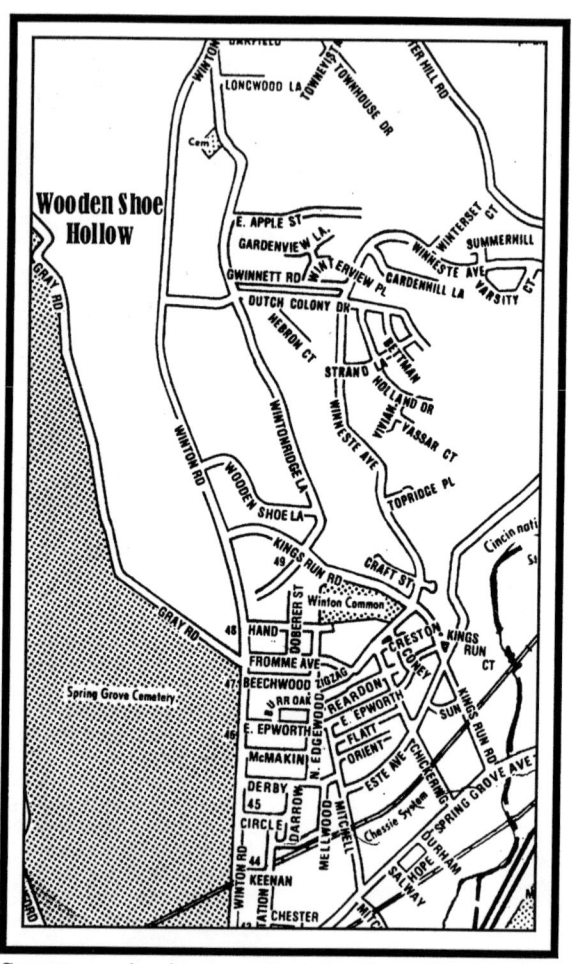

Current map showing approximate location and surrounding area of Wooden Shoe Hollow. MAP ADAPTED FROM *GRAPHIC STREET GUIDE OF GREATER CINCINNATI*, 1994-95 EDITION, PUBLISHED BY METRO GRAPHIC ARTS, INC.

Contents

PART ONE — Editor's Introduction

Editor's Foreword	xi
Illustrations	xii
Editor's Acknowledgments	xxi
Editor's Introduction	xxiii

PART TWO — The Novel

	Preface	11
I	Milk and Honey	13
II	The Crowd	17
III	An Accident	22
IV	Two Events	28
V	Christmas	36
VI	Grossmutter Hears a Story	43
VII	Rich Speaks Again	50
VIII	Lone Saturday	56
IX	While the Rain Descended	62
X	Back Water	69
XI	Of Lavender Cashmere	75
XII	Gerhard Dreams	81
XIII	Advice	87
XIV	Angling	93
XV	The Purge	102
XVI	Aftermath	109
XVII	A Shelling Party	115
XVIII	The Other Side	122
XIX	A New Year	128
XX	Rescue	138
XXI	The Elect	148

XXII	Lost Treasure	154
XXIII	Maria's Discovery	163
XXIV	Of White Satin	171
XXV	Migrant	179
XXVI	Scythe of Ice	188
XXVII	"Tip Terry"	196
XXVIII	Inwanderer	201
XXIX	Consecration	209
XXX	Sunrise and Sunset	216
XXXI	Readjustment	223
XXXII	Deliberation	228
XXXIII	New Lives for Old	236

PART THREE — Editor's Conclusion

Illustrations	247
Notes	255
Suggested Readings	265
Index	267
About the Editor	275

Part One

Editor's Introduction

Editor's Foreword

WHAT DO THE FOLLOWING have in common: *Goetta*, a Cincinnati staple food item; *Schützenfest*, Cincinnati's oldest festival; and, a preference for buildings made of *Backstein*, or brick? They are all, of course, but a few examples of German influences that have taken root and become an integral part of everyday life in the Greater Cincinnati area, and are simply taken for granted as the way things are in the Ohio Valley. More particularly, however, they are also contributions made by German-Americans with ancestral roots in northern Germany.

German immigrants came from all the German-speaking countries and regions of Europe, but the immigration from northern Germany was especially large, and as a result greatly influenced the German heritage of the area, giving it a special regional flavor and flair, including an appreciation for things like *Goetta*, *Schützenfest*, and, *Backstein*, for example.

Another expression of this north German influence may be seen in the emergence of a German-American community in Cincinnati known as Wooden Shoe Hollow, where wooden shoes were worn as they had been in Germany. And, fortunately, someone arose out of that community who wrote a novel about it.

In 1951, Charlotte Pieper published this work about life in Wooden Shoe Hollow, but it has long since been out of print. I decided to edit it for re-publication so as to make it available once again, not only because it provides us with an interesting portrait of the area, but also as it contribute to our understanding of Cincinnati's German heritage.[1] In preparing it for republication, I have included a new introduction, explanatory notes, illustrations, a selective bibliography, as well as in index to the notes.

Don Heinrich Tolzmann
University of Cincinnati

Although the Dutch Colony Drive is located on the north end of Wooden Shoe Hollow, the Hollow was a German-American, not a Dutch-American community. Non-Germans have often confused and mispronounced "deutsch" as "dutch," such as, for example, with the Pennsylvania Dutch, who are not Dutch, but German. EDITOR'S PHOTOGRAPH.

The Matthew United Church of Christ bears the German inscription: *Deutsche Evang. Prot. Mathäus Kirche*. EDITOR'S PHOTOGRAPH.

A street was named honoring the Pieper family, one of the oldest in Golf Manor. PIEPER FAMILY PHOTOGRAPH.

Mary and Fred Pieper, the sister and brother of Charlotte Pieper, standing in front of their home on Pieper Way in Golf Manor. PIEPER FAMILY PHOTOGRAPH.

Fred Pieper not only carries on the family tradition of gardening, but also makes Mettwurst for the family, and has a smokehouse in his backyard in Golf Manor. PIEPER FAMILY PHOTOGRAPH.

According to Mary Pieper, residents of Wooden Shoe Hollow referred to Wooden Shoe Hollow Lane as "Pig Tail Alley," as it is a street that winds its way through the hollow like a pig's tail. AUTHOR'S PHOTOGRAPH.

FIRST CHURCH

From their humble beginnings with meetings at the home of Mr. Poppe, followed by a rented room from Ephraim Knowlton, known as Knowlton's Hall, the German Protestant people of Cumminsville were at last in a position to lay the cornerstone for their first church in 1856 (above). Charlotte Pieper's parents were married in this church.

As the congregation grew, a larger church was needed, and on April 29, 1894, The First German Evangelical Protestant Church on Hoffner Street was dedicated (right). This church no longer stands, but the congregation continues to grow in the new church known as the First United Church of Christ at 5808 Glenview Avenue. Among other things, many of the stained glass windows from the Cumminsville church are installed in this new church in College Hill. In 2005 the First United Church of Christ will celebrate its 150th anniversary. PHOTOGRAPHS COURTESY OF VIRGINIA KREBS.

Osnabrück

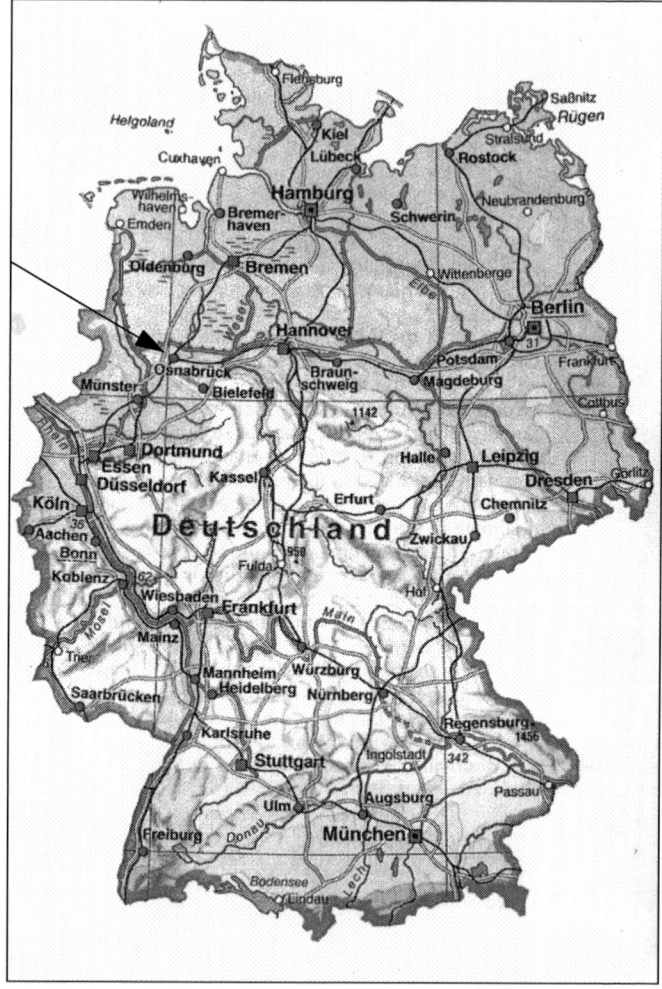

Westrup, the home town of the Pieper family, is located northeast of Osnabrück. Although Germans emigrated from a variety of areas, those from northwestern Germany were clearly in the majority that came to the greater Cincinnati area. This northwestern area can be outlined roughly by drawing a line from Hamburg in the north down through Hannover to the south, and then southwest over through Münster. This whole northwestern region of Germany can be looked on as the ancestral homeland of many German-Americans in the area. Many villages and towns have ties to the area, and some of them keep Cincinnati telephone books on file at the local museums to look up relatives. To understand Cincinnati's German heritage, it is necessary to go back to the roots in the northwestern region of Germany.

The Pieper family home in Westrup. Note the Fachwerk, or half-timber architecture, which is common to northern Germany, and which can be found in abundance in the Greater Cincinnati area. More often than not, homes in the Greater Cincinnati area that are described as English Tudor are actually German half-timber. PHOTOGRAPH FROM MARY AND FRED PIEPER

The Museum Village at Cloppenburg in Lower Saxony, provides an open air history museum that is well worth a visit to see how people in northwest Germany lived, and what their dwellings were like. PHOTOGRAPH FROM FRANCES OTT ALLEN.

One of the many beautiful half-timber buildings at Cloppenburg. PHOTOGRAPH FROM FRANCES OTT ALLEN.

Acknowledgments

MANY THANKS TO FRED AND MARY PIEPER, the brother and sister of the author of this novel, who were most helpful in providing information about their sister and family, as well as Wooden Shoe Hollow. Their kind and gracious assistance facilitated the preparation of this new edition, and was greatly appreciated.

The wooden shoes on the cover are on display at the German Heritage Museum, located in West Fork Park in Cincinnati, for those who would like to go there and actually see the originals. They belonged to John Ahlrichs, the uncle of Regina Schnetzer, and were donated to the Museum by the Schnetzer family. The explanatory note with the wooden shoes, written by Manfred Schnetzer, states that: "When John Ahlrichs immigrated in 1924 to Cincinnati from Scharrel (Saaterland), Germany, he brought with him these wooden shoes, or 'Klompen.' They were made by John Meyer of Scharrel. John Ahlrichs and his wife Gertrude Chistmann, born in Duisburg, Germany, owned and operated Ahlrichs Café at Eighth and Baymiller Streets in the old West End of Cincinnati until 1950." Thanks to the Schnetzer family for having donated these shoes to the Museum, and making them available to the general public.

Many thanks also to my wife, Patricia, and my daughter, Katherine, both of whom accompanied me on various excursions in and around Wooden Shoe Hollow, as well as throughout nearby Spring Grove, one of my favorite places in Cincinnati. A special word of thanks to the Little Miami Publishing Co., not only for its support in publishing works dealing with the German heritage, but for encouraging me to edit this work as a contribution to our appreciation and understanding of the area. Thanks also to Carol E. Mahan for research assistance, as well as to all those who provided information and photographs for this work.

D.H.T.

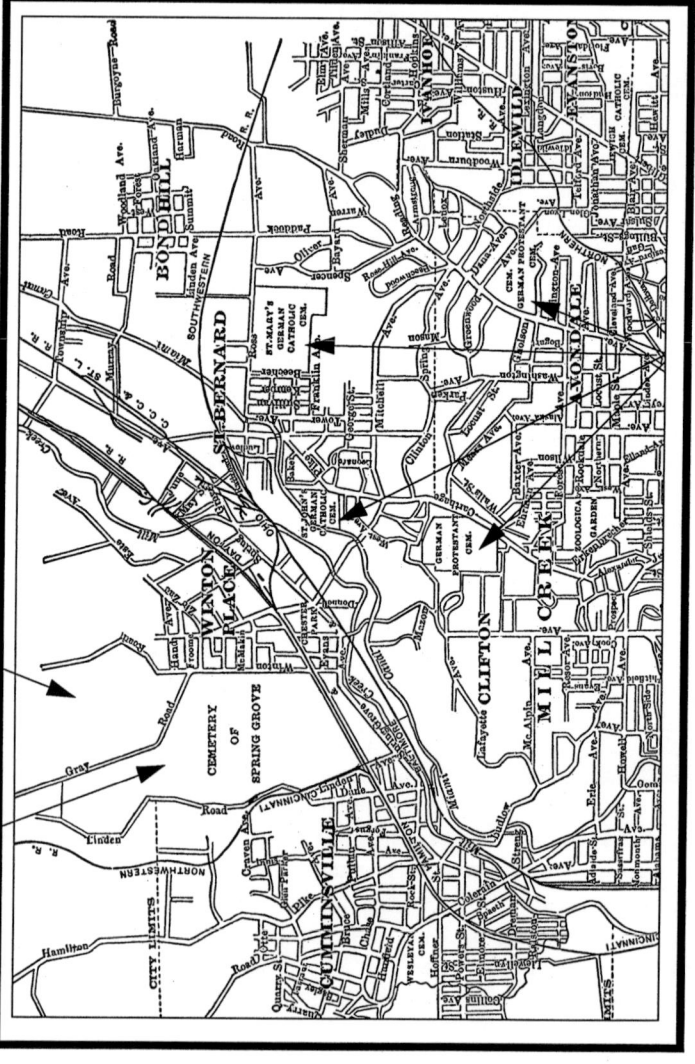

Spring Grove Cemetery   Wooden Shoe Hollow

Map from 1904. Note the many German cemeteries in this area.

Editor's Introduction

~~~~~~

The Author and the Novel

IN 1984, the *Cincinnati Enquirer* reported that "Charlotte E. Pieper, whose University of Cincinnati journalism class project about Cincinnati's German-American community blossomed into a novel in 1951, died Tuesday at Deer Park Nursing Home." The obituary stated:

> She originally wrote the story for her UC advanced writing class and the teacher, Joseph Sagmaster, a former editorial writer at the *Cincinnati Enquirer* and a former editor of the former *Times-Star*, liked it so much he urged her to expand the short story.
>
> Seven years later, she published it as a novel about Rica Heber, a woman who left Germany . . . only to find, in the wonderfully colorful Wooden Shoe community, that she could not escape herself and her problems.[2]

The obituary also indicated that this was her fourth publication, and that she also had published two plays entitled *Miracle Eternal* and *Christmas Butterfly*, as well as a worship service, *The Festival of Christian Women*. Her fourth work, however, dealt with German-American community life, and the article noted:

> "She usually wrote at night, because she was working and for a time also going to night school," said a sister, Mary Emma Pieper. "She was very methodical about everything she did. She believed in hard work, being industrious and sticking to rules. The teachers she had were very strict."

Charlotte Pieper was born in 1905 on Spring Grove Avenue in the German truck gardening settlement near Winton Place, which was the setting for her novel. She retired from the sales department of Merrell at 65.[3]

Pieper had attended the University of Cincinnati in 1933, where she received a certificate in Journalism, and later attended the Evening College there, and earned a bachelor of science degree. The novel itself was dedicated by the author to her parents, Mary Meyer Pieper and Henry Louis Pieper.

Pieper's maternal grandfather had emigrated from Hanover, and her mother was born in Wooden Shoe Hollow. Her father was also from northern Germany, and had emigrated at the age of sixteen from Westrup, a town located northeast of Osnabrück in the district of Stemwede in the state of North Rhine–Westphalia. German emigrants from the area spoke Plattdeutsch, or Low German. Often misconstrued, Low German is actually a geographical term referring to the German spoken in the lowlands of northern Germany, whereas High German refers to the German spoken in the highlands of the south.[4]

In Cincinnati, the Pieper family lived on Spring Grove Avenue, and maintained a garden filled with tomatoes, cucumbers, and other vegetables, about six acres in size. Gardeners and farmers in the area wore wooden shoes, which were available from a garden supply store at Spring Grove and Colerain Avenues, and when the store stopped carrying them, the Pieper family located the supplier of the wooden shoes in Kiel, Wisconsin, and took over supplying them for residents of the Hollow.

Wooden shoes first appeared in the twelfth to thirteenth century in northwestern Europe, where farmers wore them for field work. In Cincinnati, wooden shoes were common among German-American farmers and gardeners because they were durable, long lasting, and could take the wear and tear of fieldwork in a way that leather shoes could not. Of course, they have long since been replaced by heavy duty work shoes. However, the name "Wooden Shoe Hollow" remains as a symbolic reminder of the founding families of the area, and also of the fact that Wooden Shoe Hollow is still well known as a garden supply area. Moreover, it was Pieper's novel that helped immortalize the name for the area.

In 1910, the Pieper family moved to Wiehe Road in Golf Manor. However, the family maintained close ties to Wooden Shoe Hollow, where it had friends and family connections. Mary Pieper tells how her sister came to write the novel:

> *Wooden Shoe Hollow* might never have come into being had it not been for a strange set of circumstances. When Charlotte was in about the fourth grade of school, an aunt of hers, who was suffering from what we now call "empty nest syndrome" complained to Charlotte's mother about how hard life was with no child at home to help her. The aunt envied our mother with five daughters. And so it was decided that Charlotte would live there on Mitchell Avenue with her Aunt Minnie and Uncle George [Nippert]. Our mother was aware that Charlotte would have the benefit of more food and clothes and anything else to make her life happy. Living there on the little truck farm and going to school and church there in Winton Place gave her the experience that made it possible to write her novel. Winton Place was right next to Wooden Shoe Hollow and this was the time that these truck gardeners flourished. She had a chance to observe these people of all ages and types and later on draw on this experience to make her characters come alive.[5]

The book jacket of Pieper's novel indicates that she was

> a writer who combines the capacity to create living people with the ability to tell a gripping story. We live with her pioneer people, their lives full of toil and hardship; we see them at work and at play, and share their sorrows and laughter. When finally, through a charming story-device reminiscent of the Victorian novelists, all turns out well for Rica Heber, it is as if we have been part of a warm, sentimental friendship with all the nostalgia of treasured days not so long ago.[6]

The novel, set in Wooden Shoe Hollow, deals with the recent arrival of a German immigrant to the settlement, and her experiences there. The main character, Rica Heber, has left Germany and "aboard ship, one of those rare, chance encounters that change the currents of our lives" results in bringing her to the German-American community at Wooden Shoe Hollow. Here "desperately seeking refuge," she discovers "the bitter truth that there is no hiding place, and no amount of land or sea" that can separate her from coming to terms with the realities of her problems.[7]

Aside from telling the story of the main character, the novel is also "the portrait of the incredibly colorful community of Wooden Shoe Hollow, and such unforgettable people as Grossmutter Betz, Pastor Schicht, Hermann Toepfer, and a host of others who will linger in your memory long after you have put down this absorbing tale."[8] The novel tells how Wooden Shoe Hollow welcomed recently arrived immigrants, and provided them with a place where they could readily feel at home, where one could connect due to its German heritage. Although writing for a regional audience, her novel is of interest and value as a portrayal of German-American community life in the early twentieth century.

Why did Charlotte Pieper write the novel? According to an article by Robert Heidler that appeared when the book was published, "[t]here are as many reasons why people write books as there are authors, but basically most authors' motivation is twofold: to make money and to express something they think others should know about. Then there is a third reason, not clearly defined, but having to do with immortality—the writing of a book, or play, or verse is their 'mark' in the world, something that will live on. Such motivation is that of Cincinnati's newest author, Charlotte Pieper."[9]

What had begun originally as an article for a class in advanced writing, eventually turned into a novel. Charlotte Pieper's instructor, Joseph Sagmaster, a Rhodes scholar and associate editor at the *Times-Star*, had advised her in his evening class at the University of Cincinnati: "Charlotte, enlarge this, write it bigger. Put it in shape for a long short-story." Her thoughts were: "If it's that good, maybe polishing it up will make it better—good enough for a novel."

Wooden Shoe Hollow

An article in the local press referred to Wooden Shoe Hollow as a "peaceful spot in the inner city." This "rural wonderland surrounded by urban Cincinnati" is "quiet, almost perfectly tranquil . . . (and is located) on the northern edge of the city." It noted that "[c]hirping birds soar over the organic gardens and perch on greenhouses, staring down at the black soil and plush grass of the Mill Creek Valley, searching for their next meal." Wooden Shoe Hollow actually "is a different place, all to itself." As a resident observed, "[y]ou can stay back here for days and not see anyone you don't know." Today, the area is "composed mostly of neat, medium-sized homes with manicured lawns."[10] Like most places in urban settings, the area has suffered from the typical problems of the inner city, but is still considered a nice and neighborly place to live.

Wooden Shoe Hollow consists of about 150 acres and today "remains an isolated area with a one-lane, winding road through the tiny plots and well-kept farmhouses in a dip off Winton Road—seven miles from downtown." Many of the farmers and gardeners who settled in what is today Winton Place immigrated from the present-day German state of North Rhine–Westphalia. According to Willis R. Butz, "the land was so fertile because farmers would deliver produce to market downtown, then on the way home pass by the Spring Grove Avenue stockyards and haul manure to spread on their tiny plots." Apparently, it was Christian Hoeweler's ingenuity that transformed the area forever, when sometime around 1912 he introduced hothouses, or greenhouses, which made Wooden Shoe Hollow a major greenhouse center in the Greater Cincinnati area.[11]

The Hollow has often been viewed as an almost idyllic place, especially in the area press. One article noted that "gardeners wear contemporary shoes in Wooden Shoe Hollow today but many pastoral treasures found there by German immigrants in the nineteenth century remain. Lush soil in the eastern and original portion of Wooden Shoe Hollow still produces vegetables in abundance, fit for the most esoteric of epicurean delights. Fabulous gardening on land rimmed on three sides by thickly forested hills is as isolated in Cincinnati as any rural farming area far removed from urban activity. Yet the old section of Wooden Shoe Hollow, laced with a patchwork of narrow lanes curling to aged houses, barns, and sheds, is less than four hundred yards from Winton Road. Few motorists on that thoroughfare, one of Hamilton County's busiest, are aware of the existence of Wooden Shoe Hollow because it cannot be seen through the buffer zone of trees."[12]

The Hollow is located in the section of town known as Winton Place, which borders on several neighborhoods, including College Hill, Finneytown, Carthage, Elmwood Place, Saint Bernard, and Clifton. Within Winton Place, Wooden Shoe Hollow itself is located directly alongside Spring Grove Cemetery, which is internationally known for its landscape gardening and park-like setting. Winton and Gray roads form the two main thoroughfares in Wooden Shoe Hollow, and cross through the little valley, or hollow, which is sheltered on the west side by the beautiful and spacious nature preserve that is Spring Grove.

Winton Place itself derives its name from Matthew Winton, a

pioneer landowner, who laid out a road from his place in Springfield Township south into the Mill Creek Valley to meet with the military road connecting Cincinnati and Fort Hamilton. In the 1820s, the Miami and Erie Canal was built through the area, but it was not until Spring Grove Cemetery came into being in 1845 that the area began to grow and develop.

Railway service arrived in 1850, and soon a village began to emerge near the cemetery, attracting more settlers. In 1859, the German landscaping genius Adolph Strauch became Superintendent of Spring Grove, and made the cemetery's landscape lawn plan a national model. Many German gardeners were employed at Spring Grove, and German gardeners and farmers settled near the cemetery, concentrating in the valley north of the village. By 1900, the greenhouses of Wooden Shoe Hollow were supplying the produce for the markets in downtown Cincinnati. Greenhouses remained in the family for generations, developing a close-knit community.

Winton Place passenger station shown in 1918. Chester Park can be seen in the background. PHOTOGRAPH COURTESY OF BARBARA KEYSER GARGIULO.

Today, many of the family businesses have made the transition from the vegetable to the garden business, and these are the places where many Cincinnati residents go to get flowers, plants, seeds, shrubbery, trees, garden equipment, etc. Even today, Wooden Show Hollow maintains some of its charm and tranquility, especially due to the number of gardens and its proximity to the spacious and beautiful Spring Grove Cemetery. It certainly must have been inspirational for them to reside near Spring Grove, which also served to attract the general public to the area, and to the nearby garden, shrubbery, and nursery businesses for which Wooden Shoe Hollow became so well known.

As Superintendent of Spring Grove, Adolph Strauch not only attracted German landscape gardeners to work with him, but also recommended their services to the wealthy homeowners in Clifton, and elsewhere. Therefore, by means of his position at Spring Grove, he was responsible for attracting and drawing German gardeners and farmers to the area. Considered the father of landscape gardening in America, Strauch also contributed to an appreciation of landscape gardening that is still prevalent in the area today.

Adolph Strauch

Spring Grove is located across from Wooden Shoe Hollow, and many German gardeners worked there, as well as in nearby Clifton. EDITOR'S PHOTOGRAPH.

Strauch, it might be noted, was also involved with the planning of the park system of Cincinnati, the Zoological Gardens, as well as landscape plans for many homes in the area. Many residents of Wooden Shoe Hollow no doubt played a role in the completion of these landscaping plans.

Spring Grove's beauty is central to the area, and was commented on by H. A. Rattermann as follows: "the grand total impression received by the thoughtless musing heart, when it enters the gates of Spring Grove, is of a twofold nature. If we stand at any point in the lower part of the cemetery (the former swamp) then the eye beholds soft and poetic views in every direction, vying with each other in their pictorial beauty, surrounded on all sides by a forest landscape enclosing the pretty picture like a frame. Everything is soft and mild, like a painting of Murillo, complete loveliness, such as sublime art only may create; and yet this appears to us in Nature in its pure, true simplicity. No bombast or theatrical affectations anywhere."[13] Such is the general setting where Wooden Shoe Hollow arose.

It remains unknown when the first German settled in Wooden Shoe Hollow, but one of the first settlers there was Bernhard Strothmann. He emigrated from Hilter, which is located near Osnabrück, and settled in the Hollow in 1860. The German settlement that had begun in the 1860s as a result of Spring Grove was further encouraged in the 1870s by Asa Van Wormer. Rita Walsh describes Wooden Shoe Hollow as follows:

> tucked away in the northern part of the neighborhood between Winton Ridge Lane and Winton Road [it] possesses a long history of agriculture which continues today. The hollow and surrounding upland was leased by dairy and sheep farmers . . . in the mid-19th century then the property of Asa and Julia Van Wormer, whose home overlooked the hollow. The Van Wormer home is still extant on Winton Ridge Lane, which was originally a portion of Winton Road. Asa Van Wormer was a Court Street merchant and the benefactor of the University of Cincinnati bequeathing Cincinnati Street Railway stocks to establish the Van Wormer Library on the Clifton campus. During the 1870s, the Van Wormers began leasing small parcels in the Hollow for the specific purpose of vegetable gardening. All of their lessees were Germans who subsequently bought the parcels and the houses on them, which had mostly been built by the Van Wormers. Remarkably, the descendants of these original gardeners—Gabel, Schuhmacher, Rennegarbe and Greber—are still involved in greenhouses, presenting vast expanses of glass punctuated by tall brick smokestacks, are the most significant feature of this agricultural setting.[14]

Significance of the Novel

What is especially significant about the novel is that it illuminates the German-American community of Wooden Shoe Hollow. It con-

Asa Van Wormer at his home on Winton Ridge Lane. PHOTOGRAPH FROM THE ARCHIVES AND RARE BOOKS, BLEGEN LIBRARY, UNIVERSITY OF CINCINNATI.

nects this Cincinnati neighborhood with the ancestral homeland in northern Germany by means of its references to places, such as Osnabrück, and also by means of the frequent references to *Plattdeutsch*.

The novel connects to the chain migration to the area, or the ongoing process of immigration from that area of Germany to Cincinnati since the early nineteenth century. It might also be noted that the flow from northern Germany was a major element of the German immigration not only to Cincinnati, but also to the tri-state region of

Ohio, northern Kentucky, and southeastern Indiana, so that the novel takes on regional significance.[15]

The novel also conveys a sense of the *Zusammengehörigkeitsgetühl,* or the community's feeling of togetherness.[16] Also, a sense of the differences between German-Americans and Anglo-Americans, or Yankees, can be noted, thereby indicating how Wooden Shoe Hollow German-Americans viewed themselves as a community. The author notes this at one point when she writes of a new arrival:

> Oh, we aren't Yankees! We are German like you . . . [Yankees] are rich people who . . . have white coverlets on their beds, and they are proud, and sometimes they don't go to church. They eat fresh meat all winter long. . . . They have hired men and girls but they make them eat in the kitchen. Some of the Yankees are mean and stingy, but we have some awfully nice Yankees up in Winton Place.

Also, since the novel takes place in an area that Pieper knew firsthand, the novel takes on the character of a historical novel, since the places she refers to actually exist. This aspect gives the work a sense of historical realism, as the setting of Wooden Shoe Hollow is a real and actual place, and places mentioned are readily recognizable. Moreover, according to a family relative, Al Funke, the characters in the novel were based on people who lived in the area, and were readily recognizable.

The novel also provides a portrait of the area, and what it meant to be part of the community there before World War I, the time period in which the novel is placed. In so doing, it contributes to an understanding of the Greater Cincinnati area and the quaint and interesting area within it known as Wooden Shoe Hollow.

Residents of the Hollow certainly enjoyed the book. A newspaper article reported that residents agreed with their neighbor, Richard Friedhoff, who commented: "It's a fine book, with a love story woven into it. . . . We have love here in the Hollow, I guess, but it doesn't make the tomatoes grow any better."[17] Nonetheless, it certainly proved to be fertile ground for the emergence of a Cincinnati-German novelist—Charlotte Pieper.

This was the Winton Place Town Hall at Edgewood and Epworth Avenues. The volunteer fire department was organized in 1892 and also operated from this building until 1909. PRINTED WITH PERMISSION FROM THE CINCINNATI MUSEUM CENTER ARCHIVES.

Winton Place Engine House No. 38 at 725 Circle Avenue On December 24, 1903, after annexation to Cincinnati, this engine company was organized as a hose company with the Cincinnati Fire Department. On July 16, 1909, it was reorganized as a steam engine company and moved to a new station shown above. Around 1975 it was joined by Rescue Unit No. 38. PHOTO BY BINSTADT/ STUDIO 3, COURTESY OF BARBARA KEYSER GARGIULO.

NOTES

1. The work appeared as *Wooden Shoe Hollow* (New York: Exposition Press, 1951).
2. See the obituary "Author Pieper Dies," *Cincinnati Enquirer,* 1 November 1984. For her Bachelor of Science in Commerce at the University of Cincinnati, Pieper completed a senior thesis, "Worship Drama," (senior thesis, University of Cincinnati, 1946). Her thesis contains four original worship plays (15–70), which she defined as a play "embodying religious truth and written to be enacted before an altar. It may portray a Bible story, or it may simply dramatize a spiritual message. It is as much a vehicle of worship as are sermons, liturgy and sacraments" (1).
3. Ibid.
4. Westrup is a town located in the district of Stemwede in the state of North Rhine–Westphalia, and is east of the city of Osnabrück. Westrup is next to the town of Wehdem, where the local Evangelical Lutheran Church is located. Church records for the area are available on the World Wide Web <http://members.tripod.com/Stemweder>. Wilhelm Niermann writes that "in the nineteenth century the Stemwede area, governed by the Kingdom of Prussia, bordered the Kingdom of Hannover. This geographical proximity allowed many people to leave without official permission. A short walk took them to the Kingdom of Hannover where, without further difficulties, they continued to the emigration ports of Bremen and Bremerhaven. Since mandatory military service was lengthy in Prussia, men of military age had another reason to leave. The number of emigrants who left without official permission was as high if not higher than the number of those who left with official sanction. . . . The total population loss from 1845 to 1864 was about 500 individuals and from 1865 to 1885 about 1100." See Wilhelm F. Niermann, "Forces that Pushed People to Emigrate," World Wide Web <http://members.tripod.com/~Stemweder/emigration_from_stemwede.htm>. Those interested in the history of the area can visit the local museum, the Heimathaus, which consists of a farm house that was moved to a location near the church in Wehdem. For information on the Heimathaus, see World Wide Web <http://members.tripod.com/Stemweder/Wehdem_parish/wehdem_heimathaus.htm>.

    In the nineteenth century, nearly one hundred thousand people emigrated from the Osnabrück region to America. Commenting on this emigration, Walter D. Kamphoefner writes that "[o]f all the emigrants from the region who listed specific destinations in their permits, almost half of them were heading for Cincinnati and rural Ohio, and more than a third of them for Missouri (if one overlooks port cities that were often only way stations." He also notes that this "can be explained, above all, by favorable transport connections and chain migration." See Walter D. Kamphoefner, Peter Marschalck, and Birgit Nolte-Schuster, *Von Heuerleuten und Farmern: Die*

Auswanderung aus dem Osnabrücker Land nach Nordamerika im 19. Jahrhundert/Emigration from the Osnabrücker Region to North America in the 19th Century. Kulturregion Osnabrück, Band 12 (Bramsche: Landschaftsverband Osnabrücker Land e.V., 1999), 57.

The Haarlammert family, which originated from Ladbergen near Osnabrück, is an example of a family that maintains contacts with the old country, and has recently held family reunions in Ladbergen. These have been reported on in the German press of the region, and reflect the many contacts between the region and the Cincinnati area. For further information on genealogical research in the Westphalian region of Germany, contact Brigitte Jahnke at: JahnkeResearch@aol.com.

For further information about Low German, see Robert Lee Stockman, *Platt Düütsch=Low German: A Brief History of the People and Language.* (Alto, Mich: Platt Düütsch Press, 1998). Also, for an interesting novel about Low German farmers, see Johannes Gilhoff, *Letters of a German American Farmer: Jürnjakob Swehn Travels to America,* trans. Richard Lorenz August Trost (Iowa City, Iowa: University of Iowa Press, 2000).

5. From the written notes of Mary Pieper given to the editor, 4 January 2004.
6. From the book jacket.
7. Ibid.
8. Ibid.
9. Robert Heidler, "Suggestions Years Ago Resulted in Novel by Woman Author," *Cincinnati Times-Star,* 6 October 1951.
10. See B. G. Gregg, "Close to Home: Winton Place," *Cincinnati Enquirer,* 14 July 1997. The current state of affairs was commented on in the local press, where one article noted that some gardeners in the Hollow "blame the waning of their enterprise on the interstates that allow speedy delivery of produce grown in California and Florida, on the rising cost of fuel to heat their greenhouses, on an economy that favors mass producers over small farmers. There is not a universal exodus from the greenhouse industry. In some family greenhouse businesses outside the Hollow, there are sons who have decided to stay with the family calling. And, within the Hollow, a college-educated farmer has taken up the trade begun there by German immigrants, a sign that perhaps that way of life may be revived." The article notes that "in the meantime, the generation of gardeners there now isn't saying anything about the future of the Hollow. It will be for others to decide." See Kay Brookshire, "A Place of Families and the Soil," *Cincinnati Enquirer,* 1 August 1981, p. 8A, col. 1. This article lists the following family names from the Hollow: Friedhoff, Graber, Greber, Rosenberg, Schuhmacher.

Jim Calhoun, "Hollow Attracted Immigrants," *Cincinnati Enquirer,* 6 July 1988, p. 2A, col. 3. This article mentions the following families as residents of the Hollow: Rennegarbe, Hodde, Renz, Schuhmacher, Graber, and Pieper.

11. Ira Brock, "Pastoral Wooden Shoe Hollow Has Nineteenth Century Atmosphere," *Cincinnati Enquirer*, 13 June 1976, p. B2, col. 1. This article also makes mention of the Hodde family. William H. Hodde comments that "nobody seems to know for certain when the first Germans settled in the Hollow. What we do know for sure is that they all brought wooden shoes. . . . When I was young every adult out here had wooden shoes. They were lined and kept feet warm in winter."

For a survey of Winton Place, see Geoffrey J. Giglierano and Deborah A. Overmyer, with Frederic L. Propas, eds., *The Bicentennial Guide to Greater Cincinnati: A Portrait of Two Hundred Years* (Cincinnati: Cincinnati Historical Society, 1988), 434–51. A nineteenth century journal described Winton Place as "the first station beyond the corporate limits of Cincinnati on the railroads leading up the Valley, and lies about four miles directly north of the city proper. It is situated on the north side of the Millcreek Valley, on what was formerly known as Rolling Ridge. The ground rises gradually from the level of the railroads, to an altitude of one hundred feet, and on this slope and on the summit of the ridge, the town is built." See "Winton Place," *The Criterion* 2, no. 3 (April 1888). A mid-twentieth century article describes Winton Place as "placid, friendly, with a bygone beauty in its residential architecture, has 2,800 inhabitants, many of them sons and daughters of its origin, who think conservatively. Background is a strong Republican, Methodist and Episcopalian training, laced by a healthy slice of German thrift and 'no nonsense,' and to complete the picture, an element of Catholicism that flourished through years it trod to church in a neighboring suburb before erecting its own church in 1919." See Robert Heidler, "Winton Place," *Cincinnati Times-Star*, 1 July 1950. This article contains photographs of mailboxes in Wooden Shoe Hollow for the Hoeweler and Rahn families. Other family names mentioned are: Funke, Heckmeyer, Osterback, and Wischmeyer. A more recent article describes Winton Place as a place that "once was the rural burg that attracted famous Cincinnatians and served as the setting for their distinctive and spacious homes. Today, it retains some of that rural character. Large trees shade streets of modest homes and white and blue-collar workers say they are not afraid to walk the streets after dark. There also are busy streets, industrial facilities and even a farm or two." See Jim Sluzewski, "Community Offers Charm and History, Dateline: Winton Place," *Cincinnati Enquirer*, 22 January 1979.

Regarding Strauch, see H. A. Rattermann, *Spring Grove and Its Creator: H. A. Rattermann's Biography of Adolph Strauch*, ed. Don Heinrich Tolzmann (Cincinnati: The Ohio Book Store, 1988).

12. Rattermann, *Spring Grove*, 22–23. Rattermann notes that Strauch "was the obedient servant of true Nature, whose grandeur in its simplicity he loved to admire. He hated all make-up vapidities like sin. Nature to him was, as it

truly is, the unapproachable poetess of art. Whoever can follow Nature's majesty in its totality even in the distance? Who can comprehend its consummate wonders in its minutest details? Nature is perpetual harmony itself in its seeming irregularity and the unbounded multiformity. . . . Thus the life of Nature, constantly changing, reigns here in this solemn and quiet grove, sacred, sublime, harmonious charm, often described in prose and verse by many authors; but more deeply felt in the hearts of the many thousands of visitors that saw and enjoyed the grandeur of the creation of Adolph Strauch . . ."

In addition to training and study, Rattermann notes the importance of an inherent appreciation of aesthetics with regard to landscape gardening, which he considered an art: "A farmer may ever be as good in his place, but that will not make him a successful gardener, and the best gardener is not a master of the arborean art, if uneducated for it by sufficient botanical studies, and furthermore, unpossessed of the inherent genius which makes great men!" See Rattermann, *Spring Grove*, 22–23. It might be noted that Rattermann himself was also part of the emigration from northwest Germany to Cincinnati, and came from the village of Ankum, which sent many to the Ohio Valley region. For further information about Rattermann, see Sister Mary Edmund Spanheimer, *The German Pioneer Legacy: The Life and Work of H. A. Rattermann,* ed. by Don Heinrich Tolzmann, New German-American Studies, no. 26, (Oxford: Peter Lang Pub. Co., 2004).

13. Rattermann, *Spring Grove*.
14. Rita Walsh, *Winton Place: Historic Sites, 1989–1990* (Dayton, Oh.: Howard Paper Mills, c. 1990).
15. For a general introduction to Cincinnati's German heritage, see Don Heinrich Tolzmann, *German Heritage Guide to the Greater Cincinnati Area* (Milford, Ohio: Little Miami Pub. Co., 2003).
16. Articles in the area press often commented on the Wooden Shoe Hollow community. For example, see the following articles: "Farmers Work Overtime Under Glass," *Cincinnati Post*, 6 February 1939, p. 9, col. 5 (refers to the following family names from the Hollow: Friedhoff, Funke, and Graber; Joe Aston, "Wooden Shoe Hollow Residents Keep Sharp Eye on Crops," *Cincinnati Enquirer*, 29 March 1952, p. 6, col. 2 (mentions the following family names: Friedhoff, Hodde, Kemper, Schuhmacher); Charles Warnick, "Names Don't Change in Wooden Shoe Hollow: Descendants of German Immigrants A Century Ago Still Farm in Tiny Community Although They Have Discarded Favorite Footwear of their Industrious Forebears" *Cincinnati Enquirer*, 10 July 1955, sec. 3, p. 1, col. 1 (makes reference to the following families: Schumacher, Rennegarbe, Hodde, Graber, and Friedhoff).

Reference is made to the Varnau family, which now has Varnau's West Chester Garden Center on West Chester Road, but was originally located in Wooden Shoe Hollow in: Laura Bauerman, "Varnau's Knows How to Grow

Business," *Cincinnati Enquirer*, 28 May 2003. Finally, see Kay Brookshire, "A Place of Families and the Soil," *Cincinnati Post*, 2 August 1981, which makes reference to the following family names: Friedhoff, Graber, Greber, Rennegarbe, and Rosenberg. Brookshire wrote that ". . . the hollow's charm lies in the neat rows of white-painted greenhouses built of sturdy cypress and glad, its century-old farmhouses set in no particular order along the one-lane road built for horse drawn carts, the orderly squares of lush green plants beside patches of the dark-brown soil . . ." Also, by the same author, see "Industry Looks For Room to Grow Amidst Gardens," *Cincinnati Post*, 3 October 1984: p. 4B, col. a (makes reference to the following family names from the Hollow: Ernst, Graber, Greber, Grieme, Kettler, and Stephens).

The editor has also received a number of communications from residents of the Hollow, such as Marylyn Schnebelt, who knew the Pieper family, and had Charlotte Pieper as her Sunday school teacher at church, where both families were members. Schnebelt's family immigrated in the 1880s to 1890s from the village of Wehdem, which is near the village of Westrup, the home of the Pieper family. Robert M. Scharft also provided information on the Strothmann family that had settled in the Hollow around 1860.

17. Quoted in the article by Aston cited in footnote no. 16.

The Pieper Homestead at 6303 Stover Avenue in Golf Manor. Mary Meyer Pieper (Mrs. Henry) and five of her children who were still at home were forced to move from this home as a result of the Depression. When Charlotte's family lived in the home, the entrance was on Wiehe Road.

Part Two

The Novel

PREFACE

Wooden Shoe Hollow is a story, and the people in it are story people; yet in a sense they are very real, for just such men and women as Otto Betz and Minna Betz gardened in Wooden Shoe Hollow. There were also Ricas and Heinrichs, and, assuredly, there was a Herr Pastor.

If there was anything that set apart the people of Wooden Shoe Hollow it was their indomitable faith in God. It was a common sight in the spring to see the father of the household sowing the first radish seeds while the whole family gathered around him in prayer.

That faith had its humorous moments, too. Sunday-morning cooks were known to time their meals by the church service. When the closing "Our Father" bell was tolled on Epworth Avenue it was time to put the potatoes on to boil in Wooden Shoe Hollow. By the time the family got home from church the potatoes would then be ready to serve. That was scarcely the reason why the "Our Father" bell was rung, however. It was intended as a signal for the sick, and others who could not get to church, to join the congregation in the closing prayer.

There is a wealth of folklore about the people who lived in Wooden Shoe Hollow and in her neighboring colonies. It is the spirit of that folklore which I have tried to catch in this story.

I have told it as Mom, Pop, and Charlie and Gus, the hired men, might have told it in the summer kitchen long ago—with touches that were added January evenings when the oven was crammed with toasting sweet potatoes and toasting feet.

Charlotte Pieper

I Milk and Honey

GROSSMUTTER BETZ had come to Rica Heber out of the mist and smoke of a gray morning at the Osnabrück railway station. A tiny black bonnet was tied primly under her enthusiastic little chin. The word *Amerika* shuttled past her lips many times, but it was the first mention of the name which drew Rica to her side with breathless expectancy. "You are going to America, too?" she asked.

The old lady smiled warmly. "Ah yes," she said. "And you?"

Rica nodded, scarcely believing it possible that already she had found a companion for her journey.

Grossmutter took her over with a tender embrace. "Sweet child, we shall stay together, yes?"

Thus Grossmutter swept away the old world with its mixture of good and bad which had culminated in a catastrophe. As the boat sailed out into the Atlantic, Rica breathed freely. No one would ever know about that fateful night in Osnabrück! All the haunting unhappy memories would stay on the German shore, unless . . . unless she were discovered and pursued!

Like the children of Israel, plodding through the wilderness of Sin, and looking steadfastly forward to Canaan, Rica and Grossmutter had looked forward to their promised land all the way from Osnabrück to New York. That promised land was a garden community in Ohio, where Grossmutter was going to live with her son, Otto. Grossmutter saw no reason why Rica should not accompany her all the way. And Rica, glad to have an initial destination, traveled with her.

Rica caught her first glimpse of the little garden empire many weeks later. That glimpse etched its every detail into her perceptive mind. Wooden Shoe Hollow! Of this sweet land of milk and honey Grossmutter had chatted so pleasantly the long journey through.

The old lady's eyes were blinded with tears, and her heartbeat matched the staccato clop clop of the horses' hoofs on the stones, but for Rica's eyes there were no tears, only eagerness to see. To see everything from the lazy white clouds to the wooded hillsides.

Now the carriage dropped abruptly from the main road into a lane which wound its unconcerned way past each humble cottage and garden of Wooden Shoe Hollow.

Dew glistened on rows of hotbed glass. It lingered on endive, on the lush green of lettuce and on the dark foliage of beets.

Once more Rica looked at the worn photograph of Otto's home, which she had been clutching in her hand while riding from the Cincinnati railway station. "There it is," she cried. "Grossmutter, we are there!"

"Thank God, we are really home at last!" Grossmutter answered.

The moment the carriage stopped in his yard Otto clattered up to it in wooden shoes. "Mutter," was all he could manage for the moment. He lifted his mother from the seat.

"Mein Otto, mein Otto," she piped, pushing back the shaggy plush cap, and caressing him. Pent-up emotion of twenty years poured itself out in a second!

The summer kitchen door flew open and Otto's three children dashed across the yard in high excitement at this long-promised event—the arrival of their grandmother from Germany.

"This is Ernst, and Fritz and Hulda!" Otto said, joyfully sweeping them all into his mother's arms.

Rica, meanwhile, gathered her skirt in her hand and climbed down from the cab. She stood beside her companion, a trim picture in her ginger suit. Soft brown hair was becomingly fluffed above her forehead. A rolled-brim velvet hat sat heavily upon her youthful head. Classic features of a cameo lady were hers.

Tiny Hulda backed out of the jubilant circle presently, and smiled up at Rica. "Tante?" she queried.

Grossmutter wheeled about. "Rica, you must meet Otto . . .

and his little ones. Otto, son, this is Fräulein Heber from Osnabrück. She has no one in the land, and we made our way together."

Otto grasped Rica's hand and shook it vigorously. "Welcome to you, Fräulein Heber," he said. His weatherbeaten face beamed hospitably.

Otto's wife swung the summer kitchen door open. "What a comfort to see you again, Grossmutter," she said breathlessly. "So, so long we have waited for you!"

"This is Rica Heber from Osnabrück, Mamma," Otto explained, as Rica followed Grossmutter across the door sill. "She has no one in the land."

"You are surely welcome here," Minna Betz said warmly. "Make yourself right at home with us. It was nice of you to give Grossmutter company."

Rica protested. "It was I who was alone!"

In mere moments Rica and Grossmutter were seated in the Betz kitchen and were answering eager questions while Minna Betz prepared their lunch.

"Did you have it easy finding us?" Otto asked.

Grossmutter's eyes twinkled. "Och, no!" she said. "Here in America it gives so many dumb people! Even the street soldier in New York didn't know where to find Wooden Shoe Hollow. And the railroad soldiers were just as bad. Rica had to tell them so much, that it was in the state of Ohio, near the city of Cincinnati."

"And were there many children on the boat?" Hulda wanted to know. "Did the children bring German toys with them?"

Rica nodded.

Minna came from the pantry, carrying a cumbrous loaf of homemade bread. She placed it firmly against her breast and began sawing it. Rica noticed the sinewy arms, the massive spread of her fingers, and the solidity of her figure, which even near-approaching maternity could not disavow.

After the simply laid "bread and butter" lunch, excitement developed quickly. Word had gone from house to house that Grossmutter Betz had arrived and had brought a pretty Fräulein with her.

Neighbors streamed in and out of the Betz home to see the "inwanderers." One visitor offered to transport Rica's unopened bag to his own home, and made mention of some "dollars a week."

Otto Betz cut in with a thunderous, "Fräulein Heber stays with us!"

That was settled.

By the time evening came, Rica was already quite content to stay with the Betzes . . . father, mother, the three children . . . and the hired man. At bed time she stood before the night shelf looking about the simple bedroom with its pair of white beds, its bare floor, its rag rug. With an audible sigh of relief and gratitude she blew out the lamp and slipped under the billowy featherbed with Hulda. Sheer exhaustion quickly brought sound sleep.

Early in the morning, however, a crash awoke her. There were hurried footsteps in the hall. A clatter of pans down in the kitchen.

Peering through the darkened room she could see Grossmutter's bed unceremoniously deserted, the featherbed half resting on the floor.

What could possibly happen to disturb the peace of this complacent little valley? . . . A moment later Rica ceased wondering. Up the stairs came the sharp cries of a tiny baby—Minna's fourth child.

It was almost day break when Grossmutter tiptoed upstairs. Rica bolted out of bed.

"Awake?" Grossmutter whispered. "It is a fine girl we have, Rica. A sister for Hulda. Och, it is good we came. Minna needs us!"

"Can I help?"

"There is nothing to do now. The midwife has taken care of everything. A fine woman she is. So wonderfully kind, and so wise."

Grossmutter slipped off the loose gray wrapper and returned to her dishevelled bed. "Thank God," she sighed.

Rica could not sleep. So there was a new baby! That made four children in Otto's family. Of course she would stay . . . a little while at least . . . perhaps a long while. Who could tell? It was good to be needed somewhere, to have work and friends.

Osnabrück seemed very far away, not only in miles, but in her short life's cycle. Life could compensate for some of fate's harshness . . . some of it. So Rica reflected as the morning of her second day in Wooden Shoe Hollow began to dawn.

II The Crowd

~~~~~~

It was Saturday evening. Rica had spent the day sewing, cooking and baking, and ever it seemed to Herman Toepfer, the Betz hired man, that there was someone in the kitchen with her. But finally, after supper, came a moment when she was alone.

Herman stopped twirling the roller towel. He ambled over to Rica, shyly. "I'd like to take you to the crowd tonight," he said.

"The crowd?"

"Yes, up at the hall. It's where all the young folks go Saturday nights.

"Oh, that would be lovely, Herman. Thank you for asking me, and another time I'll surely go, but tonight I must stay with Grossmutter."

Rica smiled coyly, then went to minister to Minna and the baby. Minna had overheard their conversation. "You are to go to the crowd with Herman," she said incisively.

"Oh, no . . . some other time. Tonight I have work."

"Work?" Frau Betz repeated. A frown spread over her blanched face. "No, Rica, Saturday night young people go to the crowd. That is no more than right. Life comes upon them soon enough with its everlasting work and worry! After a while you will marry and have babies. . . . There will be no time for the crowd then. Of course you will go with Herman! . . . He is not to be put off. Herman is a fine boy, and the other girls . . ."

Minna left her speech in mid air, for her better judgment had caught up with her tongue. A moment of puzzling silence, and she continued, "You had better get ready now. Herman goes early."

Rica acquiesced. "But what shall I wear?"

"Wear . . . ? A gingham dress is all right, and an apron."

"Apron?"

"Yes, sure. Do you want them to take you for a Yankee?"

Rica didn't know who a Yankee might be, but if the hollow folk didn't like Yankees she wouldn't want to be mistaken for one. "No, I'll wear an apron," she said.

Minna yawned. "You'll like the crowd. Lusty music and plenty of dancing partners. Ours is the liveliest crowd in whole Cincinnati."

Herman was still sitting on the kitchen bench, looking out of the window at the phalanx of poled lima beans when Rica came back with her reversed decision. He was jubilant.

Hulda followed Rica upstairs. "I wish I was big enough to go to the crowd," she said wistfully. "We'd have a good time together; only I can't dance."

"Do you want to learn?"

"Yes, sure! I want to waltz fast like Mamma does, and I'd like to do the Schottische, too. You can dance proper, I know."

"Maybe the American way will be different."

"Oh, we aren't Yankees!" Hulda said. "We are German like you, Rica."

"Who are the Yankees?"

Hulda laughed merrily. "Weren't there any on the boat? They are rich people who have black buggy horses with sets in the horses' harness. They have white coverlets on their beds, and they are proud, and sometimes they don't go to church. They eat fresh meat all winter long and they use napkins at the table, and white tablecloths, even during the week! They have hired men and hired girls but they make them eat in the kitchen. And they always have pie and cake for dinner. Some of the Yankees are mean and stingy, but we have some awfully nice Yankees up in Winton Place. When I get big, I'd like to work for nice Yankees. Do you know why?"

Rica didn't know.

"Because they have lots of books, and if they are nice they let you read them," Hulda ran on breathlessly.

Rica fastened a sunburst brooch to her collar, then, with a smile of secret amusement, tied on a stiffly starched blue apron.

"You look so nice. You'll be the prettiest girl at the crowd," Hulda ventured. Herman ventured the same opinion when he saw Rica coming down the stairs. Rica dismissed it with a shrug of her shoulders.

"How long have you been working in the hollow?" Rica asked, as she and Herman sauntered down the lane.

"Since I was eleven. Herr Betz took me from the orphan home," Herman answered. "My parents both died before I started school."

"I see. My parents are dead, too," Rica said with a hint of bitterness.

Herman caught an evasive air. Perhaps he had better not ask questions about her family. Recalling scenes from the homeland always meant pain for inwanderers. He would be silent.

As they approached the hall, whose cheerful windows were lighted with spare lamps from many a Wooden Shoe Hollow home, Herman forcefully changed the subject. "You must feel at home, here, Rica. I'll make you acquainted, and dance with you whenever it isn't my turn to play. I want you to have such a good time that you won't be able to wait for next Saturday night to roll round."

Herman held the door open and Rica entered.

Before her was a long room with bare wood floor, scrubbed white and strewn with paraffin shavings. The walls were lined with rough-hewn benches. At one end of the hall was a coat rack and mirrors. At the other was a bar. A crowd of young men had already congregated there to supervise the tapping of the first keg.

A trio of girls babbled in the center of the hall.

Yust Bobke, the alternate accordionist, was limbering up his fingers.

Herman took Rica's arm and escorted her to the girls.

Sophia, a chubby red-cheeked blonde with babyish blue eyes; Hattie—thin, sharp-eyed and sober; Rosie—freckled, tongue-tied and merry. Rica met them all with the same poise and warm-hearted grace. They exchanged greetings shyly. It was seldom that a stranger came into the crowd.

The girls were dressed alike in gingham frocks and aprons.

There was an awkward silence for a moment, and then they began chattering like magpies about Germany, sea travel, and the hardship of leaving home and friends.

It was Hattie who ventured to ask, "Did you leave a sweetheart over there?"

Rica was caught off guard. She faced Hattie's blinking, inquisitive black eyes and answered, "No, I didn't have a sweetheart."

"That wasn't nice," Rosie lisped. "Of course she has a sweetheart. It just makes her feel bad to say so."

Rica protested that she had not left a sweetheart in Germany. She hoped guiltily that this one announcement would suffice for the entire crowd.

Hattie didn't want to be convinced. It would be better to be able to whisper within earshot of the boys, "Rica is engaged," for a girl like Rica had too many advantages over the other girls . . . prettiness . . . good manners . . . a ready smile, and the lure of mystery. Dancing would bring out all these attractions. Hattie sniffed and turned from the theoretical aspects of friendship to the material aspects. "Could you lend me your apron pattern?" she asked.

"Pattern?" Rica queried. "Why, I just cut it out of newspaper. You can borrow it if you like."

"Let's all cut one," suggested Rosie. "We can use new crowd aprons."

"Suppose I cut each one a different pattern. That would be nicer. We could have a blue one with white ruffles for you, Sophia . . . and a pink one with feather stitching for you, Hattie . . . and a green one with diamond-shaped pockets and a peak top for you, Rosie."

The three girls were speechless at this outburst of creative enthusiasm.

Hattie was the first to recover. "Do you mean that you can draft all those out of your head?" she challenged.

"Oh yes, I like to draft patterns," Rica said happily. "It makes them all my own."

Nobody understood, but Sophia wanted to understand. "Many thanks," she called, as she glided off into a waltz with her brother.

Rosie sat down to the business of tapping her feet to the steady rhythm of the accordion—to tap her feet and think about a new green apron with diamond-shaped pockets, while she waited for her single dance of the evening.

Herman came and took Rica.

Hattie was chosen by Emil Mueller, the aging Lancelot of the hollow. He jerked her round and round fitfully. Just ahead of these two Rica and Herman glided as one person—Rica felicitous, Herman singing ever so gayly as the accordion rolled on:

Du, du liegst mir im Herzen,
Du, du liegst mir im Sinn.

"How do you like the crowd?" Herman asked, as the dance ended.

"It is lovely," Rica answered. "Very, very lovely."

Yust laid down his accordion, flicked his lapel and strolled over to Herman. "The next dance with your girl if you will play, Herman."

"All right," Herman replied. "What shall it be?"

"*Ach, du lieber Augustin.*"

Herman took the accordion on his knee, rippled over the keys playfully and then swung into the lively tune. Rica glimpsed him frequently through little open patches across the dance hall.

Yust stamped his feet and brayed foolishly. He held Rica's shoulder in a vise-like grip. She was glad when the dance was over and she could rejoin the girls.

The evening passed quickly for Rica as she plunged wholeheartedly into fun-making with the boys and girls of Wooden Shoe Hollow. The cinders of Osnabrück were trampled under foot as she danced and sang and learned once more how truly effortless it is to enjoy living. Minna had been right in her boast. This must, of a truth, be the liveliest crowd in all Cincinnati.

On the way home, jolly Emil Mueller marched ahead of Rica and Herman, twirling a cane. His silk neckerchief fluttered about, and he assembled all the tunes of the evening into a continuous concert, switching from bass to falsetto whenever a facile spirit so moved him.

"It wouldn't seem like the crowd without Emil," Herman remarked. "Boys and girls join the crowd and after a while they marry and stop coming, but Mueller sticks!"

"But he doesn't to his girl?" Rica speculated.

"Mueller?" Herman laughed. "The whole hollow calls him 'Wooden Shoe Hollow's beau.'"

"How beastly! . . . If he doesn't choose to marry . . ." Rica defended.

"Nobody expects him to," Herman said. "He'll call himself one of the young folks as long as he can hobble down off his hill and make his rounds with all the girls in the crowd. He's a fine old fellow, even if we don't understand him."

Rica's thoughts spun about. She put herself in Herr Mueller's place. A place that she wouldn't choose deliberately. The thought chilled her spirit momentarily. They walked on in silence.

The chill disappeared, however, as the two parted company in the Betz kitchen. "Good night, Herman," Rica said. "I've had a nice time."

Herman held her hand and patted it. "You've brought me so much joy," he said, as her fingers slipped through his. She turned to go upstairs.

III *An Accident*

GROSSMUTTER AND RICA made their first appearance at Old First Church the next morning, ostensibly to give thanks to God for a safe journey to America. All plans were carefully made so that this might be the remembered occasion that it deserved to be.

The spinster music teacher of Wooden Shoe Hollow, famous for her unusual recipes, was to prepare the dinner. Emil Mueller was to drive the honored ones to church in his very stateliest carriage. It seemed there were some personal sacrifices necessary also. Herman was to stay home and "watch the place." Thus, his Sunday plans were left decidedly awry. He buried his disappointment in feeding the chickens. Fondly, he had looked forward to walking down the long aisle of Old First Church, with Rica beside him. The whole congregation would follow them with admiring eyes. Herman had projected himself into that interesting moment many times during the sleepless night after he had come home from the crowd.

Great, too, was Hulda's woe at not being permitted to attend Grossmutter's first public appearance. It would have been such pleasant excitement to be in the midst of all the handshaking, greeting and well-wishing of reunited friends, to have seen Grossmutter swishing about in her black silk dress. There was compensation for Hulda in staying at home, however. She could watch Frau Laufer, the midwife, bathe the baby—smell the sweet pungent Kummel mixed with steaming water.

As the carriage drove out of the Betz roadway Otto surveyed his modest home, deeply satisfied with its peace and stored plenty.

Herr Mueller turned about and faced his passengers. "What do you think of this wilderness of America?"

"Wonderful," was Grossmutter's awed answer.

"And does it please you, too, Fräulein Rica?"

"I am more than pleased. The country is lovely and the people are so gracious."

Mueller tipped his hat appreciatively. "Oh, you haven't seen the best, my girl. We have lots to show you. . . . How did you like the crowd last night?"

"It was the nicest dance I've ever attended."

"Well, well. So our dances are best after all!" Mueller ejaculated. "Were you from the country?"

Rica hesitated. "No, from the city."

"Where," Emil asked.

"Osnabrück."

"Osnabrück? That is a business town. Was your father a tradesman?"

Grossmutter chafed. Would the man spoil everything with his eternal question asking?

"No, Father was in service."

"Ah," Emil continued. "He died in service?"

"Afterward," Rica answered with restraint.

"Ah, that is too bad. But you left others back there?"

Rica shook her head. "Nobody of the family."

"But, I'll venture sweethearts by the score!" He burst into bucolic laughter. "Sweethearts by the score; not so, Otto? Well, there are a dozen good hired men here. All good hard-working fellows who know how to count their coppers!"

Grossmutter fretted under her breath.

Mueller chuckled. "By the way, Herman Toepfer plants straighter celery rows than any hired man in the hollow."

Rica stirred uneasily. Clearly, Emil was a menace. What would he say if he knew? . . . "Perhaps I shall not marry at all," she said diffidently.

"Nonsense!" Herr Mueller protested. "You will be married within the year, and I hope you will do me the honor of standing for your oldest boy."

At this, Otto slapped Mueller's back in glee. "Herr Mueller has a godchild in almost every home in Wooden Shoe Hollow, Rica, and always he expects more! . . . How many is it, now, Emil?"

"The fifteenth one hasn't been named yet," Mueller retorted.

The carriage now halted at a hub of avenues.

"This is Knowlton's Corner," Fritz explained. "See, Rica, there's our church, the one with the big spire!"

Herr Mueller drew up before the steep flight of stairs and his passengers alighted; they were greeted by the half of Wooden Shoe Hollow who had made it their concern to be on hand at the door of First Church when Mueller's carriage arrived.

One granny held fast to the rail, waiting for the crowd to disperse and let the newcomers go into church. Rica saw her wrinkled face lit with anticipation. "Grossmutter," she said, touching her companion's arm. "Is that an old friend over there?"

Grossmutter whirled about. "Och," she cried, darting through the throng like a mouse. "Lieschen, my Lieschen! How are you?" The two grandmothers, who had not seen each other for thirty years, and that after a bosom friendship dating back to schooldays, fussed over each other like two homing pigeons. Even Otto gulped at the sight.

Then the huge bells overhead in the tower pealed a warning. The crowd streamed into church. Wullum von Schleyer and Otto Betz disentangled their respective mothers and helped them up the stairs. Rica, holding fast to Fritz's arm, followed Otto and Grossmutter down the aisle, while Emil Mueller strutted ahead of the procession, swinging his gold-topped cane.

Rica took her seat and became engrossed in silent prayer. Grossmutter, likewise, let her thoughts soar heavenward in thanksgiving.

Otto stood erect in the pew—his face covered with his plush hat. In deep silence he delivered the long formal Sabbath morning prayer of his hymnal. This done, he seated himself beside his mother, and smiled to every chance worshiper who looked in his direction.

It was a large edifice, larger than Rica had expected, but it lacked the decorative warmth of her home church. High on the ceiling was painted an august conception of the Almighty Creator, God of seed-time and harvest, mighty Judge of men, omnipotent Father. In great majesty He sat enthroned in the clouds of Heaven.

On the left façade a white-robed angel knelt in a dark garden, and on the opposite panel was painted, in somber tones of blue and gray, the crucifixion scene. The clouds hung heavily above the three crosses, and the despair of the vigilants echoed the gloom of the heavens.

Rica gazed steadfastly at the paintings and thought unconsciously of the radiant stained-glass picture of the Good Shepherd, which glowed in the front of St. Johanneskirche in Osnabrück.

The great triple-toned bell sent out a clamorous call, followed by an organ prelude. At the hushed amen of the prelude, Pastor Schicht entered the sanctuary. Sinewy brown hands dangled out of his robe. Solemnly, he faced the congregation and pronounced the invocation which every boy and girl in Wooden Shoe Hollow could repeat with him, in the same unhurried manner. "I was glad when they said unto me, let us go into the House of the Lord!"

Devout. Sincere. Persuasive.

And presently the strong voices of the assembly burst into familiar song . . . so familiar that Rica could scarcely believe she was in America.

After the service Pastor Schicht ushered the newcomers into his study. He grasped Rica's hand and shook it vigorously. There was kindness in his eyes, keen understanding and a suspicion of wit.

"So you are from Osnabrück, Fräulein Heber?" he asked. "And you came with Grossmutter? How providential! Frau Betz needs a fine girl like you. I know you will be very happy. We are simple folk, but God blesses us abundantly, is it not so, Herr Betz?"

Otto nodded.

"If there is ever anything which I can do for you, never fear to ask it," he added, giving her hand a reassuring clasp. Rica knew that such a need was not distant.

This man she could trust. Everything about him bespoke sincerity and honesty. Nevertheless, she turned away troubled. What right had she to stand before him—daring to pretend . . . ? Conscience murmured. Her throat tightened. Would it always be like this? Why could she not free herself of guilt?

Pastor turned to Grossmutter. "Give to Frau Betz my hearty good wishes for herself and the new baby. A girl, I believe?"

"Such a tiny one she is," Grossmutter answered. "Only five pounds."

Herr Mueller sidled up to the chatting party. "Have you seen my new mare, Herr Pastor?" he asked, as a child with a new toy might ask.

Pastor hadn't and he gladly accompanied the group down to the carriage.

"A wonderful creature," he said, while stroking the new horse's sleek black coat and admiring her shapely trotting legs. "She makes a nice teammate to Molly. When you are ready to sell her let me know."

"She will serve me another ten years first, Herr Pastor," Mueller boasted, as he stepped up into the carriage, clicked the reins and rode off in high spirit.

The carriage was rolling along past Spring Grove Cemetery, when, suddenly, it gave a violent lurch. Grossmutter and Otto were thrown to the floor. Rica plunged headlong out of the vehicle and landed on her outstretched hands, shaken but unhurt.

Fritz leaped clear of the falling carriage and fell beside her into the dry roadside weeds, hardly daring to look back at the wreck.

Both horses were down with the impact of the falling vehicle. The front wheel had come off completely. Molly was trying to rise, but Betsy lay still in her traces, and whinnied piteously.

Emil rose slowly from the floor and clutched his pain-shocked arm to his breast. "Anybody hurt back there?" he gasped.

"I'm safe," Grossmutter answered tremulously. "Otto caught me . . . but you, Herr Mueller?"

"My arm," he said weakly. "You, Fräulein, are you hurt?"

Rica's voice deserted her. She scrambled to her feet and spread her hands in a gesture of reassurance.

The party climbed out of the carriage and gathered around the ill-fated Betsy.

Fritz ran down the street, shouting to the passengers in an oncoming wagon, "Herr Mueller has wrenched his arm and the new horse is badly hurt."

The driver, Wullum Yaeger, with a mighty oath, leaped from the seat. One after another, the Yaeger children hurtled over the sides of the wagon, wasting no time to lower the tail gate. Soon a crowd had gathered at the scene of the accident. Each newcomer reiterated the verdict of Yaeger—that the new horse would never rise again.

This appalling news came to Emil like the dismembering blow of a flail. He fumbled for his spangled buggy whip and walked down the road, utterly desolate. Rica, alone, was sufficiently sure of herself to follow him.

"I know how you must feel, Herr Mueller," she said. "I am deeply sorry, believe me. It is because of us that this happened. Is there anything I can do for you?"

Emil shook his head sorrowfully.

Something in her earnest voice reached through the pain. She understood . . . she knew how great was his loss . . . this young immigrant girl. Emil took her proffered hand, and her strong friendly fingers closed round his own.

IV   *Two Events*

~~~~~~

HERMAN AND OTTO had been up very early to get ready for butchering. They scrubbed and cleaned the meat grinder and the sausage stuffer and the enormous black rendering kettle.

All morning the kitchen savored of Grossmutter's home baking. The array of finished pies and cakes grew steadily until the bakery board and two shelves in the pantry were filled.

At noon the great table was opened to full length, and sixteen hungry workers sat around it to feast with gusto.

Otto was in princely humor. He had a story to tell with every fresh cup of coffee, stories that covered childish escapades in Germany, and a whole series of "outwitting peddler" episodes at the Broadway wholesale vegetable market. Minna bustled back and forth with stacks of kuchen. Now and then she interrupted Otto to correct some flaw in the story, for Minna knew his stories, all of them, from the first "He said" and "I said" to the ultimate and irrevocable "And then *he never said another word!*"

Rica followed in Minna's footsteps with the coffee pot. One by one the coffee cups were turned over. Finally, Otto clattered his cup upside down, wiped his mouth and rose. "Now we can stand it again," he said.

In the afternoon Rica and Minna inspected the dressed pigs which were hanging in the market shed. The nauseating stench of scalded skin made Rica's nostrils quiver. In the tubs floated the kidneys, livers and hearts. The pigs dangled from single trees, their scraped bellies yawning and empty as shelled pea pods.

"Aren't they beautiful?" Minna asked, stroking the back of the biggest pig. "Now let winter come only! Our smoke house and our lard crocks will be brimful!" She turned to Rica. "Have you ever made wurst?"

Rica shook her head. "No, I don't know the basting stitches about it."

"Well, that's good. Then you can learn my way. I'm particular about my wurst. I turn casings three times in fresh water, where most folks turn them but twice, and I grind the meat a little coarser and leaner, with plenty of mustard seeds and coarse pepper. That's the way to make metwurst! We don't like Yankee wurst, ground fine and pasty, and stuffed with sage. You can't keep strong and healthy on that kind of eating!"

Herman came into the shed and skirmished around in the basket of offal.

"Miss something?" Minna inquired.

"I want to make a bladder balloon for Hulda."

Rica watched Herman wash the bladder, insert a straw in it, puff it full of air and drop a few seed beans in it. "There," he said, fastening a string to the mouth of the bladder and handing it to Rica. "You can put it behind the stove. It will dry out in a couple of days."

"So thoughtful Herman is," Minna said, as she and Rica toted the basket of salted casings into the house. "A good husband he will make, Rica. You couldn't find a better in the land."

Color raced to Rica's temple. There was no ready answer, but Minna expected none, that was the troublesome part. If only she could say bravely that she did not intend to marry Herman . . . that might be necessary tomorrow, or next week, but today it was better to say nothing. Was there, after all, anything to say? Must a hired girl marry the hired man just because he had, for six weeks, taken her to the crowd?

By rationalizing, Rica might have been able to make her position seem right had some rebel force within not beaten her and given the lie to reason.

She was emotionally beset. At supper, she spilled gravy into the coffee—Herman's coffee. And whenever she looked across the table Herman's placid blue eyes met hers. It was as though he sensed her insecurity and shared it.

She turned to Hulda for respite. Hulda could always turn one's thoughts into untrammeled paths.

"Mamma is going to have the baby christened Sunday. Can you get her dress finished by then?" Hulda inquired.

"Ribbons and all," Rica assured her. "Lottchen is going to be the prettiest baby ever to be christened in Wooden Shoe Hollow!"

Hulda's eyes danced. "And little angels will come to bless her, won't they?"

"Indeed they will!"

"And there will be lots of company, too. And everybody will bring a bag of candy! Molasses kisses, cinnamon drops, lemon sticks and maybe even chocolate drops! Fritz says he and Ernst had candy for a whole week after I was christened. More than Kris Kringle brings!"

Grossmutter was listening. "One shouldn't count lambs until they are all in the fold," she said, as she placed some loose wisps of hair behind Hulda's ears. Then she addressed Rica. "We must sew a dollar bill in the christening dress. The baby shall be rich."

"Will that make her rich, Grossmutter?" Hulda asked excitedly.

"Och, child, it is only a bit of fun putting money in the baby's dress, but it is a pretty thought."

"I wish Lottchen could be rich as a Yankee!" Hulda sighed. She turned instinctively to look past the hollow and up to the hills of Winton Place.

"What was that?" Grossmutter asked sharply. "You want Lottchen to be a Yankee?"

Hulda's voice dropped apologetically. "No, Grossmutter, I said I wish she would be *rich* as a Yankee."

"That's worse, Hulda! You are a wicked girl. Would you have her godless and idle?"

"No, no, Grossmutter," Hulda protested at the point of tears. "I just want her to be rich so she won't have to clean sooty lamp chimneys and skin marble potatoes and tie radishes on the Fourth of July. That isn't wicked, it's the Golden Rule!"

"Golden Rule!" Grossmutter sputtered. "So, you not only want to make a Yankee out of your innocent little sister, but you want to be one yourself!"

Hulda's wrath leaped beyond reach. She stormed into the

kitchen and chucked cups and saucers into the dish pan with a vengeance.

Grossmutter chuckled. "What a little pepper pot!"

"Hulda is so very set on Lottchen," Rica interceded.

Grossmutter nodded. "All children dream of fairy gold even if they have no shoes for their feet. But one mustn't let them dream too much, Rica, otherwise they can never make their way in the world!"

Early the next morning the Betz household proceeded with wurst making, the services of both Ida and Anna Menke having been volunteered for the day's cooking. Minna's watchful eye was kept on the coffee pot, for she contended that old maids invariably make coffee too strong, though the rest of their cooking may be all right.

"Not so much fat, Ernst," Minna ordered, as she looked into the meat tub. "Trim it down a little more."

Ernst winked at his father, who was setting the grinder across two sturdy chairs. He motioned to the basket of fatty pieces beside him. As Minna walked away he dumped the contents back into the tub. A grin spread over the elder man's face. For once they had outwitted Minna!

But Hulda, too, had seen the incident, and, being altogether on the side of her mother and the cause of leaner sausage, she burst out, "Ernst put the fat in the meat tub, Mamma."

Minna whirled about and boxed Ernst's ears. "I want to be minded!" she said sharply.

The young culprit's hands itched to pass on that cuff. Hulda was standing tantalizingly near, but Minna was her buttress.

"Sit down, Hulda," her father said sternly. "You on this end and Fritz on the other end. And sit still both of you!"

Hulda took her seat on the grinder board as her father stuffed pink chunks of pork into the machine. It had surely been a lapse of memory on her part . . . father liked his bread soaked with sausage grease and was very much displeased at her interference. . . . This was the wrong way to start a holiday—a day free from multiplication tables and jelly bread sandwiches. She began to hum snatches of Herman's plaintive Lorelei.

"I see the cats are going to claw Hulda before sundown, if she has to whine so early in the day," said Otto.

Hulda stopped short. She resented her father's lack of musical appreciation more than she feared the shadow of the cat's claw. Promptly she curled into her shell, and was soon away from the whole scene of sausage-making—into a realm of fancy where none could follow, where little girls pattered through lovely flower gardens in spotless white slippers and embroidered dresses.

Meanwhile, Otto's sturdy arms, alternating with Herman's, turned the tubs full of pork into ground meat.

"There, now," said Minna. "We are ready to come to the table, Rica. After dinner we can begin our wurst-making in earnest."

Hulda left her banquet hall with its golden goblets and jeweled spoons to pick up a bone-handled fork and spear a giant dumpling.

After dinner there were chains of casings to be turned. Hulda's tiny hands grew red with the sting of salt water. Reluctantly, she admitted to herself that even multiplication tables of nines were much to be preferred to this.

When the last casing had been thrice turned, however, she shared in the thrill of stringing the wurst upon sticks so that they might be hung in the smokehouse.

Minna and the men had begun to cut up fat for rendering when Friech Tanzer came running up the lane.

"It is surely Pastor Schicht. And here we are in the midst of butchering!" Minna complained. "We must make order the best we can." She splashed her hands in the dishpan. "Rica, see if the baby is all right for Pastor to hold. He always goes to the cradle first."

The door opened unceremoniously. Friech yelled, "Preacher's coming."

Minna nodded and called after him, "Thank you."

When the preacher came he found a well-ordered kitchen. "How are you, Frau Betz?" he inquired, stretching a friendly hand to Minna.

Then he took Lottchen out of her cradle and sat down in the

rocker with her. "What a fine child," he said, stroking his beard and smiling broadly upon the infant.

Minna heard him saying those words again, the same words he had had for Ernst and Fritz and Hulda, and for every other baby.

"Ach, and here is little Hulda, too," Pastor Schicht said, reaching out his hand.

Hulda stood one foot upon the other and put forth a timid left hand.

"The nice hand," corrected the Pastor.

At that moment the cat's claw struck Hulda full in the face . . . Mamma had the audacity to suggest having Lottchen christened today, and that in the midst of a hog butchering. Worse . . . Pastor consented without a sign of displeasure.

Hulda shook with rage as she poked the kitchen fire. "It isn't right," she exploded.

"What isn't right?" Grossmutter interposed.

"Christening Lottchen today. It isn't holy!"

"Holy?" Grossmutter repeated.

"If it was shelling beans or fixing market it wouldn't be so bad, but *butchering!*"

Rica put a consoling arm around her. "We are wurst-making, that's a little different, isn't it?" she asked.

"No! It's all the same! Little Lottchen can never grow up to be a lady if she gets christened at a butchering!"

"Och, what a silly notion!" Grossmutter chided.

Hulda's eyes flashed angrily. "I'd think you would know better, Grossie. The little angels won't come here with everything full of speck and blood and pig meat!"

The corners of Grossmutter's mouth drooped sadly. "Poor little Lottchen!"

Hulda burst into tears. She dashed upstairs.

"Now, what is the matter?" Minna asked, coming out of the parlor just in time to see Hulda run away.

"Her world spins crooked today," Grossmutter replied indulgently.

"Temper, that's what it is!" said Minna. "I'll fix that!" She strode to the stairway. "Leave your stubbornness and come downstairs you little goat," she shouted. "Open the shutters in the par-

lor and dust around. . . . Pastor hasn't all day's time to wait for us!"
Hulda came downstairs still sobbing.

Rica melted at the sight of the child so miserably crushed and disillusioned. "Come, Hulda," she said. "We'll get the parlor ready, you and I."

They flung open the shutters, flicked the dust off the chair backs, put a new drape cloth on the organ, and a clean linen cloth on the Bible table.

"Now we must get a christening bowl for Pastor. Which one shall we use, Hulda?"

"Let me," Hulda said. "I know which one." She scrambled upon a chair and peered around in the great closet in the dining room. "Here it is . . . this blue one with the white feet . . . isn't it pretty?"

Rica took the dish. "It is *lovely*." She rinsed away the dust and rubbed it dry. "Blue as the sea, and the scallops are like whitecaps on the waves. Where did you get this bowl?"

"From the coffee man. It cost 200 coupons. I got some of them from Holtes, but most of them I got from Ida Menke for washing catsup bottles. It's my very own dish."

"Fritz!" yelled Minna. "Tell the menfolk to come in and wash up now. We are going to have the baby christened. Supper will be ready afterward. We can finish the speck tomorrow."

"What does Pastor say?" asked Otto.

"Why, he agreed it was all right. Grossmutter and Rica will stand for her. There is plenty of food in the house. Nothing fails us."

"Nothing fails us . . . !" Hilda winced under her mother's utter blindness . . . "nothing" but the long white dress with lace and ribbons, and a fringed shawl, and smiling angels hovering overhead. . . .

She pressed her sister's wee fingers, kissed them, and looked dolefully at the red polka-dot dress hanging on the cradle. Tearfully, she slipped a fresh pair of yarn booties on the tiny pink feet.

Then Rica came and put on the red dress. She carried the baby into the parlor, where the men were already standing in an awkward circle, hands behind them, and feet astride.

Hulda took her place in the doorway beside Fritz.

"Our beginning be in the Name of the Father, the Son and the Holy Ghost." Pastor's voice resembled a trumpet sounding from a hilltop into a hollow glen.

Hulda listened to the long ponderous prayer of dedication. There were so many strange words, long and eloquent. Grossmutter and Papa and Rica understood them.

The ceremony continued. "And what shall the child be named?" Pastor asked.

"Charlotta Johanna Maria Betz," Grossmutter said proudly, as Rica placed the sleeping babe in her arms.

"Charlotta Johanna Maria Betz," Pastor repeated solemnly, "I baptize thee . . ."

Now was the moment when the angels should come if they were coming to *such* a christening. The lazy November sun emerged from a cloud and sent a stray gleam of golden light into the parlor. It fell upon Herr Pastor's brown beard and on Grossmutter's happy face and Rica's coronet braid and, yes . . . surely, it was shining on little Lottchen most of all!

Hulda was overcome with joy. Currents of excitement raced up and down her spine! The angels *had* come from heaven to bless the baby. It was their halos that brought the sudden brightness into the drab parlor!

"Let us pray," said Pastor Schicht, once more reverently folding his great brown hands. They all joined in the prayer which even Hulda knew.

She whispered the phrases slowly, glancing upward now to watch her father's thick lips open and close as he muttered the petitions. Grossmutter's high voice rose above the rest. Rica's joined in the chorus—rich, mellow and serious. "For Thine is the kingdom, the power and the glory, forever and ever. Amen."

Minna bustled out of the parlor as soon as the hush of the amen was over. "Cradle the baby, Rica," she called. "We'll set the feast."

"Let me hold Lottchen," Hulda pleaded. "I'll sit right here in the big rocker . . . out of the way."

Rica lay the child in Hulda's eager arms.

Dwelling on the angelic face of the newly christened Lottchen, Hulda was, in a measure, able to forget that guests were eating fresh metwurst instead of the traditional roast beef and brown gravy with bay leaves, and that there was bacon-specked potato salad instead of drifted mashed potatoes, and snippled beans instead of creamed peas. . . . It was a little harder to forget that no one had brought a bag of candy for the children, as every well-bred christening guest should do!

Scraping chairs preceded an uninterrupted clatter of dishes. That meant that the first table had been served.

Simultaneously, Grossmutter came to take Lottchen so that Hulda could help set the second table. As Hulda came into the kitchen Rica came close and whispered, "Shut your eyes." Obediently Hulda closed them. "Now, open them!"

A pinafore pocket full of sugar cubes and a square of sweet chocolate greeted Hulda's eyes.

Rica had remembered!

Hulda slipped her arm about Rica appreciatively, and they went in to supper, just as Pastor Schicht said "good-bye" and started to Cumminsville with a fresh ham under his arm.

V Christmas

IT WAS CHRISTMAS EVE. Every house in the hollow proclaimed it. Little ones were being dressed and rehearsed to make the best possible showing besides the Yankee children at the Christmas Eve program.

Everywhere the Tannenbaum stood proudly in the window, lighted with twisted candles of every hue, and covered with mellow tinsel—mellow with Christmases of other years.

In the Betz home stood a giant balsam. All afternoon Herman

and Rica had spent dressing it. There were chains of tinsel and popcorn. There were angel faces, silver trumpets, peppermint canes and sparkling balls of red, gold, green, silver and blue. Cautiously, Rica snipped on the candleholders as the thrilling task neared its finish.

It was a glorious spectacle, from its lowest scintillating branch to the crowning star of Bethlehem at the top. Herman folded the ladder and gazed critically at the tree. He tilted his head and murmured, "How lovely! Is there anything else to be done, Rica?"

"The oranges must be unpacked. Think of it! A whole crate! Such a Christmas we shall have!"

Herman's quiet eyes beamed. "Yes, Rica, such a Christmas as would make a beggar rich. For me, it's not only Christmas, it's something more!"

"Yes?"

"You, Rica . . . you did know, didn't you?" His stout arm closed around her and she relaxed in his embrace, inexorably happy.

The shadow of Osnabrück was rashly thrown aside tonight. But one conviction held Rica—knowledge that she loved Herman with a love that she could no longer deny or withhold. She would defy Osnabrück and the whole world if necessary!

To Herman there came a giddy sense of achievement. It tingled in his finger tips, as they caressed Rica's soft brown coronet. It leaped into his eyes, which sought hers—found them appealing, adoring, inviting. It surged into his lips, which claimed hers just as Grossmutter was about to enter the parlor.

Grossmutter backed out of the door unobserved and trotted upstairs, pleased as a kitten in the yarn basket.

In the kitchen the rest of the Betz family were taking sides in a spontaneous debate between Hulda and her father, with Hulda resolving that it was all right to let little children speak Christmas pieces at the English Sunday school, and her father loudly maintaining that Wooden Shoe Hollow lambkins had no business in Yankee Sunday schools. Fritz upheld Hulda. He was just as anxious to go to the program as she.

Growing tired of the quarreling, and seeing better opportunity to make Christmas preparations with the children away, Minna cut in, "Let them go, Otto, let them go! Christmas is Christmas everywhere!"

Otto grunted and changed his course. "Alone our little ones can't go to Winton Place. For my part, I'll not be seen of God in the midst of Yankees!"

Rica and Herman came into the kitchen at that point. "I'll go with them," Rica offered, as soon as she had heard Hulda's story.

"You will understand nothing," Otto warned her. "It will be all English."

"Christmas speaks but one language and that all can understand," Rica answered.

Otto gave up.

"I'll go too," Herman added.

Merrily, the four trudged out of the hollow later that evening. Hulda, stuffily clad in two overcoats, held fast to Fritz's arm as they plowed through the snow banks on Winton Road. Rica and Herman followed closely behind them, blending their voices in "Stille Nacht, Heilige Nacht."

Hulda and Fritz started a new tune—a jolly song, new to both Rica and Herman:

Jingle bells, jingle bells

Hulda sang joyously.

Jingle bells, jingle bells

Fritz's voice raced up an octave to meet Hulda's. Laughing and quickening their paces the two young people trudged along to the merry tune.

They came to the little gray stone church and were shown inside. Stiff-collared boys and crisply sashed little girls sat in the pews, nervously awaiting their turns to speak.

This was a revelation to Rica. She was proud of tiny Lizzie Vollman, who started off the round of recitations with eight lines of poetry delivered in a manner that made every Wooden Shoe Hollow visitor proud. Not one of the Yankee children could do better!

Fritzie sat beside Maggie Vollman, enthralled both by her nearness and by the sweet singing of Gerhart Locher's violin. Fritz longed to be in Gerhart's shoes, to hold up his head proudly and play that magic instrument. . . . Such was the transcendence of love at thirteen!

Hulda stretched her neck from side to side, admiring the tasseled red-topped shoes of her Yankee classmates and wished that she, too, had a piece to say, and could sally up the aisle with a brand-new blue serge dress, red hair bows, and a red silk tie, like Virginia Templeton over there. Virginia's father sat beside her, his white hands folded on his knee. The judge's hands were always white, for they never touched manure or weeds.

And there was Hilbert Noyes, with his mother. Hilbert was the smartest and the nicest boy in Hulda's class at school, and she admired him humbly, even though he never looked at gardener lassies.

Just as there was Maggie, as Fritz's star of hope, and Hilbert Noyes in Hulda's firmament, so Rica served Herman. All the drama revolved around her, and in her wide-eyed pleasure he enveloped himself until the last carol was sung and the last piece spoken.

Fritzie and Hulda received a gift box of candy from the smiling red-haired usher at the door. Politely, they refused twice, according to Wooden Shoe Hollow etiquette, and they accepted the third offer eagerly. Hulda squeezed the box into her muff and stammered, "*Danke schön*" and "Thank you" in a single breath.

Hilbert Noyes smiled at her confusion, but the smile was friendly, and Hulda was satisfied quite.

At home Grossmutter awaited their return. From her trunk she had taken a bolt of homespun linen and slipped it into Rica's drawer.

Like a drama too quickly ended the great night passed. Hulda lay sleeeping under the tree with a tin-headed doll cuddled in her arms. At this moment she was in the presence of the Judean angels . . . and their joyful anthems of "Peace on Earth" were filling her universe. She tried to mount the golden stairs, but, somehow, the staircase kept moving ahead before she could set foot upon it.

Fritz packed his checkers back into the shiny red box and wondered sleepily what had greeted Maggie's eyes under the Vollman

Christmas tree. Somehow, he wished that it might have been a white muff lined with red satin. That would be a gift worthy of Maggie. Some day she should have such a muff, instead of a prosaic navy dunce cap with prosaic navy mittens, which in all likelihood was what she had found.

Otto yawned. "To bed everybody!"

Rica shook Hulda and helped her to her feet. Minna picked up the lamp and headed the procession upstairs, while Herman snuffed out the candles a bit regretfully. Otto strolled over to the buffet and took down the decanter of claret. "And now, Herman, we'll drink one together on Christmas!"

"*Zum Weihnachten!*" These were the words of Herman's toast, but it was to more than Christmas that he drank.

"Rica," Grossmutter was saying upstairs.

"Yes."

"Are you happy, child?"

"How happy! And you?"

"For me there never has been a sweeter Christmas."

Rica dropped beside Grossmutter's chair. "It is good we came here."

Grossmutter patted her cheek. "You must always be happy, liebling. You and Herman."

Rica looked up guiltily. "Herman and I?"

Grossmutter's white head bent back in gay laughter. "You would not tell me then that you like your young man?"

Rica blushed. "Grossmutter . . ."

"Yes?"

"Oh, it is nothing," Rica answered. "I guess it is just that I wanted to tell you that I *do* love Herman."

"Right," Grossmutter answered, kissing Rica's cheek. "Shall we say 'Good night and a merry Christmas,' then?"

Rica lingered over their words. Just that she loved Herman had not been all she wanted to tell Grossmutter. There was more, far more, pressing urgently to be confided. But it did not lend itself to the telling tonight. Not tonight. Some other time Grossmutter must know it all, the whole bitter story.

Rica forcefully put these thoughts from her mind and thought of tomorrow. The great festival at Old First, where everybody would go early in the morning. There, too, would be a beautiful tree to grace the sanctuary where Pastor would once again tell the ancient story that began so simply: "And it came to pass in those days—"

And, as Rica had anticipated, Christmas Day brought many delights to Wooden Shoe Hollow. Emil Mueller was abroad early, distributing his wonted silver dollars to fourteen godchildren. To every other child who gave his hand and solemn promise to be a good boy or girl he gave a piece of pan candy and a penny. Everywhere he was greeted kindly, and his injured arm duly inquired about. At the Betz household, where he had no godchildren as yet, Mueller paid an unofficial call to bid "Merry Christmas"—especially to Rica and Grossmutter who were celebrating their first Christmas in the land—celebrating, indeed, with stuffed goose and mincemeat pie!

That night the younger set gathered for a Yule celebration at the crowd.

Rosie, Sophia and Hattie made spectacular entries in their new aprons. Hattie basked in the admiration her pink apron with feather stitching brought her. Of all the aprons hers was the nicest, didn't even Herr Mueller think so?

Sophia smiled to Herman and slipped her dimpled hands into the ruffled bosom of her apron. "Rica helped me make it," she said.

"So nice it looks on you, Sophie," Herman answered.

The music started.

Rica and Herman were off at once.

Sophia and Rosie crossed the hall and sat down on the bench. A swain came and waltzed away with Sophia.

Rosie sat. She fluted the edge of her apron. Would tonight work a miracle? Could it? What was to be was to be . . . what use for fretting?

There was Yust staring at her. She squirmed. For his sake it would be better that she would be wearing a "scrub" apron! Nice boys like Herman never looked her way, but Yust, with his green teeth, was forever leering at her like a Peruvian monkey. Amalie Krauss slid down the bench.

"You have a nice new apron, too, haven't you, Rosie?"

"Yes. Do you like it Amalie?"

"I should say so! It's elegant!"

"I think so too, Amalie . . . will you dance with me?"

Amalie was on her feet. "I was just waiting for Chris to come back. He's out after a keg. Sure, I'll dance one with you."

They doddled off in a waltz that, to Rosie's delight, turned into a quadrille and left her dancing with Herman, while Hattie was left without a partner and Rica finished with Emil Mueller. When the dance was over Mueller escorted Rica to his eldest godchild, Gerhart Locher. "Show Rica your watch," he said with a lordly smile.

A hubbub developed instantly. The watch, with its fine gold chain, was Emil's gift to Gerhart Locher on the occasion of his eighteenth birthday.

Gerhart showed it over and over again. No one failed to admire the watch and the fancy engraving upon it. Speculation was rife. What was the meaning of this gift? Would every godchild of Emil's be thus richly endowed upon his eighteenth birthday? Or only Gerhart, because he was the first? Gerhart was truly the favorite of them all!

Rica, too, examined the watch. Of all who came to him, Rica was the one he wanted most to see it. She raised her eyes. They were still full of the admiration which the watch had evoked. "Many happy birthdays to you, Gerhart!" she said. "You must be very proud of your watch and of your godfather!"

While the girls were setting up the Christmas supper, Gerhart stood alone in the center of the hall, still admiring his gold watch and thinking of the girl who fingered it. Gerhart wanted to see Rica. Talk to her away from the babble of the crowd. Perhaps he could, if Herman played again. But Herman did not choose to play again. He chose to dance, and with Rica.

The crowd hours were spent. "Home Sweet Home" was about to be played. Rosie came to Gerhart. "I didn't get to see your watch right," she said.

"Didn't you Rosie? See?" He turned it over to show her the swirled engraving.

"My, my," gasped Rosie. "It's most good as a Yankee's, isn't it?"

Gerhart grinned. "Sure enough! And I'd say your new apron is good enough for a Yankee!"

"Oh, Gerhart . . . ! Do you mean it?"

"Of course, I mean it," Gerhart answered, taking her arm "Shall we dance?"

Rosie was intoxicated with gladness. "Yes, yes, Gerhart. Let us dance!"

The world with its candles and its music and its glad tidings of great joy kindled a warm flame in Rosie's breast. She danced with every muscle of her fat little body. Her perspiring cheeks grew redder and redder, dimming the freckle patches. She was having a fine time, and a merry Christmas indeed!

And it would have been hard to divine who, of all the Wooden Shoe Hollow folk, had known the happiest Christmas. So kindly had the spirit of the day descended upon them all.

VI Grossmutter Hears a Story

SPRING HAD COME to the hollow. While the rest of Cincinnati knew it by budding leaves and the welcome trilling of birds, Wooden Shoe Hollow had her own harbingers.

Today, the whiskey man, O'Dee, clattered along the street, reminding everyone that once again it was his own special holiday—the birthday of St. Patrick. Tradition had it, that O'Dee always treated his customers to a free drink of brandy if they would but notice his pipe and shamrock. Most of them noticed.

By the time O'Dee had come to the Betz garden his celebrating had carried him far Erinward. "Ho, Otto!" he called. "Come, have a drink on St. Patrick with me!"

Otto hustled across the yard to greet O'Dee.

Ernst Betz had been anticipating O'Dee's call. For several days he had been planning mischief apropos of the occasion. With a twist of tobacco, he had coaxed Knopf, Vollman's simpleton hired man, away from his work in the hotbeds. "Would you like a 'slook,' Knopf?" he asked.

"Yes, sure."

"Then come here and let me pin this lettuce leaf in your jacket."

"What for?" Knopf wanted to know.

"Why so O'Dee will treat," Ernst explained. "Today is St. Patrick's Day. Tell him that you're Irish, too. And here, stick this corncob pipe in your mouth for good luck!"

"Knopf no Irish!" the simpleton objected.

"Just pretend," Ernst urged. "It's easy. O'Dee won't know the difference. He's got one sitting already."

Knopf rehearsed the act several times before it met with Ernst's approval. Then he paraded out to the wagon.

O'Dee was taking a drink and did not see the simpleton approaching. He whirled about angrily at Knopf's thick-lipped greeting, flung the bottle across the yard, lunged for the unfortunate fool and bore down upon him with both fists.

"Ernst! Ernst!" screamed Knopf. "Vericht! Kerl vericht!" At which O'Dee increased the force of his blows.

Ernst did not come to Knopf's rescue, however. He peeped out of the market shed window and watched the fray he had started.

Otto laughed uproariously. "Fight like a man, Knopf," he mocked.

"An Irishman, are you?" O'Dee ranted. "I'll give you an Irishman, you yokel!" A volley of blows rained down on Knopf's head.

Suddenly, O'Dee got a surprise blow on the jaw. A blow so well aimed, and so forcefully driven that he pitched forward and sprawled on the ground. . . . It was Herman. His strong body towered above the two men at his feet.

O'Dee gathered himself together and rose, baffled and bruised. Herman's eyes were afire.

Otto stood rooted to the spot—speechless. He didn't know whether to move to the left or right. For one of the few times in his life he was definitely afraid! Afraid of Herman—timid, soft-spoken Herman. It was incredible!

Knopf's pummeling left him with a battered face. Rica hastily brought a basin and Grossmutter followed with the vinegar jug and a towel.

Herman washed the wounds while Knopf chattered incoherently about the whiskey "kerl" going crazy. "Oi, oi, Herman . . . hurts . . . hurts . . ." he whined, each time the smarting mixture of vinegar and water was dashed over his bleeding nose and mouth.

O'Dee, in the meantime, had climbed back on his wagon. Enraged, he cracked the whip over his blind sorrel's back and shouted vengeance on the whole hollow. "You can all die of dry rot down here before I bring a pint of whiskey to you! Every last stinking Dutchman of you! And if I ever catch that cracked saucer outside this place I'll kill him!"

Knopf swayed dizzily, and wept like a child. "O'Dee kill Knopf, you hear, Herman? . . . Kill Knopf! . . . My didn't do him nothing!"

"He won't kill you, Knopf. He's drunk. For my part he can keep his whiskey out of here for good!"

"That is what you say!" Otto stormed, flinging his arms in the air. "Why did you have to beat O'Dee? Now he is mad at all of us. You should have taken it easy, man!"

"And let him kill Knopf?" Herman asked with deadly candor. He looked squarely into Otto's eyes.

Rica clutched Grossmutter's arm.

"Herman did right. . . . He did *just* right!" Grossmutter said with sudden fire. "It is good somebody had sense enough to trounce O'Dee or he would have killed Knopf. If I ever catch that drunken peddler on this place again he'll have it to do with me and the teakettle!"

While Otto stalked back to the hotbeds, Herman took Knopf home. Mother Vollman promptly sent the victim to bed, refusing to be disturbed at his misfortune.

"That was your punishment for running away from your work," she said severely. "God is not mocked; whatsoever a man soweth that shall he also reap . . . !" She shut the door upon the sniffling Knopf and he tramped to the attic.

Herman fumbled at the door. "Well, I guess I'll get back home," he said, as he raised his cap. "It's a nice day, Frau Vollman."

Lizzie agreed. "Thank you for bringing the oaf home, Herman."

"I think we had better not go to Rubber Neck Hill to see Buffalo Bill's show tonight," said Rica, as Herman passed the summer kitchen door.

"You are angry with me?"

"No, Herman, not angry."

"Ashamed?" he asked uneasily.

"No, I was proud of you. You did right, but people will be talking about it, and if they see us going out together this evening they will think we are talking against Otto. We can't stop the wind from blustering outside, but we mustn't let it blow through the house."

"Yes sure. You are right, Rica. You are right."

While Herman joined the uneasy Ernst at weeding, Rica went back into the kitchen where Minna, with downcast eyes, thumped the butter churn.

The affair set a melancholy air over the household.

Hours later, at the night watch, Grossmutter turned to her companion: "What fails you, Rica?" she asked. There was earnest questing in her eyes. Rica burst into tears of shame and bewilderment.

Grossmutter held her close. "There, there!" she said, as the paroxysm of weeping died down. "What is it that troubles you so, my child? It is more than this morning's trouble?"

There was vast silence in the room. Rica battled for words. Grossmutter took her hand. "You are not afraid of me, my Rica? Whatever it is, you are not afraid to tell me?"

The words came with a rush, came so fast that Rica had to hold them back by force.

"Grossmutter, ever since we first met I've wanted to tell you that I am . . . married."

Grossmutter received the news with a tighter clasp of Rica's hand. "Yes," she said softly.

"But let me tell you all of it, now, Grossmutter. Every bit . . . ! I was running away from my husband when you met me that morning in Osnabrück. I didn't love him. We were strangers."

Grossmutter's lips parted, and one word—"Strangers?"—dropped from them.

"Yes," Rica answered. "We were strangers. Our fathers were comrades in the Kaiser's service. My mother died when I was nine. My father spent his whole life in military service. When he came home at last he was sick and crippled. Sent the housekeeper away because he had lost everything but the house in settling his gambling debts. The little pension he got we needed for living expenses. Then, one day, his comrade, Maximilian Heber, came to visit us. He and his son, Heinrich, were on their way to Berlin. He and my father were anxious to have Heinrich marry me.

"The ceremony was performed that same night. I didn't have a chance to refuse. Before we knew what had happened Maximilian had brought the clerk and we were standing before the fireplace saying strange things. I was only fifteen years old, Grossmutter, and the young man was seventeen.

"I didn't know anything about my husband except that he would some day enter the army like my father and his father. They drank afterward, and toasted the army, the emperor and our marriage. When they were all quite drunk, I slipped upstairs and cried until I could no more.

"The next morning I found Maximilian and Heinrich had gone. Father was sick. Angry, too, because I hadn't prepared supper for his guests. I dared not ask when Heinrich would return . . .

"It was months later when father told me Heinrich was in military training and Maximilian had a military post in Berlin.

"Two years dragged by, Grossmutter. Long and bitter years. My young friends stopped calling on me. They knew of my marriage and it made a difference. I had nothing to face but a future which gave no promise of being any richer than barren years already spent.

"Father died.

"After the funeral, my father-in-law made arrangements for me to stay with neighbors. In a few weeks Heinrich would have served his time and could then bring me to Berlin to make my home there.

"I sickened at the thought of leaving Osnabrück to go to Berlin. Wait for my husband to live out his youth soldiering.

"Instead of staying with the neighbors I ran away. . . . You know the rest."

"And now are you happy in America?" Grossmutter asked.

Rica met her gaze falteringly. "I think you *know* how I feel, Grossmutter."

"But, can you keep your happiness, my child? The years behind you are unfulfilled. They will press themselves into the future and demand fulfillment."

Rica's face twitched. "Grossmutter, please don't tell me I must go back. Oh, please, Grossmutter anything but that!"

"Set yourself at peace, child. There is no hurry. We must think about all this seriously. . . . Pray for guidance."

Rica's head dropped disconsolately into Grossmutter's lap. "If you knew how much I wanted to find a new world for myself. I didn't mean to be wicked."

"God knows you haven't been wicked, liebling. You have run away from a life you were too young to face. Running away was not wicked, but it has made you want to keep running away. It is not good to be a fugitive from one's self!"

"I loved my father. It was only his soldiering that I hated so bitterly. I wished that there had never been a soldier born in all the world," Rica sobbed.

"That, too, I understand, my dear. War took my own son, my Joseph. . . . Yet, let us try to see your father's heart in all this. He wanted to protect you. Your father trusted Maximilian to do things for you which he knew he himself could not. Try to understand how his deep love for an only child would make him wish to see her safely married to the son of his dearest friend. . . . He used the only means he could find to give you a home and companionship and security."

"I know, Grossmutter, but I cannot force myself to love the man he made me marry!"

Grossmutter sighed. "Are you sure you cannot love him?"

"Grossmutter, I can't!" she said desperately. "I love Herman!"

Grossmutter closed her eyes. "It must not be," she said firmly. "It must not be, my child."

Rica gasped. "What shall I do? Deny my love? Rob myself and Herman of the happiness we can give each other?"

"What seems hard is often so right." Grossmutter replied. "It is not only yourself, Rica. It is the man you vowed to love and honor all your life. . . . I am thinking of him, too, liebling."

"But he didn't ask me to make that vow, Grossmutter. He doesn't love me any more than I love him. It is hardly a marriage."

Grossie lifted Rica's chin and looked anxiously into her eyes. "Don't be tempted to talk after the world, Rica. Marriage is more than a saying of pretty words. It is a promise made before God and to Him!"

"What you are saying, Grossmutter, is that my love must always belong to the man whom German law calls my husband, that I can't give it to Herman?"

"It is not yours to give," came Grossmutter's forthright answer. "Cruel as it may seem, it is true as the day is long."

Rica moaned. "I will not go back to Germany and leave Wooden Shoe Hollow. I love this place. It is my home . . . my only home! Here I have found what it means to be happy, to love and be loved!"

"I wouldn't drive you back into your unhappy past, Rica. We must think this all over carefully before we act. I think you should tell Pastor Schicht. . . . It is not wise to keep this counsel alone."

"I should have told Pastor long ago," Rica said wearily.

"He is good and kind. He will know best." Grossmutter drew both of Rica's hands together, stroked them gently. It was she who read the Bible that night:

The Lord is my Shepherd

Long after the house was dark and quiet Rica lay in bed, distressed. Up in the woods an owl hooted plaintively. And Rica could not sleep for thinking about the painful task that lay ahead: the wretched ordeal of telling Herman that she could not marry him.

The stars shown down coldly upon her unhappiness. The young owl filled the desolate night with his lament and Rica wept, comfortless.

VII Rica Speaks Again

IN THE MORNING Rica was stabbed awake with the memory of last night's confession. Today she must tell Herman, but how? Could she tell him she no longer loved him. . . ? No! . . . That was a thought of which to be ashamed. . . .

She would tell Herman everything, just as she had told Grossmutter. He, too, would understand if she could but find the right time and place to tell him. That time came when, in the parlance of the Low German folk, they were "covering loose," immediately after breakfast.

Herman stood stock still in the hotbed row. His face turned ghastly white. Speechless, he walked on to the next row. Rica followed, pouring out the whole unfortunate story.

"What can we do?" she asked.

"Do? Why there is nothing we can do!" Sharp rebuke lashed in his voice.

Rica looked up pleadingly. "Herman, must we?"

He turned away. "Rica, say no more! . . . It is too terrible for a man to put before himself! . . . Every hour since you came has left me with no thought but of you, no plan but for you. Now, with a few words you end everything! . . . I loved you, Rica. Trusted you with all my heart! . . . And all the time you belonged to another! . . . You might as well have shot a pitchfork through me! It would have been surer riddance!"

Rica's lips were drained of color. She seized his arm savagely and cried, "Herman! I don't want to be rid of you. I love you deeply—I have suffered so long for that love! I wish it could have been otherwise!"

"Yes," he answered hoarsely. "You would have made it otherwise!" He kicked the last hotbed cover in place.

Rica turned toward the house in a state of mental stupor. Heartfuls more she had wanted to say, but words were futile. They could not obliterate the mockery of fruitless love. The cycle of day and night, summer and winter, would roll on and on mercilessly. Romance would be in the midst of the rhythm no longer. Time would be dead. She had gained nothing by fleeing Osnabrück. All she had done was to spread her blight upon Herman. . . .

Of Herman, Rica thought with every new task she started and with every one she finished, until the brooms and mops and pans were all put away at night and she picked up Lottchen to rock her to sleep.

Herman passed with a lonely, "Goodnight, Rica," and went to bed.

She rocked on dismally. Held Lottchen desperately close, as though she were her own child—her own and Herman's.

Grossmutter observed. Knew her distress. Shared the heartache.

And then, in tripped Hattie, Sophia and Rosie with their sewing bags. "Wasn't it nice today?" lisped Rosie. "The radishes just popped up like magic with the sun so warm."

Hattie saw distress in Rica's eyes. "We came to cut new work dresses," she said, wondering how best to find out where the trouble lay.

Grossmutter took Lottchen upstairs and Rica cleared the kitchen table so the girls could lay out their material. Each of them had brought five yards of snow-flecked calico. With it they brought a tattered pattern—a standard for work dresses—that had been circulating freely in Wooden Shoe Hollow for many springtimes.

The only sound in the room for a long time was the snipping of the scissors. Hattie kept her eyes riveted on Rica, observing every flutter of her lashes. "Where is Herman?" she asked.

"To bed."

"It was a hard day," Sophia observed. "These spring days make one work harder than he is used to working in the winter."

"Herman had a fight yesterday," Rosie giggled. "Maybe he got a black eye, eh, Rica?"

Sophia turned on her friend. "He did *not* get a black eye! O'Dee got the trimming he had coming!" There was no mistaking the irritation in Sophia's voice.

"What was it all about, Rica?" Hattie asked.

"Herman made the whiskey man stop beating Knopf. That's all there was to it."

"Oh."

"But O'Dee went out of the hollow mad as Herr Mueller's bull. He might get even with Herman," Rosie conjectured. "Papa says O'Dee vowed he wouldn't come again."

"Nonsense," Sophia replied. "You couldn't keep O'Dee out of Wooden Shoe Hollow. He isn't foolish enough to give up his trade down here . . . if only he was! As for Herman, he can handle O'Dee any day!"

Rica glanced up at Sophia and thrilled to what she saw there. Thrilled, winced and thrilled again.

"I didn't think Herman was such a hothead," Hattie remarked.

"A hothead!" Sophia protested. "There is nothing hotheaded about a man holding up for one who can't hold up for himself!"

"Oh, please, girls," Rica pleaded. "Let's talk about something else, shall we?"

Rosie's dimples deepened. "I know. We will talk about weddings. You start, Rica. What kind of a wedding are you and Herman going to have?"

Rica took a long time to find the simple answer: "I am not going to marry Herman, Rosie."

All three girls gasped.

"I know you are fooling," Rosie said.

"No, Rosie," Rica answered flatly. "I am not fooling. I mean what I've just said. Herman and I are not going to be married."

Sophia turned away with tear-filled eyes. The other two girls stared open-mouthed at Rica's firm rejection of Herman.

Rica gleaned Sophia's thought and was powerless to modify it. Sophia would surely hate her. Hattie and Rosie would gossip and forget, but Sophia would remember!

Soon, all Wooden Shoe Hollow would know of her giving up Herman. There would be speculations and explanations, all of them wrong, but they would persist nevertheless.

Rosie, not to be diverted, prodded Sophia. "You tell us what kind of wedding you would like to have."

"I?" Sophia asked. The long-cherished dream unspun itself without effort. "I'd like to have a lavender cashmere dress, with puffed sleeves and a lace collar, and violets in my hair. And I'd like to have all the crowd down at the hall to celebrate that night. I'd want a wash basket full of ham and cheese sandwiches, and two accordion players so we'd never have to stop dancing."

Hattie laughed outright. "That's just like you, Sophie! I'd want to be a real bride and wear a long lacy veil and a white silk dress and white slippers. And I'd want a bouquet of bridal roses and a coachman to drive me to church . . . a hack and a span of black horses. And afterward, I'd want a big dinner for my friends and then we'd go to Milwaukee on a honeymoon!"

Rosie gasped. "You talk like a Yankee, Hattie Flieger! Nobody from Wooden Shoe Hollow could have all that!"

"What if I married rich?" Hattie queried.

"Oh, you wouldn't marry anybody outside of Wooden Shoe Hollow or someone from the pasture or Back Creek, would you? How could you trust anybody else?" Rosie asked naïvely. "Now, if it were me, I'd want to be sure I was getting a good man first, and if I got one, I'd wear a pink embroidered dress and a Leghorn hat with a big plume. I'd carry an armful of red roses. I'd nod as I walked down the aisle and my plume would bob up and down."

Rica laughed, in spite of herself, at Rosie's childish ecstasy. "I'm sure you will make lovely brides, all of you."

The little group was silent, contemplating Rica's flushed countenance. Her hands relentlessly pushed a needle through the calico. It was as if, with one accord, they were asking for the secret she was holding from them. And, looking into Sophia's troubled eyes, it was very hard for Rica to keep her secret.

But keep it she did.

The girls talked about it as they walked home.

"What fails Rica?" Sophia asked, the moment they were outside the Betz kitchen door.

"She is set upon herself," Hattie said. "She doesn't want to waste her good looks on a hired man, and I can't say I blame her if she can do better."

Sophia clutched Hattie's arm frantically. "Don't say that, Hattie. Mercy, is your head that easy to turn? Promise me, you'll never, never say such a horrible thing again!"

By this time Rosie was blubbering in sympathy with Sophia. "Promise, Hattie!"

"All right," Hattie said stiffly. "I promise. . . . I didn't mean anything wrong, Sophie. . . . I'm not putting our people down. That's what you are thinking, aren't you?"

"But you would," wailed Sophia. "You'd sell your birthright for a mess of pottage, like Esau did!"

"I would not!" Hattie rasped.

Sophia was appeased. She squeezed Hattie's hand in forgiveness and dodged across the path, calling a succession of "good nights."

But once in bed, she sobbed out her sorrow and disappointment. For what reason could Rica be rejecting Herman? Didn't she know how very much he loved her? Sophia found herself wishing that Rica would never find the glamour she was seeking, would never find a finer man than Herman Toepfer. But she couldn't, for . . . there was no finer man than Herman Toepfer!

It came easily now, this self-confession of Sophia's. She had always loved Herman. It hadn't mattered that she couldn't have him for herself, as long as he had found happiness in someone else. That was what mattered. And now his joy would be gone forever. She would never see that happy light in his eyes again, that light which only Rica had been able to bring to them.

While Sophia wept, Rica talked over her problem with Grossmutter at the night watch.

She told how she had confessed everything to Herman and had left him to brood in resentment. Resentment that surely would grow into something else.

Grossmutter comforted her. "But you have begun to set things aright, liebling. This suffering will soon be over. These moments will be the ones you will be proud of. Herman, too, will see them in that light, never fear."

"I told the girls I would never marry Herman."

"That was the right thing to do, Rica, however hard it may have been. Courage breeds courage just as fear breeds fear."

"Grossmutter, there is something else."

"Yes, dear."

"It is about Sophia. . . . She loves Herman."

Grossmutter's eyes met Rica's. There was in them surprise and spontaneous sympathy.

"It may be only your fancy, child. Everybody likes Herman. Perhaps Sophia likes him a bit better than others."

"Oh, it is more than that, Grossmutter. It is deep inside. I saw it in her face tonight."

"And if it is true?"

"Then I hope Herman will find happiness in Sophia." But with Rica's bold speech a world of love rebelled. After a long silence she asked, "Grossmutter, do you think it could happen that Herman might some day love Sophia?"

The older woman hadn't the courage to answer. "We cannot tell, Rica. You and I cannot tell."

She laid the open Bible into Rica's lap. "You must not trouble yourself too much about this. Every river finds its own way to the ocean, no matter how many mountains it must flow around to get there. We will put this out of our minds now."

Rica moistened her lips and read how Jesus had called Simon and Andrew away from their nets and made them "fishers of men." Somehow, it was difficult to keep her mind upon the Bible story. The picture of Simon and Andrew was continually being obscured by another picture—Sophia, unbelievably lovely, standing beside Herman in lavender cashmere. A cluster of violets nestled in her hair. It *was* a beautiful picture!

Rica ached with all her being and, for the first time in her sojourn in America, she was homesick or thought she was.

VIII   Lone Saturday

ON FRIDAY EVENING Rica slipped over to Vollman's with her sewing bag. She and Sophia took a lamp and went into the parlor to sew and chat.

"You have been wondering about what I said last night?" Rica found the courage to ask.

Sophia nodded.

"I can't marry Herman, even though I care deeply for him. Some day I'll tell you all about it, Sophia."

Sophia's wistful blue eyes were expressive, but she offered nothing in reply to Rica's mysterious statement.

"You care for him, too, don't you?" Rica asked.

Sophia threw her arms about Rica in dismay.

"Herman loves *you*, Rica!"

"He will love you, Sophia, if *you* will let him."

Sophia shook her head. "No, Rica, you don't know Herman. He can love only once like that. . . . You've never known how rudderless he was before you came . . ."

Rica sighed. "Herman's nature is made for loving," she said. "He will love again . . . and you can make him happy, Sophia. You can take away the sting of my selfishness and my cowardice. Such love as yours can do great things!"

"Why do you condemn yourself?" Sophia challenged. "What have you done?"

Rica wavered. . . . "I have a husband in Germany," she found herself saying. . . . "I had no right to Herman's love."

Sophia burst into uncontrolled compassion. "Rica," she sobbed, "I'm glad you told me this. . . . I promise I'll never tell a soul. . . .

It will be a trust . . . and I'm not going to ask you to tell me anything more . . ."

Rica raised her head and received that promise gratefully. "Thank you, Sophia," she said. "I knew you for such a friend." Then, in spite of her dislike of talking about her past in Germany, she launched into the story once more.

The next evening Herman was distressed when Rica would not go with him to the crowd. "But, Rica," he said, "must you shut even the crowd out of your life? You are too young to deny yourself music and dancing."

"It is best, just for tonight, Herman. When I have found myself I'll go again."

Herman was at the point of staying at home himself, but before the idea had a chance to crystallize Rica shattered it. "You must be there as always, Herman."

"I don't feel like going, Rica."

"Go anyway," she pleaded. "If you don't it will be awkward for both of us, don't you see?"

Herman's lips trembled. "You know best, Rica. You know best."

When Rica put Herman's accordion into his arms and sent him to the crowd she knew that one cycle of her life was closed.

Otto Betz looked around his paper uneasily. "What is the matter, Rica?" he asked blunderingly. "Have you had words with Herman?"

"No."

"You aren't holding it over him about that fight with O'Dee? If you are, just forget it. Herman can't stand a man drunk. He's a little queer that way, but you don't have to make it worse than it is. That you don't. Herman wouldn't have lifted a finger against O'Dee if he hadn't been drunk."

"I'm not angry with Herman, Herr Betz."

Otto grunted, peered over his glasses, moved the lamp closer to his newspaper and went on reading of the activities of the old barber philosopher Zinnfade.

Mrs. Betz came bustling downstairs. "I'm on my way to the Avenue, Otto. Hanchen must be sick. She didn't go to market this morning and she fixed yesterday."

"I'll go," Rica volunteered.

"No, no. You go ahead to the crowd, Rica."

"Herman has gone already," Otto explained. "Rica doesn't want to dance tonight."

Minna stared first at Rica, then at Otto. "Not want to dance?" she repeated. "What fails you, girl?"

"I just didn't care about going to the crowd," Rica replied. "Won't you let me go to see Hanchen for you?"

"Alone?"

"Yes."

"All right then," Minna agreed halfheartedly. "Here, I've packed some balsam salve in the basket. That's for her leg. And there is herb tea, elderberry wine and zweibach. If she is very sick stop at Dr. Baum's, up in Winton Place, and tell him. Most likely, though, it is just her leg bothering her and a little balsam salve will fix it."

"And maybe some strong coffee is the medicine she needs," Otto said derisively. "Make it good and strong, Rica."

"Otto, you shouldn't talk that way. If the children should hear you.... But there, if she is on a spree, Rica, hide the jug and sober her up like Papa says."

Rica found soon enough "Papa was right." There was, however, no need of hiding the unhappy woman's jug. It was empty.

"The devil tipped it over and it all ran out," Hanchen complained soddenly. She peered down the earthen jug. "He didn't leave a drop, not a drop, for a poor old woman sick to death. It gives such mean devils in the world.... What did you bring?"

"Frau Betz sent some salve for your leg. And herb tea and zweibach."

"Nothing else?" the drunken woman asked with a grimace. "Didn't Minna send me anything to drink?"

"I'll make some fresh coffee for you," Rica said cheerfully.

"Coffee!" Hanchen wobbled across the creaking floor and spat into the stove. "Coffee can't warm my blood! I'm an old woman."

Rica took her basket in to the kitchen and thrust the elderberry wine into a musty cupboard.

Everything about the house had the same unclean, nauseating

stench, worse than the accumulated odors of hog butchering. It clung most tenaciously to Hanchen herself.

Rica flung open a window and let the cool March air sweep into the house.

"Shut the window!" Hanchen fretted. "Do you want me to catch lung fever?"

Rica took a blanket from the couch and wrapped it around the old woman. "You need fresh air, Hanchen. Sick people must have fresh air."

Then she dumped a week's collection of coffee grounds out of the grease-spattered pot on the back of the stove, scrubbed it, and filled it with fresh water.

"Now, then," she said, "While the water is getting hot we will see what we can do for you."

Hanchen grunted and hiccoughed disapproval as Rica washed her grimy face and combed out the snarled kinky coil which was perched above her forehead. When she had finished the old lady's toilet she prepared a tray of hot coffee and zweibach. Hanchen grabbed the tray and emptied it speedily, alternately crunching zweibach and gulping coffee.

It was not an appealing sight. The filthy kitchen floor invited attention. Rica scrubbed industriously. Hanchen began to sober, due partly to the coffee and partly to her contact with soap and water.

"Now, I know who you are," she grunted. "You're Otto's hired girl from Germany."

"My name is Rica. Rica Heber."

Hanchen felt no need of any acknowledgment beyond a perfunctory, "So?"

Rica looked about the room. "Is there anything else I can do for you?" she asked, taking the empty tray from Hanchen's lap.

"You can look for Hans at the saloon. A brick on his head! I sent him over to sell the onions and radishes I tied for market yesterday . . . three hours he is gone already from his poor ailing mother and doesn't come back with the greens or the money. . . . Schlingel!"

Hanchen spat on the newly scrubbed floor. "Supper he can find for himself on the free counter, while I starve!"

"I'll see if I can find him," Rica answered. She slipped on her cape and started in search of Hans. She walked past the saloon. Ill-timed and ill-pitched singing floated out of the half open door.

Rica hadn't the courage to look. She paced up and down in the hope someone would come out. When the first jovial spirit bounced the door wide open and staggered out she sprang from the sidewalk. The man followed an uncertain path up the Avenue, singing a drawling tempo of "The Three Jews." Like a scratched phonograph record he droned, "E-ee-sac-sac." Jacob was not to be recovered.

Rica darted to the back door of the saloon and knocked.

"Come in," came a strident female command.

Rica cautiously opened the swinging door. "It's Hans I'm after. Is he here?"

"Hans!" the woman yelled into the barroom. "Here's a lady come for you."

Hans slouched into the kitchen. "Where is she?"

"Out by the door. She isn't a mind to come in, I guess."

"What do you want with me?" Hans asked insolently, as he leered at Rica.

"Your mother wants you right away," Rica explained in hesitant, accented English.

"I ain't got any money. They took the greens for what the old lady owed them."

"She is waiting for you."

"When I get good and ready, I'll go, Dutchy!" Hans retorted.

Rica quickened her pace as she left the saloon door. She was almost running when she reached a lonely spot on a hilltop. Grass was carpeting the ground. It was off the homeward path ... this point to which she had come.

She fell upon the earth and wept tumultuously, unleashing a whole day's cramped heartache with her sobs in the darkness. A long time she lay there, oblivious to everything but a fierce pain in her breast. A raw slithering wind rushed over the top of Rubberneck Hill, and forced Rica to rise—shivering with cold.

At home Grossmutter Betz rocked in her chair and waited anxiously for the girl to come back from her errand of mercy.

Through an open window she could hear the faint pulsing of the accordion at the crowd, distant laughter—laughter in which Rica had no part tonight.

She wondered, as she sat, how happiness could go on in the world when Rica and Herman were parted. But youth has no time to mourn. It dances and plays on, and he who will not play and dance must sit alone with his woe.

It was not very comforting. "Dear Lord, one better day," Grossmutter interceded. "One better day."

Long after the crowd had dispersed, Rica trudged down the lane. Even Grossmutter's room was dark. Added pain. . . . She fumbled through the house, undressed and dropped into bed. Hulda crept up to her and drew away with a disappointed, "You are cold, Rickey."

It was not long until Hulda cuddled back at Rica's side, for she was no longer cold.

In the morning the household awoke to a new experience. Rica was critically ill.

Ernst was dispatched to get Dr. Baum.

Grossmutter sat by the bedside, besieged with fear.

Herman brooded over his coffee.

Hulda cried.

At length Dr. Baum arrived, and was breathlessly escorted upstairs by Minna. Long deliberation, footsteps, water splashing, strained voices. . . .

Herman's long brown fingers drummed nervously on the window sill.

Lottchen whimpered in her cradle unheeded. Otto thundered, "Hulda, are you deaf? Take the baby!"

Hulda bent over the cradle and sang a mournful lullaby.

IX *While the Rain Descended*

~~~~~~

"MILL CREEK is going over," Dr. Baum said, as he came downstairs after his daily visit with Rica. "It's just like the spring of 1883, when Camp Washington got it badly."

Otto rubbed his back against the door jamb. "I don't know, doctor," he said. "The river isn't coming up fast. The *Volksblatt* isn't warning people to move."

"The *Volksblatt* will sound a warning today, you can be sure, Otto. Back water is tricky. One never knows. It's best to be prepared."

"You can't take your sprouting seeds out of the ground, doctor. If high water comes a gardener can't run away. He's got to stay till the last!"

"But he can move his family, furniture, tools and animals. And he ought to do it in time!"

"Oh, the Avenue gardeners will have warning. They can see when it's time to move."

Otto settled himself comfortably before the stove, slid his stockinged feet into the warm oven and picked up his knitting. Mentally, he resolved to finish two more pairs of stockings while the rain lasted. Otto, like most Wooden Shoe Hollow fathers, spent his winter hours knitting stockings. Only irresponsible men left the knitting to their women folk. A woman's spare time was needed for family sewing and for crocheting miles of lace for petticoat insertions.

Herman joined Otto at the oven. Nonchalantly, he stuffed a beer bottle into a sock and set to work at darning.

Otto's steel needles clicked rhythmically. "How is Rica doing?"

"Pretty sick," Dr. Baum answered.

"But she's getting better?" Otto sucked in his lower lip. "We are crippled without Rica. Three weeks is a long time to be sick."

"And it may be three weeks more before she can get up."

"What?" Otto exploded at Dr. Baum's professional calmness. "It's no joke to be without the girl! There isn't another woman in Wooden Shoe Hollow who can match her. . . . Wash on the line by six o'clock mornings and breakfast ready. . . . Children off to school and she is outside to cover loose and give air. Like lightning it is finished and she is back setting bread and lunch fixing by midmorning."

Herman's stolid face glowed with pride.

"What fails her?" Otto persisted. "Does she need something?"

Dr. Baum thumped his kit from knee to knee and looked steadfastly at the sandy floor. "Something she needs, yes, but what it is, God knows, Otto. I don't."

Otto's neck stiffened. He muttered ironically. "If I couldn't cure people better than that, I'd go lay in straw and forget about tending sick!"

"There are some things doctors can't do," Dr. Baum retorted. "Fever isn't as easy to get over as having a baby." He winked at Minna, whose three-day lying-in-limit was well known in the hollow and abroad . . . to the despair of good Frau Laufer.

"Maybe she's worked too hard," Minna said. "A woman shouldn't overdo. I always say that."

At this, a broad grin played on Dr. Baum's face. A grin that grew broader and broader as he tipped his hat and bade the Betz family a pleasant " Good morning."

"It is perhaps nothing but homesickness the child suffers," Minna said, as she started upstairs with Rica's tray.

Herman hung the mended hose on a chair and shuffled out to the barn.

"Good-bye, Mamma, good-bye Papa," Hulda called merrily, as she plumped her sausage sandwiches into a school bag and ran after Fritz.

Otto knitted and pondered. Minna had it, that was sure! Wiser than Dr. Baum she was!

Homesickness. . . . So long it had been since Otto suffered its pangs. He recalled now the torture of those first lonesome years in the land.

Hack driving over clattery brick streets. . . . No traffic with anybody but Yankees . . . never enough potatoes to eat . . . lonesome . . . longing for Minna whom he had left behind in Westphalia. . . . Away from his mother's thatched peasant hut, away from the sheep and the rye fields.

There was that one bitter day, when, driving his Yankee mistress down Spring Grove Avenue he saw a flock of sheep being driven to the stockyard. . . . He thought wildly of his mother's sheep, and of Westphalia, and he wanted to throw up the reins then and there and hurry to the railroad station.

And New Year's Day, when he had listened to every shot, reminded of the grand autumnal shooting matches of his youth. He had bought a quart of whiskey . . . drowned out the noise of the rifles . . . rolled off the wave of homesickness in sodden sleep.

The pain finally spent itself. Relief came when, one morning, he met a gardener at the watering trough in Camp Washington. Heard him talking *Plattdeutsch* to his balky horse. It was like music to Otto's ears. He cuffed the gardener's back mightily. . . . That's how he came to learn of Wooden Shoe Hollow. That's how everything suddenly became all right with his world!

He got a job in the hollow. Saved his money. Sent for Minna. Bought this garden. Found contentment and fullness of life. What more could a man ask? A plot of good ground, a house, a devoted wife, children to rear. . . .

These had cured him of homesickness more than twenty years ago. They would cure Rica, too!

Otto put down his knitting and went to the window.

Vollman didn't need the two acres between his garden and Otto's. The patch was in weeds half the time. It would make a nice garden. . . . In his mind's eye Otto saw the garden and house already there. And the thought clamored for immediate action.

He clapped on his plush cap and went out to the barn, where Herman was currying the horse.

"I've been thinking, Herman," he began brusquely, "It's time you got married."

Herman looked up questioningly.

"Well, you have thought about it, haven't you, boy?"

"Why yes, Herr Betz, I have; only I don't think it will be very soon."

"Money? I can help you, Herman. Mamma and I . . . why sure, boy, you're just like ours. What you need to go on a garden we can give you. It's no more than right. I was just thinking what a good garden you could have on Vollman's spare ground. And maybe a little piece of Emil's for a house. We can do with one set of tools for a while. And Emil will get money out of the Bauverein for you. He's always willing that way, Emil is."

Herman circled the brush over the horse's dusty coat. It was hard to find a suitable answer, but he tried. "It is so good of you, Herr Betz. You've always been doing for me. . . . Some day I want my own garden, but not for a while . . . not yet."

"You're getting older, Herman. And women are best satisfied in their own kitchens." Otto strode out of the barn, adding over his shoulder, "You think it over, and when you are ready, I'll see that you get a fair deal."

Herman was left to his currying and his thinking. Vollman's ground was precisely the spot he had always wanted. More than ever when Rica was his girl. . . . But losing her made him lose sight of everything else that he prized. The garden? Well, it didn't seem necessary now that there would be no Rica to share it with him. But, perhaps Otto was right. . . . He ought to marry. . . .

Herman looked out of the barn window and saw the drygoods merchant come driving into the yard through the drizzling rain.

Minna bustled out to the wagon with Otto's denim jacket thrown over her head. "Ten yards of cheviot, Max," she said. "Got any that's extra strong?" For Minna there was no pleasure akin to looking at the motley collection of yard goods.

Max unearthed a bolt of dark-blue cheviot from his wagon shelves. "Strong it is, Frau Betz." He tumbled the bolt over and over, wheezing laboriously as he unwound the cloth.

Minna dropped her jacket back on her shoulders and surveyed the tiers. "Who buys all that light stuff?"

"The women in St. Bernard. They like light colors."

"For what?"

"Children's dresses and Sunday aprons, I guess."

"They must wash themselves *humpbacked!*"

"Well, they don't have outside work to do, Frau Betz. Their men all work in shops. They can wash every day if it has to be."

Minna sighed. "One dress I wouldn't say."

Her eyes lingered a moment too long on a bit of pink flowered percale. Max brought it down instantly. "You like this? It's just a yard and a quarter. Would make a nice company dress for the baby. I'll sell it for fifteen cents."

"Fifteen cents with pink stitching thread," Minna bargained. "Rica likes to stitch up baby's things."

Max fished for a skein of pink floss among his notions. "There," he said, "I'm giving it to you, but don't tell anybody. You're a good customer."

Minna nodded appreciatively. "Thanks, Max."

"How is Fräulein Rica?"

"Coming along slowly. Lung fever takes time, the doctor says."

"Too bad . . . with all your work, Frau Betz. Too bad. . . . And the rain. . . . Is that all now? I guess you could use a new corset, couldn't you?"

Minna was noncommittal.

"Because if you need one, now is the time to order it. Frau Meier and Frau Reinholt ordered theirs today." Max fingered the tape measure temptingly. "Why don't you let me get you a new one while the radishes are bringing a price? And I'll get extra laces like always."

Minna shook her head negatively, yawned and huddled the ten yards of cheviot and the bit of pink percale to her breast.

"Is that all, Frau Betz?"

The man had a distressing way of asking that question every time he made ready to close the wagon. As if it wasn't hard enough to say no when there was so much one needed and wanted, but hadn't the means to buy. One couldn't buy everything Max had to offer.

Minna carried her material upstairs to Rica.

"I've something nice for Lottchen. See?" She unfolded the remnant and laid it upon Rica's pillow. "And I got a length of stitching thread to match."

Rica's white fingers passed over the percale admiringly. "Did Max have only this piece?" she asked.

"No, he had all kinds of cloth—bright as cherries. Did you want a length?"

"Not for myself." Rica gazed out of the rain-streaked window. "I was thinking how happy Hulda would be to have a dress made of this."

"Maggie grows so fast that Hulda gets her dresses before they are half worn out . . ."

"Just once, I'd like Hulda to have a brand new one . . . it would make her so happy," Rica explained.

"Happy, yes, but she must learn to be content with what she has. Maggie Vollman's dresses are good enough!"

Minna withdrew self-righteously and left Rica to contemplate the comparative virtues of uncompromising thrift and of bringing joy to a child.

And then Ida Menke came for her daily visit. She drew up a chair and lay down her leather scroll of music. "How is it this morning, Rica?"

"Much, much better, Miss Ida. Thanks."

"I've brought you the English book I promised."

"Oh, thank you. Nobody knows how badly I've wanted to learn English. Hulda has been teaching me. If only my tongue wasn't so heavy. I can't bring the words out light and easy the way Hulda does."

Ida smiled. "Hulda's chatter is hard to follow. You are fond of her, aren't you?"

Rica nodded, and leafed through the reader. "Miss Ida, did you ever want to leave here?"

"Leave?"

"Yes. I mean to work."

"No, I never cared to work out. The folk wanted us to stay home on the garden. There weren't any boys, you know. And after Papa and Mamma went, Annie and I just naturally stayed on here. It's our home. It always will be. Annie has her sewing, and I have my music. We belong here the same as the gardeners themselves."

"I know it is your home," Rica replied. "But didn't you ever think about going somewhere and making more of your music?"

Ida smiled thoughtfully. "Oh that. To be sure," she confessed. "When I was very little and found sweetness in the first bit of organ music Mamma taught me I could have taken wings and flown out of Wooden Shoe Hollow. No genius could ever come to flower here among cabbages and beets. I was sure of that. . . . And of course, I meant to be a genius!

"But when I had to face months and months of dull finger exercises with Professor Reghoff in St. Bernard I wasn't so sure I wanted to be a genius, or could! There were always wheelbarrows of radishes to be tied, bushels of lima beans to shell, stoves full of pots and pans to clean. It was only spare minutes that were left for organ playing. I learned to treasure those minutes with my organ, just for the momentary pleasure they gave to me and Annie and Mamma and Papa. And that is how it has been ever since. . . . Annie has her sewing and I have my music."

Rica cupped her fingers over her mouth and stifled a yawn. "But don't you and Annie sometimes get lonesome for others—for children especially?"

"Gracious, no! Don't we have them with us every day? When they are not practicing with me they are fitting on clothes with Annie." Ida smiled. "Take Gerhart Locher. Ever since he first sat down at the organ beside me he has been mine . . . in a way . . .

"He was like a young eagle, impatient to fly dangerously high and far without much flying practice! One couldn't hold him. He plunged into the hardest music with the same sureness as he approached his first little waltz.

"I knew that I had little to teach the boy. So soon he was past me. And then he began talking about a violin. It made me so happy! The very thought of a gardener boy playing a violin . . . but his folks wouldn't buy the instrument . . ."

"How did he get it?"

Ida blushed prettily. "I've never told anybody this before, Rica, but I don't know why I shouldn't tell you. I called on Herr Mueller one evening and asked him to make Gerhart a present of a violin so that his parents would have to let him take lessons! Gerhart is his oldest godchild, you know. Emil is very much set on him!"

Rica chuckled. "What a dear little beggar you are, Miss Ida. What has Gerhart done to be blessed with two such guardian angels as you and Herr Mueller?"

Ida smiled slyly. "He has just been Gerhart Locher."

A merry whistle sounded below and Miss Ida jumped to her feet. "Speaking of the angels," she laughed. Scarlet tinged her smooth cheeks.

"Driving up into Winton Place, Miss Ida," Gerhart called at the window. "Want to go long?"

Ida patted Rica's hand, picked up her music and tripped downstairs.

The summer kitchen door creaked and closed.

Rica watched the two figures go out of the gate. Miss Ida, erect and airy—Gerhart, bronze, broad-shouldered, bareheaded—striding along happily beside her.

Rica curled up on her pillow and listened to the rain patter on the roof. Listened and tried mentally to fit her life pattern into Miss Ida's.

It didn't fit very well. She wasn't brave enough . . . or perhaps it was that she had no music to dispossess the flesh.

X   Back Water

HERMAN STOOD in the muddy water and swung chairs up to the tail gate of the spring wagon, where Otto was stacking them as compactly as cells in a hive.

"Such everlasting water!" Otto said. "What is to become of the Avenue? Nothing is safe!"

"The house can come to order again, but the crops are gone," Herman lamented. He gazed sorrowfully along Spring Grove Avenue, where a dismal sheet of water had risen above every row of hotbeds.

"This shall be the last time our people suffer flood. We must move everyone up to Gray Road out of danger. There is ground enough for all up there!" Otto declared.

"But the earth is fatness itself on the Avenue," Herman said. "Many and many a load of manure has been hauled here!"

Wullum Yaeger lumbered out of the house with a mattress, just as Pastor Schicht alighted from a passing wagon.

"I had not thought you, too, would have it so badly, Wullum," Pastor said, grasping Wullum's hand sympathetically.

"How far is it Back Creek, Pastor?"

"Past the foundation."

"It is a punishment," Otto said heavily. "The innocent must suffer with the guilty, not so, Pastor?"

Tears filled Wullum Yaeger's eyes. "It is the Yankees with their theater acting and their horse racing. Always scheming how to get rich!"

Pastor looked intently into Wullum's troubled face. "We must not judge them, Wullum. Many of our Yankee brothers are fine men. Let us rather search ourselves."

Herman lifted a high chair up to the wagon. "God gets tired of blessing men who return His good favor with stable-stealing and drunkenness."

Pastor tilted his head and stroked his beard. "Stable-stealing, again?"

Wullum coughed.

"It's not in Wooden Shoe Hollow, Herr Pastor," Otto said smugly.

"And not on the Avenue," Wullum added hastily. "It's back in the pasture."

"*Sonderbar*," Pastor reflected. "Somehow, always my sinners are back in the pasture . . . and when I go back in the pasture I hear the sinners are elsewhere."

Both Wullum and Otto felt the full weight of that *Sonderbar*.

Stable-stealing Pastor named a double sin, for it not only violated the moral code of the gardeners, but, with one blow, it set at naught the fifth, the eighth and the tenth commandments!

Nobody who had attended church in springtime could say that he had not been warned against the treacherous sin of stable-stealing.

A man would prefer to be caught drunk, beating his horses or winking at his neighbor's wife rather than have Pastor get news of his being implicated, even remotely, in a stable-stealing episode.

Just two years before Pastor had waged a relentless war on the vice. There had been an epidemic of it. Cases popped up "Back Creek," in the pasture, in the hollow and on the Avenue. Even docile Frogtown had suffered a backslider. Since that time, however, there had not been an open indictment of any gardener. But rumors persisted from time to time.

To any court of law, or to any society outside the pale of the gardeners, this would have appeared ridiculous, for stable-stealing, in a legal sense, was not an act of stealing at all! One "stole" a stable by offering a few dollars more than his neighbor was paying for the privilege of regularly emptying a livery stable of manure. If one bargained successfully he was an out and out "stable-stealer." And if, because of his interference, the price of the stable was raised to its present lessee, he was a "trouble maker," an indecent man who would "steal the manure off his neighbor's ground"—a brother to him, surely, who steals bread out of the mouths of babes!

It was not without reason that Pastor fought so furiously to keep his flock from bowing to the economic god of supply and demand. It destroyed the sense of loyalty and faith which he and his people needed in their pioneering.

A gardener's crops depended upon his getting a regular supply of manure. If he didn't get it his ground became impoverished and his crops failed.

Even Otto, always ready with bombast and wit, had no answer for Pastor's disappointed "Sonderbar."

Pastor sighed and plodded across the Avenue in his rubber boots. The flood waters had already gone over Hanchen's rickety stoop. In the window her big red cat lay stretched—waiting for the sun which had failed him these many days.

Inside the house Hanchen was muttering and pitching boots, hose and dirty aprons into a barrel.

"Can I help you?" Pastor asked.

"Help me?" Hanchen ejaculated. "Yes, sure. You can pray Herr Gott to spare a poor sick woman and not sweep my straggling radishes in the creek! Only a few pennies they will bring me, but without them Hanchen and Hans must starve!"

"Now, now, Hanchen," Pastor said, surveying the useless bric-a-brac which the woman was trying to save. "So bad it is not! Would you murmur against God when misfortune comes?"

He pulled out a flap-toed pair of shoes, cut and worn past repair, and dropped them upon the floor. "Don't you think it would be better to get your good things for the barrel? Bring your dishes, your clothes and bedding. Where are the garden tools?"

Hanchen laughed coarsely. "They can lay in the water and rust. I'll never need them again!"

"Never need them again?" Pastor asked, suddenly upsetting the barrel. "What kind of talk is this, Hanchen? Never need them again. . . . Where is the good uncle to buy new tools for you after the flood?"

"I mean I'm not coming back here. The hut can float down the river for all I care!"

"What here, what there!" Pastor exclaimed. "This is no time for sport!"

"I'm talking sense, Pastor!" Hanchen said. "For once in my crazy life I'm talking sense. I'm not coming back here. The place is ver-hexed! My horses die. My radishes won't grow! My boy won't work, and now the Devil comes up out of the river to torment me with his dirty creek water! I'll show the Devil he can't plague Hanchen!"

"So? And how will you show him?"

"I'm going downtown and find a nice job in a saloon. I can cook soup and Hans can get his lazy knuckles to work tending bar!" The thin purple lips parted and Hanchen sent out a hollow mocking laugh. "Let it rain and rain and rain! Let even the almighty Wooden Shoe Hollow gardeners get a taste of high water! And Gray Road, too!

"Let the Yankees do without stuff! Let them break their own backs weeding. Let them get burned black with the sun. Let them get old and stiff and sore with dew damp and icy rain! Let them drag their insides out carrying sprinkling cans up and down long rows to save a crop from burning . . .

"I'll spend my days easy, where money comes in every day, and I can get plenty to eat and drink and don't have to worry about my neighbors!"

Pastor's cheeks, which had become more and more inflated with each declaration, collapsed with a whack. "That is enough!

We will talk about this later. You and Hans are going up to Vollmans until the flood is gone. . . . Thank God that He has provided for you in this hour of need, and trust Him ever so to provide!"

Hanchen took her rebuke with dolorous head-shaking. "Forgive me, Herr Pastor," she said. "I was only beset with worry." She folded her stained gnarled fingers under her chin, like a naughty child. "I thank Herr Gott for cousin Lizzie and cousin Minnie and for the dry ground up in Wooden Shoe Hollow." Her fingers found a loose button on her wrapper, and she twisted it round and round until it dropped into her palm. "Where else is there for a poor sick woman to go with her wild-fanged boy?"

"Herr Pastor! Herr Pastor!" Hans came leaping across the threshold. "They are coming to get you in a boat. Three boats with soldiers are coming to move us."

"We are not going with the boats and soldiers," Hanchen said dully. "We are going up the hollow with Uncle Wullum."

"We don't need to go up there," Hans protested. His wild eyes opened wide. "Let's go with the soldiers, Ma. Come on!"

"You and Mamma are going where it will be better, Hans."

"I'm going with the soldiers," Hans insisted stubbornly.

Pastor came out of the hut and leaned heavily on the rail.

Herman, in the act of sliding Frau Yaeger's sewing machine into Vollman's wagon, stopped and looked up at the gray heavens from which rain drizzled tirelessly. He looked at Wullum's bitter countenance, twitching helplessly with the emotion he was trying to suppress as he flung seeds into the stagnant water.

Seeds, thought safe, but now damp and swollen. Tomato seeds, so painstakingly selected from last summer's crops. The cream of a whole lifetime of gardening. So vastly better had the fruit been that customers gladly paid double the market price for it.

Gone the magic seeds! From now on Yaeger's tomatoes would be no better than anybody's else. Once again he would be at the mercy of seedsmen. Again, the tedious waiting to see what new strains would yield. . . . Had he shared the seeds with Friech Vollman they would not now be lost. But he had withheld the best strain for himself. . . . God had come with a recompense!

"Come, Pastor," a red-bearded oarsman called. "We must hurry Back Creek. There is nothing more you can do here!"

Nothing more he could do! The group huddled together around Hanchen's porch—Hanchen, Otto, Wullum, Herman. It was not easy to leave them in their despair. They needed his help, but so did every other flood sufferer. Everywhere there was need . . . everywhere!

He climbed into the boat, just as Vollman's wagon splashed around the bend at Mitchell Avenue. Dr. Baum sat upon the seat beside Friech. "Out, too, in such weather, Pastor?" he called.

The boat bearing Pastor was quickly rowed up to Vollman's wagon to get Dr. Baum. "It's no use, Herr Vollman," Pastor said. "You can't get through with your wagon any longer. Better load up what is left here and go back to the hollow."

Vollman stood up in the wagon and surveyed the muddy inflow of water rising and sweeping down the Avenue like some hungry beast of prey.

"The water is inside the church," the oarsman said.

Pastor gripped the sides of the boat. "It is good we moved the books this morning. The walls we can paint again. . . . Old First will survive this flood as she has survived every calamity!"

Dr. Baum climbed into the boat beside the clergyman. "Let me," he said, stretching out eager hands for the oars.

"No, doctor," came the quick reply. "We've got orders to bring you to Camp Washington as fast as we can. Fever has broken out."

"Fever!"

"Yes. All the city doctors are busy. It is spreading like wildfire!"

Pastor bowed his head.

Dr. Baum sat beside him, watching the helter-skelter of refugees moving from the Avenue. Frantic dashing from window to window, to look for rescuers who were late in coming. Swollen faces, shrill voices, muddy water creeping up and up, dispossessing, overturning, destroying everything in its path. And the rain fell ceaselessly over the dismal scene.

Yet, if the men in the boat, as well as those who were fleeing the Avenue could have seen the wild rushing of the Ohio river as it tore over its banks a few miles distant, they would have taken some comfort in the lesser fury of her backwaters.

"Pastor," Dr. Baum forcefully broke into the silence, "have you seen Otto's hired girl?"

"Fräulein Rica? No, I'm sorry. I didn't get to see her. I meant to go up when we brought Wullum's furniture to Vollmans. How is she, doctor?"

"The fever is broken, Pastor, but something is holding her back. Something I cannot understand. I thought you ought to know. I've done all that I can, and so has Grossmutter Betz."

"I should have gone to see her today. I should have gone! So it goes!" Pastor chided himself. Then he turned to the oarsman. "See that stripling who is following in the next boat? See that he is put to work. He bears watching."

XI   Of Lavender Cashmere

It was all over now, Rica mused. The hammering of nails into the modest frame cottage next door. The strident sawing of beams, the merry whistling of carpenters at work.

Yes, the house was finished. Herman and Sophia's house. There it stood in the bright July sun, glistening with its snowy-white walls, its proud brick chimney and its fresh green shutters. There it stood like a white shrine in a scattering of faded red sheds and drab houses. There it stood awaiting transformation into a home. That transformation was at hand. . . . Tomorrow, smoke, like incense, would rise from that pert little chimney.

Like a pageant were these events of the past year to Rica—her illness; the apathetic stretch of convalescence, during which she cared little what happened, now that she had sacrificed her love; the turmoil of flood; Herman's quiet courtship of Sophia; their engagement; and the building of their home.

And today, the wedding! Sophia's dearest dream about to come true. . . . Herman's too?

Hulda, who had been invited to ride to church with Maggie Vollman, was posing before the mirror, frankly admiring her white dress with its lush embroidery carefully pressed out, her black-velvet Sunday sash, her choice narrow-ribbed white stockings and an utterly new pair of patent leather slippers which creaked excitingly. Best of all were the bewitching hair bows salvaged for her and for Maggie from the bride's own sashing!

"Oh, Rica," Hulda said impatiently, "Let's hurry over to Vollmans. I can't wait another minute!"

"Run along, pet," Rica answered. "I've got to wait for the carriage." She placed her gloves besides the streamer of nun's veiling, which floated from the rim of her Leghorn hat.

Hulda pattered downstairs as fast as her stiff slippers would carry her. Bursting with enthusiasm she danced around Lottchen's pillow on the kitchen floor. "Going to see a wedding, going to see a wedding, going to see Herman get married," she sang jubilantly.

Then she dropped to her knees and hugged Lottchen.

Lottchen, pleased with the world and Hulda's cooing, gurgled and clapped her chubby hands.

"Hulda ought to stay home," Ernst teased.

Hulda bristled. "Maggie's going, and I should go with her for company. Mamma Vollman said so, *now!*"

Two quick jerks and Ernst had untied both of Hulda's ribbons . . . an angry yelp from Hulda, a whimper of sympathy from Lottchen and a resounding whack from Minna followed. The door banged and Hulda was off, hurtling cabbages on her way to Vollmans and the wedding.

There was a painful silence after Hulda left. Rica gazed into the mirror . . . what met her eyes looked like the picture in Hattie's book—"Heart Bound." A picture of a lady with an armful of roses . . . nothing more. . . .

"Rica!"

She clutched her bouquet. It was Herman calling softly from the hall.

She went out to meet him.

The world was a hollow shell, ready to crumple into bits at the slightest tap on its crest.

Herman's ruddy face shone like his patent-leather-tipped wedding shoes. He fumbled with the rose Sophia had said he must wear in his lapel. "Will you pin it on for me?" he was asking.

Rica lay the bouquet in Herman's arms and with trembling hands pinned Sophia's rose in his lapel. Her lashes quivered an instant before she looked up at him.

"Rica!" he begged tremulously, as she took her bouquet.

She yielded to the desperate invitation and, for one moment, lay her head upon his shoulder and felt the rapture of his embrace. There were no words. Only a deep understanding silence, an inflow and outflow of love and sympathy, sorrow and hope—a tender rendezvous of souls.

A sob died in Rica's throat. She took the bouquet and blindly turned back to her room, while Herman went downstairs.

As Herman strode through the kitchen Minna stretched out her hand. "Be good to yourself," she said. "I hate to see you leave, Herman." Tears came.

Otto added his farewell with a cigar and a lusty, "Good luck . . . must never forget this is your home . . . whenever you need help come to us. Mamma and I will do for you as long as we are here."

Herman grasped Otto's hand and shook it vigorously. "I won't forget," he promised. "Thanks for all you have done for me all these years." There was a tremor in his voice.

Rica dropped across the bed upstairs and sobbed brokenheartedly. Grossmutter, quite prepared for this, was at her side. "Come, Liebchen," she said. "Lay down your burden . . . this is a precious day. . . . Those who love Herman and Sophia must be happy, not downcast!"

She drew Rica to her feet, smoothed down the full-flowing violet challis dress as Rica lowered the Leghorn hat upon her soft brown coronet. Grossmutter sifted the streamer into a misty mass over her shoulder. "So!" she said.

Rica went downstairs.

Herr Mueller's coach drew up outside. "Aha! Aha!" Emil chortled. "The man of the hour! How goes it with you this grand wedding day, Herman?"

Herman, who had beaten a path from the porch to the gate, responded, "Very fine, thank you."

Herman helped Rica into the coach beside Gerhart Locher and himself took the back seat.

"It was nice of you to drive us to church, Herr Mueller. Many thanks Sophia and I owe you."

"No thanks at all," Emil said pompously. "With Gerhart standing up at the wedding it is no more than right. No more than right. Besides, it isn't every Thursday we have a wedding in Wooden Shoe Hollow."

Emil was like nothing so much as a cricket, Rica mused. His elbows jutted back as he checked the reins. A high stiff collar held his head erect. He bounced up and down and chirped merrily. . . .

"And how is Fräulein Rica?" Emil inquired. "Not much like a sick girl now."

"No, I'm well again, Herr Mueller."

"The picture of health," Gerhart said.

"And a pretty picture she is, too, my boy!" Emil added, with a flourish of his whip.

Rica blushed comfortably under her hat brim. And Herman blushed uncomfortably in his solitary corner. Gerhart didn't blush at all. He ducked his head mischievously and gave Rica a fascinating oblique smile.

They had stopped before the Vollman gate.

"Here comes the bride," Emil cackled, as Sophia picked her way out of an adoring family cortege and emerged utterly sweet and lovely in her lavender cashmere.

The little sister-brother band tagged at her heels in a whirl of rapture. Sophia, a bride! A beautiful bride!

Fritz Vollman's weatherbeaten face, cleanly shaven and smarting from its unwonted razoring, reflected something of pride, something of sorrow and much of happiness.

"Here she is, Herman," he said gallantly, as he lifted Sophia up to the carriage step.

Herman's brown hand was quick to reach out for her. Admiration was in his eye. Gratitude. Tenderness.

Lizzie, who had been holding her handkerchief threateningly before her face, burst suddenly into violent weeping. Maggie, seeing her mother's woe, cried too, and Hulda's tears came unbidden in sheer sympathy.

"Come, Mamma," Herr Vollman said. "Mustn't take it so

hard." He helped his wife into the family barouche. Maggie and Hulda scrambled into the back seat. The clumsy vehicle rumbled out of the gate, following closely behind Emil's fashionable coach.

Ida and Anna Menke, staying to "watch the place," waved goodbye, Ida's glance rested upon Gerhart—young, eager, proud as he had a right to be. Anna's eyes were for Sophia. "Wasn't she grand?" she asked. "It was just right, her dress was. I needn't have fretted so about those sleeves though they *were* a trial to set! Sophia's sleeves have always been hard to fit, ever since she was a little girl."

"It was a nice wedding dress," Ida agreed. "It's truly the nicest dress you've ever made!"

Anna was satisfied. Ida knew what was good and bad about everything—music, pictures, places, people and leg-o-mutton sleeves. . . . That's what Professor Reghoff meant when he said Ida had a sensitive soul.

Often throughout the day Rica had to rouse herself to consciousness. There was that terrifying moment when the party came to a halt before the altar, that breathless second before the ceremony began.

And that same moment, intensified a hundredfold, when "Amen" echoed through space and the bells pealed out clamorously. Then came the happy interlude. Well-wishing, hand-shaking and laughter. A deluge of rice. Rosie giggling somewhere in the distance. Hattie frowning.

The tumultuous drive back to Wooden Shoe Hollow, Herman singing gayly as the wheels spun round.

Evening—crammed full of excitement—eating, drinking, dancing and singing. Swarms of people. The never-empty wash basket, full of sandwiches. The accordion playing merrily through the night.

Herman, gracious, smiling, attentive. Dancing with Sophia and singing to her.

Sophia—all animation. Risen above plainness! This was truly her hour!

And Gerhart. There was strength in his young face. And something more than strength. Rica was glad that Gerhart had been chosen to witness the wedding with her. He had been a godsend.

It was almost daybreak before the crowd began to thin. Mothers looked for their sleeping children, who were scattered on the grass, and marched them home.

One more good wish extended to Sophia and Herman, a lingering good night, and Rica, too, left the hall. With Gerhart.

"Do you like it here, Rica?" he asked, with an earnest ring in his voice.

"Like it? Why yes, Gerhart, of course!"

"Oh, I thought you would want to go other places, where life has more punch."

"But there is no better place than Wooden Shoe Hollow."

"I don't believe you really mean that. You were born for adventure and excitement like I was, Rica. You are different. . . . That's why you gave up Herman, don't you see? He is cut out to be a gardener. He'll never want anything more than a patch of ground, a house to live in, and sons and daughters to be gardeners and gardeners' wives after him and Sophia.

"You were born for a different life, Rica. . . . I'm going to make my mark in the world, and, when I do, everything I get will be yours!"

"You are too impulsive, Gerhart. You have just begun to live. You mustn't be giving yourself away so soon."

"I'm eighteen years old, almost nineteen," he said stubbornly. "I know what I'm talking about. From the first day I saw you I knew we were meant for each other. . . . I can't help it, Rica. I love you."

Rica caught her breath. "You mustn't say that, Gerhart. It isn't nice."

"But it *is* nice! And I will say it! Over and over again, because it is true!"

"You're just a boy, Gerhart. In a few years you will know what love *really* means."

"Don't you care, Rica? Not even a little?"

"I think you are a splendid fellow, Gerhart."

"I'll prove that I'm worth having for more than a splendid fellow," Gerhart replied impetuously. "I'll build a new world for you, Rica. Do you hear? A world that is rich and wonderful! Away from stables and market sheds. Where you can be the lady you were meant to be!"

Rica protested ineffectually, "You musn't think of such things, Gerhart!" And gently she put down his hands, and warded off his embrace. "Please, Gerhart," she said. "Will you go now? Good night."

As though his fingers were seared he jerked back, wheeled about and strode away angrily into the dark.

XII   Gerhart Dreams

IT WAS A WARM DROWSY EVENING. Rica sat on the porch dreaming. Across the Betz hotbeds her gaze followed Herman up and down the long celery trenches, as he poured water upon the thirsty plants and turned the dusty brown earth to rich black. Sophia stooped beside him and examined the tiny celery which she had helped transplant a few days ago.

Now they were trudging back to the house, arms about each other, heads back, laughter on their lips, warm golden sunset lighting up their happy faces. From St. Bernard came the sweet tones of the evening bells at St. Clement's Church.

Rica closed her eyes and momentarily shut out the world. This was what life could mean—peace, contentment, working together, wanting the same things and striving to get them.

And here, tucked away from the rest of the frantic world, was Wooden Shoe Hollow, a complacent haven for those who loved her and who were satisfied to live upon her quiet bounty.

Here, many a pioneer had come to break the virgin soil, plow and plant, reap and sell, rest through the winter and begin the cycle anew. With what infinite patience they had labored, those first inwanderers! What priceless legacies they had left for those who came after them; rich soil, sturdy bodies, sturdy faith in God and in each other. Here, they had built their little empire, set up their own unwritten codes, treasured them and bequeathed them, full of blessing, to their children.

Into this picture Herman and Sophia fit like the two figures in the Angelus. And so might she, too, have fit, had it not been for the army of an emperor. . . .

Music came. Soft music. Herman was sitting on the porch steps playing his accordion. Sophia's rocker creaked back and forth with the steady rhythm:

> *Du, du liegst mir im Herzen,*
> *Du, du liegst mir im Sinn.*

And as though that were not enough, Sophia picked up the refrain:

> *Ja, ja, ja, ja,*
> *Weisst nicht wie gut ich dir bin.*

Rica's fingers raced around the hem of her apron. Something within convulsed for outlet. Not jealousy. She prayed. . . . Dear God, not jealousy! Pastor Schicht's resonant voice boomed into her ears, just as it had boomed one Sunday morning not so long ago, "Thou shalt not covet!"

Grossmutter, too, sat on the porch, in silence, watching Herman and Sophia. She felt the sensations of joy and pain which had started such a conflagration in Rica's breast. Felt it as keenly as though she were seventeen instead of seventy, for in Rica's world her own was irretrievably merged.

Strange, mused Grossmutter. Pain always side by side with happiness. Denial ever lurking in the shadows of fulfillment. No escape from it. She was reminded of her own youth. Of her love for Lief, the young soldier. . . . His mad adventuresome spirit capsizing her, sweeping her away, almost away . . . and yet not quite. There had been Dietrich, clutching her back. Dietrich, and Father and Mother and home. Sheep and flax and rye . . . and, afterward, the children.

But always, in the inner self, Lief, too, had owned a place. A place nobody else had been able to fill. There, in unguarded moments, his sunny smile flashed brilliantly and his proud shoulders swaggered past her wide open eyes. Dear Lief . . . living on somewhere . . . somewhere.

Strange, indeed, how life's fabric was woven.

Herman could never be a Lief, however. He was all flesh and blood. He could never live in a mental upper room where Rica could look with pensive admiration, in the midst of daydreams. He would always be right there in the place across the way . . . sweating over his plow, banking his celery, pitching off a load of manure, sitting there on the porch at dusk, playing his accordion, smoking his pipe until the stars came out. . . . No, it could never be the same, Grossmutter concluded sadly.

"Rica," she said. "I want you to speak to Pastor Schicht. Will you do that for me?"

"I will," Rica promised. "Tomorrow, after church . . ."

"That is wise, liebling."

Then without a word Rica rose and sauntered to the woods.

Grossmutter's fond gaze followed the girl up the hillside and into the quiet green sanctuary of oak and maple trees.

Grossmutter's thought swerved to another figure stalking alone somewhere, an errant lad, a certain Heinrich Heber, who, but for a soldier's uniform, might now be at Rica's side. What did it matter? Heinrich or Lief? They were one. Pilgrims. Where were they now? What were they thinking? What filled their days and nights?"

Gerhart, from the west gable of Emil Mueller's home, saw Rica wander into the woods. He had been examining a curious old hornpipe. Hastily, he swung it upon a hook and ran downstairs.

"So long, Uncle," he shouted across the garden wall, where Emil was gathering poppy seeds.

"Have a good time, lad," Emil called. "I'll look in later." This, he said, thinking Gerhart was leaving to go to the crowd.

But Gerhart's feet were racing up the hillside like those of a young Cherokee chieftain.

"Gee, Rica!" he panted, as he caught up to her. "I'm so glad to see you. It's hard to get a chance to talk to you with the whole crowd in the way."

Rica smiled provocatively. "What is it you wanted to tell me, Gerhart?"

"What I've been telling you for a whole year now—that I'm set on you and I can't get over it, and I wouldn't want to if I could." His eyes swept over her challengingly. "At Herman's wedding last year, you said that I'd get over it, but I haven't Rica, and I never will!"

"Are you sure you aren't being a little testy? I didn't say I didn't want you to like me, Gerhart. I'm glad you do."

He ground his heel into a clump of grass. "Like me!" he said in annoyance. "Rica, I'm not a baby. I'm a man, and I've got feelings like a man!"

"All right," Rica acquiesced. "But I warn you, I don't like this fussy young man nearly as much as the one who stood up at the wedding with me. He was such a grand fellow, that one!"

Gerhart clutched a branch and sent it leaping skyward like an arrow released from a bow. "Can't you love me, Rica?"

"Not in any silly way, Gerhart, only in a sensible way."

"I don't want you to love me in a sensible way," he retorted. "All the love in this place is like hollow turnips. They kill all the romance there is to life. The things that poets sing about. That artists paint and that musicians turn into symphonies! Don't let them freeze romance out of your soul, too, Rica! It's real! It's . . . oh, geemanently, it's everything!" he pleaded.

A quivering set upon her. Every nerve trembled. "Gerhart," she said. "I don't want to hurt you, but you mustn't talk about that kind of love any more."

"Why?" came the question with innocent candor.

"You say you are a man, yet here you are asking, why, just like a curious urchin. You just mustn't, Gerhart. You will spoil everything!"

"What is everything?" he demanded sullenly.

Rica's hands dropped to her side in despair.

"What do you mean by loving in a sensible way, Rica?"

"Being interested in the things you want to do, that isn't hollow turnips, is it? Hoping you won't be discouraged by those who don't understand you and who can't possibly know what is best for you. Even fathers and mothers are that way sometimes," she added bitterly.

"Rica," he said, as he slid up the trunk beside her, "You believe I can be an engineer, don't you? That if I had the right schooling I wouldn't have to stay here and slave my life away like Papa has had to do?"

"Your father hasn't slaved his life away, Gerhart. He has worked hard, but it was work he loved. He has been very happy here, I think. Perhaps you can't be because you were meant for something else. Building things out of wood and steel and concrete. That's what you dream about, isn't it?"

"Yes, that's what I dream about. Towers and bridges and canals. Ever since I was old enough to steer a pencil across a sheet of paper. And the more I read books about it, the more I want to be an engineer. When I play my violin it takes me out of the hollow. I can see big cities with towers, beautiful long bridges spanning wide rivers, and, even, a canal down at Panama. Honest, Rica, I can see it plain as anything, a canal and steamers passing through and people cheering and flags flying. That's where I want to go. That's what I want to do. Help build the great Panama Canal!"

"You think about things like that when you are playing?"

Gerhart nodded. "Always, until you came, Rica. Now, when I play, I think of you. You are always in the midst of the ships and canals and bridges and towers."

Rica shook her head regretfully. "I don't belong there, Gerhart. You mustn't let me get mixed up in those dreams."

"But I want you in them. That's what makes them so real. Don't you understand? Without you they are just shadows of what might be, they haven't the strength to come alive."

"They *can* come alive," Rica argued. "If you want something bad enough, nothing can prevent your getting it."

"How do you know?" he demanded. "Have you always got what you wanted? Has nothing ever stopped you?"

Rica's heart stood still. She was speechless. The fire in her will smothered; she was defenseless. In tears.

"I'm sorry I said that, Rica," Gerhart apologized. "Of course you have had a hard fight. I ought to have known." He drew her into his arms. "You've had your dreams, too, and sacrificed your Wooden Shoe Hollow, wherever it was. You came across the ocean to make your dreams come true . . . have been sick and lonesome.

"You are stronger than I am, I guess. At least you've got more nerve. I stick here in the hollow and moon around like Moses' Calf, playing my violin, wishing and wishing and wishing. And that's all the farther I get!"

He stroked her head compassionately, pressed eager kisses upon her lips.

She wept on, and clung to his shoulders as though he were a rock standing firm in an eddying current.

"Rica, Rica, dearest," he murmured. "I'm sorry I was so thoughtless. See, I understand how you feel. It's all right, darling. Please don't cry."

But Gerhart couldn't understand. How could he know that it was not for Germany she wept, but for America? Not for rosy dreams that were slow in blossoming, but for dreams that had bloomed and were now shattered forever! How could he know that?

Gerhart had dreams of his own, however, and she was in them! Towers, bridges stretching across the continent, joining east and west, north and south. The Panama Canal. Excitement, adventure, romance. . . . These were the things he wanted to share with her.

It was true what he had said about hollow turnips.

Otto Betz and Minna—had they ever known really rapturous love? Vollmans? Yaegers? Old Hanchen? No, they hadn't; Gerhart was right!

But Sophia and Herman . . . Rica wept anew.

Gerhart's arm tightened around her. "Please, Rica," he said, lifting her face and searching the depths of hurt he found there. "I'm sorry, I'm *so* sorry I've made you feel this way. It's all my fault!"

"No," Rica answered, loosing herself from his embrace. "I've been foolish, Gerhart. I'm all right now. We had better go."

"Do you want to go to the crowd?"

"Yes."

They came down the hillside arm in arm. Tears dried themselves. Inner disquietude ceased. Silence was so comprehending.

When they came into the hall questions rained upon them merrily.

From Emil—"A nice crowd where you were?"
From Rosie—"We thought you had eloped for sure!"
From Hattie—"Planning to survey Uncle Emil's woods, Gerhart?"
And then laughter. Waltzing with Gerhart. Not caring what rankled or what amused the crowd. Not caring! Not caring!
Die Lorelei. Herman. Dusk. Rows of newly watered celery. *Im Grunewald.* Couples twirling. Glasses tinkling. *Prosit!* Towers—yawning bridges . . . Gerhart's fiery eyes looking down upon her. Understanding eyes. Proud . . . eager . . . fascinating!

XIII *Advice*

THE NEXT MORNING Rica had her long delayed session with Pastor Schicht. Such conferences were not unusual. Intricate personal problems—who knew better how to deal with them than the kindly Pastor? His advice was freely sought and freely given, no matter whether it was in the matter of saving a soul or buying a horse.

It would have been difficult to sum up all that had been accomplished in Pastor's long labor at First Church. No tables could show it. But, everywhere, his patience, charity, piety, his good humor bore fruit.

There was old Eva, whom he had rescued from wash tubs and sent back to the pasture, to a garden where she could be free from the steam which made her asthma worse. Eva was well now and would never forget.

There were the von Hagells, whom he had kept together through three quarrelsome generations. Once, his timely intervention prevented bloodshed in that household.

Only a week ago he had stood at the bier of father von Hagell and tried to comfort the family. Mother von Hagell was like a child whose sand castle had been swept away by a truant tide. She stood shrouded in black veils, weeping bitterly, "Papa, poor Papa!" —weeping over the man whose rage and abuse she had endured for forty years. . . . And none but Pastor knew that pain for what it really was. Only he knew the true feeling of the twelve sons and daughters milling about in a silence such as their turbulent household had never known.

And, as he had stood by the von Hagells through their crises, he had likewise been a partaker of the accumulated joys and woes of a whole community. Their hopes he knew and their temptations he recognized afar.

This morning, as he looked down upon his flock, from the pulpit, he was conscious of the immigrant girl Rica Heber. She invited notice as she looked upward, following his every gesture, every thought.

Pastor knew, then, that she was coming to him at last. He was glad.

It was easier than Rica believed could have been possible, her confession. Pastor set back in his high tapestry-covered chair in the parlor and listened to her story. Bronze Lincoln-like hands were folded on his knee. His kindly black eyes rested upon her lightly. There was understanding and a glint of admiration.

She told him her story with no interruption. About her father, old Maximilian and Heinrich. About Grossmutter . . . and there she had hesitated like a child fearful of crossing a swinging bridge. . . . All this had told itself with little effort. . . . But now came the futile part, the part that despaired of telling. Was it any use to go on? What, after all, could Pastor do? Could he lead her across the swinging bridge? What was on the other side? Not the love her heart bled for, not that, only . . . only what?

Pastor tilted his head and stroked his beard as though he had divined her question. "And now," he said, "There is the future. It is yours, and you do not know what to do with it? You haven't been altogether happy in the land, have you?"

"I have been happier here than I have ever been, Pastor. The Betz's, Wooden Shoe Hollow, and the garden . . ."

"Yes," he sighed. "You do like the garden . . . with Minna and

Otto you are as a daughter. Flesh and blood could bring you no closer, but . . ." he locked his hands grimly and looked at the carpet. "That is not enough . . . not enough when greater hope fails you!"

Rica's lips trembled. She hadn't had to tell her real problem. Pastor knew it, was searching for an answer. Oh, that he could find something on the other side of that perilous swinging bridge!

Pastor raised his head. "Have you ever felt that it was a rash thing to do, this running away from your husband? That it didn't make good order out of bad?"

"I have never been sorry I ran away," Rica answered sharply. "I couldn't have endured it."

"It?" Pastor seized the one word.

"Soldiering for a living. To face that! Pastor! The roof over our heads, the bread on our table paid for by wages earned in fighting, killing and destroying. And there would be other ugliness, drinking, gambling, and, and . . ." Suddenly her face swept crimson.

Pastor took her hand. "That," he said, "is what you feared and hated?"

"Yes. Here, people plant their crops in peace. Build, not destroy."

"God bless you for that, Rica," Pastor answered. He came directly back to his cue.

"But, are you sure your husband wants to be a soldier for life?"

"Yes. It is *in* him, for he talked about it just as eagerly as my father and his. And, like them, he was drunk the night we were married." There was a resonant sting in her voice and an angry flash in her eyes. "Don't marvel, Pastor, that I never want to see him again!"

"But, Rica, what if he didn't want to be a soldier?"

"He didn't have to follow in their footsteps if he didn't want it that way," Rica protested.

"You married the boy when you didn't want it that way," he reminded her gently. "Isn't it possible that Heinrich's wishes were just as much out of the picture as yours?"

"He didn't care about the marriage. Only that it gave him a home to come back to when he is old and pensioned out of service."

Pastor chuckled. "That would be a strange outlook for a bridegroom, my child. I have never seen such an odd one in all my life, and I have seen many. . . . Tell me, what was Heinrich like?"

"I've tried to forget," Rica confessed. "But I haven't been able to forget entirely. I never shall. His hair was cropped short. A thick dry shock stood on end above his forehead. He bulged beneath his uniform. His voice was raspy. Father said it was from a bad throat he got on the march. And he wore monstrous boots that shook the floor when he walked."

"There was nothing to admire in him?" Pastor asked with a twinkle in his black eyes. "If his uniform had fit a little better, perhaps? Or he had a scholar's haircut?"

"It wouldn't have made any difference," Rica said with a hard little smile.

Pastor fixed his gaze upon the scintillating prisms of his parlor hanging lamp. "Heinrich doesn't know that you are here in America?"

"No."

"Don't you think he should know?"

"Yes," Rica admitted hesitantly. "I wish he knew, then perhaps he could forget me. . . . But what if he didn't want to forget?"

"Let us not borrow trouble. It muddles our thinking. It would ease his mind just to know you are well and happy Rica. What must it be to have a wife and not know where she is or how she fares? Perhaps your running away has hurt him more than you are willing to let yourself believe."

Rica's fingers held fiercely to the brooch at her throat. "But I don't want to lose my whole life's happiness," she entreated.

"I am not so sure that what you are doing now is not costing you your life's happiness. Isn't it bitter freedom that you have won for yourself by fleeing to America? Freedom that makes you restless as a bee out of the hive?"

Rica agreed half-heartedly. "But what then am I to do?"

"Write to Heinrich at once and tell him that you dislike his being in the army and have gone to America."

Rica shook her head. "That would bring him after me. I should have to go back to Germany and all that I have here would be lost!"

"If it were possible to let Heinrich know you are in America without writing to him yourself would you wish it?"

"Even if you wrote to him I would be in danger. . . . He would surely find me!"

"Perhaps it would be well if he *did* find you. Some order might come of it and you should know, then, what the future held."

Dismay clouded the girl's face.

Pastor brushed back his errant sympathy and made a bold stroke. "I shall write to him, if you are willing, Rica. This silence is nothing!"

"There isn't any other way?" she asked helplessly.

Pastor stroked his beard, and looked at her in calm assurance. "It is the only way! There are two of you and with two of you the answer lies, not with one!"

A more characteristic statement Rica would never hear from him. When Pastor found his solutions he had his own strong way of putting the answer. None could argue. None tried.

"Then write to him, Pastor," she said.

The earth rocked as she gave her weak consent to this thing which threatened to rob her of everything she prized. . . . She was mad to invoke this evil upon herself! But there was Pastor, rubbing his brown fingers over the arm of his chair, smiling at her, satisfied that he was choosing the right way.

"Where," he was asking, "can I send the letter to Heinrich? Where was his home?"

"In Wehdem."

"I shall write to the village pastor in Wehdem. He will notify Heinrich that you are in America and send us any message Heinrich may wish to send."

"Thank you," Rica said. "It has been kind of you to listen."

"It is a small thing, listening, Rica. If only we can find the right answer to all this, that is what we want, isn't it?"

Rica agreed.

"There is something else," said Pastor.

"Yes?" A tinge of fear skirted Rica's smile.

"Think kindly of your husband. It is no more than right!"

Pastor's flock respected that argument almost as much as they did the ten holy "thou shalts" and "thou shalt nots." Rica, too, realized the full import of that phrase and she had no wish to run counter to it. Anything less than "thinking kindly of Heinrich" was sinful. She shuddered.

"Pray for a spirit of love and forbearance, always."

Before the session was over he, himself, led her into that spirit. His forceful taut jaw relaxed as he prayed for wisdom and faith to receive guidance and the will to follow it.

Rica felt her will follow a new course. One that gave peace if not promise. Relief . . . cleanliness . . . and she found, as she raised her head, that she was able to face Pastor, at last, without the shadow of deceit between them.

When Rica would have begun her trek to the hollow Frau Schicht protested. "You have talked a long time," she said. "You would be overcome of hunger before you half reached home. You must stay to dinner."

Rica was abashed.

Frau Schicht's ruddy face was overspread with a warm smile. "We have your own good butter beans on the table. We will be happy to have you stay. I've wanted to know you better, for a long time. It is hard to get acquainted just over a 'good morning' and a handshake, isn't it?"

Rica stayed to dinner.

Afterward, Pastor drove back to the hollow with her. "I must see Wullum Yaeger," he gave as his excuse. "See if he has heard from his sister. The flood is long past, everybody has his crops in the ground, and still no Hanchen! She cannot choose to stay in a saloon forever! What will become of Hans? Those devil-driven alleys are no place for the boy. He is weak as it is!"

"She may be ashamed to come back, Father," Frau Schicht put in. "Hanchen is headstrong. If you went after, perhaps . . ."

"Yes," Pastor answered. "Just so I've been thinking, Mamma. I'll do my best to find her. With floods every springtime . . . it is small wonder that she deserts the garden."

With that, Pastor was aware of his second son's upturned face. "Your turn, Robin?" he asked, smoothing back the sandy hair.

Robin was ready with his polite, "Yes, Father, my turn."

There wasn't room in the runabout for more than one to accompany Pastor and so the boys waited their turns to ride with him on his jaunts. It was a choice ride to Winton Place, longer and more interesting than village calls. Robin had reason to be pleased!

As the runabout approached the gardener's lane Rica was amused to see Friech Tanzer begin his wing-footed circuit.

Pastor drew in the reins, a great smile played on his rugged face. How often he smiled at this never-failing telegraph system, which was responsible for freshly aproned housewives poised in doorways, and children's voices rising into zealous choruses of "Praise the Lord" and "Since I Am a Lamb of Jesus."

Yes, there were many things Pastor knew!

XIV   *Angling*

"GREENHOUSES will never take the place of hotbeds," Wullum Yaeger insisted.

Friech Vollman smiled as he looked upon the skeletons of his greenhouses. "Some day," he ventured, "all the gardeners will have greenhouses—sure as the earth turns!"

"There will be none on my place," Wullum replied. "Winter is a time of rest—for the ground, and for us, too. If the Lord wanted us to raise greens the year round he wouldn't cover the gardens with ice and snow."

"But, why shouldn't a gardener work the year round?" Vollman asked. "In greenhouses you can raise lettuce that beats the best land lettuce. As well as the Indianapolis gardeners can make money that way, so can we in Cincinnati."

"It's risky business. . . . A year or two and your ground will be ruined, Vollman. Overworked and dead . . . and all the years you spent fertilizing and building up will be wasted."

"Then I'll bring in new ground."

Herman and Otto came upon the scene. Others followed. Soon Vollman's yard was full of gardeners who came to see what progress had been made in the building of the fantastic "winter garden." Skepticism filled the minds of many, but there were a few who looked upon the project with favor. Among them was Herman Toepfer.

"If we can raise crops all year there will be no need of pinching in the winter," he said. "Greenhouses may be the beginning of fortune for us."

Otto spliced into the conversation. "If wind doesn't blow fortune to the dump! A house of glass will clatter in ruins when the first gale whips across the country."

Vollman was not to be swayed. "Some loss there will be from year to year," he admitted. "Bare land has its losses, too, with frost and drought and hail."

To look at Friech's greenhouses was not the sole reason for this gathering. A momentous community decision was to be reached tonight. Should Winton Place build her own church? That was what the men from the Avenue, the pasture, Gray Road, and Wooden Shoe Hollow had come to decide. In Vollman's spacious parlor they held the discussion.

The time had come when a new congregation must be organized, Vollman began. Old First had grown so large through the years that it was beyond Pastor to serve her as he wished. The miles were many and Pastor was growing old. Was it fair to expect him to be at the beck and call of such a far-flung congregation?"

Otto heaved a sigh. "But nobody can take Pastor Schicht's place among us."

"Truly, no," replied Friech. "But must we be selfish because of that? There is a pastor over in Reading who has promised to help. He has a bicycle and will come to preach for us at first."

Otto grunted. "The Yankees would never stop laughing at us—having to ask a preacher to travel across Cincinnati on a bicycle . . . not even have a home to offer him . . . or a man's wages."

"The devil with the Yankees!" Yaeger exploded.

"All beginnings are hard," Vollman philosophized. "If we all work together faithfully we will soon have a church that we won't need to be ashamed of. Let's build on Winton hill, by the school."

Epworth Avenue was Wullum's choice. "Right with the Yankee churches . . . why not? It's the best location for church property."

Only one suggestion was made for a name. It came from Herman. He smoothed back his blonde hair with his rough brown hand as he rose.

"All these years we've been faithful to First Church," he said. "It would be nice to name our new church after the first of the Gospel writers—that the spirit of putting our Lord first may never leave our homes and our church. Matthew was an humble man as we are . . ."

There was silence as Herman took his seat.

"Well spoken, Herman," Otto complimented with fatherly pride.

A chorus of "It is so" echoed around the parlor to the accompaniment of nodding heads.

Thus, by common consent, the new body named itself after Matthew, the publican, and the men proceeded to elect their council.

The next afternoon the wives met at Old First for their monthly coffee. Echoes of the men's conference were heard at every table. Certainly, Winton Place should have its own church, the women agreed.

"It is much too far to go Back Creek every Sunday," Frau Vollman said. "It is not only unhandy for us, but for Pastor, too."

"No other could take Pastor's place," Minna reflected. "Nobody can . . ." But as usual, Minna found it difficult to put her thoughts into words.

"One must be sensible," Maria Locher cut in decisively. "What needs to be done needs to be done! Pastor Schicht is not Herr Gott himself! All this wishfulness will help nothing! Besides, it is ungodly. So soon as the church is built and the preacher is called we will think of the new days, not of the old."

She stopped stirring her coffee, whipped out the spoon and turned to Minna. "Could you spare Rica an afternoon? The girl is handy with the needle, isn't she? I've such a lot of school clothes to make. Can't get ahead of it."

"Rica is mighty handy with the needle," Minna answered proudly. "I'll send her over tomorrow afternoon. We aren't fixing market on Wednesday, since the beets and carrots are off the patch . . ."

"I'll expect Rica tomorrow then," Maria said abruptly. "Hope Max brings plenty of shirting in the morning."

Minna folded her plump hands over her coffee cup and stared across the social room dreamily. . . . Maria wasn't interested only in her fall sewing. . . . She had other designs.

Minna brought Rica the unexpected invitation as soon as she returned from the coffee. "Maria Locher wants you to help her get the children's clothes ready for school. I told her we weren't fixing market in mid-week now, since the land crops are through, and you could come over tomorrow afternoon."

Thus, Rica found herself in Gerhart's home early the next afternoon.

Maria Locher got to the heart of her purpose almost as soon as Rica arrived. "How long is it you've been in the land?" she asked.

"Almost two years," Rica answered.

The bobbin hummed back and forth, gathering up its slender spoolful of thread. Rica slid it into the sewing machine and reached for the brown woolen dress she was about to seam.

"You like it here, don't you?"

"Yes," Rica answered.

"You couldn't want it better," The older woman's thin colorless lips snapped shut like a spring lock.

Rica murmured agreement. Why must everybody ask that same question? Expect the same matter-of-fact answer?

"I've noticed," Frau Locher continued, "ever since Sophia

took Herman away from you that you have looked to our Gerhart."

Rica was painfully silent.

"You mustn't mind my talking to you plain out. After all, it's best. Gerhart is my boy. Papa and I have talked it over and we haven't anything against you even if you are a few years older than our son. You are decent and hard-working as any girl born right here among us. Only it is this way. We've got to know how you stand with Gerhart's ideas about learning. This nonsense about building bridges and scraping canals in some God-forsaken wilderness . . . he wastes too much time thinking about such things. A gardener boy of his age ought to be worrying about getting a stable and a stand in market, especially when he is keeping steady company. . . . We hoped you would bring him around to it."

Maria Locher's lips snapped shut and she searched Rica with kaleidoscopic eyes.

Rica ran her fingers along the layered seam, folded it in place, clamped down the presser foot, treadled lightly and sent the cloth gliding across the machine. She had a story to tell, too, but hers hadn't any such clear-cut path as Maria's, nor had it the motive. Her story hadn't been planned aforetime, it had to tell itself spontaneously. It must not raise deadly questions or seem evasive. These warning flags dropped before her highly charged thought. . . . She plunged in . . .

"Gerhart and I *have* been good friends, Frau Locher, but we aren't keeping company."

"Not keeping company?" Maria ejaculated. "You are too! I took the trouble to make sure before I asked you to come here. You don't have to be bashful. It's nothing to be ashamed of. Papa and I are agreeable, unless . . ." Maria narrowed her brows, "unless Minna Betz has something to say. If she has she can tell it to Papa and me, she doesn't have to slur behind our backs!"

In spite of Maria's studied insolence Rica kept her emotional balance, though she wanted badly to toss the dresses in a heap and walk out of the door. Not even the pitch of her voice was raised to say, "Frau Betz hasn't noticed my friendship with Gerhart. We've never spoken about him or you."

Frau Locher dropped back in her wicker rocker. "Then it's

just you want to run around for a while first? See if you can do better?" Her feet tapped the floor rhythmically.

Was there no end to this inquisition? She'd make an end! "Frau Locher," Rica said frigidly, "I can't presume to tell you what I don't know myself. As for Gerhart, this much I know: we shall never marry, though I hope we shall always be good friends. Knowing *that* I don't think you would be interested in my plans."

"Not in the least," Maria retorted. "Not in the least! You've got funny ideas, too, I can see that. Don't you suppose Gerhart will find himself a girl who will be glad to marry and settle down on a garden? There had better not be room for your kind of friendship then! Such things don't go on here in Wooden Shoe Hollow! A man sticks to his wife and his children. His neighbors he helps whenever he can, his relatives he honors too, but he doesn't keep friends hidden in corners. That he doesn't! At least, not women friends!" Dual resentment seethed within Maria's breast.

"I don't think we understand each other," Rica said. "There isn't any use talking about it." The sinews in her hand quivered. She clutched the dress and rumbled along fiercely with her sewing, keeping her head bent low over the machine.

"Well, I'll go get coffee on," said Maria. "Children are all out weeding, they are, and it's high time for lunch."

She spread the table with rows of saucerless mugs and knives. A plate of plum kuchen occupied the center.

The children paraded into the kitchen, removed their ticking aprons and dabbled in the basin of wash water, trying hard to scrub off the gluey stains of milkweed.

At table they munched cake and drank weak black coffee. Now and then they stole sheepish glances at "Gerhart's girl." Not knowing how to conduct themselves in her presence, even though it was only afternoon lunch made festive with plum kuchen, they wriggled uncomfortably in their places and hid their faces behind coffee mugs.

Gerhart returned from an errand to the Avenue. His surprise and delight at finding Rica nobody could have missed. Herr Locher, who came in with him, extended an awkward hand to the girl. Intuitively, reading in his wife's face that something had gone amiss with their plans, he slumped down in a chair and waited for Maria to lead the way.

. . . Comely girl, he couldn't help reflecting. . . . It was hard to believe that this slender delicate-featured young woman was Otto's hired girl. How could she work all the wonders Otto boasted about in market? Wash on the line by daybreak, and all the rest of the work inside and out. . . . It was hard to believe . . . she looked, well, yes, one couldn't deny it, she *did* look like a Yankee. Perhaps that was why Gerhart wanted her.

She would be the kind to appreciate violin playing and canal building. She would be on *his* side all right. Maria must have discovered that this afternoon. Gottlieb was sad, sad for reasons which he could never have justified. He was sad because Gerhart wanted this girl so badly. . . . Gerhart was always wanting things badly and getting them in spite of what they did to him. . . .

"Gee, Rica," Gerhart was saying. "I'm so glad you stopped in to see us."

"She didn't stop in to see us. I asked her to come," his mother explained. "Frau Betz was nice enough to spare her. There was so much sewing to be done, I couldn't handle it all. And we couldn't afford to send it up to Anna Menke. Markets are too lean for that this summer."

Gerhart's cheeks were aflame. There were times when he and his mother were as far apart as the two poles. This was one of those times.

He turned to Rica. "Well, you *will* come again, won't you, when there isn't sewing to do? I'd like to show you my drawings."

"Humph!" said Maria.

Gottlieb moved uneasily on his chair and twirled a checkered cap on his pudgy thumb. Disaster lurked in Maria's "humph."

"I'm sure you would like to see the drawings, Rica, even if nobody else cares to look at them."

"Yes, Gerhart, I would." Rica took extraordinary delight in saying so. "Bring them up to Betz's tomorrow night and tell me all about them. And be sure to bring your violin. I'd like to hear you play the way you did at the little English church on Christmas Eve."

Gerhart was jubilant. "Did you like the carols?"

Rica nodded. "I lived with them for days. Herman tried to play them on the accordion, but he could never capture the whole melody, so we had to satisfy ourselves with humming the snatches we remembered."

Gerhart's teeth glistened, as he smiled. "I'll play lots more for you, Rica. Beethoven and Strauss. . . . I'll do my best with them."

"Strauss!" Rica repeated ecstatically. "I love Strauss, Gerhart! And oh, how long it has been since I've heard the glorious 'Tales of the Vienna Woods.'"

"Oh, gee, Rica, I'd love playing for you. That's what makes playing worthwhile—knowing somebody is listening and feeling every mood with you."

"I know," Rica said, face aglow.

Gottlieb winced. How should the boy know that he, too, listened and understood?

"I'll be waiting for you to come and play for us tomorrow, Gerhart. I'll invite Herman and Sophie to come over, too. We'll have a grand time together."

Gerhart's pride rose higher and higher. He was filled with the desire to press Rica to his bosom right here before them all. He loved her. Wanted her.

Rica drew back from that possessiveness. "I must be getting home." She turned to Frau Locher. "Thank you for the afternoon lunch. It was so nice."

"It was nothing," Frau Locher contradicted abruptly. "For your sewing, thanks."

Again, Gerhart was offended. "I'll walk home with you, Rica," he said.

"You have beans to pick, Gerhart," Maria said.

Gerhart ignored the reminder.

He and Rica went out of the door together. Maria shot an envious glance at Rica's slim figure.

Gottlieb sat there still twirling his cap.

"Papa," Maria said, "there are six rows of beans to pick. Better get to them right away. They can't last till Saturday. If they don't sell I'll snipple them. It's none too early."

"Mamma is hard to understand," Gerhart said, in an immediate attempt to gloss over Maria's bluntness. "You must have thought her rude, Rica. I'm so sorry . . . hardly know what to say. It could have been so different this afternoon. Should have been. If only Mamma would try. It isn't that she means to be rude. She just doesn't know how to be friendly, even when she means to be."

"Don't trouble yourself, Gerhart," Rica answered. "No harm is done."

Gerhart looked at her uneasily. "I hope not, Rica, because I want you for my wife, no matter what Mamma says or thinks or does!"

"Hush, Gerhart!" Rica scolded. "There is no need for that kind of defense. As I told your mother this afternoon, I am not going to be your wife."

Gerhart gripped her arm. "Rica," he gasped, "you told Mamma *that*?"

"Yes, Gerhart, of course."

"Why did you do it?" he asked bitterly. "Oh, Rica, you don't know what you have done!"

"I think I do, Gerhart. It was only fair. She hoped I would get you to settle down on a garden . . ."

"So that was it!" Gerhart exploded. "I might have known! Of course, you couldn't agree to that kind of marriage. I wouldn't expect it! Forgive her, Rica, and me. But, please don't go on with that desolate story. It's getting to sound like Poe's old raven. I can't bear it! Some day, Rica, you and I will leave here—leave all this grubbing and *really live!* The world won't be big enough to hold our happiness!"

His fiery breath beat upon her throat.

Minna saw them approaching. She called to Grossmutter, "Come see. Things happened today at Maria's, I shouldn't wonder. See how close they walk together. Och, it is good, not so? One can't blame Maria. Who wouldn't put out her bacon to get such a helper for a daughter-in-law? Lucky woman! And luckier is Gerhart! That he were my son!"

Grossmutter answered nothing. She saw only shadows falling on the lane. Gray shadows. A man and a maid. And her heart rose in indignation at Minna Betz and Maria Locher, who thought

Rica and Gerhart were like two sheaves of wheat to be bound together at their design.

"Make nothing of it," she said at length. "Oldsters have no business meddling with young lives. Marriage now for them? Chaff! Young people think of many things besides marriage!"

"Grossmutter!" Minna reproved. "You would not say such things to the girl? Marriage is best. . . . How else will Gerhart get over these spells of thinking about going away and being an engineer? Rica can save him. She will make a fine gardener's wife."

"Chaff!" said Grossmutter.

XV *The Purge*

SUMMER WAS ON THE WANE. The Betzes were gathered around the Saturday night supper table, each person enjoying the *Stollen* in his own way. Ernst sopped it in his coffee. Hulda ferreted out the raisins to enjoy at the end of the meal and Fritz nibbled at the sugared top, then slipped the rest to Sport, the shaggy Newfoundland, who sat under the table.

Suddenly, Hulda turned to Minna with the abrupt question, "What does it mean to be in a fix?"

"What do you mean?" Minna asked.

"Like Pearl Bryan."

Minna, shocked out of speech, laid down her *Stollen*.

Otto's face turned beet red. "Where did you hear such talk, Hulda?" he sputtered.

"In a story book, Papa."

"Whose story book?"

"Maggie's. She got it from the coffee man."

"So!" Otto's fist pounded the table mightily. The dishes rocked. "What have I always said?" he shouted. "Book reading is the ruination of people! So long we've stood by and let books come into Wooden Shoe Hollow. Now we've got the boar to slay!"

Minna's bosom rose and fell in consternation.

Hulda was aghast at the storm she had aroused . . .what would Maggie say? All their precious books would be taken away. Papa would see to that. If only she hadn't asked that bothersome question. She ought to have known that "being in a fix" was terrible if Pearl Bryan had had her head cut off because of it!

"Hulda!" Otto thundered across the table.

"Yes, Papa."

"Never let me catch you saying such a sinful thing again!"

The girl fled upstairs in a panic of bewilderment.

"Are there any of the coffee man's books in this house?" Otto demanded.

"Certainly not," Minna said. "I never get anything but dishes with my coupons. Nobody has time to waste reading books here, Papa."

"That's what I wanted to know first," Otto replied. "Now I can go out and clean up the hollow. It's a good thing I didn't have to begin in my own house!" He barged out of the door.

Rica was downcast. If only Grossmutter had been there; but Grossmutter was spending a few days with the Back Creek folk, making chronological rounds of cousins.

"Hulda needs a good talking to," Minna said, as soon as the rest of the family were out of the kitchen. "It . . . it . . . makes my blood run cold to think of . . ."

Rica had come to know when Minna reached blind alleys in her speech.

"It wasn't Hulda's fault," she said. "Hulda is innocent."

"Yet, she needs to be corrected."

"I'll speak to her."

"I wish you would." Minna shrugged her broad shoulders in relief. "Better go upstairs and see to it before Papa gets back."

Rica found Hulda at the window, staring over at Vollmans, where her father had gone. Remorse, confusion and anger, like a pack of noisy dogs, had driven off Hulda's curiosity. She was no longer thinking of Pearl Bryan. She was thinking only of how she had betrayed Maggie's friendship . . . all because of a foolish question, which, in all likelihood, neither Otto nor Minna could answer anyway.

"Oh, Rica!" she wailed. "What did I do? What made Papa so mad? What is he going to do?"

"We shall have to wait and see, Hulda. It was a wicked book. You and Maggie ought not to have read it."

Hulda sobbed. "It was just a murder story, Rica. Why was it so bad? Maggie will get in trouble on account of me. She won't ever talk to me again. I know she won't, Rica. And Maggie is my very, very best friend."

Rica held out her arms. "It may not be as bad as that, darling. You mustn't be so upset. Everything will be all right after a while. You don't want to be reading bad books, do you? Or have Maggie reading them?"

Hulda shook her head. "But I tattled, Rica. I shouldn't have said anything about the book."

She pushed aside her bangs and looked squarely into Rica's face. "What did it mean, Rica? Do you know?"

"There is so much, Hulda, so very much!"

An hour later they were still upstairs, talking in low voices. Like a mountaineer beating an uncertain path Rica pushed her way past thorns and jagged rocks with Hulda. Gradually, she found her ground, winding round and round as it mounted. Presently they had come to the top . . . the top!

Hulda looked up in startled fascination. Her mouth was slightly open, her eyes like two polished jewels . . . her thoughts too occupied to wander back down the hillside to the point where Pearl Bryan had been left.

From next door Otto now returned with Vollman and Yaeger at his heels. He was still gesticulating wildly, and the two men were nodding assent.

Their voices came into the window. "I'll horsewhip the first dog who dares to bring a book into Wooden Shoe Hollow!" Otto declared.

Hulda wailed.

From house to house Otto and his aids barged in high indignation, confiscating books. Beside the Betz market shed their plunder was tossed and burned. Not only the one which had caused the furor, but many another went with it. Fairy tales, *Robinson Crusoe, Arabian Nights*—everything that did not bear the stamp of school or church went into the fire. Tears and protests could not stem the purge. Ruthless mob spirit prevailed.

"Tomorrow, Pastor Schicht shall hear about this," Otto said, tossing an armful of yellow-paged story books upon the fire. These last were from the Locher household, all books which Gerhart had received from Yankee school friends long ago.

Maria came running to the fire with a book . . . one Otto had overlooked.

Rica shouted out of the window in dismay. Instinctively, she knew what it was Maria had in her hand—the engineer's textbook. Maria had her own reasons for entering so wholeheartedly into the spirit of this mad episode!

Hardly had she tossed the book on the bonfire, when Gerhart came flying up the lane. "Mamma, don't! Please, Mamma, not that one!" he called frantically. But Maria, self-satisfied, stood empty-handed, looking into the fire where flames had already begun their devastating work on the book of bridges and towers.

Gerhart, seeing the malicious look of triumph on her face and beholding his treasure hopelessly afire, ran up the hill to his godfather.

Rica's heart pounded. What happened now depended upon Emil Mueller! If only he would act wisely!

The crowd dispersed. Disgruntled little ones, robbed of their Cinderellas, wiped away their tears and turned to their hammers and dolls. Young folks were off to the crowd, fast forgetting Pearl Bryan. Older ones pondered the shameful event, talked about it guardedly, yawned and went to bed.

For Rica, there was no crowd tonight. She scarcely heard the music when the dancing started.

Darkness crept over the hollow . . . up the hill . . . where Gerhart had gone for succor. Rica was filled with weird loneliness. This past year had brought Gerhart very close to her.

When she saw his shadowy figure coming down the hill she clutched her throat. Something had happened she knew. Not for the best. . . . She slipped downstairs, stole up to him in the lane, and took his arm.

"What is it, Gerhart? What has happened?"

"Everything," he mumbled.

She drew him to the Betz porch and sat down beside him on the step. "They burned your book. I saw that. But what else happened? What did Herr Mueller say?"

"I don't know, Rica. He said a lot of things, but nothing that matters. Said Mamma was right. I ought to be glad I've got a good home. Preached about keeping respectable. Setting a good example for innocent children. Said doing things the hollow doesn't approve of is sinful . . ."

He fell into silence.

Rica burst out, "But, didn't you tell him about the book? Doesn't he know you want to be an engineer?"

"Yes, he knows all that, but doesn't hold much for it. He promised me a garden anywhere I want if I'll give up trying to be an engineer. It was different about the violin. He helped me then. He always has, but this time he won't. It's hopeless."

"Well, I'm for you," Rica assured him.

"And I need you to help me, Rica," he said throatily. "You are all I've got left."

"No, Gerhart. You mustn't feel that way. Your folks don't understand, that's all. If they did, they would send you to school, where you could learn the things you want. They can't understand, Gerhart. It isn't their fault. Nobody else ever wanted what you want. How should they know?"

"But you understand, Rica!" he challenged.

"Yes, yes, I do, Gerhart!" Her arm slipped around his shoulder.

"Will you go away with me, tonight?"

"Gerhart!"

"I mean it! I've got to go sometime. Couldn't stand it here, after what happened tonight. Oh, Rica, please say you'll go with me!"

Rica recoiled. "You don't know what you are doing, Gerhart. "Surely, you don't want to run away!"

"I do, Rica. I've got to go!"

"Wait till morning. Don't go like this—without a word to anybody. You can go talk to Pastor Schicht tomorrow. He will help you."

Gerhart shook his head. "I wouldn't have enough nerve to go after I talked to him. Anyway, he would be on their side just like

Uncle Emil. . . . No, Rica, I've made up my mind. Let's catch the midnight train down at Winton Place. I've got enough money to get along for a while. My share of the market money I've been saving for a horse. It's almost a hundred dollars. That's enough to start." He added tenderly, "You could buy a wedding dress and new shoes. We could afford that. . . . Oh, Rica, *please* go with me! I want you so badly! I'll always work hard and save and do everything I can to make you happy."

Rica's head was spinning. "Want you so badly. . . . Everything to make you happy . . . buy a wedding dress . . ." Like telegraph code the words scuttled through her brain.

Gerhart's lips were burning against her cheek. "Rica, my darling, don't make me go away without you . . . Rica!"

Tight bands gripped her throat. She longed desperately to answer, "Yes, I'll go with you" . . . longed to tear off the shackles which bound her to a phantom soldier. But reason followed hard upon the heels of desire, and whipped her into subjection.

"Gerhart, you mustn't ask me to do this. I can't. It isn't because I don't care. Believe me. Your going away will leave me forlorn. I've come to need you just as you need me. But I can't do this thing . . . it's . . . it's not in my power," she added helplessly.

"Are you afraid, Rica?"

"No, Gerhart, not afraid. I'd gladly share every misfortune, every disappointment of the road with you. Fight for you, if necessary. And work too, but . . ."

"Then what is holding you back?" Gerhart demanded. "Is it Frau Betz? She has Grossmuter. And Hulda's getting older. She will soon be out of school."

"It would break Grossmutter's heart, Gerhart. I owe everything to her. Running away like a thief in the night would be a shameful way to show thanks, especially when she isn't here to say, 'Good-bye.'"

"Grossmutter would never stand in our way, Rica. She'd know how we love each other."

"If I left now," Rica answered, "it would throw a heavy burden on Grossmutter. That is the point, Gerhart. Not how she would feel about it . . . and little Hulda would come out of school ahead of her years . . . Fritzie too. . . . They deserve better. We mustn't cheat them, Gerhart. It would be like burning their books, only worse. You can buy back books, but you can't buy back burnt-up years!"

"But, Rica, it isn't all your responsibility! They have their father and mother. We've just each other. We've got to fight for ourselves. Our whole lives are at stake!"

"You are right, Gerhart. Our whole lives *are* at stake! That is the very reason why we must be careful. Why we can't take one false step. I'm begging you to think twice!"

"I have thought twice, and more!" he retorted. "I know what I'm doing. I'm leaving Wooden Shoe Hollow, perhaps forever! Sick and tired of it all. I've got other things to do besides pitch manure, and if my people can't see it my way, I'll have to go my way alone!"

"You haven't thought at all," Rica argued. "You are too hurt and too angry to think. After this has had time to pass over, you will see things differently. Our folks were angry tonight—indignant and confused. That's why they built the fire and burned all the books they could lay hands on. They are working off spite and hasty rage. Tomorrow they will know that what they did was wrong, that the way they felt was wrong. Perhaps they won't say so, but they will feel it, and try to make amends. If you run away tonight nothing can be set aright, for that will make you the transgressor. Don't you see how they will feel?"

"I don't care how they feel . . . now, or tomorrow," Gerhart retorted. "They can paint me as black as they like, think what they please, I'm through!"

Rica sighed. "Don't let this make you bitter, Gerhart. Don't break all the links that hold you here. They are precious. Some day you will need and want them. Only believe it!"

Gerhart sulked in silence.

"Out there in the clatter and bang of the outside world Wooden Shoe Hollow will come to you often. You will think of it early in the morning when heaven is close to us with dew and fresh sunlight. And you will think of it, too, at night, when you are through pounding and climbing and your body is sore and aching for rest. You will think, then, of the peace and quiet at home. Of every hotbed safely covered for the night. Of every house, every garden beneath the stars.

"There is something godly here, Gerhart. You will miss it when you are away. You will never be able to forget, no matter how far you go or what you do!

"You will think of Pastor, sometimes, too, I think. The things he said. And you will long for a moment to talk to him, one moment to feel his strong kind hand gripped in yours, his great heart-warming smile upon you.

"And you will think of your home, Gerhart. Your mother, your father and the little ones. You will wonder if all is well, and what they are doing!"

"You may be right, Rica, yet I must go."

"Not tonight. Not this way, Gerhart!"

"Tonight. Oh, Rica, won't you come with me?"

She bent her head.

"Tell me, yes! Rica, Rica, darling! Can't you see how much I love you? How much I need you?"

He clutched Rica savagely and drew from her one relentless kiss after another. He lay his burning face against hers, which quivered with emotion as mighty as his own, crying for release . . . crying . . . struggling to be let go. . . .

XVI *Aftermath*

THE NEXT MORNING a tempest raged. Gerhart Locher had run away! The news swept over the whole hollow before the first church bell had rung.

Gottlieb stood on the summer kitchen steps staring at the road down which Gerhart had gone. When the children stumbled downstairs with Gerhart's good-bye note, he wanted to dash to the railroad station . . . the station master might know where the boy had gone . . . but Maria forbid his going.

"Like the prodigal our son has gone and like the prodigal he shall return! There will be no running after him," Maria said bitterly, as she put on the coffee pot and spread breakfast for her smitten clan. She sent the children on their way to Sunday school with the admonition, "Don't talk to anybody about your brother. If people ask questions, say only, 'I don't know.'"

And then she forced Gottlieb into his pleated-bosom shirt and sent him to church with the same instructions. For herself, she chose to stay home.

Maggie Vollman stalked by on her way to Sunday school without so much as a glance at the Betz home. Remorse bit into Hulda's sensitive soul. "Rica," she said. "Maggie won't ever talk to me again!"

"Yes she will," Rica said halfheartedly.

That afternoon Pastor spent hours with the Lochers, while neighbors, like anxious voters at election time, waited for the outcome of the forum. They speculated about all the queer tendencies which Gerhart had displayed since childhood, such as wanting a violin and a trotting horse, and wanting to draw meaningless figures and sit with his head in a book past midnight . . . a queer one was this oldest boy of Maria and Gottlieb Locher!

While the hollow waited, gossip grew. It was Rica who had caused Gerhart's escapade. She had spurned him just as she had spurned Herman Toepfer. This was Hattie's view. Anybody could see Gerhart was set on Rica, and she had led him on, knowing all the while, that she would not marry him. . . . Oh, Rica was a coquette, all right, and the men here in Wooden Shoe Hollow had best learn that once and for all!

And Hans had a story to tell . . . how he started home from the crowd early, in search of a spider web to stanch the bleeding of his hand which had been cut by a broken beer glass.

As he neared the Betz home he heard voices, and so he stole along the hotbeds on hands and knees to hear what the robbers had to say, for, of course, they must be robbers since Minna and Otto had long since been asleep. Grossmutter was Back Creek and Ernst was at the crowd. He discovered that it was Rica and Gerhart who were quarreling on the porch and defaming each other with ugly names.

It wasn't often that Hans had a story to which people were willing to listen, but this one was palatable. He told and re-told it with ever growing enthusiasm and candor.

To Maria, herself, Hans went for the climax, as soon as Pastor's carriage had driven into the hollow.

"It's about Gerhart," he began, as Maria warily opened the screen door. "I know who it was drove him away . . . Rickey Heber . . . Betz's Rickey . . . that's who it was! I heard them fighting last night on Betz's porch, I did!"

"When?" Maria asked.

"When I come home from the crowd last night."

"Wasn't Gerhart at the crowd?"

"No, sure wasn't, Frau Locher. She either. They must have been fighting a good evening."

"What were they fighting about?" Maria demanded.

"I don't know what all, Frau Locher, but he said he was going away and he would never come back!"

Maria's jaw snapped.

"And Rickey told him to go ahead and run away and see if she'd care."

Maria encouraged Hans to continue talking about the episode. And gladly, he expanded it to meet her expectations, coming back with certainty, many times, to the convincing assertion that it was Rica who was responsible for Gerhart's flight.

By the time Pastor had paid a few more calls and finally approached the Betz garden Hans had succeeded in turning all eyes in that direction. Everybody was sure that it was indignation which took Pastor there. Even Minna was uneasy. She hustled away to Vollmans before the carriage drove into her yard.

Rica, alone, waited Pastor. Some idea she already had that she was being blamed for Gerhart's running away, but how thoroughly she was being held accountable she did not guess.

"This is too bad," Pastor said, as he came to Rica. "Too bad that Gerhart has run away."

"It was because of the book burning."

"Otto told me about that this morning. But why did that anger the boy so much? He is no rascal. He knows right from wrong!"

"You think it was right—what they did?"

"Burning evil books? Yes, child, of course they were right!"

"But *his* book, Pastor. There was nothing evil in it! There couldn't have been. It was only a study book."

"A study book? I heard nothing of this."

"An engineering book, with problems and rules and measures. It was something only Gerhart understood."

"It was burned by mistake with the others?"

"No," Rica answered quickly. "Not by *mistake,* Pastor. It was burned for *spite!*"

"So?" Pastor frowned mightily. "For spite they burned a harmless book? Does the boy's mother know this?"

Rica drew breath sharply. "It was *she* who burned it, Pastor!"

"So-o-o? . . . Is it fair to ask how you know that Frau Locher spited the boy?"

"She tossed the book on the fire because it made Gerhart ambitious to be an engineer when she wanted him to be a gardener."

Pastor nodded. "And that is the reason why he ran away?"

"Yes."

"And yet, not the whole reason, either. This would have come anyhow, book burning or no. Wooden Shoe Hollow could never have held Gerhart. He is too restless, too adventurous. It was folly to try to hold him here."

Rica remembered with pain Gerhart's morose words of last night. . . . It wouldn't do any good to talk to Pastor. He would be on "their" side.

Pastor folded his massive hands behind his head. "One of the finest boys I ever taught—Gerhart was. Studied ahead. Nobody ever had to push him. And yet there was another side to Gerhart, a dreamy side that often separated him from people and made him lonely. That's what drove him to silent study . . . I am not surprised. . . . But, where did he get this book?"

"From his Yankee friends in Winton Place."

Pastor smiled broadly. "Gerhart ever had a way with Yankees!"

"Nobody knows where he has gone, Pastor. What if something happens to him?"

"Something *is* going to happen to him, Rica. We can't and mustn't stop it. He left Wooden Shoe Hollow a raw stripling, with nothing but ambition and strong arms to fight his way. He wants to be an engineer, does he? Well, he will be an engineer, if I know the boy, and I think I do.

"He will struggle through hard years that will sap strength and will, but it won't best him. He will come back the better for it, a man whom all Wooden Shoe Hollow will be proud to welcome home."

"It's good to hear you say that, Pastor. I'm afraid nobody else feels that way, do they? Especially, his parents?"

"Not now," Pastor admitted. "He is an ungrateful prodigal to them. They can prophecy only doom. But time will change that outlook, when anger is replaced by loneliness and yearning."

"Pastor," Rica began hesitantly, "you don't think Gerhart will lose himself?"

"No, Rica. Gerhart is his own master! That much we have been able to do—give him a solid staff for his travels. Hardship and temptation can do their worst, but they will never dwarf his faith in God or his love for good and beautiful things."

Pastor stroked his beard meditatively. "Some day it will burst upon him like a sun out of clouds—the knowledge that his boyhood days were good. He will know then that his stern upbringing made him able to do the things he wanted to do. They gave him health, faith and cleanliness, without which no man succeeds."

"You know him well, Pastor," Rica faltered.

"I should be dull not to know my boys and girls. They come to me when it is easiest to know them, surface years when all that is on the inside comes to the top—doubts, questions, hopes. And the outside shapes itself into new molds, too. It is then that I can do most for them—to help pluck out spiritual cinders that would otherwise sink inside and fester the body and blister the soul.

"It was so with Gerhart. He sat opposite me, sometimes looking straight at me, with his daring black eyes, following every word. At other times he wanted to do nothing but stare vacantly out of the window, and I had to reach across the table and rap his hands and bring him back into the presence of the lesser prophets.

"This happened especially in the spring when the pear tree was all abloom outside the window and the birds were building nests and singing. To him it made little difference, then, whether they found Benjamin in the sack or Joseph's cup.

"And his confirmation day . . . I remember it as clearly as if it were yesterday. . . . 'Let the words of my mouth and the meditation of my heart be acceptable in Thy sight, oh God, my strength and my Redeemer.' . . . I can see Gerhart as he rose before me, tearful, with a smile breaking through. I knew that he was taking that blessing with him forever. . . . Do you see why I trust him to come back, why I cannot fear the outcome of all this?"

"Yes," Rica said with a surge of awe. "Yes, I do see, Pastor."

"Before long we shall hear from him. Never fear."

"Do they blame me for his running away?"

"I'm afraid so, Rica. Maria and Gottlieb do, but that will pass. Their conscience must tell them sooner or later that they are wrong, that it is not you, but they, themselves, who have driven the boy away. . . . You will be questioned. Unfortunately, Hans saw you talking to Gerhart last night."

"Hans? . . . How could he?"

"He was wandering by on his way home from the crowd. So the story goes. . . . He has kept out of my sight. Perhaps he doesn't want to tell that story to me. . . . Ah, Hans, when will people learn to understand you, poor sinner?"

Pastor had known then . . . that she and Gerhart. . . . How patiently he had waited!

"Pastor, Hans did see Gerhart here last night. After the book burning. He was upset and wanted to run away then, only . . ." she lowered her voice. "He wanted me to go with him."

Pastor looked at her in grave silence.

"I tried to keep him here, at least until morning, but it was of no use. I couldn't help his wanting me to go with him. Truly, I couldn't, Herr Pastor. I never led him to think . . . we were just friends . . . even at the crowd . . . I never . . ."

"I know, child," he rescued her with ease. "I understand all that. You needn't try to say it." He took Rica's hand. "Don't worry. Hans' story will unravel itself once he must face you. . . . And soon, too, we should be hearing from across the water."

Pastor rose to go. "Good-bye."

"Good-bye, and thank you, Pastor. Thank you for all you have done for me."

She closed the door.

Soon . . . she pondered . . . soon I shall hear from across the water . . . but what of Gerhart? Would he, too, be a fugitive from himself? A pilgrim forever seeking and never finding, forever beholding and never acquiring? Would he pay that price, too, for his zeal to set his world aright?

XVII *A Shelling Party*

~~~~~~

IT WAS MID-OCTOBER. Rica and Ernst were clearing the lima bean patch in anticipation of frost, which the *Volksblatt* promised for the night. At the end of the row Rica dropped an apronful of beans into the basket. As she did so, she glanced over the field at Sophia, who was sewing on the porch. It was not the brier quilt she was stitching . . . nor the gingham apron.

Rica darted into the thick of the patch. A cold thrust shocked her. She grappled a pole and buried her head in the thick bowered vines. Life raced on beside her . . . Herman . . . Herman, Sophia . . . and . . .

Hulda wove in and out of the poles. "Where are you, Rica?" she called.

Rica's hands released their fierce clutch on the pole and she answered huskily, "Here I am, Hulda, what is it?"

"I am going to help you, slowpoke! It will be getting dark soon."

"I am about finished," Rica answered. "Just one more row."

"I'll take the bottom and you take the top," Hulda chirped. "We'll beat Ernst, see if we don't!" And she launched into a tale of African jungles and diamond mines and elephants. Only the sounds fell upon Rica's ears.

The row was finished.

Another long job awaited them. A job that Hulda concluded would last all night. The beans had to be shelled for market.

The family fell to the task zealously, each with a pan beside him. Hulda and Fritz sat Turk fashion before the heap of lima beans on the summer kitchen floor. Ernst was perched against the wall, his knees drawn up as if he were a grasshopper ready to leap. Otto's long legs sprawled out into the center of the room.

Minna, Rica and Grossmutter were gathered around a twin heap.

Ida Menke and Herman Toepfer, too, were on hand.

"I just knew you would be having all kinds of beans to shell, when I saw Ernst and Rica picking so steadily this afternoon," Ida said. "Annie would have come too, only she must finish Hattie Flieger's dress. Hattie is going to Avondale, you know. She has a house job for the winter."

"Hattie's going to work out?" Ernst asked. "Hah! Maybe she won't think she is so high-toned when those Yankees tell her what's what!"

"Ernst!" Minna reprimanded sharply. "Mind your own business and let other people alone!"

Ernst shrugged his shoulders. "Well, it's the truth, Mamma. Hattie's head gets so big sometimes that it won't fit in a bushel basket."

Hulda tittered.

"That's enough!" Minna turned to the second offender. "Hulda, must you laugh at your own brother's dumbness? Shame on you!"

There was a moment of crushed silence. Only the ticking of the big wall clock and the snapping of pods could be heard.

Hulda tried to quell the merriment inside. It was hard thinking of Hattie's smoothly rolled hair and her talcumed nose under a bushel basket. . . . She broke forth again.

Grossmutter came to the rescue. "Let the little one laugh, Minna. She'll get a stomach-ache holding it inside."

Minna snapped pods with emphasis. "Better a stomach-ache than . . ." The thought was incomplete.

Grossmutter gave Minna a sly wink.

The episode was closed.

Curiously enough, Hulda didn't want to laugh any more.

"Are you going to take all the beans to Vaigo?" Herman asked.

"Every quart," Otto boasted.

"Do you think he will take them? Vollman is bringing some in too and Back Creek the vines were hanging heavy Sunday."

"Whether he needs them or not Vaigo will take my beans. Did I ever tell you how I brought him to time?"

Though everybody had heard the story, not once, but many, many times, Otto swung one leg across the other, brushed his mustache, and began, "It was the year I raised so many red beets. More than my peddlers could use.

"Well, I took a load down to Vaigo. He looked it over, and tried to beat me down. I said, 'Vaigo, you're getting to be a regular dead beat! I'm doing business somewhere else!'

"That made him mad. Oh, those commission men can get awfully mad . . . but he couldn't bluff me!

"I hopped right on my wagon and pulled the load around the corner to Tazzo. Tazzo was busy packing in sugar melons and the men didn't want to call him, so I told them I'd wait around for a while. Went in the restaurant for a cup coffee and flour pancake.

"And who should be in there but a fellow in the canning business. He was down Cincinnati buying up stuff. Well, I wasn't any too slow to talk business with the fellow. He was so glad to buy my load that he even paid for my pancake.

"And you should have seen Vaigo's face when I started rolling barrels down and loading up the stranger's shipping wagon. He was altogether out of himself!"

Otto slapped his knee and laughed uproariously. Hulda exchanged proud glances with Fritz. This particular story always elated her. There wasn't another gardener who could outsmart a commission man, like her father! Not one!

"How much more did you make on the load, Papa?" she asked. That, after all, was the crux of the matter.

"Almost eight dollars more than Vaigo offered me," Otto

chuckled. "And since that time I don't have any more trouble with the old *Spinnervergift!*

"He came up to me after the deal, and said, 'Why did you sell your load to a stranger? You know I'm your best customer.'

"And I says, 'My best customer is the man who pays me best!' Old Vaigo turned around and never said another word! I had him!"

The picking went on and on. Many an old story was employed to while away the tedious hours.

Every now and then Rica met Herman's soft smile or Ida's quick questioning glance.

"I guess we could stand a little lunch," Otto said with an abysmal yawn, as the last pair of baskets were emptied on his heap.

Rica was on her feet immediately.

Ida rose and followed her to the kitchen.

"I've been wanting to talk to you, Rica," she said. "About Gerhart."

Rica's face colored.

"I've a note for you. It came in my letter today. It was best that way. So nobody could talk. Here it is."

Rica jammed the envelope into her apron pocket and covered it with a handkerchief.

"How is he?" she asked breathlessly.

"Fine. He is in New Orleans, working for a steamship company. Pretty soon he will go down to Panama."

"Has he written home?"

"No, he doesn't want them to know where he is."

"He ought to tell them," Rica whispered. "It's no more than right."

Ida smiled. "I don't want you to think I'm interfering. You think lots of Gerhart, and I do too, but maybe we had better let him work this out for himself."

"But, if Frau Locher finds out! She hates me now, worse than Paris green. What would it be then?"

"She won't know you have heard from him, if no letters come here."

"But what of you?"

Ida raised her eyebrows. "That," she said, with an emphatic wave of her hand, "doesn't trouble me at all. Maria Locher's blame wouldn't crush my shoulders!"

Rica's lips parted. It seemed odd . . . such words coming from even-tempered little Miss Ida. It was mysterious, her attitude toward Gerhart—fighting for him, defying his family, to shield him.

"But his father, Miss Ida, don't you think he ought to know where Gerhart is? I . . . I can't help feeling sorry for him. Everybody knows how wretched he is, poor man."

Ida blanched. Unsteadily, her hand pushed the jagged knife through the loaf of bread. "I know," she said.

"Couldn't we tell just him? Somehow, I feel he would understand."

"No," Ida said quietly. "Much as we would like to tell Gottlieb, we just mustn't do it. Maria would see that he was holding something back and she would drive him into a corner and flag the secret out of him."

Again, Rica caught her breath in sheer surprise.

After the midnight lunch Ernst and Otto crated the beans. Quart by quart they gathered up the sea of pale green from the sheet spread out upon the bedroom carpet.

While they were packing, Rica and Ida cleared the table. A long time the two women stood in the doorway talking softly. Herman came from the barn with a lighted lantern.

"I'll take you home, Miss Ida. . . . Good night, Rica." Again that tender look of old.

"Good night, Herman."

Rica carried a lamp into the parlor. Breathlessly, she turned to the letter from Gerhart.

DEAR RICA:

I wish you were here with me in New Orleans.

I am working in the shipyards during the day, and I have an extra job at night in a shrimp cannery. It is only for a few hours. It won't be long and I'll have the money to get down to Panama. I don't want to go without you.

I got another book. It is newer and better than the old one. At the cannery there is a little time to study every night.

Oh, Rica, it is going to be wonderful to help build the Panama Canal! Think of men digging like beavers, turning land into water, building a sea road just like a highway across the land. Think of ships passing from ocean to ocean! It's power and wisdom and progress.

And thank God we can play a part in it. Doesn't it thrill you, darling? Doesn't it make you want to be here and watch it come to life?

Do come! I'll make you happy! Write and tell me you will come, and I'll take care of everything. I'm waiting, darling, and loving you more than ever!

Eternally yours,
GERHART

Rica raced through the note like a child chasing a rabbit through the woods. Then, back to the beginning she turned and re-read the letter. This time she read slowly, so that words and phrases took hold of thoughts and held them fast, as earth holds seeds till sprouting time.

Then she slipped into the kitchen and gave the letter, uncrumpled, to the brightest glowing coal under the tea kettle. Watched it turn into a tablet of fragile gray ash.

The kitchen was deathly still.

Upstairs there was more silence. Grossmutter's white hair—her furrowed face relaxed in sleep. . . . Baby Lottchen taking comfort from her tiny pink thumb. . . . Hulda, still jungle-tramping, silently beholding a mystic world such as no vagabond traveler had ever seen!

Asleep . . . dreaming . . . forgetting today . . . and forgetting tomorrow . . . all of them.

But Rica, in confusion, could not sleep, could not dream, must think of today and of tomorrow! Herman, Sophia . . . a new spirit traveling worldward . . . a sweet bright spirit . . .

And Gerhart! Strong-hearted fellow. Working day and night slavishly. Hoping, struggling to fulfill dreams that could never come true all the way. The part that could come true he must do alone, quite alone! She and Ida Menke could be merely a pair of Aarons to him.

Mightily, Rica wished that the letter had not come from New Orleans, but that it had come from across the sea; that Gerhart Locher were Heinrich Heber. Then it would be a good world, indeed! But Gerhart was not Heinrich. He was dear, brave Gerhart, fighting a lonely battle in New Orleans. And Heinrich was an interloper, a wretched ruffian, whose trade was to destroy such marvelous works as a Panama Canal, to destroy lives, too, with intrigue, hate and steel!

One bitter promise shackled her to this wastrel! A promise that she would have moved the Andes to recall!

At that moment, however, the "ruffian" was neither hating nor killing, nor laying waste. He was driving sheep to pasture in the lowlands of Germany.

In New Orleans, a weary lad was climbing stairs to his dark unhospitable room near the gulf.

His work ended, his body tired, mind dull with another night of over-study, he was coming home to rest.

He flung himself upon the cot and stared out upon the gulf. It was shimmering like a vast silver platter with rippling engravings upon its surface. That way lay Panama! Rich effulgent Panama!

And back, back across the states was Wooden Shoe Hollow and Rica. Soon she would come, his love, and there would be no more pain like this. Soon she would come, with her great heart full of love and understanding. Would turn every dismal day into a day of rhapsody. Would transform some pair of rooms here in New Orleans into Paradise!

And then, together, they would sail across that adventurous silver platter to Panama. . . . So Gerhart dreamed.

At the same hour, Herman Toepfer blew out the light of his lantern and stepped out of his wooden shoes in the stoop. Lightly, his fingers touched a bit of soft wool upon the back of a chair, as he tiptoed into the room where Sophia was asleep.

And he thought of many things.

Sophia . . . the baby who was coming . . . this house . . . the celery that had grown so well, the price it would bring, the things it would buy for Sophia, things she wanted.

A deep sigh of satisfaction.

Sophia stirred. "It took a long time," she said drowsily. "It must be almost market time."

"It is half past one," Herman said softly.

"You didn't forget to lock the stable?"

"No," Herman answered. "Everything is in order."

Sophia turned upon her pillow. "That's right, Herman," she sighed. "Everything is in order because you are home."

XVIII *The Other Side*

HEINRICH HEBER was tending sheep when a little boy came running to the fields with a letter for him.

Heinrich sighed. So this was another end! All his life seemed to be chopped up into ends and ineffectual beginnings! School, the army, discharge and now civilian life.

What twist of fate was this? Word from the Reich? Must he return to service in spite of his injured leg? From the Reich this message must have come, for nobody else knew that he had gone to Westphalia, nobody except his father.

The seal was not from Berlin, however. It was from Wehdem, his old home village. The jerky stream of letters on the envelope was not at once familiar to Heinrich.

"I hope your father didn't die," the little towheaded messenger panted, as he dropped upon the cropped grass.

Heinrich shook his head. "No, Gustave, not that."

There was a full-page letter from Pastor Sigfried of Wehdem, Heinrich's old teacher.

Dear Heinrich:

Word has come to me, through a Christian minister in America, that your wife, Rica, is living over there.

I had never heard of your marriage, my boy, and had some difficulty in understanding just how these strange circumstances came about. I am deeply sorry about the injury you received in service, and also about the separation from your wife.

My inquiry about you at military headquarters finally was answered. They reported you had been discharged six months ago because of an injured leg, and that you were recuperating at Gustave Meyer's sheep farm in Westphalia.

It is my hope that you are restored by now, Heinrich.

The American pastor asks whether you have any message. He assures you that your wife is sorry for any anxiety her sudden leaving may have caused you. She disliked your being in service, and therefore fled to America. She is working on a garden, and does not wish to return to Germany.

If there is anything which I may do for you, Heinrich, please write. It shall be an extraordinary pleasure.

Faithfully,
Reinhold Sigfried

Little Gustave sat with puckered brow waiting for Heinrich to speak. But Heinrich was silent. No word to explain why his pale cheeks suddenly turned crimson and then receded to white again. Why his eyes grew misty and his hands shook with emotion. Heinrich folded the letter and put it back into the envelope.

His troubled gaze swept over the rolling pasture. "There is nothing wrong with Father, Gustave," he said, in answer to the lad's troubled questioning.

"Is it about your leg, then? Maybe you will get some money?"

Heinrich shook his head. "Who cares about my leg?" he asked bitterly. "Who cares about anything?"

"Herr Gott!" Gustave ejaculated throatily, as he got to his feet and ran back to the cottage.

Heinrich gazed absentmindedly at his flock. So, it was the uniform of his emperor that had robbed him of Rica!

His father had worn that uniform proudly for more than thirty years. Planned for his only son to step into it and carry on!

Well, he, Heinrich had tried, hadn't he? Tried to like the whole brutal business, from the field exercises to the battlefront, and from the bugle call to the scream of shells, and from the thick odor of mess hall cooking to the stench of exploded powder. But it was of no use—he hated it! And welcomed honorable discharge even at the cost of his leg!

Heinrich looked down at that leg. There was no pain now. Nothing but a shrunken thigh muscle, which made him lame. One careless moment at drill and he had been crippled for life.

Poor Maximilian, with all his glorious dreams of commissions and bars and epaulets—to have a son who could do no better than maim himself before he ever tasted battle!

But surely, it was best that way, Heinrich had reflected many times during his convalescence. There would be other years. He could give himself wholeheartedly to life in the country—the life his mother had taught him to love. . . . Never have to part from fruitful earth. Germany needed her farmer sons, as much as she needed her soldiers!

Perhaps, in a little while, he would be well enough to buy his own farm. Raise fruits, vegetables and flowers—many, many flowers! A cow or two, sheep and geese. That would be hearty living! Some day Maximilian would come home in the country to stay. And it would be like old times again.

Days full of earth and sunshine. Coolness of dusk in the arbor —his father's long jeweled pipe sending up a haze of smoke— nights full of rest and companionship. The warmth of a hearth fire—joy of listening to his father's lively stories. All this Heinrich had been anticipating while he tended sheep for Gustave Meyer.

And now, the letter. Word, at last, from his phantom wife. That's what she had always been. Willowy memory had preserved the picture of a delicate gray-eyed girl standing beside him in a parlor in Osnabrück. She was frightened. Barely whispered the words put into her mouth by the burly clerk.

The same words, he, in bewilderment, had repeated himself. Not knowing whether it was right, not having time to think.

. . . And Maximilian—proud and happy as a prince! It had been like the making of an alliance to him. An alliance between two friendly nations wishing to guarantee each other peace and fellowship. That was the way both he and Rica's father, Friederich Herzog, felt. This marriage would bind their families together forever!

But they were wrong, for speech is powerless when insincerity directs it. Fragile—shifting as dandelion down!

But had he, Heinrich, really been insincere in the marriage? . . . Yes, he had to accept the accusation. He wanted only to please his father. That was why, without a bicker, he agreed to marry the girl; let the whole burden of refusing—if there were need of it— fall upon her shoulders. That was why, too, in high spirits, he tried to be jovial and soldierly even to the point of getting drunk . . . that's how sincere he had been!

And Rica, thrust into a marriage not of her own making, how sincere could *she* have been? Only one hesitant moment was hers. Heinrich could still see the pitiful indecision on her face, as she looked at three relentless men—all bent upon overpowering her senses, arguing in one breath that she "must."

"Must." A word hard as flint and just as cold. How could a marriage so contracted live or deserve to live?

It couldn't, of course. Rica knew that. Her regret must have been immediate. She went away. Had no part in the revelry that night. Ignored her father's pleas to come downstairs and celebrate her marriage.

Only silence came from behind that high-paneled oak door. Terrifying silence.

And Heinrich had never heard her young voice again or caught a glimpse of her sweet face.

Late that night he had left Osnabrück and his bride. That, too, was Maximilian's wish. There must be no foolish interruption to his career. A few miles away his comrades were garrisoned. A military expedition was waiting. He must march, march, march! Forget for a time that he had a bride.

Having listened to Maximilian's accounts of military life with awe and enthusiasm, Heinrich had come to feel the play of like forces within himself. Wanted to go out and brave dangers for his flag and his fatherland as three generations of Hebers had done before him.

Lustily, he learned to sing with Maximilian, *"Deutschland, Deutschland, ueber alles, ueber alles in der Welt!"*

During these days of rich companionship with his father, Heinrich ceased grieving over Mother Leah, whom he had worshiped all his life.

With the accident, however, sorrow over Leah returned, for he was *her* son, after all, and it was *her* world he loved! There wasn't a pair of hands in the hospital as gentle as hers. Nor a smile as helpful. Pain and distress and no Leah! Doubts and fears and no Leah! What agony four walls could hold!

Now he was over those jagged walls of physical suffering, but mental suffering was still ever-present.

Heinrich sighed and shivered as he looked upon his flock. If only Rica had written directly so that he could tell her how he felt about all these things—their hasty marriage, his military service, retirement. Perhaps she would understand . . . if she knew he cared . . . and was not angry, and wanted only to make amends.

But she hadn't written to him. She had sent her message through a stranger. How could he tell this man the things he really wanted to tell his wife?

What was there to do? Have the American pastor notify Rica that he had been injured so badly as to lose his place in the ranks permanently? That he was recuperating at a sheep farm?

Perhaps Rica hated sheep farms. Perhaps she would answer such a letter with wilting silence. Or, perhaps, she would come to him speedily on the wings of duty or sympathy. That would be worse!

Whatever happened, some word must go to America.

Rica had crossed the sea to escape him. That had taken courage and resourcefulness. Maximilian and Friederich had been wrong in supposing she needed a husband for support!

A barrage of questions battered at the gate of Heinrich's thought —"What was it made Rica write to him at last? Had she regrets? Did she want merely to know what sort of soldier he had made? Whether she was now an officer's wife or still an insignificant private's spouse? Was it, perhaps, that she wanted to be freed from him?

And what would Maximilian say? Would he be relieved to know that Friederich's daughter was well and happy in America—living her own life? Or would he be angry and begrudge her that happiness because she had rejected his son?"

One couldn't tell!

Heinrich concluded that, for the present, it would be best not to tell his father. See what further word would be forthcoming from Rica, after he wrote to the American pastor. That would be soon enough to tell Maximilian.

The reply to Pastor Sigfried was sent upon its way that very evening.

Dear Pastor Sigfried:

I was much surprised to receive your kind letter. Thank you for troubling to find me. I know what difficulty you must have had in getting the message to me here in Westphalia.

As you probably learned, I was discharged from the army permanently. My injured leg is now healed as completely as it can ever be.

I was married to Rica Herzog in Osnabrück four years ago. Our fathers arranged the marriage. Later that evening I rejoined my fellow students, and have not seen my wife since then.

Two years after our marriage, while I was on expedition, her father died. Before I could return she had disappeared.

Your letter brings me great relief, Pastor, and I am grateful to you.

Please tell the American pastor that I am glad Rica is well and contented, but that I should like her to return to Germany and shall be happy to arrange her passage. There will be no difficulty.

If she does not wish to come back, let him urge her to write. Say nothing about my injury.

I shall trust in your kindness and the kindness of the American pastor to send this word to my wife.

My thanks and good wishes are yours.

Gratefully,
Heinrich Heber

XIX *A New Year*

NEW YEAR'S DAY found Wooden Shoe Hollow noisily alive. Every few moments were punctuated with a shot. There were many out in the frosty air to welcome the year 1913. From house to house they went, singing, firing their rifles, helping themselves to "fat cakes" which graced every kitchen table of the circuit.

Into a bedlam of shooting and whiskey-drinking Dr. Baum descended complacently with his yellow-wheeled carriage and his sorrel mare. He was making a call upon Grossmutter Betz, who was having an attack of grippe.

From his hilltop view, Emil Mueller saw the carriage coming. Bareheaded, he hurried down the slope to get inside Betz's kitchen before the doctor arrived.

"Happy New Year!" he piped, as he burst into the kitchen. "Happy New Year, everybody! How is Grossmutter this morning?"

"She is fine," Minna answered.

"Happy New Year to you!" the family chorused.

"Haven't you been out shooting, Herr Mueller?" Hulda wanted to know. "Papa and Ernst have gone long ago."

Emil rubbed his hands over the stove. "A little too cold out for me, Hulda. I did my shooting at midnight. Shot the year 1913 in on the dot and then went to bed. Let the others have their fun." Minna handed him Otto's bottle of rock and rye.

"Thank you, Frau Betz," he cackled. "Here's to a good year for you all, from baby Lottchen to Grossie. And may it be a rich year for all of us, no floods, no hard times and no sickness!"

Dr. Baum strode into the room. "What's this?" he asked, making a sour face in Emil's direction. "Drinking to my ruin? Emil, I always counted you for a friend!"

"Friends we are," Emil chuckled, "But there isn't anybody in the hollow who wouldn't rather see your heels than your face!"

"Is that so?" Dr. Baum railed. "It's funny that you don't stay where you can see my heels, then, you old washwoman!" He studied the assortment of doughnuts on the table and seized a bloated diamond-shaped cake, brown as mahogany. Up the stairs he pounced, munching the "fat cake."

Emil found an advantageous seat near the open stairway. . . . "See Hattie Flieger is home again, isn't she, Rica? What brought her back, do you know?"

"She didn't like Avondale." That was the only answer Rica could give. Emil needn't know the real reason, which Hattie confessed at the New Year's Eve crowd, the fact that Yankees don't eat enough.

"I'm thinking Hattie will be glad to slip her feet into a pair of wooden shoes again," Emil said. "Just like Hanchen. She was glad to get away, too, that time of the flood. Vowed she'd never come back! You never saw a happier creature than she was when Pastor brought her back to Yaegers'. . . . Dr. Baum stopped over to see her, too, yesterday, I noticed."

"Hanchen's had a spell with her leg. Never had it tended to down in that saloon. An open leg is nothing to fool with. She ought to know that by now," Minna said gingerly.

Dr. Baum came downstairs with the word, "Grossmutter is doing fine. Won't need me any more."

"Say, doctor, how many gooses did you win last night?" Emil asked.

"I didn't win any. How many 'gooses' did you win?"

Emil clapped his hands. "I brought home two of them. Big boys, too! Cost me only six chances in all."

"Raffling again?" Minna inquired tartly.

"As long as I'm lucky," Emil interposed. "Doc, how much did you spend for that empty bag you took home?"

"Two dollars," Dr. Baum confessed.

Minna shook her head. "What menfolk!" she scolded. "Wasting money that way just for . . ."

Dr. Baum winked at Emil. "Well, take good care of Grossmutter, Frau Betz," he said. "She'll be good as a new dollar in a few days. . . . I must be going. Have to stop over at Yaegers' to see Hanchen."

Emil tilted his chair back to the wall. "Wonder what's become of Gerhart?" he pondered aloud, looking at Rica. "It's almost three months now since he went away. That isn't any way for a boy to act. It surely hurt at Christmas, not having him around with the rest of my godchildren. I've always tried to do the right thing by Gerhart. Nobody can deny that. If he had words at home he shouldn't take out spite on all of us.

"Take yourself, Rica," he added sympathetically. "You didn't lift a finger against him, as far as I know; why should he keep you uneasy? That's no way for a fellow to treat his girl. What if you did iron him out that night on the porch . . . of course, there was mostly wind to Hans' story. I never did get it straight."

Rica was abashed. Emil was prying for information. He was sure that she had heard from Gerhart and was keeping the news to herself.

"Better not put it that way, Herr Mueller," she said. "Gerhart and I weren't sweethearts. We were only good friends, you know."

"Get out!" Emil ejaculated. "With you already calling on his mother?"

Minna intervened. "Maria had sewing for Rica to do. . . . And what if Gerhart and Rica were sweethearts . . . it's pretty plain that they aren't any more . . . not after he ran away. There are other boys in Wooden Shoe Hollow besides Gerhart Locher, and our Rickey has sense enough to know it!"

There was unglossed irritation in Minna's tone. That's what he got for trying to settle Dr. Baum's hash by dragging in the goose raffle! Minna was touchy about things like that. One would never see Otto at a raffle!

Emil bounced to the floor with his chair. Just then Hanchen's shrill voice sounded next door.

Emil ran to the window.

Dr. Baum was fleeing Yaegers' with Hanchen at his heels. "Verhex my fine black rooster, will you?" she screamed. "I'll show you!" She landed a broom squarely on Dr. Baum's broad shoulders just as he slid into the buggy and grabbed the reins.

"Yesterday, you shook your be-deviled finger at the poor creature when he was crowing and said he'd be a good one for a pot of soup. This morning I find him dead on my doorstep! You verhexed him, all right, that's what you did! . . . Maybe you've been verhexing my poor leg too, so you can get my money! Verhexer!" she sputtered, as Dr. Baum sped out of the yard.

"Don't you dare come back, either, or I'll take worse than a broom to your hide!"

Emil ran down the lane and jumped upon the footrest of Dr. Baum's carriage. "Hanchen got fits?" he gasped.

"Whew! I don't know, Emil. She claims I verhexed her pet rooster."

"Och, she looked in the bottle too deep again. Mustn't mind her. Hanchen is as crazy as Knopf, half the time."

Dr. Baum grinned. "It's a good thing she didn't land that first blow! It would have been one happy New Year for me! . . . and dressing without goose! Guess I'll have to bring a bodyguard next time I sneak down to the hollow."

Grossmutter heard Hanchen's tirade. "For shame on the sodden creature," she fretted. "Talking so to the man when he is good enough to spend his holiday visiting sick people. . . . She ought to be whipped. Wait till I get downstairs. I'll teach the dolt about hexing!"

"We've just got you well, Grossie," Rica laughed. "Do you want to be put back abed so soon, or do you think you can best Hanchen and her broom?"

"Chaff!" said Grossmutter. "I'm not afraid of Hanchen or her broom either!" Salt and pepper flew over her egg vigorously.

That afternoon there was a reunion at Sophia's. Hattie, Rosie and Rica were invited for "flinch and supper." Hulda, too, had been invited, a bit of strategy on Sophia's part. Ever since the fatal book purge Hulda and Maggie had been estranged. Dark months they had been on both girls' calendars.

Sophia asked her little sister to come over and help "set lunch for company." Maggie came with a lace-bordered white apron over her red serge dress. She brought six of her mother's silver teaspoons and a jar of Indian relish. Into the kitchen she went . . . and there was Hulda Betz! It was a perilous moment. Neither spoke.

"I'm going to let you two alone in the kitchen," Sophia explained. "Make whatever you like."

The door closed.

Hulda was uncomfortable as a toad in tar. This wasn't fair. Maggie had been tricked into coming. She wouldn't have come if she had known . . .

Voices hummed in the next room. Rosie was giggling. Rosie was *forever* giggling!

"Maggie?"

"Yes, Hulda."

"What are we going to do?"

"Don't know."

"Want me to bake a jelly roll?"

"Would you?"

"It's the only kind I can make without a recipe."

"What should I do?"

"You can beat the eggs if you like. Four of them."

Maggie broke the eggs into a bowl and began whipping them furiously.

Hulda sifted and resifted the flour as though she were propounding a chemical formula. "Rica says you must never be lazy about sifting flour. The finer and softer it gets the lighter the cake will be. For angel food and fairy loaf the flour must be sifted four times. When you get it light as snow you have to measure it all over again." Maggie nodded understandingly as she whipped the eggs.

Hulda's mental maneuvers were many. When, at last, she slid her cake into the oven and joined Maggie at the task of skinning jacket potatoes she found the only outlet. "I've missed you so much, Mag. You don't know how much!"

"Oh yes, I do," Maggie answered. "Because I felt that way, too. For a long time."

Hulda could have shouted for joy. "It was all my fault. I didn't mean to give our secret away. Do you want to know how it happened?"

But Maggie had long since learned how it happened . . . from Fritz. "It doesn't make any difference now," she answered. "Let's just forget it."

"And be real friends again?"

"Yes, always."

Hulda sniffed. "I hate peeling onions, don't you? When I get my kitchen I'm never going to put onions in potato salad!"

"Me, either." Maggie dug into her dainty pocket for a handkerchief. "They always get in my eyes! Even when I fix them for market."

"Where did you get the braid for your dress? I never saw it in the wagon."

"It came from Germany," Maggie said proudly. "Tanta Elise sent it for Christmas. It's silk braid, and Anna Menke says it's awfully expensive. This was Sophia's dress, you know, but Miss Anna made it over so you can't tell. It's got inside pockets, see? And pleats all around the skirt!"

Hulda admired the whole creation. Beside it her own coarse brown wool dress was shapeless and barren as a burlap sack. No braid, no lace, no pleats. A row of four-eyed buttons—general utility buttons that served on Otto's jacket, Fritzie's trousers, and Grossie's wrapper just as efficiently as they did on this spiritless dress.

In the parlor the game progressed.

Rosie had been flinched so many times that she was custodian of most of the deck.

"Flinch, Rosie!" Hattie cried. "I declare, that makes me *out* again."

"Tell us about Avondale," Sophia said. "Did you meet many nice people?"

"Yes," Hattie admitted. "But I couldn't really get acquainted with them."

"What was your place like?"

"Like a castle, Sophia. Oil paintings, statues and silk drapery . . . and plates that cost ten dollars a piece."

"You broke one, didn't you?" Rosie interrupted.

Hattie bit her lip. "Who wouldn't break such dishes? It scares the wits out of you to wash them."

"I should think so," Sophia agreed. "You didn't fancy working out, did you?"

Hattie blinked and drummed her fingers on the table. "I was telling Rica last night. It would be all right if they didn't eat like sparrows! Do you know they eat only three meals a day? And no potatoes for breakfast . . . or meat either!"

"No morning lunch even?" Rosie gasped. "How can they stand it?"

"I don't know, but they do. Honest! Afternoon lunch is what I missed most. I'd get so hungry my stomach would growl until I thought I'd go crazy. And that awful sour-faced butler wouldn't let me sit down to so much as one cup of coffee!

"And at supper they stuffed. Milk gravy on everything. And hot biscuits! It's a wonder they don't get cancers in their stomachs the way they burn them with hot biscuits!"

Rica shook her head. "Our Wooden Shoe Hollow is best after all."

"Oh, I wouldn't say so," Hattie said. "Avondale isn't the only place on the map. Next fall I'm going to try Clifton. There are lots of nice places up there."

"Yankees are all alike, though," Rosie said dubiously. "Did you have any dates up Avondale?"

"I went to the picture show with the Graphophone man. It was my afternoon off, and as I came out of the house there he was putting his tools in the buggy. 'Want to ride to town, sister?' he asked."

"Sister!" Sophia ejaculated.

"Sure! That's what all the fellows in town call you."

"Oh."

"And then he said he had a piano to tune farther down the line, but it would take too long; he'd best not start it that afternoon. He took me to a picture show."

"Where was it?" Rica asked.

"Down on Vine Street. . . . The picture was about an old tramp with shuffly feet. It was so funny the way he kept getting into scrapes . . . I couldn't sit back in my seat, I was that excited!

"The tramp hung from window ledges—way high up in the air, and people threw things at him! Once I caught myself pinching my fellow's arm. I just couldn't help it! And after the show the

Graphophone man took me to an ice cream parlor. And we had a Steamboat Sue ice cream sundae! It had marshmallow syrup and nuts and bananas and cherries. It was the richest dish I ever tasted in my whole life!"

"And did you go out with him again?" Rosie asked enviously.

"No," Hattie sighed. "I thought surely he would take me out the next Thursday. I spent my whole week's wages buying a store dress with a hobble skirt. But he didn't come."

"Maybe he was busy," Sophia suggested.

Hattie's eyes flashed darkly. "Yes. . . . That's what I thought. . . . Busy fixing Graphophones other places and taking other girls out on their afternoons off. . . . Oh, well, it was nice for one afternoon, anyway," she sighed. "I wouldn't take a thousand dollars for that wonderful day." She blinked in reminiscence.

"How romantic!" Rosie whispered.

"By the way, has anybody heard from Gerhart?" Hattie asked. "I didn't get much news from Mamma while I was away."

"Not yet," Rosie answered. "He ought to be writing to somebody soon."

"There is Herr Mueller and Miss Ida," Hattie reflected. "He could write to them if he doesn't want to write to his own . . . to say nothing of you, Rica. I think it's a downright shame . . . I'm afraid he's gone wrong."

Rica shook her head. "I don't believe so," she said. "Everybody in Wooden Shoe Hollow will be proud of Gerhart some day."

"That's funny," Rosie lisped.

"What's funny?" Hattie demanded.

"What Rickey just said. Pastor Schicht told Papa the same thing."

"Maybe Gerhart has mystery friends," Hattie said tartly.

"We need to know Gerhart better," Rica put in. "He isn't like the other boys in the crowd. Not that he's any better or worse—he's just different. Gerhart is interested in music and building things. There must be people like him in the world. We can't all be gardeners."

Sophia nodded. A dot of crimson dyed each ruddy cheek. "If you were Gerhart's mother you wouldn't have burned the book, would you?"

"No. . . . I'd sent him to school where he could study the things he wanted. And when the time came to part with him I'd give him up no matter what, because if I kept him against his will I'd lose him, and if I let him go I'd keep him."

Hattie squinted across the table. She wondered if Rosie could make anything out of Rica's theory. Apparently Sophia could. . . .

Rosie's face was blank—well nigh. She wasn't thinking about Rica, or Gerhart or Hattie. She was thinking of the high romance of an afternoon in a picture show on Vine Street.

Sophia leaned forward intently. "And if you were Gerhart's mother you would have let him have his violin and books without begging?"

"Yes."

"Suppose all the Locher tribe took to wanting violins and books?" Hattie queried.

"But they haven't you know." Rica smiled at Hattie indulgently. "We all have moments when we would like to rush out into the world and taste new life, only Gerhart had more of those moments than the rest of us. Don't you see? Like you, Hattie, you've always liked style, the kind of style they have in the city. And you went to Avondale."

"Not on that account," Hattie retorted. "I went to Avondale to help out at home. There is no money coming in all winter long, and nothing for me to do but pick up clothes and sweep and wash the same old dishes all day long. That, and watch Papa knit and chew and spit. I wanted to make money."

"To buy clothes for yourself." It was Sophia's knowing comment.

"What I needed I got," Hattie came back. "Otherwise Papa would have had to buy for me."

"Otherwise," Rosie contradicted, "you would have had to do without, like the rest of us!"

Hattie was in a corner.

Rica cut in, "What I meant, Hattie, is that Gerhart has a right to want music and engineering and you have a right to want and get pretty clothes. Just because you weren't born to these things doesn't mean you can't have them. You can, if you are willing to work for them. And the rest of us mustn't think you are foolish for wanting them."

She won her point.

The game was over simultaneously.

Maggie and Hulda had a triumph to present—a light spongy cake—expertly rolled, jellied and sugared. Neither wanted to take the credit for their joint masterpiece.

"Hulda baked it," Maggie insisted.

"But Maggie rolled it," was Hulda's answer.

"I'm proud of you girls," Sophia said, drawing them together in her arms. "And I'm so glad you had a nice time this afternoon. You've had a grand start to a happy New Year, haven't you?"

They nodded sheepishly.

"Did you hear about Hanchen's running Dr. Baum out of the hollow?" Hattie asked, as the girls sat down to supper. "The poor old soul might be right. Maybe Dr. Baum *can* do more than other people, who knows? Lots of doctors can."

"Nonsense," Sophia objected. "What do you mean?"

"Frau Wolken tells how her last baby's forehead tasted salty. She thinks Dr. Baum verhexed the little one because she called Frau Laufer for the birth. The child died in its third month . . ."

"Of summer complaint, just like the Yaegers baby did that same summer," Sophia argued. "And the Yaegers never have had anybody but that English doctor from Camp Washington."

"I don't know," Hattie said. "I've heard other things, but there's no use repeating them. I wouldn't trust Dr. Baum too far . . ."

Rica said calmly, "I don't believe in hexing."

There the subject rested.

It was still early evening when Rica and Hulda came home. Grossmutter awaited them at the window upstairs. The whole afternoon she had spent rocking to and fro and reading her Bible. Now her eyes were weary.

She rather belonged to the 1800's. These early years of the new century found her a stranger, none too securely fixed for its pace.

What would the new year bring? A Scripture passage met her eye as she pondered that question.

"Grossie!" Hulda called. "What do you think? Maggie and I are friends again, friends again, friends again!"

"So the sun shines now," Grossmutter laughed. "How happy I am for that, Hulda! I was afraid you'd lost your smile for good."

"We had a nice time at Sophia's," Rica added. "And how about you, Grossie?"

"Ah, the prophets and I have had a nice afternoon."

"I baked a cake, Grossie. Here's a piece for you."

"All yourself you baked it, lamb?"

Hulda nodded.

"Wonderful," Grossmutter said. She winked at Hulda impishly. "Mamma had better look to her cake-baking honors!" And now, Rica, will you read to us from this psalm?" With trembling finger she pointed out the precious passage.

Rica read it. Her clear voice put triumph into it—a mystic communion with the everlasting Lord, the same yesterday, today, and the same forevermore!

Hulda clasped her hands about her knees, bent her head and listened.

> How precious also are Thy thoughts
> unto me, O God! How great is the
> sum of them! If I should count
> them they are more in number than
> the sand: When I awake I am still
> with Thee!

XX Rescue

MARCH SEEDING TIME was once more upon the gardeners and seedsmen from all parts of the country came into Wooden Shoe Hollow with their wares.

Up and down the soft furrows men tramped with the exalted feeling of getting the first outdoor work started. Cool, rich black earth, waiting for seeds, sunshine, rain, and the ever-recurring miracle of sprouting plants. Roots sinking, stalks pressing upward, leaves showering out on every side, demure buds opening. There was spring as every gardener knew and loved it!

There was one gardener, however, who did not share in the sublime mood of his fellows. He had the same rich soil under his feet, the same promising sunshine overhead, the same soft breeze upon his face as all the others, but he was unhappy.

The eldest son of a pioneer Hungarian gardener, Karl Metz had seen the ravages of many Mill Creek floods upon his father's garden. For himself he had bought this little parcel of ground removed from Mill Creek's treachery. Just the spot he wanted.

He had a little gray cottage, homely as an ugly duckling, but with a ruggedness that pleased its new owner, just because it, like him, was content to retire into the background of red market sheds and white houses, as a sparrow retires to gray eaves.

Yesterday he had been happy. Neighbors came to and fro, offering him hands, tools, seeds and hearty wishes for good luck here on the old Kinder homestead.

Today they circled past his patch, glanced in his direction, and hastily looked away. Not that they were unsympathetic to his needs. It wasn't that. It was just that they felt helpless in the face of circumstances. When a neighbor was sick, one could fetch a doctor for him, tend his garden, take his vegetables to market, feed his stock and look after his family. This was different. What did one do for a neighbor who, on the eve of his wedding, lost his bride?

It was no simple affair this. A gardener without a wife was as fully incapacitated for running a garden as though he were without a plow.

Last night, after a long day in the field, the bridegroom returned "Back Creek"—to Cumminsville. There his bride waited to bring him the fatal word. After careful deliberation she had decided it would be best not to marry him.

It was a joke he insisted, but a poor one. Day after tomorrow was the date. He had already notified Pastor Schicht. He was going this evening to invite a few friends for "afterward."

It was no joke, the recalcitrant bride repeated. There would be no wedding! She turned her buggy around and went home. A salesgirl in Alms and Doepke she was now and so she would remain.

It was a foolish idea to marry a gardener and slave away in dirt and despair when she could "be having it so much nicer" behind the lace counter. . . . She lifted her chin high as the carriage rolled on down the Avenue. She was free! Delivered from the certain chaos that this marriage would have brought!

The forsaken bridegroom could not comprehend the meaning of it all. Didn't women really want a home and the security of a good providing husband?

What did it matter now that he had this rich plot of ground, with a solid house upon it? He had no wife to share it with him. No wife!

And the neighbors knew it. The hollow was like a beehive. Women skirmished about everywhere, discussing the situation, condemning the vixen who had perpetrated this outrage, feeling sorry for the abandoned bridegroom. But they could improve the situation not a whit for all their conferences.

It took Emil Mueller to do that.

Emil bristled with excitement at the first suggestion of what had befallen the new neighbor. He lost no time in getting the real facts and from none other than the new neighbor himself.

It was no longer cold, but Emil clung to his customary winter wrappings. He plodded across the patch in his felt boots, dangling black overcoat and red muffler. "Good morning to you," he said, grasping the young man's hand and shaking it vigorously. "I hear you are in trouble. If you will tell me all about it, I am sure I can help you."

The young man shook his head. "There's nothing to tell and you can't help, sir. She just isn't going to marry me."

"But you got the place deeded over already, haven't you? Your tools in shape, a stable promised and a little seeding done?"

The gardener shook his head mournfully.

"Then this isn't any time for the girl to be backing out on you and you'd best not let her."

"But, I can't *make* her come."

Emil rocked up and down on his heels. "Let me call on the girl and talk it over with her. Maybe you aren't forward enough. You can't be backward in this world, young man, or you'll get licked every time! Stick up for yourself. You've got rights same as she has, and seeing your good intentions," Emil said, solemnly, as he pointed to the house and land, "I think the law will be on your side."

The Hungarian shook his head. "The law has nothing to do with it. If she doesn't want me there is nothing to do about it. . . . Guess I'll have to sell out."

"Sell out!" Emil said scathingly. "That's no answer! Get yourself another girl."

"I don't know anybody else."

Emil brightened. "I said I'd come to help you, boy, and I will! Just leave it to me. There is a wife for you somewhere."

The youth looked at his would-be benefactor intently. "Do you know a girl for me?"

"I know several of them," Emil said. "I'll hitch up my buggy and take you out calling right away. Soon as I dress respectable for business."

Karl scrubbed his stained hands, shaved, oiled his shoes, dampened down his sparse black hair and got into a greenish-gray suit.

They called on Rica first. "This is just the girl for you," Emil counselled. "Best little worker in the hollow—that is, as hired girls go. And she's got a nice way with it all. I think you might have a good chance right now. She just lost her fellow—maybe you heard about it? Gerhart Locher? Oldest of my godchildren. Got into a little trouble and ran away from home. . . . Of course, he'll come home . . . that we all know . . . but I don't think Rica will take him back. She's too proud for that. And who would blame her?"

They came to the Betz household. Rica saw them coming down the lane as she put the pillows to air. She wondered what Emil could possibly be doing out riding with the unfortunate young neighbor, but she didn't have to wonder very long, for soon Minna was calling upstairs, "Rica, Herr Mueller would like to see you."

Both men rose from the horsehair couch as Rica entered the parlor.

Karl Metz blushed furiously. He hadn't expected to see anyone this pretty . . . would he dare ask her?

But his companion launched the project with no preliminaries. "Rica," he said, sticking a thumb in each vest pocket, "We came to see if you would help this good neighbor out of a pinch."

"I'll try," Rica answered. "What is it you want of me?"

"To marry him," Emil said quickly.

Rica gave no answer. She looked from one to the other in dismay. "You've come to ask me that?" she asked. "I'd be glad to help any way, but marriage . . ."

"Oh, come, Rica," Herr Mueller coaxed. "Mustn't be so quick to refuse. Wouldn't you like a nice garden of your own and a house to run any way you please? That's what Karl Metz is offering you."

"I know," Rica answered. "It is so generous of you to offer it, Herr Metz, and I feel honored to have been asked, but I am sure somebody else will fit into your plans much better than I." She tried to smile, but could bring nothing but a sorry expression to her face.

Seeing it, the distraught young man said, "It's all right, Fräulein Rica. I don't blame you. Come on, let's go, Herr Mueller. We are just taking up her time."

Emil shrugged his shoulders. "I think you are making a big mistake, Rica."

"I think not," came Rica's resolute answer. She turned to Karl. "If we can help you in any way, we will be glad to do it. I want to wish you good luck. Hope you will soon be settled and one of us here in Wooden Shoe Hollow."

The two men rode away. "She's a strange one, that girl," said Emil. "I don't understand it. . . . Almost looks as if she doesn't want to get married. . . . There is something she isn't so sure about. Tight-lipped as she is we'll never know what it is, either." There, for Emil, lay the real rub!

"She was nice," was Karl's only comment.

"We'll try Hattie Flieger next. She's not like this one, but she'll make you a good wife, if you keep the upper hand of things. A little bit high-toned for a gardener's girl; otherwise she is all right. . . . She worked up Avondale for a spell this winter. Learned that it wasn't all cake and pie with the Yankees. All the more reason why she ought to be ready to make a go of it with you. . . . Well, we'll see."

Hattie was in the midst of housecleaning when the two men came on their naive errand. She dashed upstairs quickly and removed her dirt-streaked apron and dust cap, washed, powdered, and flecked a scent of lilac upon her hair.

Then, calmly, she sauntered into the parlor, where her father and mother had already given consent to the marriage, provided Hattie, herself, were willing. Hattie was reticent. She didn't want to say "no" without giving the offer some thought.

"Must you be in such a hurry?" she asked.

"Of course he must," Emil explained. "There is work to be done—crops started. Why should he do it all alone?"

Hattie drew up her shoulders haughtily. "Well, if it's just someone to help plant potatoes, he can get a hired man . . ."

Karl Metz's collar was choking him. He scouted for an answer. Hattie's father spoke. "What do you think of Karl's offer?"

"I don't know, Papa," she answered. "This isn't the way I want to get married. I want to be in love with the fellow I marry, have some romance, and wear a stylish dress and veil and take a honeymoon trip to Milwaukee."

Emil's left eyebrow curved upward sharply. "Who do you think will give you such a wedding?" he asked. "Not your poor papa, that's sure, with the Bauverein claiming the market money every week!"

Hattie swept out of the room in high indignation. "You've heard what I expect!" she said dramatically.

"Not even thanks does one get," Emil said in exasperation.

Amid profuse apologies from Herr and Frau Flieger the two set out once more in search of a bride.

"Best to go Back Creek," Emil said. "It's a shame little Rosie went to Indianapolis. She'd be willing to marry, Rosie would. But she will be gone a few weeks at least. . . . Taking care of her sister, Katy, in Indianapolis. . . . Another baby there, I hear. Of course, Rosie is plain, a little cross-eyed, and her face is freckly, but she's a jolly one, and goodhearted as your brother . . . most fat people are . . . but there is no use talking Rosie—we can't wait for her to get back. Your house needs a boss, same as the garden, eh, Karl?"

Karl agreed, but in the spirit that there wasn't much reason to say so. It was all so useless.

They rode from garden to garden Back Creek, stopping wherever there was an eligible daughter. And everywhere the offer of marriage was politely, but firmly declined. Too young . . . got to help at home . . . going steady with Pete Landman . . . ailing this winter . . . rather live Back Creek . . . valid excuses all of them, but they took the poor abandoned bridegroom farther and farther from his goal.

He was a wretched fellow when Emil, having exhausted his list of eligibles, taken from the ranks of friends and acquaintances, started for home.

"Just a little bad luck for one day," Emil said. "Tomorrow it will be better."

Karl refused to be uplifted. "No, it won't! There isn't anybody wants my garden or me! Nobody!"

"Do so," Emil countered. "Girls are funny with their excuses. Know what really hindered them?"

Karl didn't.

"Romance. They wanted to be courted first . . . and shown off. Get a thrill out of all the goings on ahead of time, going steady and all that."

"Guess I'll hold auction," Karl mused. "I hate to do it."

"Auction nothing! Tomorrow we'll start out early in the morning and I'll wager you a pair of boots you'll have a bride before tomorrow night."

Emil pulled the reins. "Come on, Molly," he said. "Pancakes will be cold by the time we get back. That's what we are going to have for supper—potato pancakes. Like 'em?"

Karl nodded.

"Yetta makes them good, too."

It was seldom Emil mentioned his maid. In his service she had grown from a raven-haired buxom girl of twenty to a white-haired fragile woman of fifty.

She moved about the great house quietly, in a ceaseless round of cleaning, laundering, cooking and serving.

Yetta's hands were never still. That was the way it had been ever since she came to Wooden Shoe Hollow thirty years ago.

Karl marveled at the richness of the old bachelor's home the moment he entered the door. Lush rugs and draperies, polished floors, the cleanliness of every nook and corner, brilliance of glassware, soft sheen of copper, wealth inherited and mellow with years . . . kind years.

It was in the kitchen Yetta had laid supper. Red-figured plates with the tower of Cologne in the center, and grapevine borders. A blue-checkered tablecloth, a platter of potato pancakes, a bowl of spiced peaches, currant jelly, steaming aroma-laden coffee, cream and lump sugar.

They sat down to table with Yetta seated opposite them, her eyes only for cups which needed refilling and for the platter which must be restacked occasionally from the pan in the oven.

"Tell you what," Emil said, resting his fork and knife on end, in either hand, beside his plate. "You tend to your radish-seeding tomorrow and I'll go out looking for you. And I'll wager you I'll bring a bride!"

Yetta poured more coffee into his cup.

"That's plenty, Yetta," he said with a yawn.

Yetta sat down again.

Karl smiled at her. "These are the best potato pancakes I ever ate. Coffee, too, is surely fine."

Yetta's lips turned up into a soft lovely smile. "Thank you, Herr Metz," she said.

"Yetta's all right," Emil said. "She surely is!"

"Herr Mueller's been trying to get a wife for me, I suppose you heard about it?"

"No," Yetta answered. "I haven't. He mentioned you were taking over the Kinder homestead."

"His girl kept him for a fool," Emil explained. "She won't marry him now that he has the garden."

"What a shame," Yetta answered.

"I figured someone else would step in, somebody like Rica Heber, down there at Otto's, or Hattie Flieger, or one of the girls Back Creek. But they weren't willing. Yetta," he said, "Can you figure why a girl wouldn't want to get married?"

Yetta put down her cup and looked at Emil. She answered slowly, "I don't know."

The next morning Emil was on his way before a single seed had been sown. Eastward, he traveled. It was a glorious morning for driving.

He came to the outskirts of Pleasant Ridge. There were farms here—larger places than Wooden Shoe Hollow gardens. Here there would be daughters. . . .

At a large prosperous-looking farm he made his first and only call. There was a ruddy-faced hired girl who listened to his tale of the forsaken bridegroom and sobbed in genuine sympathy for him. When the proxy suitor proposed marriage to her she accepted at once.

Emil was elated.

"You'll marry today, won't you?" he asked. "He'd rather . . . that's the way he planned it for the other one. Might be bad luck to change the day."

"Certain sure," the bride-to-be replied.

"Then I'll hustle back to Wooden Shoe Hollow and tell Karl the good news . . . that's his name . . . Karl Metz. He'll go after the license right away and come for you at three o'clock this afternoon."

"I'll be waiting down at the gate," she said.

Emil raced back over the hills to Wooden Shoe Hollow. At Karl's place he leaped from the carriage and pranced across the field like a young colt. "Lucky fellow," he said, clapping the bridegroom's back. "I've got a bride for you, a nice farmer girl. She's got sense, too, and anybody can see she's a hustler."

Emil never deserted his friend that morning. He stayed with him through shaving, shoe polishing, necktie tying, and even accompanied him to the courthouse to get the license. Proudly, he produced the girl's full name and history from the slip of paper she had given him.

"Tell me, how do I get there?" Karl asked, as they came down the courthouse steps. "Do you think I'll be able to find it alone?"

"Sure thing," Emil said, turning over the bride's slip of paper and drawing a map on one of his many building-and-loan books. "Here is Spring Grove Avenue, here is Vine Street, and here is the road up to Pleasant Ridge. Here is a big dip in the road and a hill on the other side. And here is the farmhouse. The girl will be waiting at the gate for you."

Karl clutched his marriage license. "I hope so," he answered, dread creeping into his voice.

"I'll tell you what. You take me back to the hollow and then you can have my horse and buggy to get your bride and take her to the preacher. That's the ticket."

Karl stammered. "Sure, thanks for it, Herr Mueller. You've been so good to me."

"'Tisn't anything at all," Emil assured him. "God bless you, my boy! God bless you!"

With that blessing Karl started on his journey to Pleasant Ridge.

Faithfully, he followed Mueller's directions, all the way to the dip, the hill, the farmhouse. And there, with a leap of joy, he beheld his bride waiting for him at the gate, all her worldly goods done up in one suitcase beside her.

He stopped the carriage. Asked if she were Edna.

She nodded.

He alighted and tossed the suitcase into the back seat. Helped her into the carriage. He spread the license out before her.

"Isn't it beautiful?" she asked, fingering the raised seal of the State of Ohio.

"It surely is," Karl answered. There was a season of awkward silence, while the carriage sped on Back Creek to Pastor Schicht.

That evening the bride cooked her own supper in her new home. The high excitement died down quickly. Peace settled over Wooden Shoe Hollow again.

It was Emil, however, who had to get one more thrill out of the affair. He rounded up the children into a cavalcade of tin panners. With wash tubs, boilers, pots and pans and sticks the army stole upon the honeymooners in the cottage at dusk, and filled the hollow with their raucous shouts and clanging.

Herman came with his accordion and serenaded them at the summer kitchen stoop.

Rica heard the impromptu celebration at the other end of the hollow.

She heard Otto, too, grunt over his *Volksblatt*, "It's a wonder Emil wouldn't treat a keg on it. The old cheek beard!"

XXI *The Elect*

~~~~~~

HAVING PAID HER DAILY CALL on Sophia Toepfer, Frau Laufer stopped to chat with Minna Betz. She removed the gray shawl with which she was identified everywhere in the neighborhood. "How has everything been with you?"

"Can't complain," Minna answered. "Not at all."

"How is the little one?"

"Lottchen is fine. How is Sophia's baby?"

"Fair," the midwife answered. "One would have expected Sophia to have a huskier child, though."

"Well, a girl," Minna reflected. . . . "And then, it being the first one . . ."

"Oh, I dare say she'll outstrip any bottled Yankee baby of her age." Frau Laufer chuckled, "Herman still looks at the baby as if she wasn't mortal."

Minna smiled wistfully. "Didn't I always say it? From a young skate he was like that . . . softhearted . . . not many given of such nature. Sophia doesn't know how good she has it."

While Minna and Frau Laufer chatted Rica paid a visit at Toepfers. Sophia was knitting a comforter for the baby's cradle when she came.

Herman sat beside the bed holding the baby. "I'm so glad you've come," he said. "We were just talking about you, Rica."

"We want you to stand for the baby," Sophia added. "You and Mamma."

"I can't think of anything nicer," Rica answered.

Sophia nodded happily. "Thanks. We've been such good friends ever since you came to Wooden Shoe Hollow."

Herman smiled upon his sleeping daughter. "Tell her the others, too, Sophia," he said.

"Can you guess?" Sophia's docile blue eyes were agleam.

"No, I can't guess."

"We are going to call our little girl Rica!"

"Oh! You shouldn't," Rica said. "Unless you really like the name."

"We do," Sophia assured her. "Rica Jane, that shall be her name."

"Jane?"

"That was Herman's mother's name and his grandmother's also. It goes nicely with Rica, don't you think so? Some people might think it's queer, just two short names like that, but Herman and I like it. Rica Jane Toepfer. It's perfect."

"Just perfect." Herman echoed, as he lay the child into Sophia's arms. He brushed his finger tips over the baby's silky red hair. "Well, I can't stay here," he sighed. "Carrots need weeding."

"Ours too," Rica said. "The weeds shoot up overnight, with all the showers we've been having."

"But it saves sprinkling," Herman answered laconically. "And keeps the hocksters full of water."

Rica rumbled the sweeper over the vivid blue rug on Sophia's bedroom floor and dusted the furniture. Then she brushed Sophia's flaxen hair and braided it. "I'll make the christening dress," she promised.

"You're so busy, Rica. I could get Anna Menke to sew it."

"There are evenings. We get our market finished early now. The children are home from school. I'd love to Sophia."

When Max next came Rica deliberated a long time before the open wagon, looking at the tiers of cloth.

"Not what you wanted?" Max quizzed, staring upward through his spectacles.

"I want a piece of very fine white batiste for a baby dress, and some narrow lace with a dainty pattern, and some satin rosette ribbon."

"I'll get it for you at Alms and Doepke's," Max offered.

"Don't trouble to do that," Rica said. "I'll go myself. It's special."

Max was not that easily defeated. "Just you let it to me to get the best . . . and at a good price too . . . if you don't like the goods I'll keep it for the wagon. I'll buy it tomorrow and come back the day after."

"That's asking too much."

"'Tisn't," Max argued. "I have to go to town to match some waist material anyway. Anna Menke is making Ida a brocaded waist for a birthday present. You won't let it out, will you?"

"No, I won't tell."

"Let you have a look at it, then," Max offered. He reached into his coat pocket and produced the sample Anna had given him. "Here it is. Rich stuff, isn't it?"

Rica nodded. "A whole waist of this?"

"The whole thing. She reckons it to need another half yard. The pattern calls for such big sleeves. . . . Surely will make an elegant present."

"Lovely," Rica agreed.

"Beats all, doesn't it, how those two are so set on each other? I always tell my wife, there isn't a pair of girls in whole Cincinnati who are better off than the Menke sisters."

Two days later Max returned with his special orders. He stopped first at Menke's.

Anna stole out to the wagon while Ida was giving Maggie Vollman her piano lesson. "Did you get it matched all right?" she asked excitedly.

"Sure did, Miss Anna." He produced the length of lustrous brocade. "Off the same bolt it came."

Anna rolled her apron round the material. "It was nice of you to make a special trip with it, Max." She dropped an extra dime into his hand. "Get yourself some cigars."

"Thanks," Max answered. "Want to see something pretty?" He unwrapped Rica's parcel. "It's for the Toepfer baby. Rica is going to make the christening dress. I hear she is going to stand for the little one."

Anna drew a quick sharp breath. "It's nice," she said. "Very nice, Max." Then she went inside to begin work immediately on Ida's blouse while Ida was giving a music lesson.

She was counting methodically, as Maggie Vollman played. The same practice piece over which all of Ida's pupils stumbled, stopped, and started again.

Anna tapped her feet in time with Ida's counting—"One-two-three. One-two-three." There it came out right that time, every note of it. Ida was saying cheerfully, "That's fine, Maggie. Just fine. Now, we'll take up a new piece."

"A new piece?" Maggie squealed with delight. "The 'Spring Song'! Oh, I *adore* the 'Spring Song,' Miss Ida! Do you think I'll ever learn how to play it?"

Miss Ida smiled. "I'm sure you will, Maggie, but you must practice faithfully."

"I will! I will!" Maggie promised, as she skipped down the road. "Good-bye, Miss Ida."

"Good-bye, dear."

Anna quickly put away the blouse and resumed basting a petticoat. When Ida came into the room she said in a strained small voice, "Max tells me that Rica is to make the christening dress for Sophia's baby . . ."

"Is she now?" Ida asked with quick interest. "Then we shall have to make something else." She patted Anna's hand understandingly.

Rica, too, was pleased with her special order. Her fingers itched to begin sewing the wee dress at once, but that couldn't be done, for there was market to fix. Even now, there were four wheelbarrows of carrots and beets to be tied and scrubbed.

Hulda was already occupied with plucking off yellow leaves and laying the beets in neat rows for Rica to tie. Grossmutter and Fritz were teaming their efforts on the carrot bank in the same manner.

Rica sank down upon her box and fell to tying with vigor.

That afternoon Ida Menke came over to help. She slipped a note to Rica at the first opportunity.

While Otto swept away the rubbish of rotted leaves and cleared floor space for another load of beets Rica stole away to read her letter.

Dear Rica:

Miss Ida sent me your note. I was whipped to learn you aren't coming, Rica.

For days and days I've been aching to see you and be with you again. I've been searching around here for rooms. I found two big ones near the gulf. They are not very fancy, but you could make them lovely, I know you could!

I've applied for a job with the Government. They will call me soon. The agent down at the shipyard said so. They need fellows who are willing to learn how to do the thousands of things that must be done before the Canal comes through.

There is a boy from Kansas staying at my boarding house. He wants to go to Panama, too. We made friends right away, and last Sunday we took a boat trip together on the Mississippi. Had a wonderful time. There was a minstrel band, and a lot of young people singing and dancing. Reminded me of our crowd back home. If only you had been there!

Please write again, Rica. Tell me about yourself and the crowd. The crops and market. And tell me about the little ones.

I'll be waiting anxiously to hear from you, darling.

All my love,
Gerhart

Reluctantly, Rica burned the letter, her eyes lingering on the angular sweep of the closing words—"All my love—Gerhart."

Gerhart was homesick. Not a line in actual words, but there it was just the same. Behind the words and around them. Yes, certainly, he was sick for the sight of Wooden Shoe Hollow's green summertime. Sick, too, for the crowd . . . for his little sisters and brothers. Yet, he was determined to go to Panama, alone if need be.

It was fine that he had met the boy from Kansas. Having a comrade meant something inexplicably fine. Providential. The way it had been when Grossmutter came upon the scene at Osnabrück.

Basket after basket of knobby brown radishes was carried into the shed and dumped at Rica's feet. Round and round her hands spun in the act of bunching.

Otto, with a great glow of pride, saw his wash stand crowded with banks of fresh clean vegetables. He rolled up his sleeves and began packing them into barrels—counting them by the dozen bunches and chalking the count on each barrel. Then he and Ernst stacked the barrels into the market wagon. What a magnificent towering load! And finished at dusk! In other market sheds the lanterns would glow till midnight. There was no denying he knew how to regulate his market fixing. Trained his folks. No idleness in his household!

It was well for Rica that market was finished early. It gave her an excuse to walk home with Miss Ida.

"Gerhart tells me he is waiting for you to join him in New Orleans," Ida said, as soon as they had passed through the gate.

"I can't do it," Rica answered unsteadily.

Ida was silent—expectant.

"I'll write to him at your house, if you don't mind."

Ida nodded. "Tell him just how you feel. It's no more than right," she said sadly.

Into Ida's trustworthy hands Rica left her message.

DEAR GERHART:

It grieved me to learn you were still expecting me to come to New Orleans. I didn't mean for you to think I would come.

Even though I am lonesome without you, it will be best if I stay here. I could never be happy anywhere else, Gerhart. This is my home.

Miss Ida and I shall be thinking of you every day and hoping you will be in Panama very soon with your friend.

The children are all well.

Has Ida told you the news? Herman and Sophia have a little girl. She is to be christened Sunday. And guess what her name is to be? Rica Jane! We are all so happy about it.

The crops are bearing splendidly.

We wish you every good fortune along the way. Think of us, too, won't you? And Gerhart, won't you write to your folks? They miss you terribly, especially your father.

Please try to understand why I can't come to New Orleans. In the end you will see that it was best this way.

My dearest wishes go with this letter.

Faithfully,
RICA

XXII *Lost Treasure*

~~~~~~

HANS WAS RESCUED from a gang of thieves by Pastor, who found him in a poolroom wrestling with a homeless ragamuffin who had wandered into Cincinnati via a freight car.

Very quickly Hans was transported to Wooden Shoe Hollow. He was given choice of being turned over to police or surrendering his booty. He chose the latter, in the hope of being able to break away at an early opportunity.

"Hans," Pastor said, once he had the lad in his buggy. "This isn't what you meant to do with your life, is it?"

Hans sulked in stony silence.

"There is safety with our people, Hans. Down here is only danger and restlessness."

"I don't want to be an old 'manure heinie.' For no money in the world!"

"So-o-o?" Pastor asked. "You would rather be a thief and a yokel? You would rather grovel in the foulest hole of Cincinnati than live in your uncle's good clean home? Surely, such an ox you are not, Hans!"

"I know what you think."

"It is not so important that you know what I think. Do you know what you think of *yourself?*"

For that question Hans had no answer. He was thinking of Wullum's stern preachment and of the horsewhipping Hanchen would give him once Pastor was out of sight.

But Hans had not taken his rescuer into account.

As soon as Pastor got his charge safely inside Wullum Yaeger's house he invited Wullum and Hanchen for a talk. He sat down heavily on a market stool. "I found Hans in bad company," he said soberly. "But, bad company or not, the boy thinks they are his friends and he will want to get back in their midst as soon as he can. It is your lookout to see that he doesn't get back."

"If he sets foot off the place . . ." Wullum began.

Pastor lifted his hand. "Not that way, Wullum. Make him want to stay with you. Try to satisfy him. And no horsewhipping . . . no harsh words . . ."

Hanchen stared at Pastor. The man was unfathomable as the ocean. When one expected him to be lenient he was hard as flint, and when, by turns, one expected him to be hard as flint he was yielding as clay.

"And you, Hanchen," he said, "you must be different or Wullum can do nothing for the boy. You are his mother!"

The implication was enough. Hanchen turned away sorrowfully.

Very carefully, she avoided her errant son for a few days. Wullum, who contended that there was "not a good spear of hair on Hans' head," bridled his tongue and checked his wrath as best he could.

Hans was puzzled at the impersonal good will which was directed at him by the Yaegers. The curious abeyance with which Hanchen regarded him was even more puzzling. He chafed under the mystery of it all. He was irked and restless as a tethered colt.

Plans began to whirl in his mind. Plans that had nothing to do with sobriety and making a new man of himself by weeding carrots for Uncle Wullum.

. . . Hop the train . . . get away . . . out of reach of unctuous relatives and soul savers . . . get money and break away!

He laid plans.

The Toepfer christening was to take place Sunday. All attention would center there for the day. That would be his opportunity.

Sunday came and with it a dual spirit of celebration.

St. Matthew's Church was completed and today the colonies assembled for the first Sabbath service to be held within her stately walls.

With what pride the people gathered before the towering edifice of yellow brick. Here was fulfillment of years of dreams! The triple-toned bell whose call was as melodious as that of Old First herself . . . the pipe organ . . . the spacious Ladies Aid quarters in the basement . . . the black-grilled fence . . . the crimson flower beds . . . red in token of God's undying love . . . for these, all hearts were grateful this day.

As a happy prelude to their daughter's baptism Herman and Sophia attended the church dedication, though it was Pastor Schicht whom they had invited to baptize Rica Jane later in the afternoon.

Soon after dinner Hans watched neighbors go down the lane with their contributions to the feast. He slipped into the Menke house as soon as he saw the two sisters enter Toepfer's yard. Quickly, he ransacked upstairs—found ten dollars in Ida's dresser drawer, a pair of diamond earrings, a lavalier. Downstairs, he snatched as much silver as he could carry in a sugar sack.

But his escape was thwarted.

Knopf, who was shambling down the lane, whistling "Im Bienenhaus," turned into Menke's yard and sought the hammock which was stretched between the willow trees outside the dining room window. He slid into it with a wide-faced yawn. Above his head a chickadee chirped. Knopf wagged his tongue at the bird, as he rocked back and forth.

More footsteps on the cinder path. "Miss Ida, Miss Ida!" It was Maggie Vollman calling. She had come to the kitchen door and was calling again. Since she received no answer she clattered down the steps and ran to Sophia's.

She had wanted to practice the "Spring Song" just once more in Miss Ida's presence. That was to be her contribution to the festivities—playing the "Spring Song" for the assembled citizenry of Wooden Shoe Hollow—and for Fritz Betz in particular. But the piece would have to go unpracticed now. She'd have to remember to count accurately, touch lightly on the descending notes. And there was one measure where she could glance up and catch Fritz's devoted glance.

But of all this Hans knew nothing and would have cared less. He swore to himself at Maggie and Knopf for delaying his escape. He tossed his corncob pipe on the mantel nervously, while he waited for Knopf to get up and leave. By and by the swaying hammock grew still. Knopf was asleep.

Hans tossed the sack over his shoulder. As he did so, he knocked the glowing pipe off the mantel and it fell into Miss Anna's pattern basket.

He dashed out of the side door and ran breathlessly through Yaeger's hotbed aisle, toward Mueller's house. He sped through the woods and out to Winton Road. In a clump of bushes he crouched and waited until a phaeton came down the steep descent from College Hill. He ran after the vehicle and leaped upon the storage box in the rear. There, he clung until the phaeton reached the side entrance of Spring Grove Cemetery, when he leaped to the ground.

He darted into the cemetery and walked rapidly toward Spring Grove Avenue. Spire-like monuments soared upward in the green leaves of countless tall trees. And on the lake, ducks swam leisurely in the sun-bathed water. He came out upon the Avenue. Glad to emerge from the city of the dead.

To the left the crest of Clifton towered. Yankee mansions stood up there like fortresses, safe from Mill Creek. Hans strolled along the Avenue. Took one last look at peaceful Spring Grove Cemetery, and Winton Road . . . leading back to Wooden Shoe Hollow.

Felt a little regret at his move. . . . He could never come back after this, of course . . . never come back!

He turned and ambled across the street to the grass at the railroad track. He would have to wait for a freight. That was safest. If he should buy a passenger ticket they would trace him. Have him back in no time at all. And this time there would be horse-whipping all right! The boy shuddered.

He lay in the high grass at the trackside, until a slow-moving freight came puffing and grinding toward Cumminsville.

He hopped upon a grain car and found the door bolted. His eye traveled along the long line of rumbling freight cars—all probably closed as tight as this one.

In Cumminsville the train might switch . . . that would give him a chance to get inside a car.

Meanwhile, Knopf awoke to find smoke pouring upon him. Flames were already licking their treacherous way to the second floor of the Menke house.

He rubbed his eyes and stared at the burning house, trying to recall where he was and what was happening. . . . Fire? Menke. . . . Fire. . . . Ida and Anna weren't home. . . . They were at Toepfers' for the christening. . . . Nobody knew. . . . Everybody was at the christening.

Knopf toppled out of the hammock, picked himself up and ran down the lane shouting gibberish, punctuated with sharp cries of "Fire, Fire! Idie. . . . Annie. . . . Fire!"

Perspiration poured down his face. Breathless and exhausted he came to Herman's summer kitchen door. Wild gestures were his only means of expression. Frau Vollman, mightily resenting this intrusion upon her granddaughter's christening, bustled to the door. "Go way, Knopf, or else tell what you want. Look at you all sweated up. . . . Who was chasing you?"

Knopf's tongue was tied.

"Come in and behave yourself," Lizzie said angrily. "Such calving around in the midst of a baby christening. What fails you, anyhow?"

Knopf jumped up and down on the porch, cupped both hands over his ears and strained to bring out the word—"Fire!" It came, finally, like the last drop of water wrung from a cloth.

"What?" Lizzie asked sharply.

Knopf pulled her outside and pointed down the lane where smoke was belching from Menke's windows.

"Fire!" Lizzie's piercing shriek echoed around the hollow. "Fire! Menfolk! Quick! Menke's house is burning!"

Bedlam ensued. The guests stampeded to the scene like a herd of cattle.

"Water! Water!" was the cry of agony.

Ida and Anna stood side by side in Otto's hotbed aisle, stunned out of speech. Tragedy striking again . . . like death . . . like Papa's going and Mamma's . . . this time it was the house!

Back and forth men and women rushed with buckets which they filled at the hockster. Sprayed feeble jets of water through garden hoses. All to no avail. The fire had been burning too long on the inside of the house.

Herman leaped upon his horse and rode pell-mell to Winton Place for help.

Sophia laid Rica Jane, with all her finery, into the cradle.

There was the table elongated with five leaves—reaching from one end of the room to the other. Set with sparkling cut-glass bowls, glasses and rosebud china. A new white damask cloth. And on the stove the feast was cooking. In the oven the savory roast was almost ready to serve. And the side table was arrayed with scores of pies and cakes.

A few moments ago all was joy. And now there was a chasm of sadness into which every vestige of joy was engulfed. Sophia raced down the lane after her guests, her eyes blinded with tears. She was thinking not only of four walls about to collapse; she was thinking of two lives that would be crushed with the crash of those four walls. She thought of all the lovely things the house held. The grandfather clock, with its resonant voice, the rosewood chest, the porcelain figures, the old plush lounge, the red velvet rugs . . . they and the house that sheltered them were all Ida and Anna had in this world, besides each other.

Herman came clattering back with the clanging fire wagon at his heels. As the horses tore down the crooked lane the house collapsed with a whack. Ida and Anna fell into each other's arms, sobbing and calling each other by name for solace.

Fricch Vollman came forward. "You still have the insurance your papa had, girls?"

Ida nodded. "The papers are in the iron safe in the bedroom wall."

"Then things won't be so bad," he comforted. "We will build you another house. Till it is up you can live with me."

"No, Papa," Sophia pleaded. "Let me take them. Herman and I have room. I want you Tanta," she said, embracing Anna. "I . . . I want you." And she laid her cheek upon the forlorn woman's. "Don't cry so," she said. "Come on home with me."

Anna clung to Sophia's arm as they walked back to Sophia's little white cottage. Rica and Ida followed.

Inside the house they came upon Lottchen rocking the baby and singing lustily:

> Kaffee milk unt sooker
> Koken pie unt tee.

Her baby treble soared up and down the scale. Rica Jane apparently did not like the song or the energetic rocking of her cradle. She was crying rebelliously.

As the house smoldered in ruins thoughts turned to other aspects of the misfortune. How had the fire started?

"Knopf must have done it," Maggie said, frowning at her father's idiot hired man. "He's always playing with matches and he was down at Miss Ida's. I saw him!"

"Are you sure?" Friech Vollman asked.

Maggie nodded. "I'm sure, Papa. It was this way. I went to practice the 'Spring Song' before I came here. Miss Ida was gone when I got there, but I saw Knopf in the yard."

Friech looked at Knopf. "Did you set fire to the house?" he asked.

Knopf shook his head. "Didn't do," he said, "My didn't do."

"Did you, Knopf?" Herman asked soberly.

"Didn't do!" Knopf insisted.

Angry men closed in on him from all sides. Knopf quaked like a scared rabbit. "My didn't do," he screamed. "Herr Gott, my didn't do!"

Otto grappled him at the collar. "Out with it, you jibbering fool! You should have been put in the crazy house long ago!"

"My wanted swing Knopf asleep! My didn't do!"

"I'll swing you to sleep, you liar!" Otto's broad hand whacked across the simpleton's face. Wullum Yaeger's foot sent Knopf sprawling on the ground. He groveled in the dust, still sobbing, "My didn't do."

Pastor broke into the circle and knelt beside Knopf. "Go away, all of you," he said sternly. "Let me alone with Knopf."

When they had turned away, Pastor talked to Knopf. "Tell me, Knopf," he said kindly, "were you inside Menke's house this afternoon?"

"No," Knopf stammered. "Please, Herr Pastor, no."

"You were not inside the house?" Pastor repeated, smoothing back the wretch's dusty rumpled hair. "Think hard, Knopf, perhaps you have forgotten. Were you inside the house?"

"No, no," Knopf insisted.

"But Little Maggie said you were there."

"My sleep in Idie's hammock. My likes hammocks. Sleep good."

"You came only to sleep in the hammock?"

Knopf nodded.

"Did you see anybody while you were there?"

Knopf brightened. "Seed a chickadee up in the tree."

"You didn't see any person?"

"My see only a little chickadee."

Pastor looked into Knopf's childish face, and sighed, "I believe you, Knopf lad. I believe you did see only a chickadee."

He took Knopf into the house. "Don't vex the lad," he said to the christening guests. "He had nothing to do with the fire. Of that I am quite sure!"

After the supper Ida helped wash and put away Sophia's new dishes. All the time she was thinking of her own lovely china destroyed in the holocaust.

She looked at Anna, who was sitting at the window staring tearfully across the hollow at the ghastly patch of charcoal in the distance. Smoke continued to rise from the ruins.

Ida thought with a pang of Anna's great loss—the sewing machine which she had had all these years—Papa's last gift to her. She must get another machine for Anna right away. Anna couldn't live without her sewing machine!

Anna was not thinking of her sewing machine, however. She was thinking of Ida's piano. She was wondering by what means she could possibly replace it in the midst of every other loss. If there weren't enough insurance money she'd sew by hand, borrow a machine, sew harder than ever, only Ida mustn't be without her piano! Ida couldn't live without music. . . . If only she had given Ida her brocaded waist this morning so that she could have worn it today. Now, there was no brocaded waist to give . . . even the pattern was destroyed. . . .

Pastor went home with a heavy heart that night.

Rica hovered over little Rica Jane's cradle, held the wee little warm hand a moment and picked up her scarf to go home.

Lizzie Vollman shooed her clan up the lane.

The Yaegers, too, departed. When they came home they found Hanchen disgruntled. "Dr. Baum sure has verhexed us one and all. 'Twas he who started that fire with a brand from hell itself! Even the smoke took the form of devils! There's a curse on us, a black curse!"

Wullum Yaeger shook his head and made a mental guess as to the contents of the jug behind the pantry door. "Where's Hans?" he asked.

Hanchen shrugged her shoulders. "Plague that wild-fanged one! Never did a hand's turn all day, he didn't. Slept through hell's fire and water like a ground hog. And no wonder, with the bellyful he ate at dinner!"

Wullum investigated. He came downstairs with the report. "Hans is not in bed. . . . You let him run away!"

"Run away?" Hanchen repeated stupidly. "My Hansy? Oh, Hans, how could you run away from your poor ailing mother again? Her with one leg in the grave and no one to look after her right! Come back, Hans, come back before it is too late!"

It was already "too late" however.

Switchmen on the railroad tracks near Dayton were holding their lanterns high to see what was lying there. They saw a young man's mangled body.

"The nine o'clock must have struck him," one of the switchmen said shuddering. "Mortals! What a shame! He's only a kid!"

The other switchman saw the sack lying within hand's reach of the outstretched arm of the corpse. "A tramp," he said.

With one voice the switchmen sighed, "Wonder who he was?"

XXIII   *Maria's Discovery*

~~~~~~

OTTO BETZ stopped at the schoolhouse to pick up Ida Menke, who was returning from a trip to Cincinnati.

"Any news?" Otto asked.

Ida nodded. "The insurance is settled." A tinge of resignation saddened her speech. "The new house won't come up to the one Papa built, though. Anna and I wanted a two-story brick with a slate roof, and the architect says he can't make it. He wants to build a four-room house, all on one floor."

Otto shook his head. "Don't you do it," he advised. "What's a house without an upstairs? And four rooms! Where would you put the piano?"

Ida jostled up and down upon the high seat. "I don't know. Anna will be disappointed. She likes a roomy house. But if we are going to have a slate roof we'll have to make other allowances."

Ida climbed down from the wagon at her temporary home with the Toepfers. There, Maria Locher was waiting with a letter addressed to Ida—a letter in Gerhart's own handwriting! Maria was a whirlpool of frenzy. Her narrow lips were drawn together with vacuum tightness. "Will you deny that this letter is from my son?" she asked, thrusting the envelope into Ida's hand.

"Why should I wish to deny it?" Ida asked quietly.

"And this isn't the first one. . . . You'll not deny that either."

"That," Ida replied, "I don't care to discuss with you."

"Oh, you don't!" Maria sputtered. "Do you think for a minute you can stand between my boy and me? Well, you can't!"

"Whatever rifts there are between you and Gerhart are of your own making, Maria. It's poor excuse making to blame your failures on me!"

"My failures!" Maria ejaculated. "My trials you mean! You've always stood in my way, Ida Menke! You've robbed me of what was rightfully mine!"

"I've robbed you of nothing," Ida said flatly, leveling a cool pair of eyes at her opponent.

"I'll not deny you had Gottlieb first, but I married him, don't forget!" Maria snapped.

"And you still have him, don't you?" Ida asked.

Maria swallowed. She was abashed. What words could carry the bitter truth that Gottlieb wasn't really hers? In spite of house and garden . . . in spite of nine sons and daughters . . . he hadn't really ever belonged to her. . . . For Ida to understand how such a thing could be was impossible.

Gottlieb had worked side by side with Maria faithfully, never complaining, taking good and bad years with the same unruffled spirit. As the years wore on Maria's frantic search for possession of him slackened and came to a grinding halt. Subconscious inner rebellion set in, making her a ruthless household tyrant.

Ida had been Gottlieb's first sweetheart. Long ago her parents had persuaded Gottlieb that she was too frail for the rigorous life of a gardener's wife. And so he had reluctantly given her up to music and gracious spinsterhood.

It was then that Maria Hartwig seized Gottlieb.

Whether either he or Ida regretted losing each other Maria never knew. The uncertainty was devastating. How could one be jealous of a woman who did not covet? Who seemed happy and sufficient unto herself? Not once these twenty years had Maria known Ida to cross her path, but that was not enough!

Did she sometimes cross Gottlieb's path? Stir up disquietude and longing in his silent soul? Even if it was only with the notes of a song floating across the gardens to his listening ears? Maria tortured herself constantly with such fears . . . but never before had she manifested them publicly.

"You've turned Gerhart's head. Pretended all the time that it was music that brought you together, when all the time you wanted him with you just because he was Gottlieb's son!"

Ida paled. "That isn't true, Maria. You are talking hysterical nonsense. . . . I have robbed you of neither your husband nor your son."

"It is not nonsense! It's the everlasting truth, and I'll not rest until you've made amends!"

Ida started to leave the room with her letter.

"I demand to read that letter," Maria cried, thrusting herself belligerently in Ida's path.

"I can't allow you to have it."

"I'll tear it into shreds!" Maria shrieked. "And if Otto's hired girl is in this shameful plot against me she is going to suffer for it. The Lord will punish her just like He punished you by burning your house, Ida Menke. . . . You know that was God's punishment . . . and your poor sister had to suffer it with you! Innocent ones must always suffer with the guilty!"

At that moment Herman strode into the kitchen, his face as pale as on the day he struck O'Dee for thrashing Knopf. "Frau Locher," he began, "you have shouted long enough. Let there be an end to it! While Ida Menke is living under my roof you'll not accuse her of all manner of wrongdoing. I won't stand for it. It is no crime for a teacher to receive letters from her pupils, and your saying so can't make it a crime. If the boy feels like writing to her instead of you, that is your fault not Miss Ida's. As for dragging Rica's name in the street, I warn you that has to be stopped!"

Maria jeered. "So you are still set on Rica! Even named your child after her! A fine barrel of slop before your doorstep that is! I wouldn't be so proud of it!"

"Will you leave this house and take your poisoned tongue with you?" Herman asked.

"Not until I get that letter!"

"Show me the law that gives you the right to that letter," Herman exploded.

"I'll get Pastor," Maria panted. "I don't have to put up with this. I'll get Pastor. He'll tell you what right a busybody of an old maid has to rob a mother of her child. Just you wait!"

She flounced out of the door, her long calico wrapper swishing from side to side. On to Otto Betz she stalked, her fury unabated. She found Otto sprinkling celery.

"I want to know," she said breathlessly, "if your hired girl is getting letters from my Gerhart."

Otto spit out his quid. "Not that I know of," he answered. "What makes you think so, Frau Locher?"

"I don't trust the girl."

"How so?"

"I don't trust a living soul. As well as Ida Menke is sinning against me, this girl of yours can be doing it behind my back, too. And it's likely she is!"

Otto stared at Maria. "It's likely she isn't," he retorted. "For that matter you can go ask her yourself. It's none of my business. Rica's in the house."

Maria stormed into the kitchen where Rica was kneading bread. "I've come to find out where Gerhart has gone."

Rica looked up from her pan of dough. "Why are you asking me, Frau Locher?"

"Because you know. You and Ida Menke!"

"What makes you so sure?"

"My Johnny saw a letter in Ida's mailbox. And it was from Gerhart. He came home and told me and I went up to the box and saw it with my own eyes."

"And there was a letter for me, too?"

Maria scoffed. "You weren't caught like Ida was, but I've no doubt you know as much as she. I can tell by the way you are looking at me."

"Did you come to quarrel with me?" Rica asked.

"I came to get my rights! I want to see the letters you got from Gerhart!"

"I'm sorry, I have no letters to show you," Rica answered blandly.

"It won't do you any good to hide your affairs. Sooner or later daylight must come! Just you wait till I tell Pastor!"

Grossmutter chimed in, "Do you think Pastor has nothing to do but listen to your yammering? And do you think that he would agree that it was an honest thing to have your children spy in strangers' mailboxes?"

Maria's lips sprang open. "What is the world coming to when young and old are leagued against the right?"

"Chaff!" mocked Grossmutter.

Maria sallied home.

Her unsuccessful interviews with Ida, Rica and Grossmutter Betz left her in fighting fettle. She ordered Gottlieb to hitch up the horse and buggy and take her to Pastor Schicht.

Reluctantly, Gottlieb hitched up the horse and buggy and drove to Cumminsville with his disgruntled spouse.

Pastor was rummaging through his books when they arrived. He eyed the carriage circumspectly from the attic window, then hastened downstairs to greet Herr and Frau Locher.

"It's a sin and a shame what they are doing to me," Maria sobbed. "All my life I've done what was right by everybody and now they treat me like a black sheep."

Gottlieb squirmed.

Pastor looked at the two questioningly. "Black sheep?"

Maria nodded. "The whole Avenue knows already that Gerhart is in Panama—all except his own flesh and blood. By accident we had to hear about it."

"So-o-o?" Pastor stroked his beard. "And what is Gerhart doing in Panama?"

Maria sobbed afresh. "You'll have to ask Ida Menke. She knows and won't tell. She's been standing between us and our boy all this time; else he would have been home long ago."

"Miss Ida has been hearing from him?"

"All along . . . she daren't deny it."

"You don't know that for sure, Mamma," Gottlieb put in timidly.

Pastor queried, "You did learn that he is in Panama?"

"That's where the letter was mailed."

"Well, well," Pastor mused.

Maria shook her head. "And to think he would forsake us and put his trust in Ida Menke!"

"H'm," Pastor said, "we should be grateful for that, Frau Locher. It is good he let her know where he is."

Maria disagreed. "Ida had no right to write secret letters to him."

Pastor leaned back in his chair, passed his hand over his eyes and said, "Ida Menke has been a close friend of his, Maria. An understanding friend. Never has she disappointed him."

"But she doesn't know what is best for him. All she did was to turn his head."

Pastor waited for the confession he felt Maria ought to be making. But there was no hint of contrition in her beady eyes.

"Will you be frank enough to tell me what really happened the night before Gerhart left home?" he suggested.

"He rebelled against the book burning."

"More particularly at something of his that was burned?"

"It was an engineering book," Gottlieb answered.

Maria cast a reproachful glance at Gottlieb. "No matter what it was," she said. "It was taking all the boy's time and keeping his mind off his work. Something had to be done!"

"I thought the idea of the book burning was to rid Wooden Shoe Hollow of harmful books . . ."

"We might have been a little bit hasty," Gottlieb said contritely.

Maria stood her ground. "There was nothing hasty about it!" she snapped.

Pastor's jaw was set. "Gerhart may be serious about this engineering. Perhaps forcing him back home would not be wise. Certainly burning his book was unwise!"

Maria was shocked. She clutched her handkerchief. "Come, Papa," she said, rising abruptly. "There's no use trying to get help here."

"Mamma," Gottlieb pleaded.

"Are you coming, Gottlieb?" she asked frigidly.

Pastor laid his hand upon Gottlieb's shoulder. "I'll speak to Miss Ida," he said. "She'll tell me where the boy is staying. I'll try to get him to write to you."

"Humph!" said Maria, mincing down the porch steps. "If Gerhart can't come home, he needn't write. We'll not be kept for fools!"

There was nothing further Pastor felt free to do at the moment. He climbed back to the attic . . . sorry for Gottlieb and apathetic toward his wife.

"You shouldn't have spoken about the book," Maria scolded.

"But Pastor asked what started the trouble," Gottlieb reasoned.

"Pastor asks too many questions. Lazy thieving hounds like Hans he runs after and brings back bit and bridle, but one like Gerhart he lets run in the world!"

"But he ought to go after boys like Hans, Mamma. It's no more than right."

"And it's no more than right that he help us. If it is too much trouble for him, there's help for it. There's the bicycle preacher. I'll tell him Sunday. Maybe he has the story of the prodigal son in his Bible, if Pastor Schicht hasn't!" Hate burned in her words.

"Mamma," Gottlieb protested, in a shocked voice that accused Maria of near blasphemy. They drove on in silence.

Suddenly, the two were startled by a sickly yellow light which traveled across the heavens. Gottlieb drew in the reins. "I'm afraid there is something in the air," he said ominously.

"What is it, Papa? Wind? Not a cyclone?"

Gottlieb shuddered. "God knows."

Maria dropped back in the carriage guiltily. What was it she had said to Ida about innocent suffering with the guilty? "Heaven!" she panted. "Pray that we may be delivered from this . . . this . . ."

Already the wind was rushing down upon them, whipping up the buggy top and driving against them with the fury of a tribe of crazed savages.

Blinded and paralyzed with fear, Gottlieb tore down Spring Grove Avenue until the vague outline of the C.H. & D. station appeared on the right. He pulled the reins to the right and the horse leaped under the cover of the station.

Maria, sobbing hysterically, was helped from the buggy by the station master. Helped into the sitting room, where she sat alone in the darkness of the storm and moaned. . . .

Gottlieb stood at the window in stark silence and stared at the swirling yellow world outside—flying debris and the mighty wind sucking, blasting, and driving rampantly down the Avenue and across the hills. Were the children safe inside the house at home? All of them? No matter about the garden . . . or the new greenhouses he had glazed yesterday . . . just so the children were safe inside the house. Just so all the windows were shut and little Carrie was not frightened as only she could be in a storm. A storm like this.

Now a lull descended. The wind was abating. The yellow light seemed to scatter into oblivion. The sky grew gray now . . . dark . . . darker.

Then a new fury was unleashed. Hail shot down in torrents. Like the sound of steel against steel the pellets dashed upon the brick paving of Spring Grove Avenue. All the air was thick with this rain of ice. Savage ice that had the power to cut down every growing thing and shatter every pane of glass in the greenhouse. Hailstones as big as pigeon eggs! So long the downpour lasted that Gottlieb no longer cared when it would stop. . . . The damage had been done. What good was respite now?

Maria was still in the corner choking out her petitions desperately, "Deliver us from evil!"

And in Wooden Shoe Hollow the hailstorm had completed its destructive work. Friech Vollman came outside into the chill and the melancholy of the after-storm atmosphere. All about him lay the carpet of hailstones, fast melting. Mingling with the splinters of glass . . . ruin!

He was reminded of Otto's injunction last year—"A house of glass will clatter in ruins when the first gale whips across the country."

But the greenhouses had done well. Nobody could say otherwise. What money could repay the first thrill he had had when snow was on the ground—knee deep—and inside his warm greenhouses the lettuce grew green and hearty? It was a sight to see! A contentment too deep for translation into mere words. All that was too rich to pass by. . . .

Let them say what they would . . . he would rebuild those greenhouses. And tomorrow! There would be no giving in to despair! A gardener had to have courage! And faith in God!

Rica waited for some word from Ida after Frau Locher left—

hoped for a note from Gerhart, but there was not a line forthcoming.

A whole day passed after Maria's outburst and still Ida failed to bring word.

Two evenings later Sophia brought a message. "Ida asked me to run over and tell you about the letter."

"I'm sorry it caused all the trouble," Rica said.

"It's all over now," Sophia assured her. "Pastor didn't have such a ready hand to strike the way Frau Locher expected. Pastor will not be tricked or sold. One has ever to admit that."

"How is Gerhart?"

"Fine. Happy as a prince. He landed in Panama and got a job with the government. Just the kind of job he wanted. And he says the weather is grand."

"That is good news."

"Yes. Ida was worried about him way off there in a strange country. It's been so long since she heard from him. Gerhart likes adventure."

"I'm sure he does," Rica mused.

"To you he sends greetings," Sophia added.

Rica cringed beneath her stoic smile.

XXIV *Of White Satin*

IT WAS NOW A WHOLE YEAR since Vollman's greenhouses were destroyed. They had been rebuilt and another profitable winter of gardening had rewarded that faith.

Taking courage from him, many of Vollman's neighbors erected spans of greenhouses. Herman Toepfer, who was eager to try greenhouse gardening, decided to wait one more year before increasing his Bauverein indebtedness. And Otto postponed his building till Fritz should "come out of school."

Wullum Yaeger, who was still working Friech Vollman's ground, was having a difficult time trying to sell his Spring Grove Avenue acres. No gardener would be tempted to buy land in Mill Creek's path. It must go eventually as a factory site. One day there would be factories everywhere on the Avenue, Wullum contended. And when that time came he would be out in the country on a farm— away from this whole insipid business of greenhouse gardening. Carry on his agriculture God's way!

But today the controversial subject rested, for there was a "Huchteet" in the hollow, in the language of the Plattdeutsch. And a "Huchteet" was no time to quibble over up-to-date and old-fashioned methods of gardening.

A beer wagon creaked noisily as it came to a stop at the Flieger household. Three kegs of lager were rolled down and hoisted into the market shed. Seven kegs had been delivered today, beer of light and dark varieties to satisfy the most discriminating of tastes.

Hattie glowed with pride. All her plans were taking shape nicely. Already the parlor was filled with wedding gifts. She never tired of looking at them. There was a copper wash boiler from the Betz family, an ornate gilded mirror from Emil, a turquoise granite coffeepot, crockery, a damask tablecloth, a handsome oak wardrobe, an iron roaster, and cut-glass bowls. And, as though all these household gifts from neighbors and friends were not enough, Herr and Frau Flieger had last week bought her a whole barrel of dishes! On every dish there were three bluebirds on wing.

The bluebirds, the china salesman had said, betokened happiness, whereupon Hattie's mother wiped her eyes. "Papa," she said, "can't we get this set for her?" And Papa, quite as deeply moved by the three bluebirds, bought the set.

Truly, Hattie knew herself to be a lucky bride! It was not only because of her gifts and because of the celebration that Papa was giving in her honor. There were many other things that thrilled her. The house she was to have in St. Bernard, lighted streets in the night, grocery and drygoods stores right outside her door! Not a market-fixing care in the world would be hers, for her husband-to-be was a hack driver. Every day would be Sunday!

Last week a letter had come from Aunt Hattie, saying she would be very happy to have her newly wed niece and husband visit in Milwaukee.

That completed Hattie's plans. She and Edward would see wonderful sights on their honeymoon, might even stop in Chicago! They would be envied by everybody. Rica, too, probably. That gave the plan added thrill.

And what would folks say when they saw her fashionable, white silk gown and the trailing veil of lace, with its regal coronet? Nothing so fine and rich had ever cloaked a Wooden Shoe Hollow bride in all its history.

Neighbors were not being overturned by Hattie's studied preparations, however. They were interested most of all in the bridegroom.

Hattie hadn't met him at the crowd. That didn't augur well for the match. Only once in the whirlwind courtship had she brought him to the hall. And upon that occasion she had dared to come with a parasol and gloves—and minus an apron!

It made no difference that gloves and parasols were in the height of fashion in metropolitan Cincinnati. Such things were utterly out of key at the crowd. Swains looked askance at the young Bavarian who accompanied their Hattie. Girls whispered in corners.

The stranger's deftly waxed mustache moved up and down energetically as he spoke. He danced and drank gracefully. Often, he tilted his head back and laughed with the wholehearted abandon of a child.

Where had Hattie met this man? Who was he? What did he do for a living? Those soft angular hands hadn't seen much heavy work. Nor had his smooth face been bent over garden beds. Ernst Betz promptly christened him "pale face" and "pale face" the fellow remained in Wooden Shoe Hollow, forever after!

The day after the appearance of the Bavarian at the crowd, Hattie confided her secret to Rosie. She had met Edward at Grossmutter von Hagel's funeral. He was driving a hack in which she rode to church. "It was queer wasn't it that I should have met my love at a funeral?"

Rosie agreed.

"Isn't Edward handsome?"

"Yes," lisped Rosie. "Handsome as Prince Albert."

"I know Rica will be jealous," Hattie said. "Anybody would be . . . Edward is no common man!"

Rosie sighed. "Do you think you will marry him?"

"Why, of course," Hattie gloated. "We are engaged now!"

"When will it be—the wedding?"

"I don't know," Hattie answered, blinking. "Edward and I want it real soon, though. Soon as the potatoes are in and the kraut is cut."

"Am I going to stand up for it?"

"I don't know, Rosie. You see Edward has a sister. It's no more than right that I choose her. She'll be a *lovely* bridesmaid! She has pretty black hair, just like Edward's. Wears the grandest store dresses!"

"But you want somebody else to stand up, don't you?"

"My twin cousins from over the river . . . I thought they would make it romantic. Twins are romantic when they look alike, don't you think so?"

Rosie agreed, even though she was filled with woe. Once Rica had taken the coveted place . . . this time it was a beautiful stranger and a pair of romantic cousins!

Anna Menke, too, was doomed to momentary disappointment. She was not elected to make the bridal dress. It was going to be bought ready-made in Cincinnati. That, Hattie's mother explained in a personal call of apology to Anna, was not her fault. It was simply that Hattie wanted a store dress so badly. And a store suit, too, for the honeymoon trip to Milwaukee.

"Milwaukee?" Anna asked. "My, that's a long trip, isn't it?"

Hattie's mother nodded. "Isn't it fine that the young man can take her? Sister Hattie will be so glad to see her. Sister Hattie's got it good in Milwaukee. Her husband has a shoe store. If only *my* Hattie has it that good!" Frau Flieger's voice shook with emotion. She whipped a double-tatted handkerchief out of her bosom.

"I hope she will be happy," Anna Menke said simply. "It is a shame she isn't going to live here in Wooden Shoe Hollow, but of course St. Bernard isn't far."

Frau Flieger nodded tearfully.

And so the plans spun merrily forward and the triumphant hour was at hand!

Rica, in the midst of a bevy of young people from every surrounding garden area, attended the pompous affair which, for pure sentimentalism on Hattie's part, was to be staged in Old First.

Professor Stoffregen stood aloft in the balcony and played his violin—strange tuneless pieces that nobody had ever heard before. And then, the bells clanged and the organ launched into a sonorous prelude.

Sophia sat back in the pew. Baby Rica was sitting on Herman's lap, her little head doddling up and down as she looked about this great room with its host of people. Now and again she nestled her head against her father, dizzy with the staggering sight of so many faces and a little frightened at the unseen accordion which sounded so mightily in contrast to the one her father played. Herman's strong hand held her close as she hid her tiny face in his bosom.

The pageantry of Hattie's wedding proceeded.

Down the aisle came Hattie's twin cousins from over the river. Their blue silk skirts rustled over a trio of highly starched petticoats, their cumbrous feather-laden hats of velvet drew breaths of envy on every hand.

And there was Edward's sister, whose Madonna-like face was wreathèd in a pale blue scarf which reached up high to brush her ears. Nestled in the rolls of her black hair was a camelia. Buoyantly, she moved down the aisle on Peter Landauer's arm. Peter, it seemed, was distantly related to the Bavarian Edward.

Pastor waited impatiently at the altar. This was far too much show for him!

Edward held himself erect as an armoured knight. Hattie was frigid with nervousness. She stepped falteringly, blinked relentlessly.

Rosie began to cry.

Rica's thoughts turned back to the evening when Rosie, Hattie and Sophia came to Betz's kitchen to sew. She recalled their conversation—Sophia's wish for lavender cashmere, two accordion players and a wash basket full of sandwiches. Well, Sophia had had all these and more—her cup of happiness was still overflowing.

And Hattie? Her words had been prophetic. Behold the lavish bridal finery, her man-of-the-world husband and a trip to Milwaukee, waiting . . .

But alas for Rosie! Things did not seem so promising for her.

There was only Yust, whom she loathed. Yust, with his mulish vulgarity and his braggadocio. There he sat now—on the opposite side of the church—a sardonic grin on his face, his eyes roving about wantonly.

The ceremony proceeded solemnly. Admonition. Prayer. Vows. The nasal singing of the preacher school in the balcony.

> *Jesu, geh voran*
> *Auf der Lebensbahn*

It was finished.

An afternoon and evening of celebration enlivened the hollow. In the hall a quintette of strangers provided music. There were two brass horns, a violin, a drum and a piano.

Beer kegs rolled out steadily.

Rica helped with the cooking. Such an array of food she had never seen gathered for one meal. Roast duckling, a calf, kettles full of rice, potatoes and other vegetables. A stalk of bananas. Platters full of every texture, flavor and color of cake and pie. And a baker's wedding cake with silver beads and a bridal couple perched on the top. . . . Not one thing had Hattie left undone!

There was stewing, basting, pot watching and fire tending. Acting as chef of the cuisine was Grossmutter Betz. Many of her prized recipes graced the tables.

Into this haven of cookery came Rosie.

"What fails you, child?" Grossmutter asked. "Are you going to twist those apron strings to pieces?"

"I'm sick and tired of staring at Yust's green teeth," she complained. "I wish I hadn't been in Indianapolis when Karl Metz was stood up."

"Chaff, what was not to be was not to be," said Grossmutter.

"That's what Papa says, too. I guess it's no use thinking about it anymore. It's like playing pussy in the corner, isn't it?"

"What?" asked Grossmutter.

"Nothing . . . only it's always next-door neighbor."

"What here . . . what there . . ." Grossmutter said. "There is a lid to fit every pot."

"No matter how crooked it is," Rosie finished the adage herself. And she thought of "crooked" in terms of cross-eyes and freckles, a heavy tongue and a barrelish waist. It would take a crooked lid all right! Perhaps as crooked as Yust Bobke. She shuddered.

Later that afternoon Pastor saw Rica coming down the lane with a basket of dishes. He went out to meet her.

"I was hoping to have a word with you," he said. "I have a message from Germany. Heinrich earnestly wants you to come home."

"I can't go."

"But you can write."

"It will only make things harder, Pastor. I'll never change my mind."

"Never is changeless and dead. Let's not have it that way, Rica."

"What would you have me do?"

"Write to him."

"And go back to him when he says I must?"

"That I cannot undertake to answer for you."

"Let me have one more year," she pleaded. "Another year here in Wooden Shoe Hollow. Till Hulda is through school and Lottchen is out of her baby shoes. It won't be so hard to go then."

"But in the meantime you will write to Heinrich?"

"No . . . I want this year as I have had the others—free of him."

"Shall I tell him that you will come in September? That will be a year from now."

"Next September, I promise," Rica faltered. Melancholy possessed her. "Oh, Pastor, why must this be? Why must I leave all the things I've learned to love so dearly?"

"To find what may be dearer still," came Pastor's unexpected answer. "You must not carry this as a burden. Expect kindness from life, child. There is more joy in the world than human hearts can hold. God wills it so. Only believe!"

At that point Hattie interrupted. "Rica, oh, Rica," she called, "come along with me."

Rica murmured an excuse to Pastor and followed Hattie across the road.

"I want you and Rosie to help me get ready," she said excitedly. "Edward's boss is sending the hack down for us in an hour. I must be ready."

Rosie came with the lantern and they hurried up to Hattie's home. "Isn't it thrilling?" Rosie lisped. "To think of going on a trip. Do you think you'll get homesick?"

Hattie laughed. "Of course not, Rosie."

"I got homesick in Indianapolis."

"Oh, but you weren't on a honeymoon."

"No," Rosie agreed dully. "I wasn't on a honeymoon."

The two girls helped Hattie into her blue serge suit and frilly blouse. They packed and re-packed the frocks and petticoats Hattie had bought while working in Avondale.

Soon Hattie was taking her place beside Edward in the carriage and reaching for her suitcases. "Good-bye, good-bye," she called. "Good-bye all! Mamma and Papa . . . thanks to everybody for all the nice things . . . good-bye!"

The carriage wheels ground over the cinders.

Rica and Rosie returned to the dance hall. There, festivities were now at their convivial height.

Soon they heard the train whistle as it thundered out of Winton Place on its way to Milwaukee. Rica's heart sank. . . . One more year and that whistle would be shrieking a dreary farewell into her ears.

In that moment she was sorry she made the pledge to Pastor. Sorry and exceedingly distressed!

Emil pranced up to her. "Waltz?" he asked. " 'The Beautiful Blue Danube'! . . . Ah, these musicianers know how to play it, don't they?"

"They do," Rica murmured.

Over the paraffined floor couples glided happily. The hubbub died down as the waltz proceeded. A dreamy atmosphere settled over the floor—gliding feet and quiet smiles.

"Know who that fiddler 'minds me of?" Emil asked.

"Who?"

"Can't you guess?"

"No."

"Holds up his head and swings that bow just like Gerhart!" Emil looked at his partner furtively and in the pain he read there thought he had unearthed a secret which Maria Locher would have given her every stalk of celery to know.

His knotty little hand gripped Rica the tighter as the waltz ended. He bowed graciously. "It's always such a pleasure to dance with you," he said. "Thank you, my girl. Thank you for the nicest waltz of the evening!"

"*Ein Prosit!*"

The orchestra played the stirring toast and a hundred voices thundered through the hall:

> *Ein Prosit,*
> *Ein Prosit,*
> *Der Gemütlichkeit,*
> *Ein Prosit,*
> *Ein Prosit,*
> *Der Gemüt-lich-keit!*

XXV Migrant

MAXIMILIAN was deeply satisfied with the consummation of his plans when he returned to Berlin after the marriage of his son and Rica Heber. Nothing could be better for the boy than this early marriage. It would give him stability.

Maximilian hoped Rica would be a devoted wife, just as her mother was. How proud her mother had been, sensible and courageous. Always interested in her husband's welfare. Never complained about loneliness, never tried to get Friederich to give up his high calling as a soldier of the emperor.

Maximilian remembered how she had helped her little daughter write those cheery little notes that began, "Dearest Papa," and ended "Baby Rica." Notes full of childish love and childish faith. The homely little verses she wrote to him about "spring beauties on the lawn" and "angels in the snow." They had given Friederich so much joy!

If only his own wife, Leah, had been like Friederich's, but she hadn't. Leah had ceaselessly begged him to come home. Give up soldiering. She owned Heinrich during babyhood and stripling years—yet she had not been satisfied. Lavished such care upon him as would dull the brightest boy and spoil him for rigorous living.

Then one day, quite suddenly, she was gone, and the old manor died with her. Pale-cheeked Heinrich wandered about the house and lingered in his mother's terraced rose garden—bereft and lonely. A strange self-centered child.

Maximilian realized then that he had, somehow, to win the boy. The years were going by rapidly. They had all been Leah's years. Now they were to be his!

As a soldier he began his comradeship with Heinrich. Quickly, by this means, he swaggered his way into the boy's heart, for he had been a prince of soldiers! With his tales of adventure he made Heinrich a patriot who was eager for service to the fatherland. Bit by bit Leah's rose garden faded into the background.

But all this success had been short-lived. High hopes for the boy's military career were dashed to the ground when Heinrich was wounded. It appeared there was to be nothing for him but the monotony of farming—worse . . . sheep raising!

Now came a note which brought Maximilian more alarm. Not the kind of alarm he had experienced when the lad was injured. Acute pain that had been, seeing his son suffering so gallantly, knowing he could never again put on a uniform and march with the emperor's men. That tragedy had been thorough and quick, as the severing of a branch from a tree when it is struck by lightning. Bitter resignation was its first and last fruit.

But this note carried far-reaching alarm to the old soldier. His son's bride was in America. What trickery was fate preparing? Was it not enough that the boy had been cheated out of soldierhood; must he be duped in marriage, too?

Soon after the note's arrival, Heinrich called at his father's desk in Berlin. Maximilian received his son in dismay. Winced at the sight of his unsteady footsteps—the limp he knew now would never leave!

"I've come to say good-bye, Father," Heinrich explained.

"Good-bye?" Maximilian's face twitched. "Where are you going, son?"

"To America."

There was a pause.

"Rica won't come here, and so I want to go to her."

Maximilian grasped Heinrich's hand. "You are in earnest?"

"Yes, Father."

"Duty?" It was the word every soldier comprehended.

"Hardly that. I want to see her."

His father nodded. "Friederich would want us to find Rica, though for herself she little deserves it."

Heinrich shook his head. "I don't know anything about Rica, Father. What she thinks, what she wants, how she feels, or even how she looks. I *must* know!"

"I hate to see you leave the fatherland," Maximilian said brusquely. "Many in these days wander out of the country never to return! . . . Oh, my son!"

Heinrich looked up at Maximilian's square shoulders. His eye rested upon the epaulets and iron cross. "I know I haven't made a good soldier," he said tremulously. "I'll try to make something better of myself, Father—something to justify the high hopes you've had for me."

Maximilian was moved like a stream whose current is suddenly swiftened. "How will you find Rica?" he asked.

"Through the American pastor who has befriended her in Ohio."

"Ohio? That is far away from New York. . . . I wish I could go with you to America, son. For me the country has always held fancy. It is a land to explore!" Maximilian struck his sturdy knee.

"I wish so too," Heinrich said wistfully. "It would be a glorious adventure, traveling with you."

Two days later father and son stood at the dock in Bremen, waiting for the huge liner to open her docks to the swarm of emigrants, who had come from every quarter of Germany. There were young men, like Heinrich, seeking a future. They turned eager faces westward. Old women waited complacently. Excitement was beyond their strength and will. There were bewildered young mothers and their little ones, sadly taking leave of friends.

First class, second class, third class or steerage, what did it matter how they would be transported to the New World? There was elation in every passage and a full measure of pain and sorrow as well.

Heinrich took his place among the throngs of emigrants on the boat and looked back at the shore, as they did, where loved ones waited to wave farewell.

This, thought he, was what Rica had done before him! Only there had been no one from whom she had to part at the ocean's edge. How had she felt when she embarked?

It was a calm sunny day in late September when the sea voyage began. And another sunny day followed.

But the morning of the third day brought storm to the vessel. She billowed and rocked, leaped and surged like driftwood.

The water's apron of blue disappeared. Dismal water reflected nothing but a relentless gray sky. The sea frothed and churned. Waves charged against the ship's side like a herd of angry bison.

Seasickness terrorized almost every soul on board. It was, the crew admitted, one of the worst sailing days in the ship's history. Most of the travelers took refuge in their cabin beds.

Heinrich felt none of the violence of seasickness. His was a mild discomfort, a distaste for food and a feeling of limpness. He staggered about the deck, surveying the vast stretch of noisy water.

At an entry he discovered a young woman who had collapsed beside the rail. She was thin and ghostly white. Her bony elbows jutted out of a mauve shawl. And her eyes were sunken with the unmistakable inroads of tuberculosis.

An officer opened a door nearby and Heinrich carried the stricken girl into the cabin.

She tried to quell the coughing which set upon her. "I wanted fresh air," she said feebly. "There is no air! If only the sun would come out and warm the deck. I'm so cold."

The ship's physician came.

Heinrich waited outside the cabin.

"Is the lady with you?" the physician asked, upon coming out to the passage.

"No, there wasn't anybody with her."

"She is dangerously ill. Should never have made this trip."

"May I see her?" Heinrich asked. "There may be something I can do."

The doctor shrugged his shoulders. "There is little anybody can do!" He hurried back upstairs to an overflowing hospital.

Heinrich tapped lightly on the door.

"Come in," the girl answered. "The door is not bolted."

Her face lit up when she saw Heinrich limp into the room. "It was so kind of you," she whispered, stretching out a withered little hand. "I'm glad you've come. Sit down, won't you?"

"I wanted to be sure you were all right," Heinrich explained. "Is there anything I can do?"

She nodded. "Stay with me a little while. I'm so lonely. . . . Tell me who you are and where you are going."

"My name is Heinrich Heber. I'm going to Ohio to see my wife."

The sick woman smiled wanly. "Isn't that odd?" she asked. "My name is Frances Holt and I am going to meet my sweetheart in New York. Six years ago we parted in Munich. How little did we dream that it would take six years until we would meet again! But, at last, he has sent for me. Love always waits, doesn't it?" she asked childishly.

Heinrich answered only with a quizzical smile. What a strange soul she was, he thought. Lying at death's very door and prattling innocently of love and her beloved waiting in New York. As though America could work the magic of healing a broken body when one touched upon her shores.

The next morning Heinrich called at the girl's cabin only to find an empty berth. She had been moved to the hospital during the night. Hemorrhage. Heinrich walked about the deck restlessly. He could not free himself from the picture of the stricken girl. Today there was sunshine again. The ocean rippled in sapphire waves. The sick were feeling better. Children romped on the decks with hoops, balls and mallets. Grannies dozed in the sun. Young folk paraded the decks arm in arm.

There was the playroom to explore. Poles, rings, punching bags. All being put to use by lusty athletes, strong-armed, sure-footed fellows. Heinrich longed to try a feat or two. But there was the withered muscle.

And that reminded him of his long stretch of invalidism in the base hospital. He remembered how he missed Leah during that suffering. Loneliness always brought her to mind. Heinrich wondered how she would feel about this strange journey to America? How would she feel about the hasty marriage in Osnabrück? It was hard to reconcile any of the things which had happened recently to Leah's way of living.

Late in the afternoon Heinrich visited Frances. "Are we near America?" she wanted to know. "I can't wait to reach dry land. This awful swaying up and down and rolling from side to side. I'd rather die than cross the ocean again!"

"It will not be long now," Heinrich comforted.

"Won't it be wonderful? Seeing New York coming closer and closer, with all its tall buildings looming against the sky? Like a live post card? Joseph has sent me lots of pictures of New York."

"Joseph is your sweetheart?"

She nodded happily. "We've been sweetheart's ever since we were children. We pretended we were great actors, as we played Shakespeare on his father's stage in Munich. He always wanted to play Othello, but I didn't like being Desdemona. . . . I wanted to be Juliet.

"Sometimes," she sighed, "poor Joseph would get awfully tired of playing Romeo, and then we'd stop play acting for a while and talk about America. We wanted to own a big theatre in America. Buy a nice home and fill it with costly furniture and carpets and portraits. It was to be grand as a mayor's house. Those were child dreams, but the years haven't changed them."

Heinrich smiled.

"Joseph will be great some day! He's a good actor. He pulls curtains in a show house every night. And when the show is over he hurries to a café where he sings and dances. That's how he got the money to send for me. Isn't it wonderful?" Her eyes burned with enthusiasm.

"But wait till I join him. He won't have to pull curtains any longer. He'll be right out in the middle of the stage, with the lights on him, playing the leading parts in the best shows in America!

And," she added with a touch of awe, "I hope I will be acting with him, just the way we did in Munich!"

The emotional pull of this was too great for the girl. She fell to coughing violently.

Heinrich held a glass of water to her lips. She drank in long soothing swallows. The coughing subsided. Beside her, a vigil light burned steadily. She turned over on her pillow and gazed at the glowing candle prayerfully. Then she closed her eyes and lay quite still. A lovely pair of silky black lashes lay against her blanched skin. The high temple ceased throbbing. Suddenly, she seemed like a figure of wax. Shadows of what once must have been girlish beauty appeared.

Heinrich was stirred. He wanted to hold her in his arms. That was a strange wish. It was as though he must take her to himself, thrust off disaster. There *was* disaster impending.

She opened her eyes and smiled unafraid.

"I've been talking about myself too much," she said. "Tell me about your wife and what you want to do in America. You won't mind if I close my eyes? I can listen better that way."

"I don't know where to begin," Heinrich replied. "You see I'm afraid I don't know my wife very well. We've been separated all the time. Our fathers served in the army together. They were very close friends. That's how Rica and I met."

"Rica," whispered Frances, trying the unfamiliar name on her tongue. "I like her name . . . what is she like?"

"When we were married she was a schoolgirl. Wore her hair wreathed around her head. And she had pretty gray eyes . . . I'm afraid that's all I remember."

"I hope she has grown very beautiful," Frances sighed. "I want you to have a beautiful wife and one who will love you very much." Her lips scarcely moved as she spoke.

Heinrich leaned over the pillow and lay one of Leah's comforting kisses upon the girl's lips.

Her hand brushed his shoulder. "Thank you," she said. "You have been so kind, I couldn't have made my trip without you."

Again Heinrich had the dreadful premonitory fear, but Frances was at peace.

"What will you do?" she asked. "You haven't told me."

"I'll have to wait and see what God provides," Heinrich answered. "You see here a man without a trade. Gunfire cut my profession short. . . . I was to have been a soldier."

"And now?"

"Now, I hope to be a farmer. Not very exciting, is it? Not like being a great actor?"

"Why do you want to be a farmer?" Frances asked, gazing intently at him.

Heinrich shrugged his shoulders. "I like a farmer's companions. Soil, rain, sun and open fields. They are the most precious things on earth. From them come buds, vines and fruit. Nature is the noblest partner a man can find. Nobody works as wisely and as tirelessly as she. And no one rewards one better!"

"I've never known that kind of life," Frances said wistfully. "I've only read about it in poetry." Tears hovered at the brink. "Growing things are close to God. The man who plants and cares for them must be close to Him, too. That's what you mean, isn't it?"

"Yes," Heinrich answered simply.

Frances drew a deep breath. "When Joseph and I have had our glorious day on the stage I hope we can move out in the country and have lots of flowers and pigeons. Have a flock of pink-toed pigeons—and they won't be covered with soot the way they were in Munich, neglected on the roofs—cooing sadly all the day long. My pigeons will be fat and clean."

Heinrich smiled.

When the boat reached New York there was flurry on every deck. Heinrich stood at the rail and gazed at the harbor, saw the buildings loom upon the horizon, but Frances was not there to thrill at the long dreamed of sight. She was not to be moved until she could be taken off the ship at Ellis Island.

Heinrich had said good-bye to her in the hospital, only a few moments before.

In his hand he was holding the slip of paper which bore Joseph's address. He would call there and see that all was well in the morning.

There was a great shout as the gangplank dropped. Tumult . . . feet racing down the walk . . . laughter.

Heinrich surged along with the mass joyously. America! America!

Late the next morning he called at the East Side address. But Mr. Joseph Jansky was not at home. Queer, too, the landlady remarked, since Mr. Jansky always slept the mornings. . . . A lady? No, there hadn't been a lady.

Heinrich called again that afternoon. Mr. Jansky was still not at home. If the gentleman must see him he might call at the Red Eagle Café just around the corner. Certain to catch him there nights.

To the Red Eagle, Heinrich betook himself late that evening. A bevy of girls in glittery costumes were dancing. Black silk stockings shone like lacquered ebony. In the midst of the bevy a cynical Beau Brummell danced and sang. Maudlin songs, rakish dancing, sour beer.

Heinrich called a waiter as he resisted the beer. "Is Joseph Jansky here?" he asked in heavily accented English.

"Jan? Sure, and don't you see him, Dutchman?" The waiter pointed to Beau Brummell, who was poised in a circle of dancing East Side gypsies.

Heinrich's heart sank. "This the imposing Othello?" He went to the dressing room as soon as the act was over.

Joseph eyed Heinrich critically—suspiciously. "You were a passenger on the boat?" he repeated after Heinrich. "Oh, yes, of course, the boat Frances came over on . . ."

"Is she all right?" Heinrich asked anxiously.

Jansky started at him. "Best off where she is, stranger. I didn't let her land."

"Didn't let her land?" Heinrich ejaculated.

"Course not! What would I do with her? She's a fright!"

"But the trip . . . she'll never make it."

"She made it over and she'll make it back."

This was but fulfillment of the premonition Heinrich had had yesterday . . . when he wanted to hold Frances in his arms and stay off the world! Fury seized him. "You dog!" he shouted, clouting the actor off his feet.

Before Jansky could pick himself out of the corner into which he had fallen strong hands clamped Heinrich's shoulders and he was unceremoniously hustled out of the Red Eagle under the chaperonage of the law.

And so began his life in America!

While he fretted in his cell the great liner was scrubbed and polished from stem to stern. With shrieks and snorts she turned her nose about for the journey east, bearing Frances with her.

Heinrich sat in jail, wondering how he had got there. It was an unholy potpourri. Frances, for whom love had not waited, was being thrust upon the sea like a piece of driftwood. He thought bitterly of her words—"I can't wait to reach dry land. . . . I'd rather die than cross the ocean again!"

If only they had put him aboard, too, that he might go back with her to the dismal corner of Munich from whence she had come. Comfort her. Assuage the hurt that was hers. . . . Rejected!

How keenly Heinrich knew the bitterness of rejection! Dumbly, he sat in his cell waiting for the slow wheels of justice to grind out their circle and release him . . . then what was there to be?

XXVI *Scythe of Ice*

It was Jansky who was responsible for Heinrich's release. He called at the prison to have a word with the man who "fought with him over some foolish notion."

Heinrich greeted him sullenly.

"Cooled off a little by now?" Jansky asked with a dry gust of laughter.

Heinrich did not answer.

"Come now, fellow," Jansky philosophized. "This isn't seeing America, sitting behind the bars. I've had a turn at it. It's dull business. Doesn't get you anywhere. I don't hold any grudge against you for wanting to trade a couple with me for shipping my old girl back home. Not at all. . . . Guess I know what it is to get mad. I'll have them drop the charges . . . let you go free. Shake?"

Heinrich withheld his hand. "You can do as you like," he retorted. "I'm not begging for favors."

Jansky's lithe fingers closed around the bars. "Stubborn cuss, aren't you?" he asked with a grin. "What is it makes you so stiff-necked?"

The sickish odor of stale tobacco smoke mixed with heady perfume rose to Heinrich's nostrils. "I have *some* honor," he retorted.

"Honor!" Joseph fondled the word. "Oh, of course. You brought that with you from the Old World. Honor doesn't count in America. Just keeps pockets from jingling. You don't understand why I had to send Frances home, but you will later. I was expecting the Frances I knew back there. She would have been a great help to me, but this one would be only a millstone around my neck . . . the way is hard enough here in America."

"And you can make it easier by forgetting everybody but yourself?" Heinrich asked.

"It is the only way, as you will soon learn," Joseph answered. "Remember that. It will save you many a bitter experience. As for Frances, she can go to her aunt in Munich or a hospital. She hasn't long anyway. Too bad! I loved her once, you know."

"You loved her once!" Heinrich scoffed. "You lie! Your tongue strangle you! You lie!" He turned his back upon the visitor.

Jansky shrugged his shoulders indulgently and swaggered down the dismal corridor.

Heinrich was released.

He returned to the rooming house where he had left his clothing before the ill-fated call upon Jansky.

The landlady greeted him with a bland smile. "Did you lose yourself so soon in New York? . . . Your room is taken now, I didn't know when you would be back. I'll not charge you for the second day."

She waddled off to a dark closet in the hall and lugged out Heinrich's carpetbag. "Have you some place to go now?" she asked, pushing back her dust cap and smiling at him.

"No," Heinrich answered. "I haven't."

"If you don't mind sharing a room with my boy I can take your things right upstairs. Two dollars the week and a nice room it is. Got a job?"

"No," Heinrich replied. "I don't know how long I'll be staying in New York. I want to go to Ohio. There are farms out there."

The landlady stood in the doorway, her arms akimbo. "Know folk out there?" she asked.

"Not exactly."

"Well, you better wait till spring, my boy. Ohio farms are dead in winter. Why don't you stay here? My Dan can help you to a job. And you will be right at home with us. We are German."

Heinrich stayed.

A week later as he rose in the morning the rooftops were white with frost. The air was wintry cold.

"You see," said the landlady. "It is a good thing you stayed here and have a job in the cooper shop. If this frost has hit Ohio there will be no work on the farms. It will be a hard winter!"

For the people of Wooden Shoe Hollow her words were prophetic. White frost had descended in the night and plundered every garden. Not a leaf but was touched by the greedy hand of ice!

Otto Betz's vines, heavily laden with butter beans, were bitten to death. He walked from row to row, pulling off handfuls of the glassy pods and breaking them open. The watery beans fell into his hand. Ruined. . . . No hope of salvaging any of the crop that was to carry the family through winter needs. Field crops, too, were laid low. There was nothing for the pantry but potatoes, sauerkraut and snippled beans. Barely enough money to buy flour.

Herman paced his acres restlessly. The lettuce patch lay like a slimy bog of seaweed. Heads flattened out as though crushed with a steamroller.

And the tall untrenched celery was destroyed in its prime. Fine healthy plumes. He and Sophia had planted it with so much pride and expectancy. What a blow to wake up and find it perished.

They sat at table that morning, as though death had entered the room.

The calamity of early frost spared no gardener in the Cincinnati area. Hardship faced them all, whether they lived in the fertile "Back Creek" basin, along the garden lane of Gray Road, upon the Avenue, or here in the hollow. Alike, they found themselves in dire straits. Straits too dire for the Gärtner Unterstützungsverein to mitigate.

Food, clothing, coal? How were any of these to be procured without crops to pay for them? There were many who faced that question with the first light of dawn.

Otto and Wullum Yaeger went immediately that morning to the Bauverein in St. Bernard to see if they might get a loan for the winter. But money was tight. Might loosen up after the election the officers hoped. It was too soon to tell. . . .

Frustrated, the two men stopped in a saloon for bracing. There, they emptied their pockets of the money so sorely needed at home.

It was long past midnight when they came staggering home. Down the lane they turned, arm in arm, singing in notes as wavering as their footsteps. Neighbors raised their windows to see who was disturbing the extraordinary quiet of Wooden Shoe Hollow. Quickly they banged the windows when they discovered it was Otto and Wullum returning from an all-day spree.

Minna had meanwhile kept up a bold mask. "Papa is busy somewhere," she answered to Hulda's ceaseless questioning. "Papa will soon be back," she assured Fritz, who was the soul of uneasiness.

Ernst sucked a broom straw. "Wonder where Pop's been keeping himself?" he burst out finally. "Don't take all day's time to do a little business at the Bauverein!"

Grossmutter said nothing. She was thinking of the times when Otto had had his shocks and disappointments of diverse natures as a child. Otto hadn't changed much. . . .

After supper, Grossmutter went upstairs and changed the linens on his bed, preparing for what she felt was inevitable—Otto's coming home drunk—perhaps sick.

She rocked Lottchen to sleep. Cajoled both Fritz and Hulda into going to bed.

And then she waited downstairs.

Rica slipped on her cape and went to Yaeger's. Perhaps they would know where Wullum and Otto had gone. Something must be done to relieve this suspense.

She found the Yaeger household as upset as Betz's. Frau Yaeger was sobbing like a doomed prisoner at the bar. Well she knew what to expect. It was not enough chaos for one day that the garden lay in ruins—there must be more gall in the cup . . . always more . . . and she must drink it to the last drop!

Hanchen stole about the room in her soft gaiters, sniffling. She looked like nothing so much as a witch, hanging over her cauldron. Now and then she stirred the pot of savory *Sauerkrautgemüse* in the black kettle.

One eye was sealed with the cold that was infecting it. "It's no use to try to garden," she simpered. "We've been verhexed, all of us. Flood, hail, fire and frost! In every shape the Devil plagues us! No wonder Hans lit out! My poor, poor Hans!"

Otto and Wullum were still singing when they staggered to the Betz summer kitchen door. With a pang of dismay Hulda heard them. That quality in her father's voice . . . was it time to sing foolish songs? Even Hulda knew that frost in September was nothing to sing about! She leaped out of bed and raced downstairs just in time to see the summer kitchen door swing open. Otto lost his grip on the doorknob and fell, face downward, rupturing a nasal blood vessel. A pool of blood collected under his face. Hulda trembled. Retched. Held her stomach. The room darkened. She fought for breath and toppled backward upon the stairs.

"There!" said Minna bitterly. "Such a sight for a child to see!" She left Otto and ran to Hulda's aid. "Ernst!" she called shrilly. "Come, help!"

Ernst, however, was not to be troubled by worry over a vagrant father. He snored on upstairs.

Minna panted and puffed as she carried Hulda into the parlor.

Wullum Yaeger grappled himself to the roller towel and reeled back and forth. Suddenly, he buried his face in the towel and sobbed like a child.

Minna bustled upstairs and roused Ernst. "Come!" she said fretfully. "Help Wullum Yaeger home with his kist! A spree he and Papa made of it, for sure. They don't know of day or night, and not a penny between them!"

Ernst led Wullum home much against the latter's will.

"Wullum, Wullum!" Otto pleaded as Ernst lead Wullum away. "Where are you going?" But Wullum's hazy hulk had disappeared. Otto stared stupidly across the room. "Oh, Min," he said. "Take my shoes off."

Minna banged the kitchen door behind her as she went into the parlor with kummel for Hulda.

Meanwhile, Grossmutter washed Otto's face. "Och," said she. "Shame on such schlemiels! Mocking God with drunkenness. As though that could set the world aright! Chaff! Men are such fools!"

Otto twisted in his chair. "Not so rough, Mamma," he pleaded, quite as he did when a truant urchin in Westphalia.

The blood streamed down his face.

"I hope it is sore as a carbuncle tomorrow," Grossmutter grumbled.

"Won't you please take my shoes off, Min?" Otto began again. "They are all muddy and I can't reach them. My feet are way down there. Oh, Min, please take my shoes off!"

But Minna had no notion of relenting.

It was Grossmutter who took off the muddy shoes and helped Otto to bed.

This was the kind of fruitless despair which took possession of many gardeners.

There were few who took the sober view of Herman Toepfer. Herman spent one restless day studying his problem. His Bauverein obligations were greater than any of his neighbors. His was the newest of the debts, and the greatest by that very token. He lay in the darkness of night and thought deeply. Like a messenger, solution tapped upon his weary brain. He would work out . . . the car shops . . . the desk factory . . . or at Proctor and Gamble's perhaps.

He had never done a day's work anywhere except on a garden, but he could learn. He wouldn't like sitting on a bench all day, but other men did it. It would be just a little while . . . till winter was past, and spring came again . . . spring!

The next morning he began his quest.

The car shops had no need of help. Neither had the feed store . . . or the desk factory.

There were the soap factories. Herman took heart as he walked up to the employment office of Proctor and Gamble's.

There was only one job open—an opening for a dependable night fireman.

"I'd like to have the job," Herman said eagerly. "I've helped fire greenhouse boilers for the Gray Road gardeners. I could start tonight. . . ."

There was deliberation . . . a talk with a foreman . . . and he was accepted for the job.

He drove home in high spirits. "I've got a job, Sophia," he said, sailing his cap through the room. "I've got a job for the winter. We don't have to worry!"

Sophia dropped a skillet in consternation. "Job?" she asked. "Where?"

"At Proctor and Gamble's."

"Making soap?"

"Tending the fire nights. I can sleep in the day."

"We can manage without that, Herman," Sophia pleaded. "I'd rather do with less and have you home. It doesn't seem right."

Herman swallowed. "Mustn't look at it that way," he said tenderly. "Can't be helped. It's good there is a job for me. What will a few months mean when spring brings a good green garden again?"

There were some homes, however, where the situation was not easily met. There was Wullum Yaeger, with his flood loss still weighing heavily upon him. Hanchen, whom he had taken into his home circle, fretted all day long. Not the least cause of her fretting was the fact that O'Dee no longer stopped at the door. For O'Dee's wares there was no market now, and there would be none till the radishes came again.

Pastor came to Yaegers one afternoon in November. He discovered Hanchen tossing a basket of old rotted manure upon the smouldering fire in the smokehouse.

"What are you doing, Hanchen?" he asked, as the stench of the burning manure reached his nostrils.

"Smoking wurst," she answered, banging the door.

"Strange smoke, isn't it?" Pastor asked, as he reopened the door. "Is manure something to burn in a smokehouse?"

Hanchen fanned her face with a ragged apron.

"I can't help myself, Pastor. The children eat so much. And Wullum can't say no. The wurst won't last the winter. . . . I have to fix it so they won't eat so much."

"And do you think nothing of making them sick?" Pastor thundered. The veins in his high forehead protruded.

Hanchen threw up her hands in protest. "It never made Hans sick years ago. I've been through hard times before. . . . One learns how to manage . . ."

Pastor's face blanched. "Do you mean that you fed that to Hans?"

"When I had to," Hanchen confessed. "And he grew up, too, didn't he?"

Pastor shook his head and hastened to the head of the house, who was knitting by the fireside. "Wullum," he said, "you'll have to throw away your smokehouse full of wurst. Every bit of it!"

"Throw it away?" Wullum asked. "How so?"

"Because it is not fit to eat. Hanchen has smoked it with manure!"

Wullum choked an oath. "Manure!" he gasped. "Has she gone crazy? No wonder the wurst tastes so mouldy and foul. No wonder she sneaks around with her sticks and will let no one tend the smoking! This is the last! Pastor, I'll take no more of it, and if she *is* my sister!"

Pastor picked up Wullum's ball of yarn and wound it around smoothly to the end. "It was a knavish trick, of course, but it will do no good to quarrel with Hanchen now. She thought she was helping you, Wullum, though a frog in the pond would have used more sense. We had better go Back Creek and get some meat. You've got to fill your smokehouse again."

"Can't do it," Wullum returned. "I sold the horse and harness to buy that meat. There is nothing left."

"In the spring there will be radishes," Pastor reminded him. "I think butcher Prout knows that, too!"

XXVII *"Tip Terry"*

~~~~~~

Dr. Baum had come to Betz's on his way around the hollow. There, as at other homes, he came to plead for use of antitoxin to combat the epidemic of diphtheria which followed so closely upon the havoc of frost.

Otto was adamant. His children should not be "stuck." No matter what course others would take—his children should be kept in isolation—where there would be no danger of contracting the dread "Tip Terry."

"But, Herr Betz," Dr. Baum remonstrated, "no child in Wooden Shoe Hollow is safe. There is danger in waiting. Why risk the very lives of your children when you can prevent their getting the sickness?"

"Helps nothing," Otto interjected. "If they are going to get it they will get it for all your in-spraying!"

Grossmutter swung the dipper above the *Gemüse* kettle. "And I say it *shall* be done!" she said defiantly. "It makes not a cent's worth of difference what you think of in-spraying, Otto, the doctor thinks it is best! Have a little faith in the man and do as he says, or call him not at all!"

She plunged the dipper into the kettle and ladled out a plate of the bean *Gemüse* for Dr. Baum. "Here," said Grossmutter, putting the plate beside an enormous metwurst sandwich. "Sit down and eat before you go out to deal with more bull heads. . . . You will need hot water?"

Dr. Baum nodded.

Grossmutter filled the tea kettle with fresh water and clattered coals upon the fire.

Otto shuffled out of the room.

Minna kept her eyes on her patchwork. She didn't trust herself to look up lest she betray her feelings. Grossmutter had spoken the words she had not dared ... the children ... thank God ... would be protected!

Dr. Baum bent over his soup plate gratefully and appeased the appetite which, until this moment, had not made itself felt. He hadn't touched a bite of food today. Agony ... trying to persuade parents to protect their little ones from the scourge of diphtheria ... everywhere meeting opposition ... talk of God's will ... as though God preferred little children to die ... talk of expense ... as though there could be a price on life. Going into homes where already the monstrous disease had spread ... standing face to face with death, seeing the torment of grief ... and the innocent suffering. Dr. Baum wished that he could grab every stubborn person by the throat and make him witness a few of these things!

He smiled gratefully at Grossmutter. How little did she dream what good work she had done with her decisive words and her sturdy luncheon!

Grossmutter slipped out into the bedroom where Hulda had given unmistakable evidence of her feelings in this matter of innoculation. She was crying loudly.

"What is this grief about?" Grossmutter asked.

"I don't want to get stuck," Hulda said. "Will they stick Lottchen, too?"

"Come, Hulda," Grossmutter said patiently. "I don't know what you are expecting, but it is nothing to cry about so fearfully. Dr. Baum has some wonderful medicine in his bag. It is worth more than all the riches in the world. It can save you and Lottchen and Fritz from Tip Terry. And all we need do is let Dr. Baum give it to us."

"But I don't want to be stuck," Hulda protested.

"It isn't going to hurt much," Grossmutter consoled. "Barely more than a mosquito bite. Quick as a wink it will be all over ... and you won't have to be afraid of Tip Terry! Hulda," Grossmutter said, taking the child's trembling hand, "you don't want Lottchen to get Tip Terry, do you?"

"No! No!" Hulda said contritely. She flung her arms about the baby in a fit of projected imagination—Lottchen, black with choking—her little body hot as a furnace—afterward to turn cold and stiff. That was the terrible drama of Tip Terry. Hadn't she heard enough of those horrible tales in these trying days? If one little stick could prevent that . . .

The door opened and Dr. Baum was coming. Suddenly, Hulda wasn't afraid any more. Nor did she want to hate this bald-headed paunchy fellow with the needle in his hand. She smiled to him through her tears and pressed Lottchen's firm little body close to her own, gratefully.

While Dr. Baum was packing his bag he was hastily summoned to Vollmans. "Maggie's sick," little Lizzie Vollman panted. "It's in her neck . . . Mamma says you should come over right away . . . 'cause maybe it's Tip Terry."

Their fears were tragically justified. Dr. Baum came back with the word, "Maggie has it. Frau Vollman won't have the rest of the children protected."

Grossmutter came to the front. "I'll go over and nurse the child," she said calmly. "Our little ones are out of danger. It would be best for Lizzie to take care of the other children. Will it be all right, doctor? I'll do my best to take good care of her, if you will tell me what has to be done."

Dr. Baum was as relieved as a weary traveler who sights a comfortable inn at nightfall. Grossmutter was a godsend.

As his grandmother went away with the doctor, Fritz raced upstairs to bed. He drew the cold featherbed around him, covered his head and sobbed.

Days ran their weary course. Others were stricken. There was scarcely a house where Dr. Baum's buggy was not making a daily call. By now it was evident that the antitoxin's power was not a myth. The Betz children were immune and so was little Rica Jane Toepfer. Where the measures had been taken in time Tip Terry had gained no entrance.

It was something like a passover, Hulda remarked to Rica one morning. Like the blood on Israelite door lintels.

And then came the fatal morning when Gerhart Locher's brother died. Tip Terry had claimed its seventh victim in Winton Place—the fourth for Wooden Shoe Hollow.

It was raining. Dr. Baum's shoulders were bent forward, his face ashen as he rode by on his way to Vollman's. Indelibly fixed on his mind was the picture of Gottlieb's grief by that bedside—holding on to his son's hand . . . praying desperately, calling with all the pathos of a breaking heart—"Carl, Carl . . . don't leave us!" And Maria's hysterical screams which lasted for hours after Carl had passed away. But that was all over now. The lad was gone. And the bicycle preacher was there bringing comfort.

And now the little Vollman girl. If the child recovered it would only be because of Grossmutter's ceaseless vigil at the bedside. Her intuitive good judgment never failed.

Fritz Betz waited in the cinder path for Dr. Baum's return from Vollman's. He was there a long time . . . looked more haggard than ever as he came out of the door.

Fritz stopped the carriage. "How is Maggie, doctor?" he asked tremulously. "Is she all right?"

Dr. Baum scarcely looked at Fritz's upturned face. He looked above the hollow as he answered. "She is very sick. I'll come back to see her tonight."

There would be a crisis tonight then, Fritz reflected. Crisis . . . crisis . . . crisis. All day the thought hammered in his brain. Maggie might go over that same precipice, as Carl Locher had gone over. Crisis . . . crisis . . . crisis . . . choking for breath till the Death Angel came!

And through it all there were those who had the effrontery to ask one to eat . . . to stop staring at the floor as if one were bewitched.

Supper . . . food that might as well have been ashes, and thanksgiving for food and shelter and health, while Maggie lay in the clutches of death. Otto's thanksgiving was a mechanical thing. It went on in the face of every vicissitude.

That night Dr. Baum's carriage rattled by on his way to the crisis.

Fritz crept into the dark parlor as he had done night after night during Maggie's illness. He pressed his face against the cold window pane and watched for shadows in the sickroom across the cabbage patch.

There was not only Grossmutter's familiar silhouette against the drawn shade tonight, but also Herr and Frau Vollman's and Dr. Baum, hovering over the bed.

Anguish filled Fritz's heart to bursting. He thought wildly—Maggie was going to die!! He would never see her again! They would carry her up to Vine Street Hill. He knelt by the window and sobbed.

Rica came into the dark room. He was not aware of her presence until her cool hand was on his temple, smoothing back his hair.

"Fritzie," she whispered. "Is it Maggie?"

He shook his head. His secret was safe with Rica.

"It's a long time you have had," Rica said comfortingly. "And you have been very brave about it. In the morning Maggie will be out of danger. Dr. Baum is with her now."

Rica held his head in her hands, nestled it to her breast. "We must have faith, Fritz. The wait won't seem so long or so hard if we share it with God."

Rica's hands were cool and calm. And the words she spoke in the darkness to the Father of all were good words . . . strong and full of hope. Fritz clung to Rica unashamed.

In the morning Dr. Baum's carriage was gone. The shade was up. Maggie had been saved!

Fritz was all rapture! With wholly new insight he listened to Otto's thanksgiving. Everything in the world was filled with the glory of God. Thanks! Thanks, indeed!

XXVIII *Inwanderer*

~~~~~~

ON WASHINGTON'S BIRTHDAY the preacher-school class had a holiday. Pastor found good use for the time in making preparations for Easter. In the midst of his plan-laying, he was called to the door.

The visitor, a thin lame young man, calmly announced himself as Heinrich Heber, of Germany. Pastor backed over the door sill, clutching at his beard as though he had been struck. "Not Rica's husband!" he ejaculated.

"Yes, sir."

Pastor gripped his hand. "I had not expected this," he said. "But I am happy to meet you here in Cincinnati. Come inside."

As they sat down together in the parlor, Pastor asked, "You just came over?"

"I landed in New York last autumn."

"So you've had a little experience in the country?"

Heinrich smiled wryly. "I'm afraid so."

"Not very pleasant?" Pastor ventured.

"Not in the beginning, but later the days proved more kind. I worked in a cooper shop and lived with a German family who were very congenial and most helpful to me. I rather hated to leave. But how is Rica?"

"Very fine."

"She still does not want to see me?"

"Not the fellow she left in Osnabrück." There was a twinkle in Pastor's eye. "But you are not *that* fellow, are you?"

"I'm still her husband."

"I should never have guessed it. The description doesn't fit. I can find none of the outstanding marks."

"Marks?"

"It doesn't matter," Pastor chuckled. "How could a few years make such a difference in a man? You have changed, haven't you?"

"I wasn't lame when we were married. The accident happened when I was in service. I have lost nearly a third of my weight."

That explained the mystery of the limp, which, according to Rica, should have been a heavy-booted tread. And it explained, too, the regular body contour which assuredly did not conceal bulges!"

"Suppose you tell me what happened since you married Rica."

"I've been discharged from the army because of this," Heinrich said, tapping his lame leg. "I was staying at a sheep farm when your letter came. Had been there for several months."

"A sheep farm?" Pastor asked, his face brightening. "You like farming?"

"Yes. It's what I hope to do now that my soldiering is over."

Pastor sighed in relief at this announcement. "Good, very good Heinrich!"

Heinrich looked up questioningly.

"Rica cannot help but like that," Pastor explained. "You see, she is fond of gardening. Will never tire of it as long as there is a sun to shine and dew to fall. Rica would want no other life. Not for all the kid gloves in the world! That she wouldn't!"

Heinrich's stifled sensibilities took this news as though it were a healing stream flowing over chafed flesh . . . like the sweet oil Leah poured over irate bee stings and bludgeoned knees.

But the stream was quickly dammed with another thought which flung itself into the breach. It might be true that Rica loved gardening as much as he, but what assurance was there that she would accept *him*, soldier, farmer, gardener or sheep raiser? She had run away to avoid him. Apparently she was not sorry.

Heinrich put that question before his counselor. "What do you think Rica will do when she finds I have followed her over here?"

"One cannot tell."

Heinrich's eyes met Pastor's unflinchingly. "She hates me, doesn't she?"

"I don't believe so. Perhaps she hates an imaginary creature whom she has mistaken for you."

"I must see her again!"

Pastor Schicht looked at the boy thoughtfully. "Would you be content just to see her?"

Heinrich shifted. "I think so, sir."

"You shall see her," Pastor said decisively. "Wooden Shoe Hollow is a busy place in the spring. I think Herr Locher could use you. His oldest boy is in Panama and the second oldest died this winter with diphtheria. Yes, I think Gottlieb would be glad to hire you."

To Gottlieb Locher they went immediately. As they alighted Heinrich made a strange request. "May I use my house name of Breen?" he asked.

"Surely, you may use your house name. Many do."

"And Ludwig as my given name?"

"Ludwig Breen?" Pastor asked. "Is that as you wish it?"

"If you please. It will be easier for her."

As Ludwig Breen, Heinrich entered the life stream of Wooden Shoe Hollow and her neighboring colonies.

It was Hulda who brought the news of his coming. "What do you think? Lochers have a hired man. I saw him in the hotbeds. Pastor brought him."

"A hired man?" questioned Grossmutter. "Who is he?"

"An inwanderer from Germany, and he hasn't anybody in the land . . . just like you, Rica. Isn't that strange?"

Rica smiled. "And what else did you learn?"

"He's crippled. Ernst met him. Says he'll never, never make a gardener 'cause he isn't strong enough."

"Chaff! What does Ernst know?" Grossmutter asked.

It was not until Saturday night that Ludwig came face to face with Rica. "This is Ludwig Breen," Ernst said by way of introduction. "He is staying at Locher's."

Ludwig held his breath. Rica flashed him a smile of welcome. "Herr Breen," she said lightly. "We are glad to have you at our crowd." She tilted her coroneted head to the side. A smile extended across her flushed cheek, but there was no hint of recognition.

Ludwig turned crimson. Was this a pose or could it actually be true that she did not recognize him? In a moment she was off waltzing with Emil Mueller.

"Nice fellow this young Breen, eh?" Mueller speculated.

"What part of Germany does he come from?" Rica asked.

"Haven't heard. Must ask him."

"I don't suppose he dances."

"Probably can't with that lame leg," Mueller replied.

Rosie sallied across the floor. "We want you to have a good time," she said, coming to Ludwig with pink outstretched hands. Her voice took on the dignity of polished High German. It was one of Rosie's greatest resources—her command of High German. It rose above her defects of speech.

She sat beside Ludwig on the bench. "Are you going to church with the Lochers tomorrow?"

He was.

"Will you come to our house for dinner afterward? We go to St. Matthews, too. You could go home with us if you like. Papa always likes to hear news from Germany. He's never been back since he came to America in 1870."

"Thank you. I'll come."

Rosie's freckles gathered in a cluster around her nose. "Mamma said I should invite you. . . . Do you like thick egg pies with cinnamon and nutmeg? That's what we have for Sunday dinner, after the apricots and rice."

Ludwig smiled.

Rosie's freckles receded to their wonted place. "You don't dance, do you?" she asked, tapping her feet in time to Yust's jerky playing."

"No, I'm sorry, I don't dance," he answered. "But I enjoy listening to the music and watching."

"Me too," Rosie settled against the wall. "I'd much rather sit and listen. Honest and truly I would." Under the circumstances what she said was quite true.

Ludwig's eyes followed Rica about the floor. From one arm to another she traveled. Waltz, polka, quadrille, she danced them all with equal grace. There was in her manner—pure joy of dancing. Sheer beauty of rhythm. Supple motion, melting her lithe young body into the melody. And that responsive glint in her eyes, friendly and engaging. Not at all like the frightened wistful bride he remembered.

The crowd was in a mood far more hopeful than it had been for months, now that the scourge of frost was over and, likewise, the terrifying epidemic of diphtheria.

A winter of tribulation was giving place to the brighter momentum of spring. And spring, for garden youth, was no time for despair!

Feeling that sense of joy Herman and Sophia went to the crowd, leaving the baby with Minna Betz. It was an added treat to the crowd to have Herman playing for them. Again and again he roused them to spirited singing.

No wonder Rica found such joy in her dancing tonight! Memories mingled sweetly with the music. She danced with Herman. Once more his strong hand held her and they were one. Every breath left its mark inside, not a mark of pain, but of warmth—gladness at dancing with Herman, as of old.

And for him the night was golden also. By his shy glance of admiration it was plain. Treasured because it brought back memories of other days at the crowd. It was good to meet with comrades again, to dance and sing. Sophia was enjoying the reunion also. They must come often. No reason why they should deny themselves this fellowship.

During the intermission talk drifted to Gerhart. Would he come home now? Hadn't he had enough of adventure?

Like droning bees around honeysuckle, gossip persisted in coming back to Gerhart no matter how many other topics were discussed.

Rica alone felt that he would not come back. The Panama Canal was not finished. Months of work remained to be done. The *Volksblatt* said so. And while the great task was unfinished, Gerhart would remain there, even if he longed desperately for a sight of Wooden Shoe Hollow and those who called it home.

Rica looked across the hall. Sitting over there on the bench beside Rosie was the young man who was to take Gerhart's place here at home. He was a strange fellow, with his quiet, preoccupied manner. Was it just her imagination that his eye rested rather frequently upon her? But, no, turn after turn, she met his absorbed gaze as she danced around the hall.

It was as though he were an owl perched in a treetop watching the revels of so many chattering squirrels and frisking hares below. But he was not owlish. The simile ended there.

There was something vaguely familiar about the lad. Reminded her of someone—but who? Ludwig Breen; the name carried no mental bypaths. Breen, Ludwig Breen? There was something about him she ought to know. Her subconscious was insistent. But amid lamps and laughter, the subconscious could not speak its best. The conscious, which concerned itself with the deep flowing wave in the boy's hair, a lame leg, eyes full of suffering, cheeks sunken with recent illness, all these decried the murmurs of subconscious and said arbitrarily, "You have never seen Ludwig Breen before!"

Rosie had taken a fancy to him. Her eyes were crossed upon him in a state of perpetual fascination. And Yust was glaring behind his accordion. There were others who saw Rosie's mounting interest in Gottlieb's new hired man. The crowd's practical jokestress was one of them.

She coaxed a male accomplice to ask Rosie for a dance. Rosie, flustered but pleased, sallied forth to waltz. Then Annie sent for Ludwig Breen and presented him with a flaked cocoanut custard pie. "It's from Rosie," she said. "She was backward about giving it to you herself. Here, have a piece." She sliced a quarter of the pie and laid it in his hand.

"Many thanks," Ludwig said.

In a moment his teeth were tangled in the meshes of cotton concealed in the custard. The crowd was in an uproar. Annie scored again with the good old cotton pie!

Ludwig's face burned. So the fat cross-eyed girl had played a trick on him! He put down the pie and extracted the cotton from his teeth.

Yust Bobke whistled and clapped his hands in glee. "*Hoo*ray! *Hoo*ray!" he brayed. "*Hoo*ray for the Bavarian!"

Everybody was having a good time. It was a harmless prank. Ludwig grinned back at them. Perhaps now that he had been initiated he would be one of them. That was the way it had been in the army.

Rica was smiling impishly at him. What part had she played in this?

Suddenly, a bevy of young fellows seized him and hoisted him upon their shoulders. Herman pulled out his accordion to full length and began to play the time-honored march of the crowd—the rollicking song of good fellowship filled the hall.

Ich hatt' einen Kameraden
Einen besser'n find'st du nicht.

There was the goose step and the snap of American "left foot—right foot" as the crowd joined the parade:

Gloria, Gloria,
Gloria, Victoria!

they sang with the crescendo of youth.

Ludwig rode the crest of the wave and felt within himself exaltation such as he had seldom experienced in his life. The noisy hall was suddenly blurred before him.

Marching in the parade behind him was Rica. Unless she was a clever actress . . . she did not know him. He would be free to win her—not by law—but by self. That held challenge. She did not know!

Before the evening was over Ludwig had his chance to talk to her. She came across the smoke-filled hall fanning her face. An impish smile was still at large.

She sat beside him. "Are you having a good time?"

"I've never had a better."

"Good. That is what we hope. Do you like America?"

"Oh yes, Fräulein . . ."

"Heber." Rica supplied the name with ease.

"You are from Germany, also, I've heard," Ludwig began.

"Yes, I came here a few years ago. One soon becomes acquainted in Wooden Shoe Hollow. Would you believe I've almost forgotten what Germany is like? Tell me, do the wagons roll through the cobbled streets as busily as ever? And do the markets have trays stacked high with snapskuchen and sweet wood?"

"I haven't seen the markets," Ludwig answered. "I came from the peasant lands where there was nothing but sheep."

"And how were the sheep?" Rica asked.

"The sheep fared better than their shepherd," Ludwig answered, matching her playful mood. "And that is why I came to America."

"And left your poor sheep to fend for themselves?"

"Germany is full of shepherds."

"And America is full of sheep, though Wooden Shoe Hollow has only a pair of goats to its credit."

Rica's coronet braid lay about her head neatly. A starched ruffle sat pertly around her throat. Nestled in the ruffle was a pin Ludwig remembered. A sunburst pin of gold set with diamond jets. It had reminded him, during the wedding ceremony, of a jeweled octopus. The pin seemed like a magic link—joining together past, present and future.

"I hope you will learn to like it here as much as I have," Rica was saying. "There isn't another place like it on any continent."

Rosie, dismayed by the trick played on her as well as on Ludwig, could not stem her tears of woe and anger. She hated Annie, the smart aleck, for crushing this priceless bud of friendship before it could come to blossom . . . the fairest bud on the bush. But such is woman's ruthlessness, Rosie philosophized sadly. Unable to control her emotions she ran from the hall.

Ludwig wouldn't come to dinner tomorrow. That was sure! And it had been going so nicely. For one brief hour her world had been agog and aglitter with the sunshine of romance; now it hurtled on through gray space devoid of light and romance. Rosie wept bitterly.

XXIX *Consecration*

~~~~~~

IT WAS THE EVE of presentation of confirmands at St. Matthew's Church. Back and forth in the catechism Minna turned, putting Hulda and Fritz through a final grilling in preparation for tomorrow's public examination.

"Fritz, you will have to speak louder, back in church they'll never hear you! And Hulda, stop twisting your fingers. If you do that tomorrow you'll have your handkerchief in shreds. Keep your mind on your lessons and you will be all right!"

"What if I get scared?" Hulda asked.

"Scared of what?" Minna asked. "There isn't anything to be scared of, *if* you know your lessons. I hope you will both do better than Ernst. . . . It is no pleasure to sit in the pew and listen to your children when they don't know where the next word is coming from. That it isn't!"

Nor was it a pleasure for the unfortunate candidate, Hulda noted mentally.

Minna laid aside the little book. "Well, we've gone all through the catechism. Now study your Bible history."

While Hulda and Fritz recited miracles and parables and beatitudes and checked the deeds of apostles, prophets and patriarchs, Minna proudly laid out the clothing they were to wear tomorrow.

The anxiety was soon over. All the class did very well before the congregation and the "bicycle" preacher was proud of them.

A week later Minna stood at the ironing board pressing Hulda's white dress with all its flounces and ruffles. The rack held three petticoats which were to bring out the loveliness of the frock. There was so much to be done, for tomorrow the children would be confirmed.

Rica brushed Hulda's sparse hair vigorously. It had been washed and sunned all afternoon at the window. With even strokes Rica brushed and massaged until Hulda's scalp tingled. Then Grossmutter came with a plate of water and began wetting strands and putting them into crimpers.

Fritzie watched the proceedings. That was what came of being a girl. All Minna needed to do for him was to lay out his new suit, the ceremonious white gloves and the white bow tie.

What would Maggie think of him in a white bow tie and gloves? Fritz's heart smote him whenever he thought how he had almost lost Maggie a few months ago. Tomorrow, they would be confirmed . . . together.

Next morning Friech and Lizzie Vollman took the three confirmands to Church in the barouche. Otto took the rest of the two families in his market wagon. He also stopped to pick up Ludwig Breen.

Ludwig leaped into the wagon and sat beside Rica. Lottchen, who was seated on Rica's lap, smiled and reached for the tie pin which sat temptingly on his gay cravat.

"No, no, baby," Rica warned, as she put down the little fingers. "Bites."

Lottchen's eyebrows shot up in surprise. "Bites?" She laughed scornfully as she seized the pin and put the ruby set to her mouth.

"Come, Lottchen," Rica said. "Give the uncle his pin."

Lottchen refused to part with her treasure.

The incident was forgotten. When, later in the day, Rica thought of it, the pin was missing. She was chagrined.

That afternoon she slipped away from the reception which brought many neighbors and relatives to the home to honor Hulda and Fritz. She went to the Lochers to apologize to Ludwig for the loss of his pin.

In the household there was a simple reception in honor of Louise Locher, the oldest daughter. Only a few close relatives had been bidden.

Maria's hat lay on the parlor table. The veil spilled over the table edge like a black waterfall. Rica looked at the veil. With a pang she thought of the lad whose loss it betokened . . . and she thought, too, of Gerhart, for whom hearts must ache anew today.

Louise had received a letter from Gerhart. The first letter he had sent home. Would Rica like to see it? It was right inside her song book.

DEAREST LOUISE:

I wish I could be with you today, but there are hundreds of miles between us, and that is impossible. So, I'll send you my best brotherly wishes for your Confirmation Day. Think of me, will you, Louise?

I know how much Carl is missed. It was an awful shock to hear of his death. I would have come home, but it was too late when the news came. I had no rest until Pastor's letter arrived. Thought of all of you day and night.

Pastor tells me he has found a good hired man for Papa.

Louise, tell Papa I'm going to try to help as much as I can. I'm sending him $2.00, and an extra $1.00 for you.

I hope that you will have a beautiful Confirmation Day.

Your loving brother,
GERHART

Rica read the note with a tingle of excitement. So Gerhart was engrossed with his work on the Panama Canal . . . she wondered if he still thought of her.

Ludwig came downstairs.

"I'm so sorry baby lost your pin," Rica said. "I've searched the wagon, but it isn't to be found."

"That's all right," Ludwig answered. "You needn't worry."

"It may have been valuable."

"It wasn't," he said. "Certainly not as valuable as that." He pointed to Rica's sunburst pin.

"This?" Rica asked. "It's just a piece of jewelry my mother had."

"It's very pretty," Ludwig commented.

Maria came with cherry cordial and cocoanut cake. She nodded her head perfunctorily when Rica congratulated her upon Louise's confirmation.

In Panama Gerhart had little time to think of home. Although it was Sunday a crisis made it necessary for the men to be out working on the canal.

Supplies were rushed in from the north. Picks flew. Shovels dug deep into the earth to widen and deepen the ditch that was ultimately to be a stream. Tomorrow, government men would arrive to survey the progress of the canal. Influential men. All must be on the job, working like Trojans to pull the horse within their gates.

Gerhart had hoped to help survey today, but all hands were needed in the trenches. The digging had to be at the post by sundown. Orders. To those who had been digging for days the post was like a goal post.

Perspiration and grime covered their faces, callouses padded their thick fingers and they were well-nigh exhausted. Still their shovels swung up and down with a rhythm like that of boatmen. Here and there some weary lad would climb out of the ditch and lay prone upon his back to rest for a while, gather wind and energy. The hot sun beat down upon their bronzed backs as they worked.

A Negro climbed up to rest beside Gerhart. "Ah feels so tired, ah could jus' lay mah pick down forevah . . . 'pears lak there's no end to diggin', suh . . . ah is so tired . . . ah jus' wants to sing."

And sing he did. Low pleading in his colorful voice. The hot trench bank became, for the moment, a "Praise House" in Georgia, where he formerly sang in the choir:

> Mah Lordy calls me
> He calls me by the thunder,
> The trumpet sounds
> Within a-mah soul.

The cry of a race was in his song. Something utterly simple and childlike. There was a rapture in his red swollen eyes and a rhythm in the bony feet, which swayed from horizontal to perpendicular with each beat of the song.

Gerhart gazed at him in fascination. He was strangely drawn to the man's unguessed spiritual reservoir. A contrast, to be sure, was this kind of singing to the somber chorales of his own religious experience. Yet there was unity of spirit underlying the two divergent moods.

Gerhart thought of home. Of Louise who was to kneel at the altar today. His own blessing came back on the wings of the Negro's spiritual:

> Let the words of my mouth and
> The meditation of my heart be
> Acceptable in Thy sight, O God,
> My strength and my Redeemer!

The current of his thought digressed to Pastor Schicht as he looked at preacher school. That twinkle in his eye when he was in the mood to tease, the sharp look of disapproval, too, and the slow pleased emphasis he placed upon his comment—"Sehr, *sehr gut!*"

It was just like Pastor to concern himself about the gardening problem at home . . . find a helper.

The Negro picked up his chorus:

> Steal away
> Steal away,
> Steal away to Jesus.
> Steal away
> Steal away
> Steal away home.

Gerhart quivered. His brother Carl's face seemed close beside him, as close as when they lay side by side in bed as little boys. Realization bore in upon him heavily. He would never again see Carl's face beside him on a pillow. Home would never be the same. Going home could never be complete reunion. His brother would be missing . . . always missing.

Gerhart brushed his hand across his face and wiped away the mingled tears and perspiration as he leaped into the ditch. The Negro sang on wearily, plaintively:

> Steal away,
> Steal away
> Steal away to Jesus.

Later that evening a tired army of diggers laid down their tools. A long hard day of labor it had been, but they looked in contentment at the flag flying at the top of the pole which marked their conquest! One day nearer to the sea. One day nearer.

"Locher," the division officer called, as Gerhart lit his lantern to go back to the barracks. "Come with me to the office. We've some things to talk over."

Gerhart followed his officer up the path, to the office of the construction company.

"Sit down and have a smoke."

"I don't smoke," Gerhart said. "It takes my wind. A fellow needs his wind—digging."

The officer grinned. "I think you've had your last day of it."

"Sir?"

"Digging, I mean. You go with the engineering unit tomorrow."

"I?" Gerhart repeated.

"Yes. Tony tells me you are anxious to break into that work."

"I surely am, sir. Do you think I will be able to make it? I haven't had the training."

"My boy, any fellow who has blasted and sweat and dug as you have—without a mutter—is every inch an engineer! Your friend has shown me some of your sketches. You are decidedly on the right trestle!" He took Gerhart's calloused hand and shook it heartily.

Gerhart raced to the barracks jubilantly. The tired feeling was gone. If it were morning now he could march right out with the engineers and go to work! But it was evening. Gerhart sank upon his sheeted cot and sighed . . . Palm Sunday. . . . A day of rejoicing, palms, hosannas . . . and he had spent it digging in a ditch!

Louise must have looked grown-up in her long white dress . . . a carnation in her hair.

In an obscure corner of Munich, Palm Sunday came also with its melody and devotion.

Frances Holt lay in bed listening to the brazen clock ticking away the hours. Her aunt came into the room. "Just awake?" she asked.

"No, I've been awake a long time, Aunt Agatha. I could hear the music faintly and the bells. It was lovely."

"Here is a palm," Aunt Agatha said. "It is *such* a lovely morning, my dear."

Frances reached for the palm and fingered it lovingly. "I wonder if there are bells like ours in New York."

Aunt Agatha winced. "I wouldn't be thinking of New York, Frances dear. Think of Munich, the fun we shall have going to the theater when you are well again!"

"I wonder," Frances went on, "if he heard the bells this morning. I prayed for him."

Her aunt stopped over the bed and kissed her tenderly. "Can you never forget?" she sighed.

All day the clock ticked away beside the bed.

Late in the afternoon Aunt Agatha visited with the neighbors. The room darkened slowly and soon only the rosy glow of the vigil light shone through the shadows.

Soft restful night.

It was easy to find . . . God . . . alone this way.

When Aunt Agatha returned Frances lay as if asleep. Palm in hand she had gone into His presence, leaving her candle flickering in the dark.

XXX *Sunrise and Sunset*

LOTTCHEN TODDLED up and down the hotbed rows in search of the pink basket which Hulda assured her the Easter bunny had brought.

In every garden children scampered. Cries of "Here's mine, here's mine," resounded through the glen.

"Here's mine," Lottchen piped, when she spied her basket hanging upon the pump handle. She clapped her hands in delight at the array of surprises in the nest. A looking-glass egg, yellow chicks, colored eggs and a huge chocolate rabbit!

And there was the thrill of watching the Easter lamb dance in the sun. Through smoked glass she stared in fascination at the fiery ball spinning around up in the heavens. "The Easter lamb! The Easter lamb!" she sang. "Grossie, the Easter lamb is dancing in the sun!"

"To be sure!" Grossmutter answered, peering through the glass. "Once again, the Easter lamb dances for good little children."

Emil Mueller tripped down the hill whistling "Morgenrot." A market basket swung upon his arm.

Yetta stood at the window and watched him. How many years had she not colored eggs and baked cookies for Emil's treat to the children? It was something of a rite—unpacking the cooky cutters, cutting out chicks, ducks and bunnies, decorating them with yellow icing; tinting large white eggs which took colors matchlessly —lush reds, purple, azure blue, and lettuce green. Hers was the joy of creating—Emil's the joy of giving.

Yetta watched him go from house to house with his basket. Emil was dining out today, and she would make her annual pilgrimage to Hamilton to visit with her brother Stephen and his family. Emil would take her down to the C.H. and D. station as soon as he came home. He always did. . . .

The Easter dance at the hall was the largest there had been all winter. Ludwig met new people at every turn. There were visitors from the Avenue and "Back Creek" crowds. All were one family in the crowded hall.

Herman played his accordion merrily. He danced with Sophia as though their romance had just begun. There was contagion in his smile, exuberance in his song, exaltation in his nimble fingers. The Plattdeutsch summed it all in the one word *"Lustigkeit."*

Rica learned the reason for Herman's unusual *Lustigkeit* when she waltzed with Sophia. "There is going to be another one," Sophia whispered. "I've known for a time, but I didn't want to tell Herman while things were so bad; but now that winter is over, there is nothing to worry about. Tomorrow he will go to the factory for the last time."

"You are very happy, aren't you?" Rica asked.

"As a cream-fed cat," Sophia answered. "Nothing fails Herman, baby and I. Nothing in the whole wide world. By next fall we shall have our little boy. I can hardly wait, Rica. It is so wonderful!"

Rica smiled and then turned away quickly with tear-filled eyes. Next fall she would be in Germany. . . .

The music stopped and the two friends parted.

Ludwig came to Rica, fidgeting with his tie as he crossed the hall. Rica slipped a smooth knot. "There," she said, "now, you look like a regular Amerikaner!"

"What else do I need?" Ludwig asked.

"A hat."

"Instead of my cap?"

"Yes."

"What else?"

"A striped shirt."

"And a new tongue?"

Rica laughed. "The tongue will come later, Ludwig."

"Did it for you?"

"With Hulda's help."

"I'm afraid I can't learn English from the Locher children. They are as timid as mice."

"How do you like gardening?"

"I do like it," Ludwig answered. "Better than anything I have ever done."

"Truly?" asked Rica. The fleeting thought—that expression—where had she seen it before . . . ? "What part of Germany was your home?" she asked.

"My childhood home was in Frankfort. I remember it best. After that I lived in Berlin until it was time to serve.

Rica started at the mention of service. "You?" she asked. In the same moment she was sorry for needlessly hurting him.

"I didn't last very long," Ludwig admitted. "But I tried."

So then his lameness was *not* a lifelong affliction. Ludwig must have chafed under the necessity of giving up his adventurous life. Became a shepherd out of necessity. Yes, Ludwig, too, was running away from disappointment. That's why he was here in America. She smiled wistfully at this kindred spirit as she rose to dance with Herman.

Ludwig leaned against the wall. Looked after her. There was that haunting glance again. Strange. Very, very strange.

Herman sang as he danced. Soon everybody was singing the old ballad "Lorelei." Ludwig, alone, was silent—pensive.

Herman's favorite song, it had always been. Ever since he had first heard it from his mother's lips as she drove from door to door in Camp Washington, with her blind horse and huckster wagon.

Tonight Herman was singing his beloved "Lorelei" for the last time.

Easter Monday was like an afterthought of Sunday. The sun shone brightly. The holiday spirit was abroad. Children were home from school. There were few who gardened on this traditional semi-holiday.

But no matter how Wooden Shoe Hollow took its calendar, the

world of industry knew this day only as another Monday, the beginning of a busy week. Herman was on his way to work at dusk.

As he reached the top of the hill he turned and looked down upon the hollow, back at his little white house, emerging from the shadows. Tonight was the last night he would need to spend away from home. Tomorrow morning he would be a gardener again, not a shop man. He would be turning up earth, raking it fine and smooth. God grant that the crops would grow well this year. Tomorrow evening he would rest in his Morris chair, with little Rica Jane on his lap and Sophia beside him.

Rica and Hulda joined Otto in a shopping excursion Back Creek. Hulda's shoes were in need of soles, but Otto had no time to repair them since it was seeding time. Thus, for one of the rare times in her life, Hulda was to have the thrill of getting shoes back from the shoemaker's. The edges would be trimmed neatly and there would be tassels, too. The shoemaker always embellished plain-looking shoes with bright tassels.

Otto was driving Back Creek to get seeds and tools. He had passed the word along to his neighbors. And now he had rakes, seeds, pipes, glass, putty and axle grease to bring home with him for them. He was to stop at the blacksmith shop, too, and have the horse shod.

During this time Rica would be attending to the list of purchases for the wives. Sulphur, sassafras, tea, middlings, corset laces and ticking.

As the wagon lumbered past Locher's garden Ludwig called to them and came limping through the hotbeds with a dollar. "Heard you were going Back Creek," he said. "Will you please get me a striped shirt?"

Rica's dimples deepened as she took the bill. "I'll be glad to, Ludwig," she said.

Otto clucked and drove on. "That beats everything," he said. "In the land only a few weeks and he is after Yankee trappings already. Why does he want a *striped* shirt anyway, Rickey?"

"No young fellow wants to look as if he had just landed," Rica replied.

"That beats all," Otto reiterated. "It surely does. Why, when

I came over I wore my old clothes four years before buying so much as a suit of underwear. Had enough to scratch to pay off my trip, without buying *striped* shirts!"

"I don't think Herr Breen is poor," Hulda said. "Wouldn't surprise me if he was an aristocrat!"

Rica and Hulda enjoyed their shopping excursion. One by one the articles were checked off the list, until they came to the shirt. From counter to counter Rica wandered. She deliberated, studied and compared. Finally, she decided to sew the shirt herself. It was a better plan, for there were delightful silk-striped shirtings to be had.

She selected green silk-striped material. She couldn't resist the temptation to buy a green tie to match the shirt. Of course, Ludwig hadn't asked for a tie . . . Hulda distinctly remembered.

And then Rica had a special bit of business of her own. "Come, Hulda," she said. "Let's stop at the jewelry store."

There they waited while the jeweler transformed Rica's sunburst pin into a tie pin for Ludwig.

"Isn't this old?" the jeweler asked.

"I suppose it is."

"If you would care to sell it," he suggested. "I'd give you ten dollars."

"Ten dollars?" Rica repeated. "It isn't worth that much, is it? I knew it was gold."

"It isn't the gold, or the diamond jets . . . it's the expert craftsmanship. This is surely the handiwork of some old Danish silversmith. It has all the characteristics. Want it made up or want to sell it?"

Hulda looked at Rica—her eyes wide open.

Rica's cheeks were afire. She rubbed her finger tips along the edges, and then placed the pin back in the jeweler's hand. "As long as it isn't the stones that are valuable . . . please make it up."

Hulda's amazement grew to indignation. Ten dollars was ten dollars! A whole month's wages, in fact, that's what it was! And Rica was giving it up to this crippled inwanderer just because Lottchen lost his "stick pin." It wasn't either fair or necessary. There were other "stick pins" to be had for fifty cents. The clockmaker who came to Wooden Shoe Hollow once a year had beautifully studded ones in his velvet case. Some of them cost less than fifty cents!

"Where did you get the pin?" Hulda wanted to know, as they walked down the Avenue to get the shoes which by now were red tasseled and shined as well as soled.

"It was my mother's. She wore it more than any other pin in her jewel box. It must have been my grandmother's originally. Grandmother came to Germany from Copenhagen when she was a bride. Hulda, will you keep this secret with me . . . about the pin?"

Hulda nodded.

The two sauntered down Colerain Avenue to the watering trough, where Otto was waiting for them.

When they reached home Ludwig was the first to call for his package.

"I hope you won't mind," Rica said. "The shirting was so much prettier that I bought it. I'll make the shirt for you." She handed him the pin. "This is to replace the one baby lost."

Ludwig reddened. "I'll surely treasure the pin, Rica, but I wouldn't have wanted you to do this." There was a sensitive quiver at his mouth.

Rica laughed lightly. "Nothing to fret about," she said. "It's no more than right. . . . I'll make the shirt before Saturday."

"No hurry," Ludwig said. "It's so nice of you to make it for me. If it's finished by Pentecost, that will be all right."

Rica smiled. Finished by Pentecost . . . the day, when in the old country, every young man wanted to looked his best. The day of betrothals and high churchly dignities. Ludwig should have his shirt for Pentecost!

Maria Locher was alert. When Ludwig came into supper she asked pointedly, "Didn't you get the shirt?"

"Rica is going to sew it for me."

"Humph!" said Maria. "At it again! . . . I wouldn't trust that girl if I were you, Ludwig. She takes every man for a fool, that one! My Gerhart, too. Look how she ruined him. Got him so set on her that he didn't know his own soul any more. Now he runs the wide world around looking for he doesn't know what. Herman Toepfer, too. The more the merrier! She's just a common flirt. Take my advice, boy, and stay away from her!"

Ludwig fumbled at the roller towel. His throat ached. It was as though he had been lashed and driven through fire and hail. He made a pretense of eating supper, then fled upstairs and flung the pin into a chest drawer. Anger seethed inside. Humiliation. Inner darkness in which there was no glimmer of hope.

The woman wouldn't lie about her own son . . . no matter what was true about Herman Toepfer.

Worst of all Ludwig wanted Rica now. Loved her. Sought her as unswervingly as a satellite seeks its planet. To follow any other orbit would mean destruction.

Had he stayed in Germany he would not have known, but now there could be no escape from the bondage of his love for Rica. Maria's warning had come too late!

Meanwhile, Rica was at the opposite end of the scale. She spread out her material upon the table in Grossmutter's room. She placed the new tie upon it. "Like it?" she asked.

Grossmutter fingered the silk stripe. "So this is the style now," she said. "Yes, I'm afraid I do like it."

Rica's scissors were already at work. Out of Ernst's old shirt she was making a pattern.

"Ludwig is only a slight man. Not as husky as our Ernst," Grossmutter commented.

"But his shoulders are broad. Hadn't you noticed, Grossie?"

Grossmutter looked at the girl quizzically, but Rica went on snipping unperturbed.

Suddenly, there was fierce knocking at the door downstairs. A scream—a strange man's voice answering Minna's scream. "Come quickly," he was saying, "the wife has collapsed."

Minna whipped on her shawl and dashed down the pathway to Toepfer's.

"What is the matter down there?" Grossmutter called.

Otto called up the stairs in a small choked voice—"Men from Procter and Gamble. They say Herman was killed at work. Burned to death . . ." The door creaked. Otto ran across the land to Sophia's dim light.

XXXI Readjustment

ON THURSDAY AFTERNOON Wooden Shoe Hollow, as one family, paid a last tribute to Herman Toepfer.

Sophia, whose sorrow none could assuage, lay back on her pillows and watched the procession move from her door, bearing Herman away from her forever. . . . The long black cortege ascended the hill slowly. . . . She could not go with him on this last journey, for the tragedy which robbed her of him robbed her also of the little son who was to have come in the autumn. She lay ill. Only faithful Anna Meuke remained with her during the sad hours of that afternoon.

In the first carriage the elder Vollmans sat in stony grief at the tragedy which had struck with such sudden fury. Over and over Lizzie sobbed, "It just can't be, oh, it can't be, Papa."

And Friech Vollman shook his head. "Seems like yesterday Herman came for our Sophie and we were all so happy. Who would have thought this waited for them so soon? Poor innocent ones . . ."

Rica sat numbly in the carriage with the Betz family. Minna and Otto sobbed continuously. It had been no idle boast that Herman was as their own son!

Grossmutter was thinking of the land which Herman would never till again. Of Sophia, who would have to bear her burdens alone from this day forth. Grossmutter, who had been widowed when young, knew the weight of that burden. The Psalmist was right—"Man is as grass."

Upon Rica there sat a hush like that of the deserted village, and that was her mood. There was no frenzied projection into the future, only looking backward—thinking of many yesterdays and the mingled pain and happiness they had shared in those yesterdays. . . . Herman's first kiss under the shimmering Christmas tree . . . the moment when she pinned the rosebud in his lapel on his wedding day . . . countless times when she had danced with him at the crowd . . . listening to him singing and playing his accordion. . . . Could death take all this away?

And Rica thought of Sophia. Sophia, who loved Herman ever since love had meaning for her. All the world was embodied in him. Could she make whole a life so stripped of its motive power? It wasn't things that counted with Sophia. Rica knew that. Things Procter and Gamble could provide. Hadn't they promised every assistance? But that would not bring Herman back to her.

Pastor was deeply grieved. Never a death in his flock but took a kind of inner strength from him. Now . . . it was Herman. Snatched from life at the very crest of manhood. Herman crystallized every high ideal of Wooden Shoe Hollow in his person. He had lived with courage and sanity. He was generous and kind, and had loved his own with true Christian love. Never had there labored a finer lad in the gardens of Cincinnati. If they had all followed his faithful example there would never have been such sins as drunkenness and stable stealing and Sabbath carpentry!

And, as he lived, so had he died.

To save a building left in his care, Herman gave his life. And to save those who might be in danger behind the wall he shouted, clamored and beat down a door. He had fallen into a cauldron which instantly snuffed out his life.

That alarm saved his fellow workers from horrible death by explosion and fire. The building was saved, but he had perished!

What need for eulogy? God knew the soul of Herman Toepfer. And these, his friends, knew it also. Nevertheless there were words which must be said:

Herman Rudolph Toepfer—son of Wilhelm and Jane Middlekamp Toepfer. Born August 20, 1888, in Düsseldorf, Germany. Came to America as a baby. Orphaned when seven years old, and was received into the Mount Auburn Orphanage, whence Otto and Minna Betz had taken him at the age of eleven years. (Otto's thick set jaw quivered. Minna sobbed afresh.)

Was confirmed at Old First, where also he had stood as a bridegroom and plighted troth to Sophia Vollman just three summers ago.

Herman's life had been an example for all, for his charity, meekness, earnest labor. Who had not been blessed by knowing Herman Toepfer?

Now that he had gone to his eternal home there was a holy obligation to fulfill. Herman had left a widow and child. "If you have loved this man," Pastor Schicht pleaded, "then let these, his own, never suffer hardship which you can prevent."

Pastor dwelt upon the words of Jesus, "Blessed are the pure in heart, for they shall see God."

The last farewells were said.

Friends filed past the casket in reverent silence, gazed sadly at the mold which lay there. This was not Herman. The members of the Gärtner Unterstützungsverein lay their hands upon his charred ones, mercifully gloved.

Tragedy! How well these men knew it. Death . . . it came unbidden always to take the finest of crops, the finest of men. There were old pioneers, upon whose thin white hair the blue stained glass of the church windows cast a pallor. Their slow doddering footsteps mingled with the steady tread of the younger brethren. On every shoulder was the silver-fringed badge of mourning of the society.

From St. Matthew's Church the cortege moved on to Vine Street Cemetery—where many another gardener lay at rest. Behind the stone chapel they laid him. At the foot of his mother's grave. There the solemn commitment was made: "Ashes to ashes —dust to dust." The chaplain of the gardeners' association read the brief service of his order. Like a phalanx of guards the men stood bareheaded in attendance. Under their feet the grass was bursting forth in fresh green.

Among those who were gathered at the grave was Ludwig. As he turned about he faced Rica. The ghostly whiteness of her face shocked him. She was leaning heavily upon Ernst's arm. The last hour had shaken her composure badly. She *had* loved Herman. It hadn't been vanity and conquest. Maria Locher had erred. Ludwig's tangled feeling vibrated like a steel string.

Rica took up her cross and returned to Wooden Shoe Hollow with Minna, Otto and Grossmutter. She went, at once, to Sophia. She was there when Pastor arrived after the funeral service.

"Come in, Pastor," she said. "Sophia is waiting for you."

The anguish of David was upon Sophia:

> My tears have been my meat
> Day and night
> While they continually say unto me
> Where is now thy God?

Out of the pain and distress of her suffering Sophia soon felt the strength of Pastor's prayer sustain her. Grave, enduring words of the Saviour:

> I am the resurrection and the life.

Anna Menke and Rica came into the room. Knopf was sitting on the floor turning leaves in Rica Jane's picture book, while the baby looked at the pictures.

"Knopf stay by, Herr Pastor," he said. "Knopf stay by Sophia."

"That's a fine fellow," Pastor answered.

"He wants to stay here all the time," Sophia said.

"Stay by," Knopf repeated from his corner. "Knopf must stay by. Not? Herman gone to Himmel now. Knopf stay by!"

Some animal sense of need had driven the idiot to come to Sophia that afternoon. She had defended him against many a cuff while she lived in her parents' home. And Herman had been a guardian friend. That much was not past Knopf's memory and comprehension. He looked at Pastor for approval. Anxiety pressed him.

"Knopf chop wood," he reasoned. "Knopf sprinkle celery. Knopf pump wash box. . . . Knopf stay by, not?"

"You shall stay if Papa will let you," Sophia answered listlessly.

"You do not want to give up the garden, Frau Toepfer?"

A startled look came over Sophia's wan face. "I can't give it up, Pastor! Herman wouldn't want me to part with it, now or ever!"

Pastor's black eyes glistened with quick tears. "Very well," he answered. "Surely, the place is yours and no one can take it from you. There will always be those who will help you."

"Not a thing must be changed," Sophia said. "The celery rows he laid out, the flower garden he planted and the hotbeds. Just the way he made it that's how I want to keep it. It's all baby will ever have of her father," she sobbed.

Knopf picked up the baby and carried her to Sophia's arm. "Knopf stay by," he chattered. "Knopf stay by Sophie."

Pastor laid his broad hand upon Knopf's shoulders. "That is a man, Knopf."

And so it was arranged.

Knopf dragged his cot across the land and carried it to Sophia's attic.

A gleam of light shot through his life. Sophia was never to know regret for having taken him into her home.

From that day forth he toiled tirelessly, carried out every task faithfully and asked no reward but his daily food and clothing.

And each night before he went to bed he knelt at the attic window and looked out at one bright red star. Herman's star. He prayed half to Herr Gott and half to Herman. Always, he wanted to know if what he had done that day had pleased Herman. And the red star shone down in a way that made Knopf believe that Herman was satisfied.

"Herman," he sighed frequently, upon leaving his reverie, "Knopf want to go to Himmel by and by. Tell lieber Gott, please Herman."

Sophia looked up at her friends—Pastor, Knopf, Anna and Rica—and sighed gratefully for them all.

Life was not altogether empty, nor would Herman be wholly absent. He would be present in every familiar object in the house. In every growing plant outdoors. And, most of all, in the music of baby Rica's voice, and in the sweetness of her smile that was as much like his as her one tiny hand was like the other!

XXXII *Deliberation*

IN JUNE there was great excitement in the hollow. Minna and Otto's family had been increased by two. The twins, whose premature arrival had jeopardized their lives, were to be hastily baptized Lillie and Christoph, under the sponsorship of Emil Mueller and his housekeeper.

Ludwig Breen was dispatched to bring Pastor Schicht. After Ludwig told Pastor of his errand, and after Pastor was settled in the Mueller carriage, he was at a loss for conversation. He rather dreaded the subject he knew was on Pastor's mind.

"I've been wondering about you. How have things been churning?" Pastor asked.

Ludwig shook his head disconsolately. "I'm afraid I'm not to have much luck."

"Luck? What here! What there!"

"It's her other affairs, Pastor. How could I ever know that she really wanted me . . . if I had to be one of many . . ."

"Nonsense," Pastor argued. "Must you make a haystack out of a straw?"

Ludwig's blue eyes turned searchingly upon Pastor.

"Do you think there is only a straw?"

"To be sure. Rica has had her admirers as any other young girl, but she had never forgotten her marriage, my boy. That she hasn't!"

"Perhaps not, but she loved others and hated me for being in the way."

"Not you," Pastor corrected. "The marriage, yes. After all, it was not of her making."

"Or mine, either."

"I know that. Have you regrets?"

The question left Ludwig like a traveler uncertain of his direction at a forked highway. "No," he answered. "I would be happy to have Rica for my wife . . . if I could just be sure she loved me."

"Tell me, what makes you believe she wouldn't. Has she spoken?"

"No. She has been friendly, but she was like that to him, too, wasn't she?"

"Him?"

"The Locher boy."

"Oh. You've heard stories about Gerhart? I can very well guess the rest, Ludwig. Would you like to hear my story? Perhaps it will be different."

Ludwig nodded.

"Gerhart is a fine lad. His only tragedy is that of being forever misunderstood. He was foreordained to be a gardener, according to his mother, but he wanted to be an engineer. With such tension the drum was bound to break. It was best. Now Gerhart can do the work God gave him the talent and the heart to do. It is well."

"I can understand that, Pastor. Being born to soldiering was just as much a snare for me."

Pastor gazed at the north horizon of industry. He was silent and then began talking in that introspective manner of his. "And now," he said, "we shall see order come of it, Ludwig. There is not one of us whose life pattern is not fully known by the Master Weaver. God is ever ready to help. It is not that He cannot give aid. It is so often that we cannot take! We pray for an ear of corn and when God gives us a kernel we bemoan our barren bins and show Him no thanks!

"Yet in the kernel is our ear of corn, if we would but plant it in faith and thank God for His goodness. We should see how He would add blessing to blessing and yield us our corn at harvest time.

"God's way is not always our way. His is the way of wisdom and patience. And ours, Ludwig, is the way of foolishness and impatience . . . a way of seeing in the mirror darkly."

Again the two men sat in absorbed silence. Then Pastor continued, "Rica has found contentment here, and so may you also. Prove to her that you are not the irresponsible wayfarer she thinks you to be. Win her. Does it take an old man to tell a young man how to do that?" A sly smile puckered the corner of Pastor's mouth.

Ludwig shifted uncomfortably. "I'll try," he answered.

"Remember," Pastor said, "it is not only *your* happiness in the making, but hers also. I think you are sincere in saying you love Rica."

"I am," Ludwig confessed.

They arrived at the hollow, where Emil Mueller was prancing up and down the parlor floor impatiently. Yetta, who had been summoned to meet the emergency, already was holding the tiny girl baby on her lap. There she sat in her prim black taffeta with a meticulous lace collar, her snowy hair drawn back smoothly from her forehead.

For Rica life was more complex after the twins came. Lottchen was by turns intrigued and indignant at the arrival of the twin babies. Intrigued, because there was so much excitement about the house, and indignant because Grossmutter and Rica rather neglected her in the constant care of the new babies.

Rica spent her time outdoors weeding and market fixing. The crops bore heavily. It seemed as though nature was trying to make up for her caprices of flood and frost. All hands were busy. And when there was any time to spare Rica was needed at Sophia's.

Often, in the midst of her work, Rica thought of the promise to Pastor. In September she must go back to Germany. Every day brought the dread time nearer.

Pastor spoke no more of it. He was a man of faithfulness and he expected faithfulness from others. She must go! In spite of Minna's needing her, in spite of all her own inner rebellion!

Then there was Ludwig Breen. After she had adjusted herself to her first emotional frustration and had learned to look with calm and contentment at Herman's and Sophia's happiness, and after she had fought down the impulse to return Gerhart's fiery love, along came Ludwig and disrupted her peace of mind once more!

Unheralded, he had come from Germany. Just as she had come. He took up his work and shortly became as one of the lifelong residents.

He hadn't been as shy as Herman. It hadn't taken him long to become acquainted at the crowd in spite of his handicap—and it had been a handicap—being High German. Many never got over it. They remained outsiders. But Ludwig had gotten over that difficulty easily, by using Plattdeutsch as rapidly as he could learn it.

That pleased everybody.

He had bought new clothes, and submerged his old self in every way. Perhaps that was why she had been drawn to him from the first. That was what she, too, had tried to do—create a new world for herself.

There was that feeling of having met Ludwig before, some place. It was an unreasonably persistent feeling which hadn't any foundation.

Where could she have met him? She had never been in Berlin, save for a few visits with her father. Could it have been on one of those jaunts? Ludwig had just come to America; therefore it could not have been from the crossing that she remembered him.

Mysterious, too, how he had shunned her after Herman's death. Whatever the cause of that apathy it had vanished as mysteriously as it had come.

Again, he was showing every attention to her at the crowd, but it was always as though he were holding something back. He talked of gardening when all the time there were other thoughts clearly written in his puckered brow, other wishes in his winsome smile.

And she could not turn away from him.

It was madness . . . sheer madness permitting herself to be drifted downstream again. As though there had not been enough heartache the other times. . . . She must guard against this new temptation.

What would Pastor say if he knew? Perhaps Providence was pulling her away from the fire. Sending her back to Germany, where she belonged. One more summer stretched out invitingly before her. And then autumn would come and she must go. Must become Frau Heinrich Heber. Would that be better than this eternal anguish of tasting forbidden love?

She confided in Grossmutter one evening. During recent weeks Grossmutter had seen the storm approaching. She had felt its nearness in every mood of Rica's; the long silent gaze into space, the frequent sighs, the retreat from her friends. All this had happened before. It was a relief to have the ice broken.

"Grossie, what shall I do?" Rica began. "I don't want to go back to Osnabrück, but I must."

"What is it that worries you, liebling? Some new distress?"

"Oh, Grossie, I'll never know any peace, I'm afraid. You and Pastor were right."

"Have you spoken to Pastor?"

"Yes. . . . That is what I want to tell you. I promised him at Hattie's wedding that I would go back to Germany this year, in September. The time has gone so quickly. September will be here soon."

"Does Heinrich know of your coming?"

"Yes. Pastor has told him. I dread it so, Grossmutter. Going over there to a man I don't love, when . . ."

The unfinished thought was complete in the elder woman's mind.

"We will miss you, Rica, but I know you will come back and bring him with you."

Rica shook her head. "He is a soldier, Grossie. He wouldn't leave Germany."

Grossmutter rocked in her chair. "I wish there was a way to bring order without your having to leave the country."

"I haven't told you about Ludwig," she said. "It will not be easy to part from him, Grossmutter. He has been a wonderful friend."

"And he would like to be more?"

Rica could not answer.

"You think of him constantly," Grossmutter ventured. "Against your will? Just as it was with Herman?"

Rica nodded.

"And he thinks of you constantly, which hurts worse."

"I didn't know, Grossmutter. Not at first. I wanted to make it easier for him to get along in America. It is a hard road when you come to a strange land. You and I know that. We had each other, but Ludwig had nobody. And when he had become one of us, it couldn't be the same. It couldn't!"

At the crowd on Saturday, following Rica's announcement to Grossmutter, Ludwig came with his wonted happy smile. "What makes you so sober, Rica?" he asked.

"Am I sober?"

"As Job in ashes. Let's take a walk. You've been dancing quite enough for one evening."

Rica slipped on her scarf and followed him outside.

"What's wrong?" Ludwig questioned. "You haven't been yourself."

"Why do you ask?"

"Because it concerns me. Everything you do, everything you feel concerns me."

"Do you always take such an interest in your friends? Or are you out grape-plucking for me?"

Ludwig took her hand. "It has gone far beyond grape-plucking now."

"Ludwig!"

"It's true, Rica. Ever since I came here I've had my heart set on you. You may as well have the truth."

"But, Ludwig."

"Never mind about saying—'I'm sorry it can't be.'"

Rica lips parted in surprise.

Ludwig continued forcefully. "I say it can be! You shall see, my dearest!"

"That is enough!" Rica's vexation turned to quick anger. She turned about abruptly and darted up the lane to the hall.

The lamps were burning high and the reflectors shimmered along the wall.

Rosie saw her pounce into the door. And she saw Ludwig follow, looking just as confused and excited as she. Rosie wormed through the crowd and came to Rica. "What is the matter?" she asked. "What fails you and Ludwig?"

"Nothing at all," Rica said irritably.

Rosie turned away, hurt. Yust was coming. There was no escape. Dance with him she must. "It is the last dance," Rosie said, as he seized her. His sickening beer-laden breath repulsed her. When the dance was over Rosie tore away from Yust as one possessed. Through the crowd she darted. Out of the door and to Sophia Toepfer.

Sophia was patching Knopf's shirt when Rosie burst into the kitchen.

"Oh, Sophie," she wailed. "I'm just sick all over."

"Sick?"

"It's Yust. I hate him and he keeps following me."

Sophia slipped off her thimble and poured coffee. "Here, take a cup and you will feel better," she said.

"I'm not going to the crowd any more."

"Yes, you will," Sophia answered. "You mustn't stay home because of Yust. You can turn him to the wind some other way."

Rosie daubed her eyes and proceeded to the second point of her discontent. "Rica is going to keep Ludwig for a fool."

"Best not to look too deep in Rica's affairs," Sophia advised. "You don't know what all. There may be reasons why she doesn't want to keep company."

"She is going to keep him for a fool, I know!"

"What makes you believe that?" Sophia asked.

"She had words with him tonight. When I asked what was wrong she wouldn't give answer."

"Don't worry," Sophia said. "Everything will be all right in the end." A shadow of pain crossed her florid face. . . . Was Rica in love again?

Rica, at that moment, was making up her mind to see Pastor next day. Must not let this affair get beyond her. The sinister threat was already clouding her horizon. Ludwig's words buffeted in her ear—set her pulse beating wildly—"Everything you do, everything you feel concerns me."

She did not hesitate to repeat the exact words to Pastor next day, so determined was she to clear her decks.

She wondered at the soft smile on Pastor's face. Was he being indulgent now that he knew she would be leaving soon?

"May I ask, Rica, how does this young Breen strike your fancy? Could you accept his attention if you were free?"

Her heart hurtled high. "I . . . I . . ." she stammered. "Why?"

"Was my question unfair?" he teased.

This was a new mood.

"He's a nice young man, Pastor. I can say nothing else."

"Could you care for him?"

Rica was abashed. "Perhaps I could," she confessed.

"That is good," Pastor said with shocking frankness. "Because I had taken a strong liking to the boy."

What curious bypaths was Pastor's fancy taking? Was he growing weary of her problem? "What shall I do, Pastor?" she asked. "Ludwig's attention may grow very embarrassing before I leave."

Pastor stroked his beard. "I would say nothing for the present," he answered. "You can be friends, can't you, for a few months more?"

Rica grew restive. "I don't know. I haven't been very successful so far, at pretending."

"Pretending?" Pastor laughed so heartily that tears came to his eyes. "Forgive my laughter, Rica, but it is seldom I meet someone with my own limitations. We should be grateful that we are not destined to be actors!" Then he became sober again. "Is there anything you would like me to do for you?"

"Yes. Mail this letter to Heinrich for me. Since there is no other way out, I'll have to leave in September."

"It will be a pleasure to send it," Pastor said. "We shall expect good from it. A pleasant Sabbath to you, Rica."

"And to you also," Rica replied.

Ludwig, too, it seemed had needed Pastor this morning. As Rica rejoined Rosie at the bottom of the steps, Ludwig limped into the vestry. Pastor slipped the note into his hand. "I shall leave this with you," he whispered. "Make good with it, son."

Ludwig stared at the finely addressed envelope. "What?" he ejaculated. "You have told her?"

"No. This was meant to go across the water, but since there is no water to cross . . ."

Ludwig chuckled. "All thanks to you, Pastor."

"Not to me," Pastor answered jovially. "To your wife. Whatever the note says, privately, I want to add she thinks very well of Ludwig Breen. Have a care and see that she continues to think well of him."

"I'll surely try."

"God's blessing on you both."

"Thank you," Ludwig replied.

XXXIII *New Lives for Old*

~~~~~~~~~~~~~~~~~~~~~~~~~~~~~~~~~~~~~~~

RICA AND LUDWIG came to the crest of Rubberneck Hill to watch the Buffalo Bill show assemble on the grounds below. Here they sat in the grass and saw the horses gallop about the race track with the cowboy riders going through their breathtaking stunts in preparation for the show which was soon to begin.

On this spot lovers were wont to gather on summer evenings and look down at the park lights.

A few years later, when a lake was added to Chester Park, many came to watch the lights glimmer in the water and see the Blue Streak hurtle through make-believe mountains. It has been said that many a proposal can be traced to the spell of some wonderful evening up on Rubberneck Hill.

And though there was neither lake nor moonlight this afternoon, there was nevertheless a spell over Rica and Ludwig.

They had come to see Buffalo Bill's widely hailed rodeo. They had done the incredible—taken an afternoon off during the week; however, both the Locher and Betz gardens were properly weeded and it was not a market day.

Rica was thinking of her approaching departure. September was but three weeks away . . . soon there would be instructions from Germany.

She planned to tell Ludwig after the show today. Before the show she would enjoy every precious moment up here on the bluff. She wanted these moments to take back with her to Berlin. They must be golden moments—worth preserving.

Ludwig's face twitched as he watched her. What was the strange drama going on within her mind. Would he dare pry a confession from her?

"Rica," he said, bursting in upon her train of thought, "what do you honestly think of me?"

"What a strange question," she said, frightened as a deer caught poised at a stream. "What makes you ask?"

"Because I want to know," he said. "Tell me, Rica, do you love me?"

She drew up her shoulders and faced him. The happiness faded from her face . . . bitterness took its place. "Why did you have to spoil this lovely afternoon? I had meant it to be all golden."

"Have I spoiled it?"

She nodded.

"How?"

"I don't know, Ludwig. It just happened. Couldn't you have been satisfied just as it was?"

"No! I had to know . . . now!" His tone was stern.

"I shan't answer, Ludwig. There is no need!"

"You will! I want to hear you say it! It isn't what I feel or you feel that counts. It is what we are willing to confess. We live in a material world, you and I. We are not spirits!"

Rica was morose.

"Tell me just once that you do love me. After that say what you will . . . I'll try to be content."

"Just that?" Rica mocked. "No, Ludwig. You don't mean it."

"But I *do!* His brow knit darkly above his flashing eyes. "You *must* tell me *now!*"

She drew back from those commanding eyes with a cry. Suddenly, she was no longer on Rubberneck Hill. She was back in Osnabrück. She was fifteen . . . and in her father's parlor. This piercing pair of eyes was looking down upon her. There was the same tense jaw, the same knit brow, the identical voice saying, "You must!"

She drew back from his embrace as though she had been lashed. "You, you . . . are not Ludwig Breen," she gasped.

The knit brow smoothed itself. The sinister look was gone. "Then who am *I!*"

"You are Heinrich Heber!"

Ludwig was tense. Waiting her approbation. . . .

She came forward to meet him. The hillside rocked. Years rolled aside like leaves in the wind. One turbulent kiss filled the void of empty years.

They were oblivious to Buffalo Bill and his horses. Questions rained. Droll answers. Uncontrolled laughter. Suppressed tears.

"I should have known," Rica said. "There was always a feeling that I had known you somewhere before, Ludwig. I fitted you into many shoes . . . the butcher boy, the trolley conductor and the sexton. But the shoes never fit . . . and no wonder! How did you get out of service?"

"My leg was injured in drill," came the grim answer.

"Was it long before it healed?" Rica asked gently.

"Many months."

"It must have been torture, especially when you knew you would lose your rank."

He shook his head. "I never wanted to be a soldier," he confessed. "I was glad to get out of the army."

She swayed with the impact of that confession. "Ludwig, had I known that! Things would have been much different for us."

"Would they have been, Rica?"

"I shouldn't then have acted the fool."

He caught a half pouting, half coquettish smile to his lips. "We'll hear no more of fools, darling."

"It makes my head spin thinking of all this. It is all such a tangle. . . . What will Pastor Schicht say? Do you know I have promised him to go back to Germany?"

"You told me in the letter. Remember?" he teased.

"You used Pastor for your plot!"

"Didn't you?"

She laughed, "But you tricked me, Ludwig."

"The use of my house name?" Ludwig asked. "I did that so that you would not be humiliated if you should not wish me to be known to your friends. Then, when you, yourself, did not recognize me I was tempted to win you without the help of old ties. Was that wrong?"

"No," she answered. "You chose the best way. You had none of the old barriers to hurdle. To me, you were a new person—interesting because of your mystery. It would have been hard to recognize you as the man I married. You have changed so much."

"I know," Ludwig said quietly.

"You are so much thinner. And your hair. It has changed your entire person, Ludwig. It was like a brush the other way."

Ludwig laughed. "If I had kept my military crop you would have known me?"

"Never cut it close like that again," Rica warned. "Never sheer off those thick curls, especially this wayward fellow." She slipped a finger through the ringlet and brushed it upward upon his forehead.

"You have changed, too," Ludwig said. "You were just a schoolgirl, then. Terribly frightened at the prospect of becoming Frau Heinrich Heber. And sorry for it all, afterward. I wanted to speak to you, but I never had the chance after you went away. That was the way you made me remember you . . . frightened . . . stubborn . . . tearful."

"It was a bitter experience for both of us," Rica said. "Let's try to forget."

He held her close and they sat in satisfying silence.

"Where is your father?" Rica asked at length.

"In Berlin. Soon he will be pensioned."

"Did he approve your coming to America?"

"Yes, but it was not easy for him. I've been such a disappointment. Getting wounded and discharged from the army."

"Do you think he would come to America?"

"For a visit perhaps. Oh, Rica, you would thrill to his stories. He has seen so much, been so many places—a prince of princes my father is! Marco Polo could thrill me no more! I wish I could have known him better when I was a boy."

Rica nodded. "What will folks say? And Grossie?"

"Grossie knows all about it," Ludwig confessed. "You see she and I had a long talk some time ago. She suspected the truth about me. Remember when I came up to see you on a Sunday afternoon and you were over at Sophia's house? I stayed there talking to Grossmutter Betz until you came. Grossie never minced words. She asked me point-blank if I were not Heinrich Heber."

"How could she have guessed when even I didn't recognize you?" Rica asked dazedly.

"That leaves me puzzled, too," Ludwig replied. "When I asked her how she knew, she just smiled and said, 'By every token. By the way you were acting. By the way Pastor regarded you. . . . I knew from the first there was something between you and Pastor. . . . And if there had not been the outward signs I think I should have known you, anyhow . . . lightning draws, the wind has its course and there are currents in other spheres, too. Unseen, they may be, but they are felt!' Mysterious how she knew."

Rica nodded. "She was always so sure that everything would turn out right."

There was a great fanfare of trumpets below. Rica and Ludwig scrambled to their feet and hurried down to the back entrance to the park.

Already the show had begun and the crowd was cheering. A medley of bareback riders rode into the arena. Buffalo Bill, himself, thundered in on his pompous mount and every boyish heart thrilled at the spectacle.

Here was the West of storybooks. Land of lariat and steer, mountain, plain, ranch and mine.

Clouds of dust plumed up from flying hoofs. Scarlet pennants flashed high in the air, the brass horns shone as they turned in the sun—

Ta-ra-ra boom de aye!

they blared. The spectators' feet pounded the earth in unison. This was new. Rica held fast to Ludwig's arm.

There were plaintive songs, sad sweet words sung to the accompaniment of guitars and banjos. A new rhythm they brought. The music of the West.

And when it was over the spectators rushed out to the tents to see Buffalo Bill and his men. The stands were deserted quickly. Rica and Ludwig found themselves alone.

"I can't wait to tell Grossmutter and all the rest. What will they say?" Rica asked excitedly. "Can't you just hear the commotion when we march down into the hollow today and tell them that we are married? No more secrets, no more gossip, no more speculation and heartache."

Ludwig pressed her hand. "And we shall have our own garden and our own house."

"In Wooden Shoe Hollow. . . . The Fliegers have too much ground now that Hattie left. Hattie says they want to sell two acres. That would be enough for us . . . without a hired man. And it is close to Sophia."

"Build a brick house on it, eh?"

Rica nodded enthusiastically. "With a summer kitchen on the side. And a big sunny parlor and a porch."

They planned excitedly as they walked up Spring Grove Avenue. Suddenly, a buggy whip dangled before their startled faces. It was Pastor Schicht driving up in his carriage.

"A nice day for parading the Avenue," he said. "What are we celebrating in the middle of the week?"

"We've been to the Wild West Show," Ludwig answered. "The Buffalo Bill circus in Chester Park."

"So?" Pastor inquired. "And how was it?"

"Some beautiful horses, Pastor!"

"Did you see the *Schimmel?*" Pastor asked. "Ah, there is a horse! But only for the saddle."

"You saw the show, too?" Rica asked.

Pastor winked mischievously. "I watched them go in," he said. He didn't add that his one purpose in coming down the Avenue was to see Buffalo Bill's famous horses.

"Going back home? Climb in and I'll take you back to the hollow."

Rica and Ludwig climbed into the carriage, each waiting for the other to speak.

Pastor stroked his beard thoughtfully. The reins lay loose in his energetic brown hands. "Any news?" he asked.

"Yes." It was Rica who answered. "I'm not going back to Germany."

"No?"

"It's utterly useless to try to find Heinrich Heber in Germany, Pastor."

"Why?"

"The wretch landed this afternoon!"

The two burst into laughter. Pastor drew in the reins. "So Heinrich landed. And what does he say?"

"He and his wife have plans," Ludwig answered. "Plans to have a house and garden in Wooden Shoe Hollow. On Herr Flieger's place."

"Very good," Pastor said. "This makes me glad through and through! You will be happy," he prophesied. "It will be like—"

"Like the land of milk and honey," Rica interrupted. "Grossie and I called it that before we set eyes upon it."

There ran through Rica's mind the old Arabian poem which she had learned as a child, and which bound up for her all thought and feeling for her adopted land. It was almost as if the ancient bard had, from his seventh-century vista seen a vision of Wooden Shoe Hollow when he sang:

> I wandered by a goodly town
> Beset with many a garden fair,
> And asked of one who gathered down
> Large fruit how long the town was there.
> He spoke, nor chose his hand to stay,
> The town was here for many a day,
> And will be here forever and aye.

Pastor leaned back in the carriage and let Dolly canter up Mitchell Avenue, past the car shops. He thought of this strange drama now brought to a close, of his part in bringing it to fulfillment. He recalled how Rica had come here with Grossmutter Betz. He couldn't help glancing at her now . . . at the woman she had grown to be in these eventful years.

All had ended very well for her. She was worthy of her happiness, and so was the young man beside her.

They were passing St. Matthew's Church, on Epworth Avenue.

Here most of his flock worshipped now. They would always be his people, however, even though they now had their own pastor in residence.

As the carriage rolled past the church, whistles from Procter and Gamble's began to scream. The lumberyard whistle joined in the call. From all sides there was the sudden jargon of clanging bells and shrieking whistles. All Winton Place echoed with the tumult which was noisier than a New Year's celebration.

"What can it be?" Rica asked.

Pastor leaned out of the carriage. "What is it?" he asked. A gangling lad ran beside the buggy. "It's finished!" he shouted. "The Panama Canal, sir! It is finished!"

Part Three

Editor's Conclusion

A sign in Wooden Shoe Hollow. EDITOR'S PHOTOGRAPH.

The A. J. Rahn Greenhouse in Wooden Shoe Hollow. Today the family is involved in flower gardening. PHOTOGRAPH COURTESY OF SUSAN RAHN.

Larry Rahn shown with a harvest of tomatoes when the family farmed vegetables. PHOTOGRAPH COURTESY OF SUSAN RAHN.

The Osterbrock Greenhouse and Florist in Wooden Shoe Hollow. EDITOR'S PHOTOGRAPH.

A Goetz truck like those used in the Hollow in the 1920s. PHOTOGRAPH FROM AL FUNKE.

Funke's greenhouse in Wooden Shoe Hollow. EDITOR'S PHOTOGRAPH.

Funke's Greenhouses in the 1930s. PHOTOGRAPH FROM AL FUNKE.

"Back before the City decided we couldn't keep livestock here anymore the growers had the basic compliments of chickens, hogs, goats, horses, cattle, etc. Farm kids knew well and good where chicken and bacon come from." PHOTOGRAPH AND QUOTE FROM AL FUNKE.

From the 1940s–At the end of the day, "folks on the farm would gather and discuss the day and what the plan for tomorrow was." PHOTOGRAPH FROM AL FUNKE.

"From an early age the children of the area learned the skills needed to become good growers." PHOTOGRAPH FROM AL FUNKE.

"There is always plenty to do, lettuce to cut, tomatoes to pick, trucks to load, etc. This picture shows Goetz's front field with Funke's Greenhouses in the background. Funke's owns this field today." From Funke's Greenhouses. PHOTOGRAPH FROM AL FUNKE.

"The building behind Will is the boiler shed. Large coal fired steam boilers were the primary head source for greenhouses of this era. We still have one although in 1970 the EPA forced us to install gas burners. Just as well since the price of coal skyrocked in the '70s and the labor associated with these old oal units was intense. Every morning the cinders (clinkers) had to be shoveled out by hand." PHOTOGRAPH FROM AL FUNKE.

Five of the Pieper siblings purchased this home at 6305 Elbrook after the Depression forced them to lose the family home on Wiehe Road. Charlotte lived here when she wrote *Wooden Shoe Hollow*. PHOTOGRAPH FROM THE PIEPER FAMILY.

William Pieper on the left wearing wooden shoes in the field at the Pieper homestead on Wiehe Road. Elbrook Avenue is in the background. Herman Pieper, above, at the Wiehe Road home.

From left—Henry Pieper holding grandson David MacDonald; Mary Meyer Pieper; and their niece, Henrietta Pelzer. The three Pieper brothers shown on this page emigrated together from Germany. After trying to farm near Spring Grove Avenue, they purchased land in Golf Manor to continue farming on higher ground, becoming pioneers of the Golf Manor area. PHOTOGRAPHS ON THIS PAGE FROM MARY AND FRED PIEPER.

Notes

Ed. Note: References are to the pagination of the novel.

7 *Epworth Avenue* Street located off of Winton Road east of Spring Grove.

13 *Osnabrück to New York to Ohio* This was a standard emigration route—from a location in Germany to the port city of Bremerhaven, and from there to New York, and then on to a destination in the United States. For a history of the German immigration to America, see Don Heinrich Tolzmann, *The German-American Experience* (Amherst, N.Y.: Humanity Books, 2000).

15 *Here in America it gives so many dumb people* This is a direct translation from German: "Hier in Amerika gibt es so viele Dummköpfe!"

17 *Herman goes early* Another example of Germanized English, derived from: "Herman geht früh."

18 *Yankees* Pieper refers to Anglo-Americans as Yankees, or as the English to contrast them and their views with German-Americans. Both groups held different views on a variety of issues, such as prohibition, bilingual education, the Continental versus the Puritan Sunday, and World War I. Regarding these issues, see Tolzmann, *German-American Experience*, 187ff.

21 *Du, Du liegst mir im Herzen & Ach, Du lieber Augustin* Two popular German folk songs, which reflect the popularity of German customs and traditions. For a selection of German folk music, see Ernst-Lothar von Knorr, *Deutsche Volkslieder: 168 Volkslieder und volkstümliche Lieder* (Stuttgart: Reclam, 1993).

22 *Old First Church* A reference to the First United Church of Christ at 1628 Hoffner Street, often referred to as the Hoffner Street Church, which was founded as: Die Erste Deutsche Evangelische Protestantische Gemeinde in Cumminsville. See Giglierano and Overmyer, *The Bicentennial Guide*, 267.

24 *Knowlton's Corner* Located in Cumminsville, where Hamilton, Spring Grove, and Colerain Avenues meet Ludlow Avenue and Hoffner Street, "it has several factories and a number of soaring churches. Hamilton Avenue, once the old St. Clair–Wayne trail to Hamilton, is its main shopping street, and it teems with the heavy traffic characteristic of arterial highways in Cincinnati." At the corner of Spring Grove and Hamilton Avenue, Ephraim Knowlton had built a store in 1830, and he later became the first postmaster in Cumminsville. See *The WPA Guide to Cincinnati, With a New Introduction by Zane L. Miller and a New Preface by Harry Graff* (reprint, 1943; Cincinnati: Cincinnati Historical Society, 1987), 395.

25 *St. Johanneskirche in Osnabrück* Regarding the church, as well as the history of Osnabrück, see Ludwig Hofmeyer, *Chronik der Stadt Osnabrück* (Osnabrück: Meinders and Elstermann, 1964).

26 *Spring Grove* Artist Emma Calve said of Cincinnati, "[o]nly a place with a heart and soul could make for their dead a more magnificent park than any which exists for their living." See *WPA Guide*, 424. Adolph Strauch, superintendent of Spring Grove, described the landscaping reforms he introduced as the "landscape lawn plan," and called for a return to the "aesthetics of the beautiful." In his view, a rural cemetery "should form the most interesting of all places for contemplative recreation," and everything in it should be tasteful, classical, and poetical." See Tolzmann, ed., *Spring Grove and its Creator*, vii. Spring Grove encompasses 782 acres, and nearly 200,000 persons have been interred there, ranging from ordinary citizens to the most prominent of the area.

28 *Butchering* This section deals with the German custom of butchering, and making sausages and other cuts of meat. For a good description of this, see Mac E. Barrick, *German-American Folklore* (Little Rock, Ark.: August House Publishers, 1987), 151–53.

31 *Lorelei* A well-known poem by Heinrich Heine. For a biography of Heine, see Louis Untermyer, *Heinrich Heine, Paradox and Poet* (New York: Harcourt, Brace, 1937).

34 *Speck* The German word for bacon.

36 *Christmas* Here reference is made to German Christmas customs, certainly a central part of German-American family life. For an overview of German Christmas customs and traditions, see LaVern J. Rippley, *Of German Ways* (Minneapolis: Dillon, 1970), 193ff.

43 *St. Patrick* By making reference to the patron saint of the Irish, Pieper takes note here of the second largest ethnic group in Cincinnati, the Irish-Americans.

47 *Kaiser's Service* This relates to service in the German army, which was one factor causing Germans to emigrate. For a survey of the causes of

the German emigration, see Tolzmann, *German-American Experience*, esp. 151ff.

50 *Low German Folk* The novel focuses on Low Germans, who are contrasted not only with Yankees, but also with High German-speaking German-Americans. For an introductory history of the topic, see Robert Lee Stockman, *Platt Düütsch/Low German: A Brief History of the People and Language* (Alto, Mich.: Platt Düütsch Press, 1998). Also, see Johannes Gilhoff, *Letters of a German-American Farmer: Jürnjakob Swehn Travels To America* trans. Richard Lorenz August Trost (Iowa City: University of Iowa Press, 2000). Also, see Richard Lorenz August Trost, *Growing Up Plattdütsch in America* (DesMoines, Iowa, 2000).

62 *Mill Creek* Running south of Winton Place and Spring Grove, this creek eventually feeds into the Ohio River. Some of the heavy industry in Cincinnati is located along its path. See *WPA Guide*, 409.

62 *Camp Washington* "During the mobilization of troops for the Mexican War of 1846, the First and Second Ohio Regiments encamped in this position of the Mill Creek Valley, which was largely a woods at the time. The site was named Camp Washington, and the same appellation was given to a settlement which sprang up near by, around the present intersection of Hopple Street and Colerain Avenue. All the territory in this vicinity was annexed to Cincinnati in 1870, but the name Camp Washington still clings to this busy neighborhood of thickly sown small old homes and shops." See *WPA Guide*, 428.

62 *Volksblatt* This was a major German-American newspaper in Cincinnati that was founded in 1836 and was published until 1919. See Don Heinrich Tolzmann, *Cincinnati's German Heritage* (Bowie, Md.: Heritage Books, Inc., 1994), pt.3, 101–02.

65 *Bauverein* This community is German for "building society." Such societies were formed by German-Americans, and usually met at neighborhood saloons, where on Fridays, the members would deposit their savings with the society's treasurer. Eventually, these would develop into neighborhood building and loan banks that would lend out funds for those building homes. They reflected the German orientation towards thriftiness. Almost every neighborhood throughout the area had a building and loan bank, and altogether there were close to three hundred of them by mid-twentieth century. Since that time, they have declined in number due to the consolidation of banks. However, the retention of the name "building and loan" harkens back to their German origins. For information on the early history of banking in Cincinnati, see Ernst Henry Hagner, "Banking Situation in Cincinnati," (thesis, Commercial Engineer, University of Cincinnati, 1928), and also Olga Alma Knocke, "Some Aspects of Banking in Cincinnati," (thesis, Commercial Engineer, University of Cincinnati, 1929).

65   *St. Bernard* This community borders on Winton Place, and was "settled 1794, platted 1843, incorporated 1878, and rated a city 1912. This is another municipality within the borders of Cincinnati and without room for further expansion. For the most part it consists of shops strung all along Vine Street, and comparatively new suburban homes with well-trimmed lawns and shrubbery. . . . Saint Bernard is one of the newer communities along Mill Creek. The arrival of German families about a generation before the Civil War gave Saint Bernard its first group of aggressive settlers. A starch plant established in 1859 by Andrew Erkenbrecher, founder of the Cincinnati Zoological Garden, provided steady work for most of the community. . . . Leader of the Germans here was John Bernard Schroeder (1808–53) who, together with an associate, platted the village. Legend ascribes the naming of the town to nostalgic newcomers who imagined that local hills resembled the Alps in miniature. It is more likely that Schroeder, donor of the land and funds for the church, gave the village the name of his patron saint." See *WPA Guide*, 419.

70   *Sonderbar* German for "strange."

74   *Mitchell Avenue* From Spring Grove, this runs directly north into Winton Place.

74   *Ohio River* Located several miles south of Winton Place, with Mill Creek flowing into it in the south. For a history of the Ohio River, see John Ed Pearce, *The Ohio River* (Lexington, Kentucky: University of Kentucky Press, 1989).

81   *St. Clement's Church* Located at the southeast corner of Vine and Church Streets, this is "the third local church structure of that name. Built in 1870, this building was remodeled in 1897. It is designed in a modified Gothic style, with square clock tower and steeple, and stuccoed to resemble stone. It adjoins the Franciscan monastery (1915) and the parochial school (1923)." See *WPA Guide*, 420–21.

85   *Panama Canal* Preliminary work on the canal began in 1905 and opened for traffic in 1914. The canal was a major topic of interest for the time period of the novel. See Richard B. Morris and Jeffrey B. Morris, eds., *Encyclopedia of American History* Bicentennial Edition (New York: Harper & Row, 1976), 353.

93   *Indianapolis* Located approximately one hundred miles west of Cincinnati. Regarding German-Americans there, see George Theodore Probst, *The Germans in Indianapolis, 1840–1918*, rev. and illus. Eberhard Reichmann (Indianapolis: German-American Center, Indiana University-Purdue University & Indiana German Heritage Society, 1989).

98   *Plum Kuchen* A popular homemade cake.

99 *English Church* This, of course, refers to a church of the Anglo-Americans, and was most likely Winton Place United Methodist Church, located at 700 East Epworth Avenue.

101 *Poe* Reference to a poem (*The Raven*) by Edgar Allen Poe. One well-known translation was done by Edwin H. Zeydel, head of the German Department at the University of Cincinnati. See Edwin H. Zeydel, "Der Rabe von Edgar Allen Poe," in Hermann Barnstorff, *Festschrift zum goldenen Jubiläum des Deutschen Literarischen Klubs von Cincinnati, 1877/1927* (Cincinnati: Deutscher Literarischer Klub von Cincinnati, 1927), 74–76.

119 *New Orleans* By means of the Ohio and Mississippi rivers Cincinnati has always had direct connections with New Orleans, which served as a port of entry for German immigrants headed for Cincinnati. Of more than 300,000 German immigrants who arrived at New Orleans in the latter half of the nineteenth century, more than ten percent moved on to the Ohio Valley. See Don Heinrich Tolzmann, ed., *Louisiana's German Heritage: Louis Voss' Introductory History* (Bowie, Md.: Heritage Books, Inc., 1994), 82.

122 *The Reich* A reference to Germany, or the German Empire, before World War I, which is the time period of the novel. For an introductory history of Germany, see Eleanor L. Turk, *The History of Germany* (Westport, Conn.: Grenwood Press, 1999).

122 *Westphalia* The northwest German state where Osnabrück is located.

126 *Deutschland, Deutschland ueber alles* The first stanza of the German national anthem, written by the German poet Hoffmann von Fallersleben. For further information on the anthem, see LaVern J. Rippley, *Of German Ways* (Minneapolis, Dillon, 1970), 76–79.

128 *1913* The first time the author refers to a date, although other references place the work before the World War I. For a history of the world war experience of German-Americans, see Tolzmann, *Cincinnati's German Heritage*, pt. 2.

134 *Avondale* Located about four miles northeast of downtown Cincinnati, Avondale was an independent village until 1896, when it was annexed by Cincinnati. After annexation many moved to the area, especially German Jews who "settled in northern Avondale and erected large, tastefully styled homes on rolling, landscaped lawns." See *WPA Guide*, 343.

134 *Vine Street* This was "the spinal column of the city, and the traditional demesne of Bacchus and Gambrinus. From Over-the-Rhine, the big German colony north of lower Central Parkway, a spirit of gaiety wafted over the entire city. This robust jollity flowered to perfection in the 1890s, when the fun-loving character of the city made some call it "the Paris of America." See *WPA Guide*, 105. Also, see Cliff Radel, "A Peek

Behind the Sauerkraut Curtain," *The Cincinnati Enquirer*, 20 May 2003. Radel writes that to both sides of town "Vine Street is the dividing line, the sauerkraut curtain separating east and west, creating myths about it being the line of demarcation between the swank and the old-fashioned, change versus staying pat."

135 *Graphophones* Literally this term means "the pencil of sound," and was an early name used for the phonograph.

139 *Hungarian* Reference to a German from Hungary, of which there were many in Cincinnati. Known as Donauschwaben, or Danube Swabians, they are the second largest group of Germans in the area after those of north German stock. See Rebecca S. Rodgers, "The Donauschwaben: History, Development, and Culture of an Immigrant People," (master's thesis, University of Cincinnati, 1984).

139 *Cumminsville* This is an old Mill Creek Valley suburb.

139 *Alms & Doepke* A department store established by German-Americans William H. Alms, a Union Army veteran, and William F. Doekpke, and located on Central Parkway. Today, the building is used for the offices of Hamilton County.

145 *Pleasant Ridge* Located on the northeast side of Cincinnati, Pleasant Ridge is adjacent to Kennedy Heights, "which is larger but quite similar in nature. Pleasant Ridge derives its name from its historic Presbyterian burial ground, which was dedicated as Pleasant Ridge Cemetery in 1795. The village remained a rural community until the turn of the present [twentieth] century. Annexation to Cincinnati came in 1912 and Pleasant Ridge blossomed forth with expensive homes and, around its edges, large estates," *WPA Guide*, 325.

147 *Seal of the State of Ohio* This state seal has undergone many changes over time, with the current one having been adopted in 1967, and modified in 1996.

155 *St. Matthew's Church* German-Americans organized this church as Matthew's German Evangelical Protestant Church, which today is the Matthew United Church of Christ. Located at 717 East Epworth Avenue, the brick building was dedicated in 1912, and carries a German inscription over the main entrance door. The church was formed after about thirty families belonging to the Hoffner Street church in Northside decided to organize their own congregation in 1909. The growth of the church paralleled the growth and development of Wooden Shoe Hollow. See Giglierano and Overmeyer, *Bicentennial Guide*, 444–45. Regarding the Hoffner Street church, see the note for p. 22.

157 *Clifton* Located to the south of Winton Place, many well-to-do Cincinnatians built substantial homes in Clifton with finely landscaped lawns. German-American gardeners often found employment there, and Pieper

refers to the area as a Yankee, or Anglo, neighborhood. For a history of Clifton, see Zane L. Miller, *Visions of Place: The City, Neighborhoods, Suburbs, and Cincinnati's Clifton, 1850–2000* (Columbus: Ohio State University Press, 2001).

176 *Jesu, geh voran* A well-known German Protestant hymn.

179 *Ein Prosit* The well-known toast to the spirit of Gemütlichkeit, especially popular at German-American festivities.

181 *Bremen* Bremen/Bremerhaven was a major port city for immigration to America. See *Bremen und Bremerhaven als Auswandererhaefen* (Bremerhaven: Foerderverein Deutsches Auswanderermuseum, 1988). Bremerhaven is the site of the future German emigration museum.

186 *Ellis Island* From 1892 to 1923, at least 12 million people entered the United States via Ellis Island, and more than 100 million Americans have ancestors who arrived there. See *Visiting Ellis Island: A Souvenir of the Ellis Island Immigration Museum* (New York: Collier Books, 1992).

187 *Dutchman* German-Americans are often erroneously referred to as "Dutch," such as, for example, the Pennsylvania Germans who are often called "Dutch." This misunderstanding has its origin in the fact that non-Germans could not pronounce the German word for German "deutsch," and mispronounced it as "dutch." Germans were first erroneously called Dutch at Jamestown, Virginia, by Captain John Smith. See Tolzmann, *German-American Experience*, 31ff.

191 *Gärtner-Unterstützungsverein* The German Gardeners Beneficial Society, which provided benefits in time of sickness and death for its members and their families. Such beneficial societies prospered, and provided the kinds of benefits that were not available from other sources.

192 *Sauerkrautgemüse* German for "Sauerkraut vegetables."

196 *Gemüse* German for "vegetables."

201 *Washington's Birthday* A popular day of commemoration by means of which German-Americans celebrated their patriotism. See Tolzmann, *Cincinnati's German Heritage*, pt. 4, 34ff.

204 *To America in 1870* This refers to immigration during the Franco-Prussian War, and which most likely was motivated by the desire to flee military service. For a history of this war, see David Wetzel, *A Duel of the Giants: Bismarck, Napoleon III, and the Origins of the Franco-Prussian War* (Madison, Wis.: University of Wisconsin Press, 2001).

207 *Ich hatt' einen Kameraden* A well-known poem by German poet Ludwig Uhland commemorating a comrade lost during battle, and often sung or recited at memorial services. Regarding Uhland, see John G. Robertson, *A History of German Literature*, 5th ed. rev. and enl. Edna

Purdie with the Assistance of W. I. Lucas and M. O'C. Walshe (London: British Book Centre, 1968), 134ff.

207 *Germany* The reference here to Germany emphasizes that German-Americans have found fulfillment and happiness in the New World.

212 *Black Dialect* The inclusion of Black dialect relates to the African-American population in Cincinnati. Regarding their history, see Wendell P. Dabney, *Cincinnati's Colored Citizens: Historical, Sociological, and Biographical* (Cincinnati: Davney Pub. Co., 1926). Dabney includes several references to German-Americans, including their involvement in the underground railway. He notes in general of them: "In 1888, the German population formed a most important element, enough to make a large city—more than a hundred thousand. It is liberty loving and distinguished for thrift and intelligence. The Germans are devoted patrons of education and the arts, and especially music. German is taught in the public school," (27).

216 *Morgenrot* German for "dawn," or sunrise.

217 *Lustigkeit* German for "gaiety," or merriment.

218 *Frankfort & Berlin* Two major German cities, with the latter, of course, the German capital city.

221 *Colerain Ave.* A major north-south street located west of Winton Place that leads to northwest Cincinnati, where many German-Americans settled.

224 *Mt. Auburn Orphanage* Mt. Auburn "was Cincinnati's original hilltop suburb—the first area outside the basin to which the city's wealthy migrated. Mt. Auburn consisted of the property lying between McMillan Street on the north, McMicken Avenue and Liberty Street on the south, Reading Road on the east, and Vine Street on the West." See Giglierano and Overmyer, *The Bicentennial Guide*, 188.

225 *Vine Street Cemetery* This is located just south of Winton Place, and to the east of Clifton. Before World War I, it had a German name, the German Evangelical Protestant Cemetery, but like many places, the German name was dropped, and the cemetery took on the name of the street where it was located. See Mary H. Remler, ed., *Hamilton County, Ohio Burial Records: Vol. 3 Vine Street Hill Cemetery, 1852–1977* (Cincinnati: Hamilton County Chapter of Ohio Genealogical Society, 1991).

231 *High German/Handicap* Here Pieper provides some insight into the outlook of north Germans and how they feel more at ease with other Low German-speakers. For a history of the German language, see John T. Waterman, *A History of the German Language: With Special Reference to the Cultural and Social Forces that Shaped the Standard Literary Language*, rev. ed. (Seattle: University of Washington Press, 1976).

236 *Buffalo Bill* The Wild West Show of Buffalo Bill often performed in Cincinnati at places such as the Cincinnati Zoological Gardens and Heuck's Opera House. See Robert Heuck II, *Hubert Heuck and His Opera Houses* (Cincinnati: Florence McKee Heuck, 1992), and also Robert A. Carter, *Buffalo Bill Cody: The Man Behind the Legend* (New York: J. Wiley, 2000).

236 *Chester Park* This was located at the north side of Spring Grove Avenue at Platt Avenue, and "contained until 1941 one of Cincinnati's most popular swimming pools and skating rinks. The park, originally panned as a driving resort, was named in 1875 by its founder, Capt. George N. Stone, after one of his race horses, Chester. . . . In the early 1900s grand opera was presented at the park, with the actors staying at a tavern on Chester Avenue. . . . In the center was a large lake bisected by a midway, so that boating could be enjoyed on one side and swimming on the other. Circling the lake was the boardwalk, with all the fun devices and eating places necessary to produce a carnival spirit." See *WPA Guide*, 422–23. Also, see Robert J. Wimberg, *Amusement Parks of Greater Cincinnati and Northern Kentucky* (Cincinnati: The Ohio Book Store, 2002).

241 *Schimmel* German for a white horse.

243 *Procter & Gamble* This is the largest producer of household products, and was begun in 1837 when William Procter and James Gamble joined together to sell soap and candles. During the time period of the novel, they were headquartered in St. Bernard. Its plant there covered 200 acres, and it employed about 3,000 workers. They worked in a complex of 53 stone buildings of various sizes "intermingled with a heterogeneous collection of tanks, smokestacks, and railroad tracks. Behind a high fence are landscaped grounds containing playfields." See *WPA Guide*, 420. Procter and Gamble was not only the major employer in the area, but it also had connections to the German-American community as Gamble's son married the daughter of Rev. William Nast, the head of the German Methodist Church. See Carl Wittke, *William Nast: Patriarch of German Methodism* (Detroit: Wayne State University Press, 1959).

Suggested Readings

〰〰〰〰〰〰〰〰〰〰〰〰〰〰〰〰〰〰〰〰〰〰〰〰〰〰〰〰〰〰〰〰

FOR AN INTRODUCTION to German-American authors and their works, see the editor's *German-American Literature* (1977), which includes essays on several Cincinnati-German authors. Of the many works published by them the following are especially interesting.

Emil Klauprecht's historical novel deals with life in the nineteenth century in Cincinnati before the Civil War, and was a bestseller when it was published in 1855. It is available in translation as *Cincinnati, or the Mysteries of the West: Emil Klauprecht's German-American Novel*, translated by Steven Rowan and edited by Don Heinrich Tolzmann. New German-American Studies, Vol. 10. (New York: Peter Lang Pub. Co., 1996). Klauprecht also wrote a history of the area, published in 1864, which is available in translation as *German Chronicle in the History of the Ohio Valley and its Capital City, Cincinnati, in Particular*. Translated by Dale V. Lally and edited by Don Heinrich Tolzmann. (Bowie, Md.: Heritage Books, Inc., 1992). Taken together, both of Klauprecht's works provide a pre-Civil War picture of Cincinnati German life.

Twentieth-century life is covered in a novel by Ralph C. Wood, a Cincinnatian of German descent who, like Pieper, wrote a novel in German describing life in Wooden Shoe Hollow. He obtained his M.A. in German at the University of Cincinnati before going on to take his Ph.D. at Cornell University and then becoming a noted scholar in the field of German-American Studies. See Wood's *Klumpendal (Wooden Shoe Valley): Ernstes und Heiteres aus dem Leben einer deutschen Gemeinde in den USA*. (Wolfshagen-Scharbeutz/ Lübecker Bucht: F. Westphal, 1955).

There are many other works that do not deal with local themes, but are also of interest. Most of them are in German, but several have been translated, while others were published in English. The novel *The Secret of the Andes: A Romance* (Cincinnati: Robert Clark & Co., 1879) by Friedrich Hassaurek, a German-American newspaper editor, provides an example of a nineteenth century adventure novel that has been translated from German.

There are several English-language works by Gustav Eckstein, a University of Cincinnati physician, who was an active member of the Cincinnati

Turnverein. Some became bestsellers, such as *Kettle*. (New York: Harper, 1933). A reviewer at the *New York Times* wrote of this novel that "no protest against the fate of the artist at the hands of wealth and efficiency has been more powerful . . ."

These titles illuminate the kinds of works that German-American authors in the area have published. For further information about the German heritage of the area, see: Don Heinrich Tolzmann, *German Heritage Guide to the Greater Cincinnati Area*. (Milford, Ohio: Little Miami Publishing Co., 2003).

Index

In order to facilitate further research, authors and publications are included in this index. Authors are printed in small capitals and publications are printed in italics.

Numerics

1913 259

A

A. J. Rahn Greenhouse, 248
African-American population 262
Ahlrichs Café xxi
Ahlrichs, John, xxi
Alms & Doepke, 260
Alms, William H. 260
America, immigration to xxxv
Amusement Parks of Greater Cincinnati and Northern Kentucky (Wimberg) 263
Anglo-Americans xxxii
Anglo-Americans, 259
Ankum, Germany, xxxviii
ASTON, JOE, xxxviii
Avondale, 259

B

BARNSTORFF, HERMANN 259
BARRICK, MAC E., 256
BAUERMAN, LAURA, xxxviii
Bauverein, 257
Bicentennial Guide to Greater Cincinnati, A Portrait of Two Hundred Years, The (Giglierano, Overmyer, Propas), xxxvii, 255, 260, 262
Black Dialect 262
Bremen 261
Bremen und Bremerhaven als Auswandererhaefen 261
Bremen, port of (Germany) xxxv
Bremerhaven, Germany 255
Bremerhaven, port of (Germany) xxxv
BROCK, IRA, xxxvii
BROOKSHIRE, KAY, xxxvi, xxxix
Buffalo Bill 263
Buffalo Bill Cody, The Man Behind the Legend (Carter) 263
building and loan banks, 257
Butchering, 256
Butz, Willis R., xxvii

C

CALHOUN, JIM, xxxvi
Calve, Emma, 256
Camp Washington, 257
CARTER, ROBERT A., 263
Carthage, xxvii
Chester Park 263
Chester Park, 263
Chistmann, Gertrude, xxi
Christmas Butterfly xxiii

Christmas, 256
Chronik der Stadt Osnabrück (Hofmeyer), 256
Cincinnati Enquirer, xxiii, xxxv–xxxix, 260
Cincinnati Fire Department xxxiv
Cincinnati park system, xxix
Cincinnati Post, xxxviii–xxxix
Cincinnati Street Railway stocks, xxx
Cincinnati Times-Star, xxxvi–xxxvii
Cincinnati Zoological Gardens, 258, 263
Cincinnati, Ohio (as a destination for immigrants), xxxv
Cincinnati, Ohio, xxviii
Cincinnati, or the Mysteries of the West, Emil Klauprecht's German-American Novel, 265
Cincinnati's Colored Citizens, Historical, Sociological, and Biographical (Dabney) 262
Cincinnati's German Heritage (Tolzmann), 257, 261
Clifton campus, xxx
Clifton, xxvii, 261
Clifton, 260
Colerain Ave. 262
College Hill (Ohio), xxvii
College Hill, xvi
Criterion, The xxxvii
Cumminsville, xvi, 255–256
Cumminsville, 260

D

DABNEY, WENDELL P., 262
Danube Swabians, 260
Deer Park Nursing Home xxiii
department store 260
Deutsche Volkslieder 168 Volkslieder und volkstumliche Lieder (Knorr), 255
Deutschland, Deutschland ueber alles, 259

Doekpke, William F. 260
Donauschwaben, 260
Du, Du liegst mir im Herzen & Ach, Du lieber Augustin 255
Duel of the Giants Bismarck, Napoleon III, and the Origins of the Franco-Prussian War, A (Wetzel) 261
Duisburg, Germany, xxi
Dutchman 261

E

ECKSTEIN, GUSTAV, 265
Ein Prosit, 261
Ellis Island 261
Elmwood Place (Ohio), xxvii
encampment, 257
Encyclopedia of American History (Morris & Morris), 258
English Church, 259
Epworth Avenue, 255
Erkenbrecher, Andrew, 258
Ernst, xxxix
Erste Deutsche Evangelische Protestantische Gemeinde, Die, 255
Evangelical Lutheran Church, xxxv

F

FALLERSLEBEN, HOFFMANN VON, 259
Festival of Christian Women, The xxiii
Festschrift zum goldenen Jubiläum des Deutschen Literarischen Klubs von Cincinnati, 1877/1927 (Barnstorff), 259
Finneytown (Ohio), xxvii
First Church xvi
First German Evangelical Protestant Church, The, xvi
First Ohio Regiment 257
first postmaster in Cumminsville, 256
First United Church of Christ, xvi, 255

Fort Hamilton, xxviii
Franco-Prussian War, immigration during the 261
Frankfort & Berlin 262
Friedhoff Richard, xxxii
Friedhoff, xxxvi, xxxviii–xxxix
Funke xxxvii–xxxviii
Al xxxii
Funke's Greenhouses 250, 252

G

Gabel, xxx
Gamble, James 263
Gärtner-Unterstützungsverein, 261
Gemüse, 261
Gemütlichkeit, 261
German Chronicle in the History of the Ohio Valley and its Capital City, Cincinnati, in Particular (Klauprecht) 265
German Empire 259
German Evangelical Protestant Cemetery 262
German folk songs, 255
German Gardeners Beneficial Society, The 261
German Heritage Guide to the Greater Cincinnati Area (Tolzmann), xxxviii, 266
German Heritage Museum xxi
German Methodist Church 263
German Pioneer Legacy The Life and Work of H. A. Rattermann, The (Tolzmann), xxxvii
German Ways, Of (Rippley), 259
German-American Experience (Tolzmann) 255, 257, 261
German-American Folklore (Barrick), 256
German-American gardeners 260
German-American Literature 265
German-Americans xxxii
Germans in Indianapolis, The (Probst), 258
Germany 262
GIGLIERANO, GEOFFREY J., xxxvii
GILHOFF, JOHANNES, xxxvi, 257
Goetz truck 249
Goetz's front field 252
Golf Manor xxiv
Golf Manor pioneers, 254
Golf Manor, xiii–xiv
Graber, xxxvi, xxxviii–xxxix
Graphophones, 260
Gray Road, xxvii
Greber, xxx, xxxvi, xxxix
GREGG, B. G., xxxvi
Grieme, xxxix
Growing Up Plattdütsch in America (Trost), 257

H

Haarlammert family, xxxvi
HAGNER, HENRY, 257
half-timber building, xx
Hamilton County, Ohio Burial Records, Vol. 3 Vine Street Hill Cemetery (Remler) 262
Hannover, Kingdom of, xxxv
Hanover, Germany, xxiv
HASSAUREK, FRIEDRICH, 265
Heber, Rica xxiii, xxv
Heckmeyer, xxxvii
HEIDLER, ROBERT, xxvi, xxxvi–xxxvii
Heimathaus xxxv
Heine, Heinrich, 256
Heinrich Heine, Paradox and Poet (Untermyer), 256
Here in America it gives so many dumb people, 255
Herman goes early 255
HEUCK, ROBERT, II, 263
Heuck's Opera House 263
High German xxiv
High German/Handicap 262
highlands of the south (Germany),

language of the, xxiv
Hilter, Germany, xxx
History of German Literature, A (Robertson) 261
History of Germany, The (Turk), 259
History of the German Language, With Special Reference to the Cultural and Social Forces that Shaped the Standard Literary Language, The (Waterman) 262
Hodde
 xxxvi, xxxviii
 William H. xxxvii
Hodde family xxxvii
Hoeweler, xxxvii
Hoeweler, Christian xxvii
Hoffner Street Church, 255, 260
HOFMEYER, LUDWIG, 256
Hubert Heuck and His Opera Houses (Heuck II) 263
Hungarian, 260
Hungary, German from 260
hymn 261

I

Ich hatt' einen Kameraden 261
immigration during the Franco-Prussian War 261
Indianapolis, 258
Irish-Americans 256

J

Jahnke, Brigitte, xxxvi
Jamestown, Virginia, 261
Jesu, geh voran, 261

K

Kaiser's Service, 256
KAMPHOEFNER, WALTER D., xxxv
Kemper, xxxviii
Kennedy Heights, 260
Kettle (Eckstein), 266
Kettler, xxxix
Kiel, Wisconsin, xxiv
Kingdom of Hannover xxxv

Kingdom of Prussia xxxv
KLAUPRECHT, EMIL, 265
Klompen xxi
Klumpendal (Wooden Shoe Valley) Ernstes und Heiteres aus dem Leben einer deutschen Gemeinde in den USA (Wood), 265
KNOCKE, OLGA ALMA, 257
KNORR, ERNST-LOTHAR VON, 255
Knowlton, Ephraim xvi
Knowlton, Ephraim, 256
Knowlton's Corner, 256
Knowlton's Hall, xvi

L

Ladbergen, Germany, xxxvi
LALLY, DALE V., 265
Letters of a German-American Farmer
Jürnjakob Swehn Travels To America (Gilhoff), xxxvi, 257
Lorelei, 256
Louisiana's German Heritage
Louis Voss' Introductory History (Tolzmann), 259
Low German xxiv, xxxvi
Low German farmers, novel about, xxxvi
Low German Folk, 257
lowlands of northern Germany, language of the, xxiv
LUCAS, W. I., 262
Lustigkeit 262

M

MacDonald, David, 254
map of Germany, xviii
MARSCHALCK, PETER, xxxv
Matthew United Church of Christ, 260
Matthew's German Evangelical Protestant Church, 260
Merrell, xxiv
Mexican War of 1846 257
Meyer, John, xxi

Meyer, Mary (Mrs. Henry Pieper) 254
Miami and Erie Canal xxviii
Mill Creek 258
Mill Creek Valley, xxvi, xxviii, xxxvii, 257
Mill Creek, 257
MILLER, ZANE L., 261
Miracle Eternal xxiii
Missouri (as a destination for immigrants), xxxv
Mitchell Avenue xxv
Mitchell Avenue, 258
Morgenrot 262
MORRIS, JEFFREY B., 258
MORRIS, RICHARD B., 258
Mt. Auburn 262
Mt. Auburn Orphanage 262
Murillo, xxx
Museum Village at Cloppenburg in Lower Saxony, the, xx

N

Nast, Rev. William 263
New Orleans 259
New Orleans, 259
New York, 255
NIERMANN, WILHELM F., xxxv
NOLTE-SCHUSTER, BIRGIT, xxxv
North Rhine–Westphalia, state of (Germany) xxiv, xxvii, xxxv
northern Kentucky xxxii
Northside 260

O

Of German Ways (Rippley), 256
Ohio xxxii
Ohio River, 258
Ohio River, The (Pearce), 258
Old First Church. 255
Osnabrück region, Germany (emigration from) xxxv
Osnabrück to New York to Ohio, 255
Osnabrück, Germany, xxiv, xxx–xxxi, xxxv–xxxvi, 259
Osterback, xxxvii

Osterbrock Greenhouse and Florist 249
OVERMYER, DEBORAH A., xxxvii

P

Panama Canal, 258
PEARCE, JOHN ED, 258
Pelzer, Henrietta, 254
Pennsylvania Germans 261
Pieper
  xxxvi
  Charlotte E., xxiii–xxvi, xxxii, xxxix
  Charlotte, xxxii
  Henry Louis xxiv
  Mary xxv, xxxvi
  Mary Emma xxiii
  Mary Meyer xxiv
Pieper family xxxix
Pieper family home in Westrup, Germany, xix
Pieper home, 253
Pieper Way street sign, xiii
Pieper, Charlotte xiii
Pieper, Charlotte, 253
Pieper, Fred, xiii–xiv
Pieper, Henry, 254
Pieper, Herman, 254
Pieper, Mary xiii
Pieper, Mary Meyer 254
Pieper, William, 254
Pig Tail Alley xv
Platt Düütsch=Low German A Brief History of the People and Language (Stockman), xxxvi, 257
Plattdeutsch, xxiv, xxxi
Pleasant Ridge Cemetery 260
Pleasant Ridge, 260
Plum Kuchen, 258
Poe, 259
POE, EDGAR ALLEN, 259
Popp, Mr., xvi
port city 261
port of entry 259

Presbyterian burial ground, 260
PROBST, GEORGE THEODORE, 258
Procter & Gamble 263
Procter, William 263
PROPAS, FREDERIC L., xxxvii
Prussia, Kingdom of, xxxv
PURDIE, EDNA, 262
R
RADEL, CLIFF, 259
Rahn, xxxvii
Rahn, A. J. 248
Rahn, Larry, 248
RATTERMANN, H. A., xxix, xxxvii–xxxviii
Raven, The (Poe) 259
Reich, The, 259
REICHMANN, EBERHARD, 258
REMLER, MARY H., 262
Rennegarbe, xxx, xxxvi, xxxviii
Renz, xxxvi
RIPPLEY, LAVERN J., 256, 259
ROBERTSON, JOHN G. 261
RODGERS, REBECCA S. 260
Rolling Ridge xxxvii
Rosenberg, xxxvi, xxxix
ROWAN, STEVEN, 265
rural Ohio (as a destination for immigrants), xxxv
S
Sagmaster, Joseph, xxiii, xxvi
Sauerkrautgemüse, 261
Scharft, Robert M., xxxix
Scharrel, Germany, xxi
Schimmel 263
Schnebelt, Marylyn, xxxix
Schnetzer
    Manfred, xxi
    Regina, xxi
Schroeder 258
Schuhmacher, xxx, xxxvi, xxxviii
Schumacher, xxxviii
Seal of the State of Ohio, 260
Second Ohio Regiment, 257
Secret of the Andes

A Romance, The (Hassaurek), 265
SLUZEWSKI, JIM, xxxvii
Smith, Captain John, 261
Sonderbar, 258
southeastern Indiana xxxii
SPANHEIMER, SISTER MARY EDMUND, xxxviii
Speck 256
Spring Grove 256
Spring Grove and Its Creator H. A. Rattermann's Biography of Adolph Strauch (Ratterman), xxxvii–xxxviii, 256
Spring Grove Avenue stockyards xxvii
Spring Grove Cemetery, xxvii–xxviii
Springfield Township, xxviii
St. Bernard 258
St. Bernard, xxvii, 258, 263
St. Clair–Wayne trail to Hamilton, 256
St. Clement's Church, 258
St. Johanneskirche in Osnabrück, 256
St. Matthew's Church, 260
St. Patrick, 256
Stemwede, district of (Germany), xxiv, xxxv
Stephens, xxxix
STOCKMAN, ROBERT LEE, xxxvi, 257
Stone, George N. 263
Strauch, Adolph, xxviii–xxix, xxxvii, 256
Strothmann family xxxix
Strothmann, Bernhard, xxx
T
Times-Star xxiii, xxvi
To America in 1870 261
toast 261
TOLZMANN, DON HEINRICH, xxxvii–xxxviii, 255, 257, 259, 261,

265–266
TROST, RICHARD LORENZ AUGUST, xxxvi, 257
TURK, ELEANOR L., 259

U

UHLAND, LUDWIG, 261
underground railway 262
University of Cincinnati, xxx
UNTERMYER, LOUIS, 256

V

Van Wormer
  Asa, xxx
  home, xxx
  Julia, xxx
  Library, xxx
Varnau family xxxviii
Varnau's West Chester Garden Center xxxviii
Vine Street, 259
Visions of Place
  The City, Neighborhoods, Suburbs, and Cincinnati's Clifton, 1850–2000 (Miller), 261
Visiting Ellis Island, A Souvenir of the Ellis Island Immigration Museum 261
Volksblatt, 257
volunteer fire department xxxiii
Von Heuerleuten und Farmern
  Die Auswanderung aus dem Osnabrücker Land nach Nordamerika im 19. Jahrhundert/ Emigration from the Osnabrücker Region to North America in the 19th Century (Kamphoefner et al.) xxxv

W

Walsh, Rita, xxx
WALSH, RITA, xxxviii
WALSHE, M. O'C., 262
Warnick, Charles, xxxviii
Washington's Birthday 261
WATERMAN, JOHN T., 262
Wehdem, Germany, xxxv, xxxix

West Chester Garden Center xxxviii
Westphalia, 259
Westphalian region, of Germany, xxxvi
Westrup, Germany, xxiv, xxxv, xxxix
WETZEL, DAVID, 261
Wild West Show 263
William Nast, Patriarch of German Methodism (Wittke), 263
WIMBERG, ROBERT J. 263
Winton
  Matthew xxvii
Winton Place
  Historic Sites, 1989–1990 (Walsh), xxxviii
Winton Place Engine House No. 38 xxxiv
Winton Place Town Hall xxxiii
Winton Place United Methodist Church, 259
Winton Place, xxiv–xxv, xxvii, xxxii, xxxvii, 258, 260
Winton Ridge Lane, xxx
Winton Road, xxvii, xxx
Wischmeyer, xxxvii
WITTKE, CARL, 263
WOOD, RALPH C., 265
Wooden Shoe Hollow xxiv, xxvi–xxvii, xxix, xxxii
Wooden Shoe Hollow (Pieper) xxxv
wooden shoes xxiv
World War I, 259
WPA Guide to Cincinnati, With a New Introduction by Zane L. Miller and a New Preface by Harry Graff, The, 256–260, 263

Y

Yankees 255
Yankees, xxxii

Z

ZEYDEL, EDWIN H., 259
Zoological Gardens, xxix
Zusammengehörigkeitsgetühl, xxxii

About the Editor

DON HEINRICH TOLZMANN is the Curator of the German-Americana Collection and Director of the German-American Studies Program at the University of Cincinnati. He is the author and editor of numerous works relating to German-American history and culture.

Dr. Tolzmann is shown standing next to the Cincinnati monument that honors Friedrich Hecker, a leader of the 1848 Revolution in Germany. In Cincinnati, Hecker and other Forty-eighters established the first Turner Society in America, which helped found the frontier settlement of New Ulm, Minnesota, in the 1850s.